THE PLATINUM COLLECTION: AFFAIRS TO REMEMBER

THE PLATINUM COLLECTION

January 2018

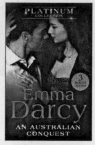

February 2018

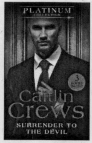

March 2018

April 2018

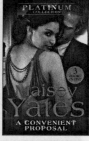

May 2018

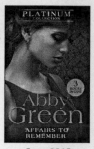

June 2018

THE PLATINUM COLLECTION: AFFAIRS TO REMEMBER

ABBY
GREEN

Published in Great Britain 2017
By Mills & Boon, an imprint of HarperCollins*Publishers*
1 London Bridge Street, London, SE1 9GF

THE PLATINUM COLLECTION: AFFAIRS TO REMEMBER
© 2018 Harlequin Books S.A.

When Falcone's World Stops Turning © 2014 Abby Green
When Christakos Meets His Match © 2014 Abby Green
When Da Silva Breaks the Rules © 2014 Abby Green

ISBN: 978-0-263-93567-7

09-0618

WHEN FALCONE'S WORLD STOPS TURNING

This is for Gervaise Landy without whose influence I would most likely still be speaking into a walkie talkie outside an actor's trailer in a car park somewhere, in the rain, trying to explain what the delay is. Thank you for all the great conversations about Mills & Boon and that first memorable one in particular all those years ago. As soon as we recognised a fellow M&B fanatic in each other we were kindred spirits. You were the one who put the idea in my head in the first place about writing for Mills & Boon, and you were the one with the tape on how to write one, which I still have, and which I will return to you as soon as you promise me you're going to sit down and finish that manuscript. With much love and thanks for sowing the seed of a dream in my head!

In thanking Gervaise, I also have to dedicate this book to Caitríona Ní Mhurchú at whose party I first met Gervaise. From the age of sixteen I have idolized this glamorous, confident, sexy, intelligent woman so if you see any of those traits in my heroines, it comes from a deep well of inspiration.

Irish author **Abby Green** threw in a very glamorous career in film and TV – which really consisted of a lot of standing in the rain outside actors' trailers – to pursue her love of romance. After she'd bombarded Mills & Boon with manuscripts they kindly accepted one, and an author was born. She lives in Dublin, Ireland, and loves any excuse for distraction. Visit www.abby-green. com or e-mail abbygreenauthor@gmail.com.

PROLOGUE

RAFAELE FALCONE LOOKED at the coffin deep inside the open grave. The earth they'd thrown in was scattered on top, along with some lone flowers left by departing friends and acquaintances. Some of them had been men, inordinately upset. Evidently there was some truth to the rumours that the stunning Esperanza Christakos had taken lovers during her third marriage.

Rafaele felt many conflicting emotions, apart from the obvious grief for his dead mother. He couldn't say that they'd ever had a close relationship; she'd been eternally elusive and had carried an air of melancholy about her. She'd also been beautiful. Beautiful enough to send his own father mad with grief when she left him.

The kind of woman who'd had the ability to make grown men completely lose all sense of dignity and of themselves. Not something that would ever happen to *him*. His single-minded focus was on his career and rebuilding the Falcone motor empire. Beautiful women were a pleasant diversion—nothing more. None of his lovers were ever under any illusions and expected nothing more than the transitory pleasure of his company.

His conscience pricked at this confident assertion—there had only been one lover who had taken him close to the edge but that was an experience he didn't dwell on… not any more.

His half-brother, Alexio Christakos, turned to him now and smiled tightly. Rafaele felt a familiar ache in his chest. He loved his half-brother, and had done from the moment he'd been born, but their relationship wasn't easy. It had been hard for Rafaele to witness his brother growing up, sure in the knowledge of his father's success and support—so different from his own experience with his father. He'd felt resentful for a long time, which hadn't been helped by his stepfather's obvious antipathy towards the son that wasn't his.

They both turned and walked away from the grave, engrossed in their own thoughts. Their mother had bequeathed to both her sons her distinctive green eyes, although Alexio's were a shade more golden than Rafaele's striking light green. Rafaele's hair was thicker and a darker brown next to his brother's short-cut ebony-black hair.

Differing only slightly in height, they were both a few inches over six foot. Rafaele's build was broad and powerful. His brother's just as powerful, but leaner. Dark stubble shadowed Rafaele's firm jawline today, and when they came to a stop near the cars Alexio observed it, remarking dryly, 'You couldn't even clean up for the funeral?'

The tightness in Rafaele's chest when he'd stood at the grave was easing slightly now. He curbed the urge to be defensive, to hide the vulnerability he felt, and faced his brother, drawling with a definite glint in his eye, 'I got out of bed too late.'

He couldn't explain to his brother how he'd instinctively sought the momentary escape he would find in the response of an eager woman, preferring not to dwell on how his mother's death had made him feel. Preferring not to dwell on how it had brought up vivid memories of when she'd walked out on his father so many years ago, leaving him a broken man. He was still bitter, adamantly refusing to pay his respects to his ex-wife today despite Rafaele's efforts to persuade him to come.

Alexio, oblivious to Rafaele's inner tumult, shook his head and smiled wryly. 'Unbelievable. You've only been in Athens for two days—no wonder you wanted to stay in a hotel and not at my apartment...'

Rafaele pushed aside the dark memories and quirked a mocking brow at his brother, about to dish out some of the same, when he saw a latecomer arrive. The words died on his lips and Alexio's smile faded as he turned to follow Rafaele's gaze.

A very tall, stern-faced stranger was staring at them both. And yet...he looked incredibly familiar. It was almost like looking into a mirror. Or at Alexio...if he had dark blond hair. It was his eyes, though, that sent a shiver through Rafaele. Green, much like his and Alexio's, except with a slight difference—a darker green, almost hazel. Another take on their mother's eyes...? But how could that be?

Rafaele bristled at this stranger's almost belligerent stance. 'May we help you?' he asked coolly.

The man's eyes flickered over them both, and then to the open grave in the distance. He asked, with a derisive curl to his lip, 'Are there any more of us?'

Rafaele looked at Alexio, who was frowning, and said, '*Us*? What are you talking about?'

The man looked at Rafaele. 'You don't remember, do you?'

The faintest of memories was coming back: he was standing on a doorstep with his mother. A huge imposing door was opening and there was a boy, a few years older than him, with blond hair and huge eyes.

The man's voice sounded rough in the still air. 'She brought you to my house. You must have been nearly three. I was almost seven. She wanted to take me with her then, but I wouldn't leave. Not after she'd abandoned me.'

Rafaele felt cold all over. In a slightly hoarse voice he asked, 'Who *are* you?'

The man smiled, but it didn't meet his eyes. 'I'm your older brother—*half-brother.* My name is Cesar Da Silva. I came today to pay my respects to the woman who gave me life...not that she deserved it. I was curious to see if any more would crawl out of the woodwork, but it looks like it's just us.'

Alexio erupted beside Rafaele. 'What the *hell*—?'

Rafaele was too stunned to move. He knew the Da Silva name. Cesar was behind the renowned and extremely successful Da Silva Global Corporation. His mind boggled to think that he might have met him and not known that they were brothers. With a sickening sense of inevitability, he didn't doubt a word this man had just said. Their fraternal similarities were too obvious. They could be non-identical triplets.

That half-memory, half-dream had always been all too real—he'd just never known for sure, because whenever he'd mentioned it to his mother she'd always changed the subject. Much in the way she had never discussed her life in her native Spain before she'd met his father in Paris, where she'd been a model.

Rafaele gestured to his brother, 'This is Alexio Christakos...our younger brother.'

Cesar Da Silva looked at him with nothing but ice in his eyes. 'Three brothers by three fathers...and yet she didn't abandon either of *you* to the wolves.'

He stepped forward then, and Alexio stepped forward too. The two men stood almost nose to nose, with Cesar topping his youngest brother in height only by an inch.

Cesar, his jaw as rigid as Alexio's, gritted out, 'I didn't come here to fight you, brother. I have no issue with either of you.'

Alexio's mouth thinned. 'Only with our dead mother, *if* what you say is true.'

Cesar smiled, but it was thin and bitter. 'Oh, it's true, all right — more's the pity.'

He stepped around Alexio then, and walked to the open grave. He took something out of his pocket and dropped it down into the dark space, where it fell onto the coffin with a distant hollow thud. He stood there for a long moment and then came back, his face expressionless.

After a charged silent moment between the three men he turned to stride away and got into the back of a waiting dark silver limousine, which moved off smoothly.

Rafaele turned to Alexio, who looked back at him, gob-smacked.

'What the…?' he trailed off.

Rafaele just shook his head. 'I don't know…'

He looked back to the space where the car had been and reeled with this cataclysmic knowledge.

CHAPTER ONE

Three months later...

'Sam, sorry to bother you, but there's a call for you on line one...someone with a very deep voice and a sexy foreign accent.'

Sam went very still. *Deep voice...sexy foreign accent.* The words sent a shiver of foreboding down her spine and a lick of something much hotter through her pelvis. She told herself she was being ridiculous and looked up from the results she'd been reading to see the secretary of the research department at the London university.

Kind eyes twinkled mischievously in a matronly face. 'Did you get up to something at the weekend? Or should I say some*one*?'

Again that shiver went down Sam's spine, but she just smiled at Gertie. 'Chance would be a fine thing. I spent all weekend working on Milo's playschool nature project with him.'

The secretary smiled and said indulgently, 'You know I live in hope, Sam. You and Milo need a gorgeous man to come and take care of you.'

Sam gritted her teeth and kept smiling, restraining herself from pointing out how well she and Milo were doing without a man. Now she couldn't wait to take the call. 'Did you say line one?'

Gertie winked and disappeared, and Sam took a deep breath before picking up the phone and pressing the flashing button. 'Dr Samantha Rourke here.'

There was silence for a few seconds, and then came the voice. Low, deep, sexy—and infinitely memorable. *'Ciao, Samantha, it's Rafaele...'*

The prickle of foreboding became a slap in the face. He was the only one apart from her father who had ever called her Samantha—unless it had been *Sam* in the throes of passion. All the blood in her body seemed to drain south, to the floor. Anger, guilt, emotional pain, lust and an awful treacherous tenderness flooded her in a confusing tumult.

She only realised she hadn't responded when the voice came again, cooler. 'Rafaele Falcone...perhaps you don't remember?'

As if that was humanly possible!

Her hand gripped the phone and she managed to get out, 'No... I mean, yes. I remember.'

Sam wanted to laugh hysterically. How could she forget the man when she looked into a miniature replica of his face and green eyes every day?

'Bene,' came the smooth answer. 'How are you, Sam? You're a doctor now?'

'Yes...' Sam's heart was doing funny things, beating so hard she felt breathless. 'I got my doctorate after...' She faltered and the words reverberated in her head unspoken. *After you came into my life and blew it to smithereens.* She fought valiantly for control and said in a stronger voice, 'I got my doctorate since I saw you last. How can I help you?'

Again a bubble of hysteria rose up in her: *how about helping him by telling him he has a son?*

'I am here in London because we've set up a UK base for Falcone Motors.'

'That's...nice,' Sam said, a little redundantly.

The magnitude of who she was talking to seemed to

hit her all of a sudden and she went icy all over. Rafaele Falcone. Here in London. He'd tracked her down. Why? *Milo*. Her son, her world. *His son*.

Sam's first irrational thought was that he must know, and then she forced herself to calm down. No way would Rafaele Falcone be calling her up sounding so blasé if he knew. She needed to get rid of him, though—fast. And then think.

'Look…it's nice to hear from you, but I'm quite busy at the moment…'

Rafaele's voice took on a cool edge again. 'You're not curious as to why I've contacted you?'

That sliver of fear snaked down Sam's spine again as an image of her adorable dark-haired son came into her mind's eye.

'I…well…I guess I am.' She couldn't have sounded less enthusiastic.

Rafaele's voice was almost arctic now. 'I was going to offer you a position with Falcone Motors. The research you're currently conducting is exactly in the area we want to develop.'

Sheer blind panic gripped Sam's innards at his words. She'd worked for this man once before and nothing had been the same since. Her tone frigid, she said, 'I'm afraid that's impossible. I'm committed to working on behalf of the university.'

Silence for a few taut seconds and then Rafaele responded with a terse, 'I see.'

Sam could tell that Rafaele had expected her to drop at his feet in a swoon of gratitude, even just at the offer of a job, if nothing more personal. It was the effect he had on most women. He hadn't changed. In spite of what had happened between them.

The words he'd left lingering in the air when he'd walked away from her resonated as if it had happened yesterday: *'It's for the best,* cara. *After all, it wasn't as if this was ever anything serious, was it?'*

He'd so obviously wanted her to agree with him that Sam had done so, in a flat and emotionless voice. Her body had seemed drained of all feeling. Relief had been a tangible force around him. It was something that she hadn't forgotten and which had helped her to believe she'd made the right decision to take full responsibility for Milo on her own. Even so, her conscience pricked her now: *you should have told him.*

Panic galvanised Sam, so that Rafaele Falcone's offer of a job barely impinged on her consciousness. 'Look, I really am quite busy. If you don't mind…?'

'You're not even interested in discussing this?'

Sam recalled the bile that had risen within her when Rafaele had made his uninterest in her all too clear and bit out curtly, 'No, I'm not interested. Goodbye, Signor Falcone.'

Goodbye, Signor Falcone, and this from a woman he knew intimately.

Rafaele looked at the phone in his hand for a long moment. Not comprehending the fact that she had just hung up on him. Women did not hang up on him.

Rafaele put the phone down and his mouth firmed. But Samantha Rourke had never been like other women. She'd been different from the start. He felt restless and got up from his seat to pace over to the huge window that overlooked operations at his new UK base on the outskirts of London. But for once his attention wasn't on operations.

She'd come to his factory in Italy as an intern after completing her Masters in Mechanical Automotive Engineering. The youngest and only woman in a group of men. Scarily bright and intelligent. He would have had no compunction hiring her on the spot and paying her whatever she asked just to keep her working for him…but he'd become distracted.

Distracted by her sexily studious air and her tall, slim body. Distracted by the mannish clothes she'd insisted on wearing which had made him want to peel them off to see the curves hinted at but hidden underneath. Distracted by her flawless pale Celtic skin and those huge almond-shaped eyes set in delicate features. Grey eyes…like a stormy sea.

Distracted by the way she would look at him and blush when he caught her eye, the way she would catch her lower lip between small white teeth. Distracted by that fall of inky black hair which she'd kept tucking behind her ear. And, as time had worn on, distracted by the slow-burning licking flames of desire that had grown hotter and stronger every time he saw her.

Rafaele had fought it. He hadn't liked it—and especially not in the workplace. There were plenty of females working in his factory and yet none of them had ever turned his head. His life was run on strict lines and he'd always kept his personal life well away from his work. But she had been so far removed from the kind of woman he normally went for: polished, sophisticated. Worldly wise. Women who were sexy and knew it and knew what to do with it. Cynical, like him.

Sam had been none of those things. Except sexy. And he'd known she didn't know that. She'd seemed to have absolutely no awareness of the fact that men's gazes lingered on her as she passed by. It had enraged Rafaele. The hot spurt of possessiveness had been an alien concept to him. Before they'd even kissed!

In the end sexual frustration had been such a tight ball of need inside him that one day he'd called her to his office and, without being able to say a word, had taken her face in his hands and kissed her, drowning in an intoxicating sweetness he'd never tasted before.

Even now that memory alone had an effect on Rafaele's libido and body. He cursed. He'd thought of her months ago, at his mother's funeral. He thought of her more often than he liked to admit. Sam was the one who had taken him too close to the edge. They had shared more than just a brief sexual history. They had almost shared...*a child*.

Even now a shiver of fear snaked down Rafaele's spine. How close he'd come to dealing with something he never wanted to deal with. That was what he needed to remember.

He swung around and stared blankly into his huge office. Clearly she wanted nothing to do with him, and he should want to have nothing to do with her.

He should not have given in to the compulsion to track her down. He should steer well clear of Samantha Rourke and put her out of his mind. For good.

Samantha woke up on Saturday morning when a small warm body burrowed into the bed beside her. She smiled sleepily and wrapped her arms around her sturdy son, breathing in his sweet scent.

'Morning, handsome.'

'Morning, Mummy, I love you.'

Sam's heart clenched so hard for a second that she caught her breath. She kissed the top of his head. 'I love you too, sweetheart.'

Milo pulled his head back and Sam cracked open an eye and grimaced at the morning light.

He giggled. 'You're funny.'

Sam started to tickle Milo and he screeched with glee. Soon they were both wide awake and he was scrambling back out of the bed to clatter down the stairs.

She shouted after him. 'Don't turn on the TV yet!'

She heard him stop and could imagine his thwarted expression, and then he called back, 'Okay. I'll look at my book.'

Sam's heart clenched again. He would too. She knew when she went downstairs he'd be looking at his book studiously, even though he couldn't really read yet. He was such a good boy. Such a bright boy. Sometimes it scared her, how intelligent he was, because she felt as if she didn't have the means to handle it.

Bridie, her father's housekeeper, who had stayed on after he'd died two years previously, would often look at her with those far too shrewd Irish eyes and say, 'Well, where do you think he got it from? His grandfather was a professor of physics and you had your head in books from the age of two.'

Then she would sniff in that way she had and say, 'Now, obviously, as I don't know anything about his father, I can't speculate on that side of things...' which was Sam's cue to give her a baleful look and change the subject.

If it hadn't been for Bridie O'Sullivan, though, Sam reminded herself as she got out of bed, she would never have been able to get the PhD which had got her onto the lucrative research programme at the university, and which now helped pay for food, clothes *and* Bridie's wonderful care for Milo five days a week.

Bridie lived in the granny flat that had been built onto the side of the house some years before.

As Sam tied the belt on her robe, and prepared to go downstairs to get breakfast ready for herself and Milo, she tried to suppress the resurgence of guilt. The guilt that had been eating at her insides all week since she'd had *that* phone call. The guilt that had been a constant presence for four years, if she was completely honest with herself.

It unsettled her so much that she slept badly every night, tortured with memories while awake and by dreams while asleep, full of lurid images. *Hot* images. She woke tangled in the sheets, her skin damp with sweat, her heart racing, her head aching.

Rafaele Falcone. The man who had shown her just how colourless her world had been before demonstrating how easily he could deposit her back into perpetual greyness. As if she'd had no right to experience such a lavish, sensual dream.

Even now she wondered what on earth it had been about her that had caught his eye. But whatever it had been, to her everlasting shame, she would never forgive herself for believing that it had been more. For falling for him like some lovestruck teenager.

She reassured herself for the umpteenth time that week that he didn't deserve to know about Milo because he'd never wanted him in the first place. She would never forget how his face had leached of all colour when she'd told him she was pregnant.

Sam sagged back onto the side of the bed, the onslaught of memories coming too thick and fast to escape. He'd been away on a trip for three weeks and during that time Sam had found out she was pregnant. He'd asked to see her as soon as he'd returned, and after three weeks of no contact Sam hadn't been able to stop her heart from pumping with anticipation. Maybe he hadn't meant what he'd said before he'd gone on the trip...

'It might be no harm, cara, for us to spend some time apart. My work is beginning to suffer...you're far too distracting...'

But when she'd walked into his office he'd looked stern. Serious. Before she could lose her nerve Sam had blurted out, 'I have to tell you something.'

He'd looked at her warily. 'Go on, then.'

Sam had blushed and nervously twisted her hands, suddenly wondering if she was completely crazy to have a feeling of optimism that he might welcome her news. They'd only spent a month together. One heady, glorious month. Four weeks. Was that really enough time—?

'Sam?'

She'd looked at him, taken a deep breath and dived in. 'Rafaele…I'm pregnant.'

The words had hung ominously between them and a thick silence had grown. Rafaele's face had leached of all colour and Sam had known in that instant with cold clarity that she'd been a complete fool. About everything.

He'd literally gone white, his eyes standing out starkly green against the pallor. She'd thought he might faint and had moved towards him, but he'd put out a hand and asked hoarsely, 'How?'

She'd stopped in her tracks, but hadn't been able to halt the spread of ice in her veins. 'I think…when we were careless.'

An understatement for the amount of times they had been careless…in the shower, in the living room of Rafaele's *palazzo* when they'd been too impatient to make it to the bedroom, in the kitchen of her flat one evening, when he'd pushed her up against the counter and pulled down her trousers…

Sam had felt hot and mortified all at once. It felt so… *lurid* now. So desperate. It had been *sex*, not romance. Had she ever really known him? The vulnerability she'd felt in that moment was a searing everlasting memory.

He'd looked at her accusingly. 'You said you were on the pill.'

Sam got defensive. 'I was—I *am*. But I told you it was a low-dosage pill not specifically for contraception. And I had that twenty-four-hour bug a few weeks ago…'

Rafaele had sat down heavily into his chair. He looked as if he'd aged ten years in ten seconds. 'This can't be happening,' he'd muttered, as if Sam weren't even there.

She had tried to control her emotions, stop them from overwhelming her. 'It's as much of a shock to me as it obviously is to you.'

He'd looked up at her then and his face had tightened. 'Are you sure it's a shock? How do I know this wasn't planned in some attempt to trap me?'

Sam had almost staggered backwards, her mouth open, but nothing had come out. Eventually she'd managed, 'You think...you truly think I did this on purpose?'

Rafaele had stood up and started to pace, some colour coming back into his cheeks, highlighting that stunning bone structure. He'd laughed in a way that had chilled Sam right to her core, because she'd never heard him laugh like that before. Harsh.

He'd faced her. 'It's not unheard of, you know, for a woman who wants to ensure herself a lifetime of security from a rich man.'

The depth of this heretofore unrevealed cynicism had sent her reeling. Sam had stalked up to Rafaele's desk, her hands clenched to fists. 'You absolute *bastard*. I would never do such a thing.'

And then she'd had a flash of his expression and his demeanour when she'd come into the room, before she'd given him a chance to speak. A very bitter and dark truth had sunk in.

'You were going to tell me it was over, weren't you? That's why you asked to see me.'

Rafaele had had the grace to avoid her eye for a moment, but then he'd looked at her, his face devoid of expression.

'Yes.'

That was all. One word. Confirmation that Sam had been living in cloud cuckoo land, believing that what she'd shared with one of the world's perennial playboys had been *different*.

She'd been so overcome with conflicting emotions and turmoil at his attitude to her news and his stark lack of emotion that she'd been afraid if she tried to speak she'd start crying. So she'd run out of his office. Not even caring that she'd humiliated herself beyond all saving.

She'd hidden in her tiny apartment, avoiding Rafaele, avoiding his repeated attempts to get her to open the door.

And then it had started. The bleeding and the awful cramping pain. Terrified, Sam had finally opened the door to him, her physical pain momentarily eclipsing the emotional pain.

She'd looked at Rafaele and said starkly, 'I'm bleeding.'

He'd taken her to a clinic, grim and pale, but Sam hadn't really noticed. Her hands had been clutching her belly as she'd found herself willing the tiny clump of cells to live, no matter what. For someone who hadn't ever seriously contemplated having children, because she'd lost her own mother young and had grown up with an emotionally absent father, in that moment Sam had felt a primitive need to become a mother so strong that it had shaken her to her core.

At the clinic the kindly doctor had informed her that she wasn't, in fact, miscarrying. She was just experiencing heavier spotting than might be normal. He'd said the cramps were probably stress-induced and reassured her that with rest and avoiding vexatious situations she should go on to have a perfectly normal and healthy pregnancy.

The relief had been overwhelming. Until Sam had remembered that Rafaele was outside the door, pacing up and down, looking grim. He was a 'vexatious situation' personified. She could remember feeling the cramps come back even then, at the very prospect of having to deal with him, and again that visceral feeling had arisen: the need to protect her child.

She'd dreaded telling him that she hadn't miscarried after all.

And then a nurse had left the room, leaving the door ajar, and Rafaele's voice had floated distinctly into the room from just outside.

Everything within her stilling, Sam had heard him say tightly, *'I'm just caught up with something at the moment... No, it's not important... I will resolve this as soon as I can and get back to you.'*

And just like that the small, traitorous flame of hope she'd not even been aware she was pathetically harbouring had been extinguished. Obviously because of doctor/patient confidentiality Rafaele was none the wiser as to whether or not she'd actually miscarried. He believed that she had.

He'd terminated his conversation and come into the room. Sam had looked out of the window, feeling as if she was breaking apart inside. She'd forced herself to be calm and not stressed. The baby was paramount now.

Rafaele had stopped by the bed. 'Sam...'

Sam hadn't looked at him. She'd just answered, 'What?'

She'd heard him sigh. 'Look, I'm sorry...really sorry that this has happened. We should never have become involved.'

Sam had felt empty. 'No,' she'd agreed, 'we shouldn't have.'

Even then a small voice had urged her to put him straight, but she'd felt so angry in that moment and had already felt her stress levels rising, her body starting to cramp. Dangerous for the baby.

Feeling panicked, she'd finally turned her head to acknowledge Rafaele and said, 'Look, what's done is done. It's over. I have to stay in for a night for observation but I'm leaving tomorrow. I'm going home.'

Rafaele had been pale but Sam had felt like reaching

up to slap him. He felt no more for her than he did for the fact that as far as he was aware he'd just lost a baby. He just wanted to be rid of her. *'I will resolve this as soon as I can...'*

'Just go, Rafaele, leave me be.' *Please,* she'd begged silently, feeling those stress levels rising. Her hands had tightened on the bedcover, knuckles white.

Rafaele had just looked at her, those green eyes unfathomable. 'It's for the best, *cara.* Believe me... You are young...you have your career ahead of you. After all, it wasn't as if this was ever anything serious, was it?'

Sam's mouth had twisted and she'd resolved in that moment to do her utmost to focus on her career...and her baby. No matter what it took. 'Of course not. Now, please, just *go.*'

Sam's control had felt so brittle she'd been afraid it would snap at any moment and he'd see the true depth of her agony.

Rafaele had stepped back a pace. 'I will arrange for your travel home. You won't have to worry about anything.'

Sam had stifled a semi-hysterical giggle at the thought of the monumental task and life-change ahead of her. She'd nodded abruptly. 'Fine.'

Rafaele had been almost at the door by then, relief a tangible aura around him. 'Goodbye, Sam.'

Feeling a sob rise, and choking it down with all of her will and strength, Sam had managed a cool-sounding, 'Goodbye, Rafaele.' And then she'd turned her head, because her eyes had been stinging. She'd heard the door close softly and a huge sob had ripped out of her chest, and tears, hot and salty, had flowed down her cheeks.

By the time Sam had been at home for a week she'd begun veering wildly between the urge to tell Rafaele the truth and the urge to protect herself from further pain. Then she'd seen on some vacuous celebrity TV channel that Rafaele was already out and about with some gorgeous Italian TV personality, smiling that devilishly sexy smile. As she'd looked at Rafaele, smiling for the TV cameras, his arm around the waist of the sinuous dark-haired Latin beauty, she'd known that she could never tell him because he simply wasn't interested.

'*Mummy, I want Cheerios!*'

Sam blinked and came back to reality. Milo. Breakfast. She pushed aside the memories, tried to ignore the guilt and got up to attend to her son.

That evening when the doorbell rang Sam looked up from washing the dinner things in the sink. Milo was playing happily on the floor in the sitting room with his cars, oblivious. As she went to answer it she assured herself it was probably just Bridie, who had forgotten her keys to the flat again.

But when she opened the door on the dusky late winter evening it wasn't Bridie, who stood at five foot two inches in heels. It was someone over a foot taller and infinitely more masculine.

Rafaele Falcone.

For a long, breathless moment, the information simply wouldn't compute. Suspended in time, Sam seemed to be able to take in details almost dispassionately. Faded jeans. Battered leather jacket. Thin wool jumper. Thick dark brown hair which still had a tendency to curl a little too much over his collar. The high forehead. The deep-set startling green eyes. The patrician bump of his nose, giving him that indelible air of arrogance. The stunning bone structure and that golden olive skin that placed him somewhere more exotic than cold, wet England.

And his mouth. That gorgeous, sculpted-for-wicked-things mouth. It always looked on the verge of tipping into a sexy half-smile, full of the promise of sensual nirvana.

Unless it was pulled into a grim line, as it had been when she had seen him last.

Reality slammed into Sam like a fist to her gut. She actually sucked in a breath, only realising then that she'd been starving her lungs for long seconds while she gawped at him like a groupie.

'Samantha.'

His voice lodged her even more firmly in reality. And the burning intensity of his green eyes as they swept down her body. Sam became acutely aware of her weekend uniform of skinny jeans, thick socks and a very worn plaid shirt. Her hair was scraped up into a bun and she wore no make-up.

Rafaele smiled. 'Still a tomboy, I see. Despite my best efforts.'

A memory exploded into Sam's consciousness. Rafaele, in his *palazzo*, presenting her with a huge white box. Under what had seemed like acres and acres of silver tissue paper a swathe of material had appeared.

Sam had lifted it out to reveal a breathtaking evening gown. Rafaele had stripped her himself and dressed her again. One-shouldered and figure-hugging, in black and flesh-coloured stripes, the dress had accentuated her hips, her breasts, and a long slit had revealed her legs. Then he'd taken her out to one of Milan's most exclusive restaurants. They'd been the last to leave, somewhere around four o'clock in the morning, drunk on sparkling wine and lust, and he'd taken her home to his *palazzo*...

'Still a tomboy, I see...'

The memory vanished and the backdrop of Sam's very suburban street behind Rafaele came back into view.

Sexy smile. 'Aren't you going to ask me in? It's cold out here.'

Sam's hand clenched tight around the door. *Milo.* Panic rushed into her blood. Finally. Rousing her.

'Now isn't a good time. I don't know why you've come here. I thought I made it clear the other day that I'm not interested.'

Sam forced herself to look at him. Four years had passed and in that time she'd changed utterly. She felt older, more jaded. Whereas Rafaele only looked even more gorgeous. The unfairness of it galvanised her. He'd known nothing of her life the last few years. *Because you didn't tell him*, a voice pointed out.

'Why did you come here, Rafaele? I'm sure you have more important things to do on a Saturday evening.'

The bitterness in Sam's voice surprised her.

Rafaele's jaw tightened, but he answered smoothly. 'I thought if I came to see you in person you might be persuaded to listen to my offer.'

A dull flush accentuated Rafaele's cheekbones, but Sam was barely aware of it as she heard a high-pitched 'Mummy!' which was accompanied by small feet running at full speed behind her.

She felt Milo land at her legs, clasping his arms around them, and could almost visualise his little round face peeping out to see who was at the door. Like trying in vain to halt an oncoming train, Sam said in a thready voice, 'Like I said, now really isn't a good time.'

She could see awareness dawn on Rafaele's face as he obviously took in the fact of a child. He started to speak stiltedly. 'I'm sorry. I should have thought… Of course it's been years…you must be married by now. Children…'

Then his eyes slid down and she saw them widen. She didn't have to look to know that Milo was now standing beside her, one chubby hand clinging onto her leg. Wide green eyes would be staring innocently up into eyes the exact same shade of green. Unusual. Lots of people commented on how unusual they were.

Rafaele stared at Milo for what seemed like an age. He

frowned and then looked as if someone had just hit him in the belly...dazed. He looked up at Sam and she knew exactly what he was seeing as clearly as if she was standing apart, observing the interplay. Her eyes were wide and stricken, set in a face leached of all colour. Pale as parchment. Panicked. *Guilty.*

And just like that, something in his eyes turned to ice and she knew that he knew.

CHAPTER TWO

'MUMMY, CAN WE watch the cars on TV now?'

Sam put her hand to Milo's head and said faintly, 'Why don't you go on and I'll be there in a minute, okay?'

Milo ran off again and the silence grew taut between Sam and Rafaele. He knew. She felt it in her bones. He'd known as soon as he'd looked into his son's eyes. So identical. She hated that something about his immediate recognition of his own son made something soften inside her.

He was looking at her so hard she felt it like a physical brand on her skin. Hot.

'Let me in, Samantha. Now.'

Feeling shaky and clammy all at once, Sam stepped back and opened the door. Rafaele came in, his tall, powerful form dwarfing the hallway. He smelt of light spices and something musky, and through the shock Sam's blood jumped in recognition.

She shut the door and walked quickly to the kitchen at the end of the hall, passing where Milo sat cross-legged in front of the TV watching a popular car programme. His favourite.

She was about to pull the door shut when a curt voice behind her instructed, 'Leave it.'

She dropped her hand and tensed. Rafaele was looking at Milo as he sat enraptured by the cars on the screen. He was holding about three of his favourite toy cars in his hands. If his eyes and pale olive skin hadn't been a fatal giveaway then this might have been the worst kind of ironic joke.

Sam stepped back and walked into the kitchen. She couldn't feel her legs. She felt sick, light-headed. She turned around to see Rafaele follow her in and close the door behind him, not shutting it completely.

Rafaele was white beneath his dark colouring. And he looked murderous.

He bit out, 'This is where you tell me that by some extraordinary feat of genetic coincidence that little boy in there *isn't* three years and approximately three months old. That he *didn't* inherit exactly the same colour eyes that I inherited from my own mother. That he *isn't* my son.'

Sam opened her mouth. 'He is...' Even now, at this last second, her brain searched desperately for something to cling onto. Some way this could be justified. *He was his father.* She couldn't do it. She didn't have the right any more. She'd never had the right. 'He is your son.'

Silence, stretching taut and stark, and then he repeated, 'He is my son?'

Sam just nodded. Nausea was churning in her belly now. The full implications of this were starting to hit home.

Rafaele emitted a long stream of Italian invective and Sam winced because she recognised some of the cruder words—they were pretty universal. Her belly was so tight she put a hand to it unconsciously. She watched as Rafaele struggled to take this in. The enormity of it.

'No wonder you were so keen to get rid of me the other day.'

He paced back and forth in the tiny space. She could feel his anger and tension as it lashed out like a live electrical wire, snapping at her feet.

Suddenly he stopped and looked at her. 'Are you married?'

Sam shook her head painfully. 'No.'

'And what if I hadn't decided to pay you a visit? Would you have let me remain in blissful ignorance for ever?'

Stricken, Sam whispered, 'I don't…I don't know.' Even as she admitted that, though, the knowledge seeped in. She wouldn't have been able to live with the guilt. She would have told him.

He pinned her to the spot with that light green gaze which had once devoured her alive and was now colder than the arctic.

'You bitch.'

Sam flinched. He might as well have slapped her across the face. It had the same effect. The words were so coldly and implacably delivered.

'You didn't want a baby,' she whispered, unable to inject more force into her voice.

'So you just lied to me?'

Sam could feel her cheeks burning now, with shame. 'I thought it was a miscarriage, as did you. But at the clinic, after the doctor had done his examination, he told me that I wasn't miscarrying.'

Rafaele crossed his arms and she could see his hands clenched to fists. She shivered at the threat of violence even though she knew he would never hit her. But she sensed he wanted to hit something.

'You knew then and yet you barefaced lied to me and let me walk away.'

Clutching at the smallest of straws, Sam said shakily, 'I didn't lie…you assumed…I just didn't tell you.'

'And the reason you didn't inform me was because…?'

'You didn't…didn't want to know.' The words felt flimsy and ineffectual now. Petty.

'Based on…?'

It was as if he couldn't quite get out full sentences, Sam felt his rage strangling his words.

Her brain felt heavy. 'Because of how you reacted when I told you in the first place…'

Sam recalled the indescribable pain of realising that Rafaele had been about to break it off with her. His abject shock at the prospect of her pregnancy. It gave her some much needed strength. 'And because of what you said afterwards…at the clinic. I heard you on the phone.'

Rafaele frowned and it was a glower. 'What did I say?'

Sam's sliver of strength started to drain away again like a traitor. 'You were talking to someone. You said you were caught up in something *unimportant*.' Even now those words scored at Sam's insides like a knife.

Rafaele's expression turned nuclear. His arms dropped, his hands were fists. '*Dio*, Samantha. I can't even recall that conversation. No doubt I just said something—anything—to placate one of my assistants. I thought you'd just miscarried. Do you really think I was about to announce *that* in an innocuous phone call?'

Sam gulped and had to admit reluctantly, 'Maybe… maybe not. But how did I know that? All I could hear was your relief that you didn't have to worry about a baby holding your life up and your eagerness to leave.'

He all but exploded. 'Need I remind you that I was also in shock, and at that point I thought there was no baby!'

Sam was breathing hard and Rafaele looked as if he was about to kick aside the kitchen table between them to come and throttle her.

Just then a small, unsure voice emerged from the doorway. 'Mummy?'

Immediately Sam's world refracted down to Milo, who stood in the doorway. He'd opened it unnoticed by them and was looking from one to the other, his lower lip quivering ominously at the explosive tension.

Sam flew over and picked him up and he clung to her.

Her conscience struck her. He was always a little intimidated by men because he wasn't around them much.

'Why is the man still here?' he asked now, slanting sidelong looks to Rafaele and curling into Sam's body as much as he could.

Sam stroked his back reassuringly and tried to sound normal. 'This is just an old friend of Mummy's. He's stopped by to say hello, that's all. He's leaving now.'

'Okay,' Milo replied, happier now. 'Can we look at cars?'

Sam looked at him and forced a smile, 'Just as soon as I say goodbye to Mr Falcone, okay?'

'Okey-dokey.' Milo used his new favourite phrase that he'd picked up in playschool, squirmed back out of Sam's arms and ran out of the kitchen again.

Sam watched Rafaele struggle to take it all in. Myriad explosive emotions crossing his face.

'You'll have to go,' she entreated. 'It'll only confuse and upset him if you stay.'

Rafaele closed the distance between them and Sam instinctively moved back, but the oven was behind her. Rafaele's scent enveloped her, musky and male. Her heart pounded.

'This is not over, Samantha. I'll leave now, because I don't want to upset the boy, but you'll be hearing from me.'

After a long searing moment, during which she wasn't sure how she didn't combust from the anger being directed at her, Rafaele turned on his heel and left, stopping briefly at the sitting room door to look in at Milo again.

He cast one blistering look back at Sam and then he was out through the front door and gone. Sam heard the powerful throttle of an engine as it roared to life and then mercifully faded again.

It was then that she started to shake all over. Grasping

for a chair to hold onto, she sank down into it, her teeth starting to chatter.

'Mummeeee!' came a plaintive wail from the sitting room.

Sam called out, 'I'll be there in one second, I promise.'

The last thing she needed was for Milo to see her in this state. Her brain was numb. She couldn't even quite take in what had just happened—the fact that she'd seen Rafaele again for the first time since those cataclysmic days.

When she was finally feeling a little more in control she went in to Milo and sat down on the floor beside him. Without even taking his eyes off the TV he crawled into her lap and Sam's heart constricted. She kissed his head.

Rafaele's words came back to her: *This is not over, Samantha. I'll leave now, because I don't want to upset the boy, but you'll be hearing from me.'*

She shivered. She didn't even want to think of what she'd be facing when she heard from Rafaele again.

On Monday morning Sam filed into the conference room at the university and took a seat at the long table for the weekly budget meeting. Her eyes were gritty with tiredness. Unsurprisingly she hadn't slept all weekend, on tenterhooks waiting for Rafaele to appear again like a spectre. In her more fanciful moments she'd imagined that she'd dreamt it all up: the phone call; his appearance at the house. *Coming face to face with his son.* A small, snide voice pointed out that it was no less than she deserved but she pushed it down.

Robustly she told herself that if she'd had to go back in time she would have done the same again, because if she hadn't surely the stress of Rafaele being reluctantly bound to her and a baby would have resulted in a miscarriage for real?

Gertie, the secretary, arrived then and sat down breathlessly next to Sam. She said urgently, 'You'll never guess what's happened over the weekend...'

Sam looked at her, used to Gertie's penchant for gossip. She didn't want to hear some salacious story involving students and professors behaving badly, but the older woman's face suddenly composed itself and Sam looked to see that the head of their department had walked into the room.

And then her heart stopped. Because right on his heels was another man. *Rafaele*.

For a second Sam thought she might faint. She was instantly light-headed. She had to put her hands on the edge of the table and grip it as she watched in mounting horror and shock as Rafaele coolly and calmly strode into the room, looking as out of place in this unadorned academic environment as an exotic peacock on a grubby high street.

He didn't even glance her way. He took a seat at the head of the table alongside their boss, looking stupendously handsome and sexy. He sat back, casually undoing a button on his pristine suit jacket with a big hand, long fingers...

Sam was mesmerised.

This had to be a dream, she thought to herself frantically. She'd wake up any moment. But Gertie was elbowing her none too discreetly and saying *sotto voce*, 'This is what I was about to tell you.'

The stern glare of their boss quelled any chat and then, with devastating inevitability, Sam's stricken gaze met Rafaele's and she knew it wasn't a dream. There was a distinct gleam of triumph in those green depths, and a more than smug smile was playing around that firmly sculpted mouth.

Her boss was standing up and clearing his throat. Sam couldn't look away from Rafaele, and he didn't remove his gaze from hers, as if forcing her to take in every word now being spoken, but she only heard snippets.

'Falcone Industries...most successful...honoured that

Mr Falcone has decided to fund this research out of his own pocket...delighted at this announcement...funding guaranteed for as long as it takes.'

Then Rafaele got up to address the room. There were about thirteen people and, predictably, you could have heard a pin drop as his charismatic effect held everyone in thrall. He'd finally moved his gaze from Sam and she felt as if she could breathe again, albeit painfully. Her heart was racing and she took in nothing of what he said, trying to wrap her sluggish brain around the ramifications of this shocking development.

'Samantha...'

Sam looked up, dazed, to see her boss was now addressing her, and that Rafaele had sat down. She hadn't noticed, nor heard a word.

'I'm sorry, Bill, what did you say?' She was amazed she'd managed to speak.

'I *said*,' he repeated with exaggerated patience, clearly disgruntled that she appeared to be on another planet while in such illustrious company, 'that as of next week you will be working from the Falcone factory. You're to oversee setting up a research facility there which will work in tandem with the one here in the university.'

He directed himself to the others again while this bomb detonated within Sam's solar plexus.

'I don't think I need to point out the significance of being allowed to conduct this research within a functioning factory, and especially one as prestigious as Falcone Motors. It'll put us streets ahead of other research in this area and, being assured of Falcone funding for at least five years, we're practically guaranteed success.'

Sam couldn't take any more. She rose up in a blind panic, managed to mumble something vague about needing air and fled the room.

* * *

Rafaele watched Sam leave dispassionately. Since the other evening he'd been in shock. Functioning, but in shock. His anger and rage was too volcanic to release, fearsome in its intensity. And fearsome for Rafaele if he contemplated for a second why his emotions were so deep and hot.

Sam's boss beside him emitted a grunt of displeasure at her hasty departure, but Rafaele felt nothing but satisfaction to be causing her a modicum of the turbulence in his own gut. Through his shock Rafaele had felt a visceral need to push Sam off her axis as much as she'd pushed him off his.

He recalled bitterly how reluctant she'd been to talk to him in the first place about the job he was offering, all the while knowing her secret. Harbouring his son. With one phone call to his team Rafaele had put in motion this audacious plan to take over the research programme at her university and had relished this meeting.

While Sam's boss continued his speech Rafaele retreated inwardly, but anyone looking at him would have seen only fierce concentration.

He breathed in and realised that he hadn't taken a proper breath since he'd seen Sam looking at him with that stricken expression on her face in the doorway of her house the other evening. The initial punch to his gut he'd received when he'd first thought that Sam was married, with someone else's child, was galling to remember—and more exposing than he liked to admit.

Nothing excused her from withholding his son from him for more than three years. Rafaele had been about Milo's age when his world had imploded. When he'd witnessed his father, on his knees, sobbing, prostrating himself at Rafaele's mother's feet, begging her not to leave him.

'I love you. What am I if you leave? I am nothing. I have nothing...'

'Get up, Umberto,' she'd said. *'You shame yourself in front of our son. What kind of a man will he be with a crying, snivelling wretch for a father?'*

What kind of a man would he be?

Rafaele felt tight inside. The kind of man who knew that the most important things in life were building a solid foundation. Security. Success. He'd vowed never to allow anything to reduce him to nothing, as his father had been reduced, with not even his pride to keep him standing. Emotions were dangerous. They had the power to derail you completely. He knew how fickle women were, how easily they could walk away. Or keep you from your child.

Rafaele had driven back to Sam's house on Sunday, fired up, ready to confront her again, but just as he'd pulled up he'd seen them leaving the house. Milo had been pushing a scooter. He'd followed them to a small local park and watched like a fugitive as they played. Dark emotions had twisted inside him as he'd watched Sam's effortless long-legged grace and ease. He'd known that if he hadn't reappeared in their lives this would have just been another banal Sunday morning routine trip to the park.

Seeing his son's small sturdy body, watching him running around, laughing gleefully, something alien inside him had swelled. It was…pride. And something else that he couldn't name. But it had reminded him of that day again—the darkest in his memory—when his mother had gripped his hand painfully tight and pulled him in her wake out of their family *palazzo* outside Milan, leaving his father sobbing uncontrollably on the ground. A pathetic, broken man.

That was one of the reasons Rafaele had never wanted to have children. Knowing how vulnerable they were had always felt like too huge a responsibility to bear. No one knew better than he how events even at that young age could shape your life. And so he'd never expected that, when faced with his son, there would be such a torrent of feelings within him, each one binding him invisibly and indelibly to this person he didn't even know properly yet. Or that when he'd watched him running around the other day there would be a surge of something so primal and protective that he just knew without question, instantly, that he would do anything to prevent his son from coming into harm's way.

From far too early an age Rafaele had been made aware that the absence of a father corroded at your insides like an acid.

Resolve firmed like a ball of concrete inside him. There was no way on this earth that he was going to walk away from his son now and give him a taste of what he'd suffered.

Cutting off Sam's boss curtly, Rafaele stood up and muttered an excuse, and left the room. There was only one person he wanted to hear talk right now.

Sam's stomach felt raw after she'd lost her breakfast, minute as it had been, into a toilet in the ladies' room. She felt shaky, weak, and looked as pale as death in the reflection of the cracked mirror. She splashed water on her face and rinsed her mouth out, knowing that she had to go back out there and face—

The door suddenly swung open and Sam stood up straight, hands gripping the side of the sink. For once she prayed it might be Gertie, even though she knew it wasn't when every tiny hair seemed to prickle on her skin.

She turned around and saw Rafaele, looking very tall and very dark as he leant back against the door, hands thrust deep into his pockets. Even now her body sang, recognising the man who had introduced her to her own sensuality, and she clamped down on the rogue response, bitterly aware that not even the harsh fluorescent lighting could strip away his sheer good looks.

Welcome anger rose up and Sam seized on it, crossing her arms over her chest. Her voice felt rough, raw. 'What the hell do you think you're playing at, Rafaele? How dare you come in here and use your might to get back at me? These are people you're playing with—people who have invested long years of study into their area—and suddenly you sweep in and promise them a glimpse of future success when we both know—'

'Enough.'

Rafaele's voice sounded harsh in the echoing silence of the cavernous tiled ladies' bathroom.

'I am fully committed to following through on my promise of funding and support to this university.' His mouth tightened. 'Unless you've already forgotten, I *had* contacted you initially to ask you to work for me. I had every intention of using your expertise to further this very research for my own ends.'

He shrugged minutely. 'There's nothing new in that— any motor company worth its salt is on the lookout for new research and ways of beating the competition with new technology. You have single-handedly elevated this research to a far more advanced level than any other facility, in a university or otherwise.'

His words sent Sam no sense of professional satisfaction. She was still in shock. 'That may be the case,' she bit out tightly, 'but now that you know about Milo you're seeking to get back at me personally.'

She couldn't keep the bitterness from her voice.

'It just so happens that you have the means to be able to come in and take over the entire department to do your bidding.'

Fresh panic gripped her when she recalled her boss saying something about Sam herself going to work from his factory. Her arms grew tighter over her chest when she recalled the hothouse environment of working in Rafaele's Milan factory four years ago and how easily he'd seduced her. The thought of going back into a similar environment, even if Rafaele would prefer to throttle her than sleep with her, made her clammy.

'I will not be going to work for you. I will remain here at the university.'

Rafaele took a few paces forward and Sam saw the light of something like steel in his eyes and his expression. Her belly sank even as her skin tightened with betraying awareness.

'You *will* be coming to work for me—or I will pull out of this agreement and all of your colleagues are back to square one. Your boss has informed me that if I hadn't come along with the promise of funding he was going to have to let some people go. He can't keep everyone on the payroll due to reduced projected funding this year. You would have been informed of that at this very meeting.'

Vaguely Sam was aware of the veracity of what he said. It had been rumoured for weeks. Once again she was struck by how little she'd appreciated how ruthless Rafaele was. 'You bastard,' she breathed.

Rafaele looked supremely unperturbed. 'Hardly, when I'm saving jobs. It's very simple if you do the right thing and accede to my wishes. And this is just the start of it, Samantha.'

Ice invaded her bloodstream. 'Start of what?'

To her shock she realised belatedly how close Rafaele had come when he reached out a hand and cupped her jaw. She felt the strength of that hand, the faint calluses which reminded her of how he loved tinkering with engines despite his status. It was one of the things that had endeared him to her from the start.

In an instant an awful physical yearning rose up within

her. Every cell in her body was reacting joyously to a touch she'd never thought she'd experience again. She was melting, getting hot. Damp.

Softly, he sliced open the wound in her heart. 'The start of payback, Samantha. You owe me for depriving me of my son for more than three years and I will never let you forget it.'

For a moment Rafaele almost forgot where he was, who he was talking to. The feel of Sam's skin under his hand was like silk, her jaw as delicate as the finest spun Murano glass. He had an almost overwhelming urge to keep sliding his hand around to the back of her neck, to tug her towards him so that he could feel her pressed against him and crush that pink rosebud mouth under his— Suddenly Rafaele realised what he was doing.

With a guttural curse he took his hand away and stepped back. Sam was looking at him with huge grey eyes, her face as pale as parchment with two pink spots in each cheek.

She blinked, almost as if she'd been caught in a similar spell, and then something in her eyes cleared. The anger was gone.

She changed tack, entreated him. She held out a hand and her voice was husky. 'Please, Rafaele, we need to talk about this—'

'No.' The word was harsh, abrupt, and it cut her off effectively. Everything within Rafaele had seized at her attempt to try and take advantage of a moment when she might have perceived weakness on his part. To play on his conscience. With the shadows under her eyes making her look fragile and vulnerable.

He'd witnessed his mother for years, using her wiles to fool men into thinking she was vulnerable, fragile. Only to see how her expression would harden again once they were no longer looking and she'd got what she wanted. She'd been so cold the day she'd left his father, showing not an ounce of remorse.

Once, he mightn't have believed Sam was like that, but that was before she'd kept his son from him, demonstrating equal, if not worse, callousness.

Rafaele took another step back and hated that he felt the need to do so. That volcanic anger was well and truly erupting now. He gritted out, 'If you were a man...'

Sam tensed and her chin lifted. Gone was the soft look of before, the husky entreaty.

'If I were a man...what? You'd thrash me? Well, what's stopping you?'

Rafaele could see where her hands had clenched to fists by her side. He looked at her disgustedly. 'Because I don't raise my hands to women—or anyone, for that matter. But I felt like it for the first time when I realised that boy was my son.'

He couldn't stop the words spilling out. That initial shock was infusing him all over again.

'My *son*, Sam, my flesh and blood. He's a Falcone. *Dio*. How could you have played God like that? What gave you the right to believe you had the answer? That you alone could decide to just cut me out of his life?'

Sam seemed to tense even more, her chin going higher. Those spots of red deepened, highlighting her delicate bone structure. 'Do I need to remind you *again* that you practically tripped over your feet in your hurry to get out of the clinic that day? You could barely disguise your relief when you thought there was nothing to worry about. You just assumed the worst. It didn't even occur to you to question whether or not I'd actually had a miscarriage, because you didn't want a baby.'

Rafaele coloured, his conscience pricked by the reminder of how eager he'd been to get away from those huge bruised eyes, the raw emotion. The shock. The awareness that Sam had strayed too far under his skin.

Tightly he admitted, 'I never had any intention of having children. But you gave me no reason to doubt the inevitable conclusion of what we'd both believed to be a miscarriage.'

Sam choked out, 'You were quite happy to wash your hands of me, so don't blame me now if I felt the best course was to leave you out of my decision-making process.'

Rafaele looked at Sam across the few feet that separated them and all he could see was her eyes. Huge, and as grey as the rolling English clouds. She was sucking him in again but he wouldn't let her. She'd wilfully misdirected him into believing she'd miscarried when all the while she'd held the knowledge of their baby, *living*, in her belly.

He shook his head. 'That's just not good enough.'

Sam's voice took on a defensive edge. 'I was hardly encouraged to get in touch and tell you the truth when I saw you with another woman only a week after that day.'

She was breathing heavily under her shirt and he could see her breasts rise and fall. A flash of heat went straight to his groin and Rafaele crushed it ruthlessly. He focused on her face and tried to forget that he actually hadn't slept with another woman for about a year after Sam had left, despite appearances and despite his best efforts. Every time he'd come close something inside him had shut down. And since then…? His experiences with women had been anything but satisfactory. To be reminded of this now was galling.

He narrowed his eyes. 'Don't you dare try to put this on me now, just to deflect your own guilt.'

But the guilt that had struck Rafaele wouldn't be banished, much as he wanted it to be. Damn her! He wouldn't let her do this to him now. She'd borne his child. His son. And said nothing.

Sam's voice was bitter. 'God forbid that I would forget what our relationship was about. *Sex*. That was pretty much it, wasn't it? Forget conversation, or anything more intimate than being naked in bed. It wasn't as if you didn't make that abundantly clear, Rafaele, telling me over and over again not to fall for you because you weren't *about* that.'

'But you did anyway, didn't you?' Rafaele couldn't keep the accusing note out of his voice and he saw Sam blanch.

'I thought I loved you.' Her mouth twisted. 'After all, you were my first lover, and isn't it normal for a virgin to develop an attachment to her first? Isn't that one of the helpful warnings you gave me?'

Rafaele saw nothing right then but a memory of Sam's naked and flushed body as she'd lain on his bed before him, her breasts high and round, her narrow waist, long legs. Skin so pure and white it had reminded him of alabaster—except she'd been living, breathing, so passionate. And she'd been innocent. He'd never forget how it had felt to sink into that slick, tight heat for the first time. It was his most erotic memory. Her gasp of shock turning to pleasure.

She continued, 'But don't worry. I soon got over it and realised how shallow those feelings were. Once I was faced with the reality of pregnancy and a baby.'

'A reality,' Rafaele gritted out, angry at that memory and at how easily it had slipped past his guard, 'that you decided to face *alone*.'

Reacting against her ability to scramble his thought-processes, Rafaele changed tack.

'Was it a punishment, Sam? Hmm?' He answered himself. 'Punishment for my being finished with you? For not wanting more? For letting you go? For not wanting to have a baby because that's not what our relationship was about?'

Rafaele couldn't stop the demon inside him.

'I think the problem is that you fell for me and you were angry because I didn't fall for you, so you decided to punish me. It's so obvious...'

CHAPTER THREE

SAM CLOSED the distance between them, her hand lifted and she hit Rafaele across the face before she even registered the impulse to do so. She realised in the sickeningly taut silence afterwards that she'd reacted because he'd spoken her worst fears out loud. Here in this awful, stark, echoey room.

With a guttural curse, and his cheek flaring red where Sam had hit him, Rafaele hauled her into his arms and his mouth was on hers. He was kissing her angrily, roughly.

It took a second for Sam to get over the shock, but what happened next wasn't the reaction she would have chosen if she'd had half a brain cell still working. Her reaction came from her treacherous body and overrode her brain completely.

She started kissing him back, matching his anger with her own. For exposing her. For saying those words out loud. For making her feel even more ashamed and confused. For being *here*. For making her want him. For making her remember. For kissing her just to dominate her and prove how much she still wanted him.

Her hands were clutching Rafaele's jacket. She tasted blood and yet it wasn't pain that registered. It was passion, and it sent her senses spiralling out of all control. Rafaele's hands were bruisingly hard on her arms and tears pricked behind Sam's eyelids at the tumult of desire mixed with frustration.

She opened her eyes to see swirling green oceans. Rafaele pulled away jerkily and Sam could hear nothing but the thunder of her own heartbeat and her ragged breathing. She was still clutching his jacket and she let go, her hands shaking.

'You're bleeding...'

The fact that Rafaele's voice was rough was no comfort. He was just angry, not overcome with passion.

Sam reached up and touched her lip and winced when it stung slightly. Her mouth felt swollen. She knew she had to get out of there before he saw something. Before he saw that very close behind her anger in that exchange had been an awful yearning for something else.

'I have to go. They'll be wondering where we are.' Her insides were heaving, roiling. She was terrified she might be sick again, and this time all over Rafaele's immaculate shoes. She couldn't look at him.

'Sam—'

'No.' She cut him off and looked at him. 'Not here.'

His jaw tightened. 'Fine. I'll send a car for you this evening. We'll talk at my place.'

Sam was too much in shock to argue. Too much had happened—too much physicality. Too much of a reminder that he aroused more passion in her just by looking at him than she'd ever felt in her life with anyone else. She simply didn't have it in her right then to say anything other than a very reluctant, 'Fine.' She needed to get away from this man before he exposed her completely.

That evening, Sam waited for Rafaele in an exclusive townhouse in the middle of Mayfair, demesne of the rich and famous. Anger and an awful sense of futility had simmered in her belly all day as she'd had to put up with her colleagues excitedly discussing the great opportunity Rafaele Falcone had presented them with while knowing that it was only to ensure he gained as much control of her life as he could.

She was afraid of the volatility of her emotions after what had happened in that bathroom earlier and, worse, at the thought of working for him again. She forced herself to take deep breaths and focused on her surroundings. Luxurious sofas and chairs, dressed in shades of grey and white and cream. Low coffee tables and sleek furnishings. Seriously intimidating.

She felt very scruffy as she was still in her work uniform of narrow black trousers, white shirt and black jacket. Flat shoes. Hair pulled back. No make-up. These surroundings were made for a much more sensual woman. A woman who would drape herself seductively on a couch in a beautiful silk dress and wait for her lover.

It reminded Sam painfully of Rafaele's *palazzo* on the outskirts of Milan, where sometimes she had fooled herself into believing nothing existed beyond those four walls. And that she was one of those beautiful seductive women.

'Sorry to keep you waiting.'

Sam whirled around so abruptly when she heard his voice that she felt dizzy. She realised she was clutching her leather bag to her chest like a shield and lowered it.

She really wasn't prepared to see Rafaele again so soon, and that swirling cauldron of emotions within her was spiked with a mix of anger and ever-present shame. And the memory of that angry kiss. Her lips were still sensitive. He looked like the Devil himself, emerging from the shadows of the doorway. Tall, broad, hard, muscled. And mean. His face was harsh, his mouth unsmiling. Making a mockery of his apology for keeping her waiting.

Nothing had changed from earlier. But despite her anger Sam's conscience stung. Tightly, she said, 'I'm sorry...for hitting you earlier. I don't know what came over me...but what you said...it was wrong.'

Liar. She burned inside. She might as well have held her tongue. She was lying to herself as much as to him.

Rafaele came further in. Grim. 'I deserved it. I provoked you.'

Sam blanched and looked at him. She hadn't expected that, and somewhere treacherous a part of her melted.

He walked past her and over to a drinks board, helping himself to something amber that swirled in the bottom of a bulbous glass. He looked at her over his shoulder, making heat flood her cheeks. She hadn't even realised that she'd been making a thorough inspection of his broad back, tapering down to lean hips and firm buttocks.

'Drink?'

She shook her head hurriedly and got out a choked, 'No. Thank you.'

'Suit yourself.' He gestured to a nearby couch. 'Sit down, Sam—and you can put down your bag. You look as if your fingers might break.'

She looked down stupidly to see white knuckles through the skin of her fingers where they gripped the leather. Forcing herself to take a breath, she moved jerkily over to the couch and perched on the edge, resisting the design of it, which wanted to seduce her into a more relaxed pose.

Rafaele came and sat down opposite her, clearly far more relaxed than her as he sank back into the couch, resting one arm across the top. Sam fought the desire to look and see how his shirt must be stretched across his chest.

'What kind of a name is Milo anyway? Irish?'

Sam blinked. It took a minute for his words to sink in because they were so unexpected. 'It's...it was my grandfather's name.'

Sam was vaguely surprised he remembered that detail of her heritage. She was one generation removed from Ireland, actually, having been born and brought up in England because her parents had moved there after her brilliant father had been offered a job at a London university.

Sam sensed his anger building again. 'I did intend to tell you…some day. I would never have withheld that information from Milo for ever.'

Rafaele snorted a harsh laugh. 'That's big of you. You would have waited until he'd built up a childhood full of resentment about his absent father and I wouldn't have even known.'

Rafaele sat forward and put down his glass with a clatter. He ran his hand impatiently through his hair, making it flop messily onto his forehead. Sam's insides clenched when she remembered how she'd once felt comfortable running her hands through his hair, using it to hold him in place when he'd had his face buried between—

Shame flared inside her at the way her thoughts were going. She should be thinking of Milo and extricating them both from the threat that Rafaele posed, not remembering lurid X-rated memories.

In a smaller voice she admitted, 'I've been living day to day…it didn't seem to be urgent right now. He…he doesn't ask about his father.'

Rafaele stood up, towering over her. 'I'd say it became urgent about the time you gave birth, Sam. Don't you think he must be wondering why other kids have fathers and he doesn't?'

Words were locked in Sam's throat. Milo mightn't have mentioned anything yet, but she had noticed him looking at his friends in playschool when their fathers picked them up. It wouldn't be long before he'd start asking questions.

She stood up too, not liking feeling so intimidated.

Rafaele bit back the anger that threatened to spill over and keep spilling. Looking as vulnerable, if not more so than she had earlier, Sam said tightly, 'Look, I can't stay too long. My minder is doing me a favour. Can we just… get to what we need to discuss?'

He'd been unable to get Sam's pale face out of his mind all day. Or the way he'd hauled her into his arms like a Neanderthal, all but backing her up against that sink to ravish her in a tacky bathroom. The feel of her against him, under his mouth, had dragged him back to a place he'd locked away deep inside, unleashing a cavalcade of desire more hot and urgent than anything he'd ever encountered.

He struggled to curb some of the intense emotion he was feeling.

'What's going to happen is this: I am going to be a father to my son and you will do everything in your power to facilitate that—because if you don't, Samantha, I won't hesitate to use full legal force against you.'

Rafaele delivered his ultimatum and Sam just looked at him, trying not to let him see how his words shook her to her core. *'I won't hesitate to use full legal force against you.'*

'What exactly do you mean, Rafaele? You can't threaten me like this.'

Rafaele came close to Sam—close enough for his scent to wind around her, prompting a vivid memory of how it had felt to have her mouth crushed under his earlier that day. He looked at her for such a long, taut moment that she stopped breathing. And then he moved back to the couch to sit down again and regarded her like a lounging pasha.

'It's not a threat. It's very much a promise. I want to be in Milo's life. I am his father. We deserve to get to know one another. He needs to *know* that I am his father.'

Panic boosted Sam's adrenalin. She couldn't have sat down if she'd wanted to. Every muscle was locked. 'You can't just barge in and announce that you're his father. He won't understand. It'll upset him.'

Rafaele arched a brow. 'And whose fault is that? Who

kept this knowledge from him and from me? One person, Sam. *You.* And now you have to deal with the consequences.'

'Yes,' Sam admitted bitterly, 'I recognise that, and you've already made your sphere of influence obvious—but not at the cost of my son's happiness and sense of security.'

Rafaele leant forward. 'You have cost our son his happiness and security already. You've wilfully cost him three years of knowing he had a father. You've already irreparably damaged his development.'

Our son. Sam's insides contracted painfully. She was feeling shocked again at the very evident emotion on Rafaele's face. Quickly masked, though, as if he was surprised by his own vehemence.

'So what are you proposing, Rafaele?'

A part of Sam, deep down inside, marvelled at that moment that there had ever been intimacy between them. That she had ever lain beside him in bed and gazed deep into his eyes. On their last night together...before he'd gone on his business trip...she'd reached out and touched his face as if learning every feature. He'd taken her hand and pressed a kiss to her palm, and there had been something she'd never seen before darkening his eyes, making her breath grow short and her heart pound...

'What I'm proposing is that, as I'm due to be here in England for the foreseeable future, I want to be a part of Milo's daily life so that he can get to know me.'

Sam struggled to take it in. '"The foreseeable future"? What does that mean? You can't get to know him and then just walk away, Rafaele, when your business is done.'

Rafaele stood up and put his hands deep in his pockets, as if he was having second thoughts about physical violence. Silkily he replied, 'Oh, don't worry, Sam, I have no intention of walking away—ever—no matter where my business takes me. Milo is my son just as much as he is yours. You've had unfettered access to him for over three years of his life and you will never deny me access again. I want him here—with me.'

Sam's mouth opened and closed again before she could manage to articulate, 'Here with you? But that's preposterous. He's *three!*'

Rafaele clarified with clear reluctance, 'Naturally you would also have to come.'

Sam emitted a scared laugh, because even though what Rafaele was saying was insane he sounded eminently reasonable. 'Oh, thanks! Should I be grateful that you would allow me to stay with my son?'

Rafaele's face darkened. 'I think any judge in any courtroom would look unfavourably upon a mother who kept her son from his father for no apparent good reason.'

Sam blanched and tried to appeal to him. 'Rafaele, we can't just…uproot and move in with you. It's not practical.' And the very thought of spending any more time alone with this man than she had to scared the living daylights out of her.

His voice sounded unbearably harsh. 'I am going to be under the same roof as my son, as his father, and I will not negotiate on that. You can either be part of it or not. Obviously it will be easier if you are. And, as we're going to be working together again, it can only be more practical.'

Anger surged again at Rafaele's reminder of that small detail and his intractability. 'You're being completely unreasonable. Of course I need to be with my son…*that's* non-negotiable.'

Rafaele took a step closer, and even though his hands were in his pockets Sam felt the threat reach out to touch her.

'Well, then, you have a measure of how I'm feeling, Samantha. I will expect you back here with your bags and

Milo by this time tomorrow evening or else we take it to the courts and they will decide how he will divide his time between us.' He added, 'You've proved that you believe one parent is dispensable—what's to stop me testing out the theory with you?'

Sam gritted out, 'I do recognise that you've missed out on time with Milo…and I should have told you before now. But I had my reasons and I believed they were valid.'

'Very noble of you, Samantha,' Rafaele mocked, with an edge.

Trying to concentrate and not be distracted by him, she said, 'It's just not practical for us to come here. This might be your home, and it's beautiful—'

'It's not mine,' Rafaele bit out. 'It belongs to a friend. I'm renting it.'

Sam lifted her hands in an unconscious plea for him to listen. 'All the more reason why this isn't a good idea—it's not even your permanent home. Milo is settled into a good routine where we are. We have a granny flat attached to the house and that's where Bridie lives.'

Rafaele arched a brow. 'His minder?'

Sam nodded. 'She was my father's housekeeper since I was two, after my mother died. She cared for me while I grew up and she stayed on after my father passed away two years ago.'

'I'm sorry,' Rafaele offered stiffly, 'I didn't know.'

'Thank you…' Sam acknowledged. 'The thing is,' she continued while she had Rafaele's attention, 'Bridie has known Milo since he was born. She…helped me.'

Sam coloured as she imagined the acerbic retorts going through Rafaele's mind and she rushed on. 'We have a good arrangement. Regular affordable childcare like I have is gold dust in London.'

Rafaele asserted, 'I don't think I need to point out that

affording childcare would be the least of your worries if you let me organise it.'

Sam was tense enough to crack, and all of a sudden she felt incredibly light-headed. She must have shown it, because immediately Rafaele was beside her, holding her arm and frowning.

'What is it? *Dio*, Sam, you look like death warmed up.'

His use of *Sam* caught her somewhere vulnerable. She cursed herself inwardly. She was no wilting ninny and she hated that Rafaele was seeing her like this. She pulled away from his strong grip jerkily. 'I'm fine…'

Rafaele all but forcibly manoeuvred her to the couch and made her sit down again. Then he went to the drinks cabinet and poured some brandy into a glass. Coming back, he handed it to her.

Hating herself for needing the fortification, Sam took it. She took a sip, and as the pungent and strong alcohol filtered down her throat and into her belly, felt a bit steadier. She put the glass down and looked directly at Rafaele, where he too had taken his seat again, opposite her.

'Look, you've said yourself that you're just renting this place. It would be insane to uproot Milo from the only home he's known since he was a baby.' She pressed on, 'My father's house is perfectly comfortable. Bridie lives right next door. His playschool is at the end of the road. We have a nearby park. He goes swimming at the weekends to the local pool. He plays with the children from the surrounding houses. It's a safe area. Everyone looks out for everyone and they all love Milo.'

Rafaele's face was unreadable. Sam took a breath. She'd just spoken as if in a lecture, in a series of bullet points. Never more than right now did she appreciate just how much Rafaele could upset their lives if he wanted to. And it was entirely her fault.

He drawled, 'The picture you paint is positively idyllic.'

She flushed at the sarcasm in his voice. 'We're lucky to be in a good area.'

'How have you managed financially?'

Rafaele's question blindsided Sam for a minute. 'It... well, it wasn't easy at first. I had to defer my PhD for a year. My father was ill... But I had some savings to tide us over. And he had his pension. When he died the mortgage was protected, so that was paid off. Bridie looked after Milo while I did my doctorate and I was lucky enough to be taken onto the research programme soon afterwards. We get by. We have enough.'

Unmistakable pride straightened Sam's spine. Rafaele could see it in the set of her shoulders and he had to hand it to her—grudgingly. She hadn't come running to him looking for a hand-out as soon as she'd known her pregnancy was viable. He didn't know any woman who wouldn't have taken advantage of that fact. And yet Sam had been determined to go it alone.

'Would you have come to me if you'd needed money?'

Rafaele could see her go pale at the prospect and something dark rushed to his gut. She would have preferred to struggle than to see him again. Since last Saturday's cataclysmic revelation Rafaele had been avoiding looking at the fact that he'd felt so compelled to see Sam again he'd ignored his earlier warning to himself to stay away and had gone to her house with more than a sense of anticipation in his belly. It had been something bordering much closer to a *need*. He'd tried to ignore it, but he'd been incensed that she'd been so dismissive. Uninterested.

Rafaele stood up. 'I fail to see what all this has to do with me getting what I want—which is my son.'

Sam stood up too, her cheeks flushing, making her eyes stand out like glittering pools of grey. Desire, dark and urgent, speared Rafaele.

'That's just it. You don't get it, do you? It's not about you or me. It's about Milo and what's best for *him*. He's not a pawn, Rafaele, you can't just move him around at will to get back at me. His needs must come first.'

Rafaele felt stung at her tirade. She had the right to maternal indignation because she'd experienced the bonding process. He hadn't. But he knew that she was right. He couldn't just waltz in and pluck his son out of his routine, much as he wanted to. But he hated her for this.

Tightly he asked, 'So what is your suggestion, then?'

The relief that moved across her expressive fine features made him even angrier. Did she really think it would be this easy?

'We leave Milo where he is, at home with me. And you can come and see him…we'll work something out while you're here in England…and then, once we see how it goes, we can work out a longer term arrangement. After all, you won't be here for ever…'

He could see her spying her bag nearby and she moved to get it. His eyes were drawn against his will to her tall, slim form as she bent and then straightened, her breasts pushing against her shirt, reminding him of how badly he'd ached to touch them for the first time, and what it had felt like to cup their firm weight, made perfectly to fit his palms. The fact that the memory was so vivid was not welcome.

Sam was the only woman who'd ever had this ability to make him feel slightly out of his comfort zone. Coasting on the edge of extreme danger. And not the kind he liked, where he ultimately had control, say in a car.

Danger zone or no danger zone, something primal gripped Rafaele deep inside at seeing Sam preparing to leave, looking so relieved—as if she could just lay it all on the line like this and he'd agree.

She was backing away, tucking some loose hair behind her ear, and it was that one simple familiar gesture that pushed Rafaele over an edge. 'Do you really think it's that easy? That I'll simply agree to your terms?'

She stopped. 'You can't do this, Rafaele—insist on having it your way. It's not fair on Milo. If he's going to get to know you then it should be in his own safe environment. He's going to be confused as it is.'

Rafaele moved closer to Sam, almost against his will. 'And whose fault is that?' he reminded her, as an audacious plan formed in his brain. 'What do you hope for, Sam? That after a couple of visits I'll grow bored and you'll be left in peace?'

She swallowed visibly and looked faintly guilty. 'Of course not.'

But *she did*. He could tell. She hoped that this was just a passing display of anger and might. She was probably congratulating herself on the fact that he now knew and that she and her son—*his son*—would be left in peace to get on with their lives once he'd lost interest.

Suddenly Rafaele wanted to insert himself deep into Sam's life. *Deep into her*. He remembered what that had felt like too—that moment of exquisite suspension when neither of them could draw in a breath because he was embedded so deep inside her—

'This will work *my way* or no way,' he gritted out, ruthlessly crushing those incendiary images, exerting a control over his body he rarely had to call on.

'Rafaele—'

'No, Samantha. I will concede that you are right that Milo must come first, so I agree that he should stay where he is most secure.'

'You do?'

Rafaele didn't even bother to agree again, he just continued, 'So, with that concern in mind, I will compromise.'

She swallowed again. Now she looked nervous. *Good. She should*. Rafaele smiled and got a fleeting moment of satisfaction from the way her eyes dropped to his mouth and flared with something hot.

'I'll move in with you.'

Sam's eyes met his and grew wider. He saw her struggling to compute the information. She even shook her head slightly.

'I'm sorry… I don't think I heard you properly… You said you'll what?'

Rafaele smiled even more widely now, enjoying himself for the first time in days. 'You heard me fine, Samantha, I said I'll move in with you. Then you will have no reason to deny me access to my son as I'll be doing everything in my power to accommodate you—isn't that right?'

Sam felt as if she was suspended in time, disbelieving of what she'd just heard. But then the smug look on Rafaele's face told her she hadn't misheard. *Twice.*

'But…you can't. I mean…' Her brain seemed to have turned to slush. 'There's no room.'

Rafaele quirked a brow. 'It looks like a decent-sized house to me. I would imagine there's at least three bedrooms? All I need is one.'

Sam cursed his accuracy and diverted her thoughts away from remembering Rafaele's palatial bedroom in his *palazzo*, with the bed big enough for a football team. They'd covered every inch of it.

Stiffly she said, 'It's not a good idea. You wouldn't be comfortable. It's not exactly up to this standard.' She gestured with her arm to take in the surrounding opulence.

Rafaele grimaced. 'This place is too big for just me.' And then his eyes glinted with sheer wickedness. 'I find my preferences running to much more modest requirements all of a sudden.'

Sam felt old bitterness rise. No doubt he meant much in the same way his preferences had become more 'modest' when he'd found himself briefly in thrall to her. Seduced, presumably, by her complete naivety and innocence because he'd become momentarily jaded by the far more sophisticated women he usually went for. This had been evidenced by the fact that he'd never even taken her out in too public a social setting, preferring to keep their dates secluded and *secret*.

Sam shook her head, the mere thought of Rafaele in her house for an extended period making her seize inwardly. Not to mention the fact that he expected her to work for him.

'No. This is not going to happen. Maybe if you moved closer—'

Suddenly Rafaele was far too close and Sam's words faltered. Any hint of wickedness was gone.

'No, Samantha. I am moving in with you and there is nothing you can do or say to put me off this course. I've missed important milestones already in my son's life and I'm not about to miss another moment.'

Shakily Sam said, 'Please, there must be another way to do this.'

Rafaele stepped even closer. Sam could smell him now and see the lighter flecks of green in his eyes. See the dark shadowing of stubble on his jaw. He'd always needed to shave twice a day. Her insides cramped.

'The reason you don't want me to stay, Sam... It wouldn't be because there's still something there...would it?'

Had his voice grown huskier or was it her imagination? Sam just looked at him and blinked. His eyes were molten green, hot. And she was on fire. It was only when she saw something very cynical and dark in their depths that she managed to shake herself free of his spell. She was terrified he'd touch her again, like earlier, and stepped back, feeling cold all over.

The thought that she'd given herself away, that he might

analyse her reaction and suspect that there had been some-thing deeper there than anger made her sick with morti-fication and shame.

In as cool a voice as she could muster, Sam said, 'Don't be ridiculous, Rafaele. I'm no more attracted to you any more than you are to me. That died long ago.'

His eyes flashed. 'So there should be no problem with my sharing your house to facilitate me getting to know my son, who you have kept from me for the last three years?'

It wasn't really a question. Much as in the way he had ridden roughshod over her department at work, ensuring she would be under his control. With a sinking sense of inevitability Sam knew that if she fought Rafaele further he'd only dig his heels in deeper and deeper. And perhaps he'd even feel like toying with her again, proving a point, and perhaps this time she'd really give herself away.

The thought made her go clammy. She must never forget his cruel rejection or let him know how badly he'd hurt her.

She reassured herself that he was a workaholic, after all, so she'd probably barely see him. And for all his lofty talk she didn't seriously see him lasting for longer than a week in the leafy but very boring London suburbs.

A man like Rafaele—son of an Italian count and a re-nowned Spanish beauty—was accustomed to beautiful things and especially beautiful women. Accustomed to getting what he wanted.

Seizing on that, and also anticipating his realisation that her house would not be a haven for his mistresses and would soon bore him to tears, Sam lifted her chin and said, 'When do you propose to move in?'

CHAPTER FOUR

FOUR DAYS LATER it was Friday evening, and Sam was tense enough to crack in two, waiting for Rafaele's appearance. He was moving in tonight, and all week his staff had been arriving at the house to prepare it for his arrival.

When she'd come home from his house the previous Monday evening she'd had to come clean and tell Bridie what had happened. The older woman had reacted with admirable nonchalance.

'He's his father, you say?'

'Yes,' Sam had replied, *sotto voce*, giving Bridie a look to tell her to be mindful of small ears nearby as Milo had been in the sitting room, watching a cartoon before bed.

Unfortunately Bridie had been enjoying this revelation far too much. She'd taken a sip of tea and then repeated, 'His father... Well, I never, Sam. You're a dark one, aren't you? I always thought it might have been a waiter or a mechanic at the factory or something...but it's actually himself—the Falcone boss...'

Sam had gritted out, 'He's only moving in temporarily. He'll be bored within a week, believe me.'

Bridie had sniffed disapprovingly. 'Well, let's hope not for Milo's sake.'

Sam's hands stilled under the water now, as she washed the dinner dishes. She could hear Milo's chatter to Bridie nearby. She was doing this for him. She had to stop thinking about herself and think of him. It was the only way she'd get through this, because if she focused for a second on what it meant for her to be thrown into such close proximity with Rafaele again she felt the urgent compulsion to run fast and far away.

Bridie bustled into the kitchen then, and Sam noticed her badly disguised expression of anticipation. She might have smiled if she'd been able.

'You really don't have to wait till he gets here.'

The housekeeper smiled at her sunnily and started drying dishes. 'Oh, I wouldn't miss this for the world, Sam. It's better than the Pope's visit to Dublin back in the seventies.'

Suddenly the low, powerful throb of an engine became obvious outside. To Sam's chagrin she found that she was automatically trying to analyse the nuances of the sound, figuring out the components of the engine.

Milo's ears must have pricked up, because he came into the kitchen excitedly and announced, 'Car!'

They didn't have a car themselves, much to his constant disappointment, and Sam couldn't stop him running towards the door now. When the bell rang her palms grew sweaty. Before she could move, though, Bridie was beating her to it, and Sam only noticed then that Bridie, who never wore an apron, had put one on. She wanted to roll her eyes.

But then the door opened and Sam's world condensed down to the tall dark figure filling the frame against the dusky evening. She hadn't seen him since Monday and she hated the way her heart leapt in her chest.

Milo said with some surprise from beside Bridie, 'It's the man.' And then, completely oblivious to the atmosphere, 'Do you have a car?'

Rafaele's gaze had zeroed in immediately on Sam, and she was glad now that she had the buffer of Bridie at the door. Bridie was doing her thing now, extending her hand, introducing herself, practically twinkling with Irish charm.

Lots of *'sure'* and *'Won't you come in out of that cold?'*.
Ridiculously, Sam felt betrayed.

Rafaele stepped in and Sam's chest constricted. He
looked so alien, foreign. Too gorgeous for this environment. Finally she found her legs and moved forward to pick
Milo up. His eyes were huge as he took Rafaele in, again.

Milo repeated his question. 'Do you have a car, mister?'

Rafaele looked at Milo and Sam could see how his
cheeks flared with colour. His eyes took on a glow that
she'd never seen before...or maybe she thought she had...
once. Her arms tightened fractionally around Milo. Bridie
had bustled off somewhere, saying something about tea
and coffee. Now it was just the three of them.

His voice was so deep it resonated within Sam.

'Yes, I do have a car... I'm Rafaele...and what's your
name?'

The fact that Rafaele's voice had gone husky made
Sam's guilt rush to the fore again. Milo buried his head
in Sam's neck, his little arms tight around her neck.

She said to Milo's obscured face, 'Don't you remember me telling you that Mr Falcone would be moving in to
live with us for a while?' Milo nodded against her neck,
still hiding. She looked back at Rafaele. 'He's just a bit shy
with strangers at first.'

Rafaele's eyes flashed dangerously at that reminder of
his status and Sam said quickly, 'You can leave your jacket
and things in the hall.'

He started to divest himself of his expensive black coat,
revealing a dark suit underneath. Bridie reappeared then,
unusually pink in the cheeks, and took Milo from Sam's
arms, saying, 'I think it's bedtime for someone...there's
refreshments in the drawing room.'

Sam wanted to roll her eyes again. Since when had Bridie referred to the main reception room as *the drawing*

room? Or said *refreshments*? Or got pink in the cheeks from preparing tea?

She called after them. 'I'll be up to read a story in a little while.'

All she could hear, though, was Milo's plaintive, 'I want to see the car,' and Bridie reassuring him briskly that he could see it in the morning if he was a good boy and brushed his teeth before bed.

Hating Rafaele right then, for imposing himself on them like this and upsetting their equilibrium, Sam forced herself to look at him and bit out, 'I'll give you a tour, shall I?'

Rafaele smiled, but it didn't reach his eyes. 'That would be lovely.'

As perfunctorily as she could, while uncomfortably aware of Rafaele breathing down her neck, Sam showed him around the ground floor of the house.

He stopped in the study and took in the impressive array of equipment set up for his benefit, surprising her by saying, 'This was your father's study?'

'Yes,' Sam answered, more huskily than she would have liked, caught by a sudden upsurge of emotion at remembering her scatty, absent-minded father spending hours on end in here, oblivious to everything. Her chest tightened. *Oblivious to his daughter.*

'They should not have set up in here…it's not appropriate.'

Sam looked at Rafaele, surprised by this assertion. By this evidence of sensitivity.

'No…it's fine. It's been lying empty. It should be used.' Her mouth twisted wryly. 'Believe me, you could have set all this up here while he was still alive and he wouldn't have even noticed.'

Feeling exposed under Rafaele's incisive green gaze, Sam backed out of the room.

'Upstairs. I'll show you your room.'

She hurried up the stairs, very aware of Rafaele behind her, conscious of her drab work uniform. Again.

She opened and closed doors with almost indecent speed, and they passed where Milo was chattering nineteen to the dozen with Bridie as she helped him brush his teeth in the bathroom, standing on a little box so he could reach the sink.

Rafaele stopped outside for a long moment, and when he finally turned to keep following Sam she shivered at the look of censure in his eyes. That brief moment of sensitivity had evidently passed.

When she didn't open the door to her bedroom, but just gestured at it with clear reluctance, Rafaele pushed past her and opened the door. He looked in for a long moment, before slanting her an unmistakably mocking look. She burned inside with humiliation and hated to imagine what he must think of the room. It hadn't been redecorated since she'd left home for college and still sported dusky pink rose wallpaper.

The faded décor now seemed to scream out her innermost teenage fantasies of *not* being the school nerd, of her deeply secret wish to be just like all the other girls. No wonder Rafaele had seduced her so easily. He'd unwittingly tapped into the closet feminine romantic that Sam had repressed her whole life in a bid to be accepted by her father, turning herself into a studious tomboy.

Aghast to be thinking of this now, she swallowed her mortification, reached past Rafaele and pulled the door firmly closed in his face. Then she led him to his room.

Thankfully it was at the other end of the house from her room and Milo's, which was opposite hers. And, even better, it had an *en suite* bathroom. After that cataclysmic moment in the university the other day she had no intention of running into a half-naked Rafaele on his way to the bathroom.

Rafaele barely gave the room a cursory once-over. As she led him back downstairs Sam sent up another silent prayer that he was already chafing to get back to his own rarefied world, where his every whim was indulged before he'd even articulated it out loud.

Bridie had indeed set out tea and coffee in the front room. Sam poured coffee and handed it to him, watching warily as he sat down on the comfy but decidedly thread-bare sofa.

He looked around, taking in the homely furnishings. 'You have a nice house.'

Sam took a seat as far away from Rafaele as possible. She all but snorted. 'Hardly what you're used to.'

He levelled her a look that would have sent his minions running. 'I'm not a snob, Samantha. I may have had a priv-ileged upbringing, but when I set out to resurrect Falcone Industries I had nothing but the shirt on my back. I lived in an apartment the size of your porch and worked three jobs to put myself through college.'

Sam frowned, a little blindsided by this revelation. 'But your stepfather—he was a Greek billionaire…'

Rafaele's mouth twisted. 'Who hated my guts because I wasn't his son. The only reason he put me through school at all was because of my mother. He washed his hands of me as soon as he could and I paid him back every cent he'd doled out for my education.'

He'd never told her this before—had always shied away from talking about personal things. She'd always assumed that he'd been given a hand-out to restart Falcone Indus-tries. It was one of the most well-documented resurrections of a company in recent times. Spectacular in its success. She recalled his mother ringing from time to time, and their clipped conversations largely conducted in Spanish, which was her first language.

At a loss to know what to say, Sam went for the easiest thing. 'How *is* your mother?'

Rafaele's face tightened almost imperceptibly but Sam noticed.

'She died three months ago. A heart attack.'

'I'm sorry, Rafaele,' Sam responded. 'I had no idea…' She gestured helplessly. 'I must have missed it in the papers.'

His Spanish mother had been a world-renowned beauty and feted model. Her marriages and lovers had been well documented. The rumour was that she had cruelly left Rafaele's father when it had become apparent that he'd lost everything except his title. But this was only hearsay that Sam had picked up when she'd gone to Milan to work for Falcone Industries as an intern.

Rafaele shook his head, his mouth thin. 'It was overshadowed by the economic crisis in Greece so it barely made the papers—something we welcomed.'

Sam could remember how much Rafaele had hated press intrusion and the constant glare of the paparazzi lens. He put down his cup and stood abruptly. Sam looked up, her breath sticking in her throat for a minute as he loomed so large and intimidating. *Gorgeous*. Lord, how was she going to get through even twenty-four hours of him living under the same roof, just down the hall? Did he still sleep naked—?

'…will you tell him?'

Sam flushed hotly when she registered Rafaele looking at her expectantly. He'd just asked her a question and she'd been so busy speculating on whether or not he still slept naked that she hadn't heard him.

She stood up so quickly her knees banged against the coffee table and she winced. 'Tell who what?'

Rafaele looked irritated. 'When are you going to tell Milo that I am his father?'

Sam crossed her arms over breasts that felt heavy and tingly. 'I think…I think when he's got used to you being here. When he's got to know you a bit…then we can tell him.' She cursed herself for once again proving that her mind was all too easily swayed by this man.

He nodded. 'I think that's fair enough.'

Sam breathed out, struck somewhere vulnerable at seeing Rafaele intent on putting Milo's needs first, over his wish to punish her.

Just then Bridie put her head around the door. 'I'm off, love, and Milo is waiting for his story. If you need me over the weekend just call me. Nice to meet you, Mr Falcone.'

Sam moved towards the door, more in a bid to get away from Rafaele than a desire to see Bridie out, but the older woman waved her back with a definite glint in her eyes.

'Stay where you are.'

Rafaele murmured goodnight and then Bridie was gone. Sam heard the sound of the front door opening and closing. And now she really was alone in the house with the man she'd hoped never to see again and her son. *Milo.* The incongruity of Rafaele Falcone, international billionaire and playboy, here in her suburban house, was overwhelming to say the least.

She backed towards the door. 'I should go to Milo. He'll come looking for me if I don't.' Why did she suddenly sound as if she'd just been running?

Rafaele inclined his head. 'I have some work to attend to, if you don't mind me using the study?'

Sam was relieved at the prospect of some space. 'Of course not.'

And then she fled, taking the stairs two at a time as she had when she'd been a teenager.

Rafaele heard Sam take the stairs at a gallop and shook his head. He looked around the room again. Definitely not the milieu he was accustomed to, in spite of his defence to

Sam. Those gruelling years when he'd done nothing but work, study, sleep and repeat were a blur now.

He felt slightly shell-shocked at how easily he'd told Sam something he never discussed. It was no secret that he'd turned his back on his stepfather to resurrect his family legacy, but people invariably drew their own conclusions.

His mouth tightened. He'd resisted the urge to spill his guts before—had been content to distract them both from talking by concentrating on the physical. Avoiding a deeper intimacy at all costs.

Rafaele cursed and ran his hands through his hair, feeling constricted in his suit. He'd come straight here from a meeting in town. As soon as he'd walked in through the front door he'd felt the house closing in around him claustrophobically and he'd had a bizarre urge to turn on his heel, get back into his car and drive very fast in the opposite direction.

For a wild few seconds when he'd looked at Sam waiting in the hall the only thing he'd been able to remember was how he'd all but devoured her only days before. He'd assured himself that he could just send in his lawyers and have her dictated to, punished for not telling him about Milo.

But then he'd seen Milo, held in her arms, and the claustrophobia had disappeared. *That* was why he was here. Because he didn't want more months to go by before he got a chance to let his son know who he was. More months added on top of the three years he'd already missed. Rafaele had never really forgiven his own father for falling apart and checking out of his life so spectacularly. For investing so much in a woman who had never loved him. For allowing himself to turn into something maudlin and useless.

For years Rafaele had been jealous of his younger

brother, Alexio, who had grown up bathed in his father's love and support. So much so, however, that Rafaele knew how stifling Alexio had found it, prompting him to turn his back on his own inheritance. He smiled grimly to himself. Maybe that just proved one could never be happy?

He made his way to the study and sat down behind the desk, firing up various machines. He stopped abruptly when he heard movement above his head. His heart twisted at the realisation that he must be underneath Milo's room. Obeying an urge he couldn't ignore, Rafaele stood up and walked out of the room and up the stairs, as silent as a panther.

He saw the half-open door of Milo's room and stopped when he could see inside. The scene made him suck in a breath. Sam was leaning back against a headboard painted in bright colours with Milo in her embrace. She held a book open in front of them and was reading aloud, putting on funny voices, making Milo giggle.

Rafaele had forgotten that she wore glasses to read and write. They made her look seriously studious, but also seriously sexy. Her mouth was plump and pink. Even in the plain white shirt and trousers her slim curves were evident. This sight of her was hugely disconcerting. He'd never expected to see her in this situation. And yet something about it called to him—an echo of an emotion he'd crushed ruthlessly when she'd first told him she was pregnant. Before the shock had hit, and the cynical suspicion that she'd planned it, had come something far more disturbing. Something fragile and alien.

He hated her right then for still having an effect on him. For still making him want her. For invading his imagination when he'd least expected it over the last four years. He would find it hard to recall his last lover's name right now, but Sam…her name had always been indelible. And this was utterly galling when she'd proved to be as treacherous as his own mother in her own way. When she'd kept the most precious thing from him. His son.

For a moment Rafaele questioned his sanity in deciding to take over funding the research programme at the university in a bid to get to Sam. But then he remembered looking down into Milo's green eyes and recognising his own DNA like a beacon winking back at him.

As much as there was a valid reason behind his rationale, it had also come from that deeper place not linked solely to rationale and he hated to admit that.

His eyes went to his son and Rafaele put a hand to his chest, where an ache was forming. He would make it his life's mission to keep Sam from sidelining him from his own son's life. Whatever it took. Even if it meant spending twenty-four hours a day with her. He could resist her. How could he desire a woman who had denied him his most basic right of all? His own flesh and blood.

Later, when Sam was in bed, the familiar creakings of the old house which normally comforted her sounded sinister. Rafaele Falcone was separated from her only by some bricks and mortar. And reality was slowly sinking in. Her new reality. Living and working with Rafaele Falcone. She suspected that he'd flexed his muscles to get her to work for him as much to irritate her as for any *bona fide* professional reason, even if that was why he'd first contacted her.

The thought of going back into that factory environment made her feel clammy. Although she'd loved it the first time around—it had been so exciting, getting an internship with one of the most innovative and successful motor companies in the world.

Rafaele had made his initial fortune by devising a computer software program which aided in the design of cars, and that was how he'd first come onto the scene, stunning the world with its success. That was how he'd been able to fund getting Falcone Motors off the ground again—injecting it with new life, turning around the perception of the Falcone car as outdated and prehistoric. Now Falcone cars were the most coveted on the race track *and* on the roads.

And Sam had been in the thick of it, working on new cutting edge designs, figuring out the most fuel-efficient engine systems. From her very first day, though, she'd been aware of Rafaele. She'd gone bright red whenever she saw him, never expecting him to be as gorgeous in the flesh as he was in press photos.

He'd surprised her by being very hands-on, not afraid to get dirty himself, and invariably he knew more than all of them put together, displaying an awesome intelligence and intellect. And, in a notoriously male-dominated industry, she'd met more females working in his factory than she'd encountered in all her years as a student. Clearly when he said equal opportunities he meant it.

Sam had found that each day she was seeking him out… only to look away like a naive schoolgirl if he met her gaze, which he'd appeared to do more and more often. She'd been innocent—literally. A childhood spent with an emotionally distant father and with her head buried in books hadn't made for a well-rounded adolescence. While her peers had been experimenting with boys Sam had been trying in vain to connect with her scatty but brilliant father. Bridie had been in despair, and had all but given up encouraging Sam to get out and enjoy herself, not to worry so much about studying or her father.

The irony of it all was that while the more predominantly masculine areas *did* appeal to her—hence her subsequent career—she'd always longed to feel more feminine. And it was this very secret desire that Rafaele had unwittingly tapped into so effectively. Just by looking at her, he had made Sam feel like a woman for the first time in her life.

One of their first conversations had been over an intricate engine. The other interns and engineers had walked away momentarily and Sam had been about to follow them when Rafaele had caught her wrist. He'd let her go again almost immediately but her skin had burned for hours afterwards, along with the fire in her belly.

'So,' he'd drawled in that sexy voice, 'where did your interest and love for engines come from, Miss Rourke?'

The *Miss Rourke* had sounded gently mocking, as if some sort of secret code had passed between them. Sam had been mesmerised and it had taken a second for her to answer. She'd shrugged, looking away from the penetrating gaze that had seemed to see her in a way that was both exhilarating and terrifying.

'My father is a professor of physics, so I've grown up surrounded by science. And my grandmother...his mother...she was Irish, but she ended up in England during the Second World War, working in the factories on cars. Apparently she loved it and had a natural affinity for working with engines—so much so that she kept her job after the war for a few years, before returning home to marry.' She'd shrugged again. 'I guess it ran in the family.'

Sam looked back at her young naive self now and cringed. She'd been so transparent, so easy to seduce. It had taken one earth-shattering kiss in Rafaele's office and she'd opened herself up for him, had forgotten everything her upbringing had taught her about protecting herself from emotionally unavailable people.

He'd whispered to her that she was sensual, sexy, beautiful, and she'd melted. A girl who had grown up denying her very sexuality had had no defence mechanism in place to deal with someone as practised and polished and seductive as Rafaele.

She'd fallen for him quicker than Alice in Wonderland had fallen down the rabbit hole. And her world had changed as utterly as Alice's: beautiful dresses, intoxicating dates—one night he'd even flown them to Venice in his helicopter for dinner.

And then there had been the sex. He'd taken her innocence with a tenderness she never would have expected of a consummate seducer. It had been mind-blowing, addictive. Almost overwhelming for Sam, who had never imagined her boring, almost boyish body could arouse someone—never mind a man like Rafaele Falcone, who had his pick of the world's most beautiful women.

During their short-lived affair, even though he'd told her, 'Samantha…don't fall for me. Don't hope for something more because I have nothing to give someone like you…' she hadn't listened. She'd told herself that he had to feel *something*, because when they made love it felt as if they transcended everything that bound them to this earth and touched something profound.

At the time, though, she'd laughed and said airily, belying her own naivety, 'Relax, Rafaele! It is possible, you know, for not every woman you meet to fall in love with you. I know what this is. It's just sex.'

She'd made herself say it out loud, even though it had been like turning a knife towards her own belly and thrusting it deep. Because she'd been so far out of her depth by then she might as well have been in the middle of the Atlantic Ocean. She'd been lying, of course. She'd proved to be as humiliatingly susceptible to Rafaele's lethal charm as the next hapless woman.

If anything, he'd given her a life lesson and a half. For a brief moment she'd lost her head and forgotten that if it looked like a dream and felt like a dream, then it probably was a dream. Her real world was far more banal and she'd always been destined to return to it. Milo or no Milo.

Punching the pillow beneath her head now, as if she could punch the memories away too, Sam closed her eyes and promised herself that not for a second would she ever betray just how badly that man had hurt her.

'Mummy, the man is still here. He's downstairs in the book room.'

Sam responded to the none-too-gentle shaking of her son and opened her eyes. She'd finally fallen asleep somewhere around dawn. *Again*. Milo's eyes were huge in his face and Sam struggled to sit up, pulling him into her, feeling her stomach clench at the reminder of who was here.

'I told you that he'd be moving in with us for a while, don't you remember?' she prompted sleepily.

Milo nodded and then asked, 'But where's *his* house?'

Sam smiled wryly. Little did her son know that his father had a veritable portfolio of houses around the world.

'He doesn't have a house here in London.'

'Okay.' Milo clambered out of the bed and looked at her winsomely. 'Can we get Cheerios now?'

Sam got out of bed and reached for her robe—and then thought better of it when she imagined Rafaele giving its threadbare appearance a caustic once-over. No doubt he would wonder what on earth he'd ever seen in her.

Hating to be so influenced by what he might think, Sam reached for jeans and a thin sweatshirt and yanked her sleep-mussed hair into a ponytail. No make-up. She cursed herself. She wasn't trying to seduce Rafaele, for crying out loud.

Milo was jumping around now and then stopped. 'Do you...do you think he'll eat Cheerios too?' He looked comically stricken. 'What if he eats *my* Cheerios?'

Sam bent down and tweaked Milo's nose. 'He won't touch your Cheerios while I'm around. Anyway, I happen to know for a fact that he only likes coffee for breakfast.'

Something poignant gripped her as she remembered

lazy mornings when Rafaele would take great pleasure in feeding her but not himself, much to her amusement.

'Ugh,' declared Milo, already setting off out of the room, 'Coffee is *yuck*.'

Sam heard him go downstairs, sounding like a herd of baby elephants, and took a deep breath before following him. The study door was ajar, and as she passed she could hear the low deep tones that had an instant effect on her insides.

Milo was pointing with his finger and saying in a very loud stage whisper, 'He's in there.'

Sam just nodded and put a finger to her lips, then herded Milo towards the kitchen, where he quickly got distracted helping to set the table.

And even though she knew Rafaele was in the house she still wasn't prepared when she turned around and saw him standing in the doorway, looking dark and gorgeous in faded jeans and a thin jumper. It did little to disguise the inherent strength of his very powerful masculine form, akin to that of an athlete. He was so *sexy*. With that unmistakable foreign edge that no English man could ever hope to pull off.

The memory of his initial effect on her four years ago was still raw, but she forced herself to say civilly, 'Good morning. I hope you slept well?'

He smiled faintly but she noticed it barely touched those luminous green eyes. 'Like a log.'

Milo piped up, 'That's silly. *Logs* can't sleep.'

Rafaele looked at his son and again Sam noticed the way something in his face and eyes softened. He came into the kitchen and sat down at the table near Milo. 'Oh, really? What should I say, then?'

Milo was embarrassed now with the attention and started squirming in his chair. 'Aunty Bridie says she sleeps like a baby, and babies sleep all the time.'

'Okay,' Rafaele said. 'I slept like a baby. Is that right?'

Milo was still embarrassed and avoided Rafaele's eyes, but then curiosity got the better of him and he squinted him a look. 'You sound funny.'

Rafaele smiled. 'That's because I come from a place called Italy…so I speak Italian. That's why I sound funny.'

Milo looked at Sam. 'Mummy, how come we don't sound like the man?'

Sam avoided Rafaele's eyes. She put Milo's bowl of cereal down in front of him and chided gently, 'His name is Rafaele.' And then, 'Because we come from England and we speak English. To some people *we* would sound funny.'

But Milo was already engrossed in his food, oblivious to the undercurrents between the two adults in the small kitchen. Sam risked a glance at Rafaele and blanched. His look said it all: *The reason he thinks I sound funny is because you've denied him his heritage.*

Sam turned to the coffee machine as if it was the most interesting thing on the planet and said, too brightly, 'Would you like some coffee?'

She heard a chair scrape and looked around to see Rafaele standing up. 'I had some earlier. I have to go to the factory for a while today but I'll be back later. Don't worry about dinner or anything like that—I have to go out tonight to a function.'

'Oh.' Sam rested her hands on the counter behind her. She hated the sudden deflated feeling in her solar plexus. But hadn't she expected this? So why was she feeling disappointed? And angry?

The words spilled out before she could stop them. 'I forgot that weekends for you are just as important as any other day.' *Except for when he'd spent that whole last weekend in bed with her, and diverted his phone calls.*

Rafaele's eyes flashed. 'We're taking in delivery of some specially manufactured parts today and I need to

make sure they're up to spec because we start putting
them into new cars next week. Something,' he drawled,
with that light of triumph in his eyes, '*you'll* be dealing
with next week when you come to work.'

Sam's insides clenched hard even as a treacherous
flicker of interest caught her. She'd forgotten for a moment.

Before she could respond, Rafaele had dismissed her
and was bending down to Milo's eye level. His ears had
inevitably pricked up at the mention of cars. 'I was thinking that maybe tomorrow you'd like to come for a drive
in my car?'

Milo's eyes lit up and he immediately looked at Sam
with such a pleading expression that she would have had
to be made of stone to resist.

'Okay...*if* Rafaele still feels like it tomorrow. He might
be tired, though, or—'

He cut her off with ice in his voice. 'I won't be tired.'

'But you're going out tonight,' Sam reminded him.

Immediately her head was filled with visions of Rafaele
and some blonde—of him creeping back into the house
like a recalcitrant student at dawn, dishevelled and with
stubble lining his jaw.

But he was shaking his head and the look in his eye
was mocking, as if he could read her shameful thoughts.
'I won't be tired,' he repeated.

He was walking out of the kitchen when Sam thought
of something and followed him. He looked back at her
as he put on his leather coat and she held out a key. 'The
spare front door key.'

He came and reached for it and their fingers touched.
A sizzle of electricity shot up Sam's arm and she snatched
her hand back as if burnt, causing the key to drop to the
ground. Cheeks burning with humiliation, she bent and
picked it up before Rafaele could and handed it to him
again, avoiding his eye.

And then, to her everlasting relief, he was out of the door. She turned around and breathed in deep, barely aware of Milo running to the reception room window so he could see the car pull away. She had to get a hold of herself around this man or she'd be a quivering wreck by the end of a week.

CHAPTER FIVE

WHEN SAM HEARD the telltale purr of a powerful engine as she lay in bed that night she looked at her clock in disbelief. It was before midnight and Rafaele was home? *Home.* She grimaced at how easily that had slipped into her mind.

Feeling like a teenager, but unable to help herself, she got out of bed and went to her window, pulling back the curtain ever so slightly. Her heart was thumping. Rafaele hadn't got out of the car yet, and even from here she could see his hands gripping the steering wheel tightly.

Sam had the uncanny feeling that he was imagining the wheel was her neck. Then suddenly the door opened and he got out, unfolding his huge frame from the sleek low-slung vehicle. In any other instance Sam would have sighed in sheer awe at the stunningly designed lines.

She stopped breathing as she took in Rafaele, just standing there for a moment. He wore a tuxedo. Sam knew from past experience that he had a dressing room and fully stocked wardrobe at his office. His shirt was open at the throat, his bow tie hanging rakishly undone.

Rafaele shut the car door and then surprised her by leaning back against the car and putting his hands deep in his pockets, crossing his long legs at the ankle. He looked down, and something about him was so intensely *lonely* that Sam felt like a voyeur. She hated the way her heart clenched.

She'd been so stunned to see him again that she hadn't really contemplated how much of a shock it must have been for him discovering he had a son. He would never forgive her.

Sam quickly shut the curtain again and climbed back into bed, feeling cold from the inside. Eventually she heard the opening and closing of the front door, and then heavy footsteps. She held her breath for a moment when she fancied they stopped outside her door, and then, when she heard the faintest sounds of another door closing, let her breath out in a shuddery whoosh.

About an hour later Sam gave up any pretence of trying to sleep. She threw back the covers and padded softly out of her bedroom. All was quiet and still. She looked in on Milo, who was sprawled across his bed fast asleep, and then made her way to the kitchen to get some water. She was halfway into the room before she realised she wasn't alone.

She gave a small yelp of shock when she saw Rafaele in the corner of the kitchen, in low-slung faded jeans, bare feet and a T-shirt, calmly lifting a coffee cup to his lips.

She put a hand to her rapid heart. 'You scared me. I thought you were in bed.'

Rafaele arched a brow mockingly. 'Don't tell me—you couldn't sleep until you knew I was home safe?'

Sam scowled and hated that he'd caught her like this: sleep-mussed, wearing nothing but brief pants and a threadbare V-necked T-shirt.

Anger rushed through her. Anger at the day she'd spent with her thoughts revolving sickeningly around one person—*him*. Anger that she had to face him like this in what she would have once considered her sanctuary. And, worst of all, anger at herself for not having told him about Milo when she should have.

Feeling emotional, and terrified he'd see it, she stalked

to the sink. 'I'm just getting some water. I couldn't sleep and it has nothing to do with you coming home or not.'

Liar.

Sam heard his voice over the gush of water.

'I couldn't sleep either.'

Sam remembered the intensely lonely air about him as he'd waited outside before coming in. Now she felt guilty for having witnessed it. She held the glass of water in both hands and turned, feeling disorientated.

She looked at the coffee cup and remarked dryly, 'Well, that's hardly likely to help matters.'

Rafaele shrugged and drained the coffee, the strong column of his throat working. He put the cup down. 'When I couldn't sleep I came down to do some work.'

His gaze narrowed on her then, and Sam's skin prickled. She gripped the glass tighter.

He drawled, 'But as I'm just a guest in your house perhaps I should ask for permission?'

Sam's anger was back just like that. Anger at herself for thinking she'd seen Rafaele vulnerable even for a moment. 'But you're not really a guest, are you? You're here to punish me, to make me pay for not telling you about your son.'

Feeling agitated, Sam put down the glass, sloshing some water over the side. She clenched her hands and rounded on Rafaele. 'I'm sorry, okay? I'm sorry that I didn't tell you about Milo. I should have, and I didn't. And I'm sorry.'

Rafaele went very still and put his hands in his pockets. The air thickened between them and swirled with electricity. He looked relaxed, but Sam could tell he was as tense as she was.

'Why?'

One word, a simple question, and Sam felt something crumble inside her. He hadn't actually asked her that yet. He'd asked her *how* she could have, but not why.

She looked down and put her arms around herself in an

unconscious gesture of defence, unaware of how it pushed her breasts up and unaware of how Rafaele's eyes dropped there for a moment or the flush that darkened his cheek-bones. She was only aware of her own inner turmoil. She would never be brave enough to tell him of her hurt and her own secret suspicion that it had been that weak emotion that had been her main motivator. She was too ashamed.

She steeled herself and looked up. Rafaele's eyes glittered in the gloom. 'It was for all the reasons I've already told you, Rafaele. I was in shock. I'd almost lost my baby only days after finding out that I was pregnant in the first place. It was all…too much. And I truly believed you had no interest—that you would prefer if I just went away and didn't bother you again.'

She almost quailed at the way his jaw tightened but went on. 'My father was not really there for me. Ever. Even though he brought me up and we lived in this house together. He didn't know how to relate to me. What I needed. I think…I thought I was doing the right thing by keeping Milo from a similar experience.'

Rafaele crossed his arms too, making his muscles bunch. It felt as if something was fizzing between them under the words. A subtext that was alive. All she could see was that powerful body. Lean and hard.

'You had no right.'

Sam looked at him, willing down the way her body insisted on being divorced from her mind, becoming aroused as if nothing had happened between them. As if he didn't hate her.

'I know,' she said flatly. 'But it happened, and you're going to have to let it go or Milo will pick up on it—especially now you're living here too.'

Anger surged within Rafaele at her pronouncement. He uncrossed his arms, unable to disguise his frustration. Sam was standing before him, and despite the charged atmosphere and the words between them he was acutely aware that all he wanted to do was rip that flimsy T-shirt over her head and position her on the counter behind her so that he could thrust deep into her and obliterate all the questions and turmoil in his head.

When she'd walked into the room all he'd seen had been the tantalising shape of her firm breasts, their pointed tips visible through the thin fabric. Her sleep-mussed hair had reminded him of when she'd been on top of him, riding him, her head falling back...

Desire was like a wild thing inside him, clawing for fulfilment. It wasn't helped by the fact that in a bid to prove that Sam *didn't* have this unique effect on him, he'd found himself hitting on his friend's mistress at the function earlier. Flirting with her, handing her his card—desperate to provoke some response in his flatlining libido. He'd acted completely out of character, managed to insult his friend Andreas Xenakis, and he'd proved nothing.

Except that he wanted this woman more than ever.

He hated her. But he wanted her. And he wanted his son.

'Let it go?' he asked now with deceptive softness, and something in him exulted when he saw how Sam paled slightly. 'I think I've more than proved myself to be accommodating where my son and your deception are concerned.'

Rafaele knew he was reacting to Sam's almost patronising tone and to his anger at this inconvenient desire.

His lip curled. 'Do you really think I would be here in the suburbs with you if it wasn't in my son's best interests? Do you really think I want you working at the factory for any reason other than because I want to keep you where I can see your every treacherous move?'

She paled even more at that, and Rafaele felt something lance him deep inside, but he couldn't stop.

'You've put us all in this position by choosing the path

that you did. By believing that you knew best. Well, now I know best and you're just going to have to live with it. *You're* going to have to let it go, Samantha.'

The hurt Sam felt at Rafaele's words shamed her. He looked as hard and obdurate as a granite block just feet away. And as unyielding. The thought of them ever reaching some sort of amicable agreement felt like the biggest and most ludicrous fantasy on earth. And yet between her legs her panties chafed uncomfortably against swollen slick folds of flesh. She wanted to scream out her frustration at her wayward body.

Just before he'd fallen asleep earlier Milo had asked, in a small, hesitant voice, 'Will the man...I mean Rafelli... will he remember to take me in the car tomorrow?'

Anger at Rafaele's assertion that he was doing his utmost to think of Milo when all he seemed to be concerned about was needling her made her lash out. 'You might feel like you're sacrificing your glamorous life for your son, Rafaele, but when will you get bored and want out? Milo has been talking about you all day. He's terrified you won't remember to take him out in the car tomorrow. He's fast heading for hero-worship territory and he'll be devastated if you keep leading him on this path only to disappear from his life.'

Sam was breathing heavily. 'This is what I wanted to avoid all along. Milo's vulnerable. He doesn't understand what's going on between us. You can punish me all you want, Rafaele, but it's Milo who matters now. And I can't say sorry again.'

Rafaele was completely unreadable, but Sam sensed his tension spike.

'What makes you think that I am going to disappear from Milo's life?'

The words were softly delivered, but Sam could sense the volcanic anger behind them.

'You know what I mean. You're not going to stay here for ever. You'll leave sooner or later. Milo will be confused. Upset.'

Sam was aware that she could have been talking about herself, about what had happened to her.

Panic at the way Rafaele took a step closer made Sam's breath choppy. Instinctively she moved back. 'I think this was a very bad idea. I think you should move out before he gets too attached. You can visit us. That way he won't be so upset when you leave…we'll have proper boundaries.'

'Boundaries, you say?' His accent sounded thicker. 'Like the kind of boundaries you put around yourself and my son when you decided that it would be a good idea not to inform me of his existence?'

'You're just…not about commitment, Rafaele. You said it yourself to me over and over again. And a child is all about commitment—a lifetime of it.'

Rafaele was so close now that she could see veritable sparks shooting from those green depths.

His voice was low and blistering. 'How dare you patronise me? You have had the experience of giving birth to a baby and all the natural bonding that goes with it—a bonding experience *you* decided to deny me. I now have the task of bonding with my son when his personality is practically formed. He has missed out on the natural bonding between a father and son. You have deprived us both of that.'

He stopped in front of her and Sam found it hard to concentrate when she could smell his musky heat. The anger within her was vying with something far hotter and more dangerous.

'I can give my son a lifetime of commitment. That is not a problem. If and when I do leave this place he will know I am his father. He will be as much a part of me and my life as the very air I breathe.'

His eyes pinned her to the spot.

'Know this, Sam. I am in Milo's life now, and yours, and I'm not going away. I am his father and I am not shirking that responsibility. You and I are going to have to learn to co-exist.'

Sam's arms were so tight now that she felt she might be constricting the bloodflow to her brain. 'I'm willing to try to co-exist, Rafaele. But sooner or later you'll have to forgive me, or we'll never move on.'

Rafaele stood for a long moment after Sam had left, his heart still racing. She had no idea how close he'd come to reaching for her, pulling her into him so that he could taste her again.

Sooner or later you'll have to forgive me.

For the first time Rafaele didn't feel the intense anger surge. Instead he thought of Sam's stricken pale features that day in the clinic. He remembered his own sense of panic, and the awful shameful relief when he could run away, far and fast, and put Sam and the emotions she'd evoked within him behind him.

For the first time he had to ask the question: if he'd been in her position would he have done the same thing? If he'd believed that his baby was unwanted by one parent? It wasn't so black and white any more. Rafaele had to admit to the role he'd played.

Completely unbidden a memory came to him of something Sam had told him one night while they'd been lying in bed. It was something he avoided like the plague—the post-coital intimacy that women seemed engineered to pursue—but this hadn't been like that. Sam had started telling him something and then stopped. He'd urged her on.

It was her mention of her relationship with her father just a short while before that had brought it back to him. She'd told him then of how one night, when she'd been about six, she'd not been able to sleep. She'd come downstairs and found her father weeping silently over a picture of his late wife—Sam's mother.

Sam had said, 'He was talking to her...the picture...asking her what to do with me, asking her how he could cope because I was a girl. He said, *"If she was a boy I'd know what to do...but I don't know what to do or say to her."'*

Sam had sighed deeply. 'So I went upstairs to the bathroom that night, found a pair of scissors and cut all my hair off. It used to fall to my waist. When our housekeeper saw me in the morning she screamed and dropped a plate.'

Sam's mouth had twisted sadly. 'My father, though, he didn't even notice—too distracted with a problem he was trying to solve. I thought I could try to be a son for him...'

Rafaele could remember a falling sensation. Sam's inherent lack of self-confidence in her innate sensuality had all made sense. He too had known what it was like to have an absentee father. Even though he'd spent time with his father growing up, the man had been so embittered by his wife leaving him that he'd been no use to Rafaele and had rarely expressed much interest in his son. In some small part Rafaele knew that even resurrecting the family car industry had been a kind of effort to connect with his father.

It had been that weekend that Rafaele had let Sam stay in his *palazzo*. It had been that weekend that he'd postponed an important business trip because he'd wanted her too much to leave. And it was after that weekend, once he'd gained some distance from her, that he'd realised just how dangerous she was to him.

And he'd just proved that nothing had changed. She was still just as dangerous and he must never forget it.

The following day Milo was practically bursting with excitement at being in Rafaele's car. It was the latest model of the Falcone road car—the third to be rolled out since Rafaele had taken control of the bankrupt company.

It was completely impractical as far as children went, but Rafaele had surprised Sam. She'd seen that he'd got a child's car seat from somewhere and had it fitted into the backseat. Every time Sam looked around Milo just grinned at her like a loon. She shook her head ruefully as Rafaele negotiated out of the driveway and onto the main road with confident ease.

Sam tried to ignore his big hands on the wheel and gearstick. But there was something undeniably sexy about a man who handled a car well—and especially one like this, which was more like an art form than a car. Rafaele was a confident driver, and not the kind of person who felt the need for speed just to impress.

Happy sounds were coming from the back of the car—Milo imitating the engine. Sam felt a flutter near her heart and blocked it out. *Dangerous.* She still felt tense after that impassioned exchange the previous evening. Predictably, she hadn't been able to sleep well and she felt fuzzy now. She'd avoided looking directly at Rafaele this morning over breakfast, preferring to let Milo take centre stage, demanding the attention of this new, charismatic person in their midst.

Rafaele had seemed equally keen to be distracted, and Sam could only wonder if he'd taken anything of what she'd said to heart. Was he prepared to forgive her at all?

Sam noticed that Milo had gone silent behind them and looked back to see that he'd fallen asleep. Rafaele glanced her way and Sam quickly looked forward again, saying a little too breathlessly for her liking, 'He was so excited about today… He doesn't really nap any more but sometimes it catches up with him.'

She was babbling, and the thought of increased proximity to Rafaele when she started working with him tomorrow made her feel panicky. She steeled herself and turned to his proud profile. The profile of a great line of aristocratic Italian ancestors.

'Look, Rafaele...about me working at the factory...' She saw his jaw clench and rushed on. 'You said yourself last night that you're only doing it to keep me where you can see me. I can work perfectly well from the university. After last night I can't see how our working together will improve things.'

His hands clenched on the wheel now, and Sam looked at them, so strong and large. She recalled how hot they'd felt exploring her body.

Distracted, she almost missed it when Rafaele said in a low voice, with clear reluctance, 'I shouldn't have said that. It wasn't entirely true.'

Sam gulped and looked back at him. 'It wasn't?' Somewhere a tiny flame lit inside her, and against every atom of self-preservation she couldn't douse it.

'After all,' he reminded her, 'I contacted you about working for me before I knew about Milo and you refused to listen.'

The panic she'd felt then was still vivid. 'Yes,' she said faintly. 'I...it was a shock to hear from you.'

Rafaele slanted her a look and said dryly, 'You don't say.' He looked at the road again. 'But the fact remains that I knew about your research. You were mentioned in an article in *Automotive Monthly* and I realised that you were leading the field in research into kinetic energy recovery systems.'

The little flame inside Sam sputtered. Of *course* he hadn't been motivated by anything other than professional interest. 'I see,' she responded. 'And that's why you wanted to contact me?'

Rafaele shrugged minutely, his broad shoulders moving sinuously under his leather jacket, battered and worn to an almost sensual texture. *Dammit...* Sam cursed herself. Why did everything have to return to all things physical even when he was wounding her with his words? She looked away resolutely.

He continued, 'I knew we were setting up in England, I figured you were still based here... It seemed like a logical choice to ask you to work for us again...'

Out of the corner of Sam's eye she saw Rafaele's hands tighten on the wheel again. His jaw clenched and then released.

'About last night—you were right. I agree that the past is past and we need to move on. I don't want Milo to pick up on the tension between us any more than you do.'

Something dangerous swooped inside Sam at hearing him acknowledge this. She recognised the mammoth effort he must be making to concede this.

'Thank you,' she said huskily. 'And I'll have to trust that you won't do anything to hurt Milo.'

The car was stopped at a red light now and Rafaele looked at her. 'Yes, you will. Hurting my son is the last thing in the world I want to do. It won't happen.'

The fierce light in his eyes awed Sam into silence. Eventually, she nodded, her throat feeling tight. 'Okay.'

A car horn tooted from behind them, and with unhurried nonchalance Rafaele released her from his gaze and moved on.

After a while Rafaele said in a low voice, 'And you *will* be coming to work with me, Sam...because I want you to.'

After a long moment Sam replied again. 'Okay.' In her wayward imagination she fancied that something had finally shifted between them, alleviating the ever-present tension.

They were silent for much of the rest of the journey, but something inside Sam had lessened slightly. And yet conversely she felt more vulnerable than ever.

She noticed that they were pulling into what looked like a stately home and raised a questioning brow at Rafaele, who answered, 'I asked my assistant to look up some things. It's an open house at weekends and they have a working farm. I thought Milo might like to see it.'

Milo had woken up a short while before, and from the backseat came an excited, 'Look, Mummy! Horsies!'

Sam saw Rafaele look to his son in the rearview mirror and the way his mouth curved into a smile. Her chest tightened and she explained, 'It's his other favourite thing in the world apart from cars. You're killing two birds with one stone.'

Rafaele looked at her for a long moment, his eyes lingering on her mouth until it tingled. Sam grew hot and flustered. Why was he teasing her with looks like this when he couldn't be less interested? Was it just something he turned on automatically when any woman with a pulse was nearby? It made her think of that angry kiss—how instantly she'd gone up in flames when he'd only been proving a point.

'Shouldn't you look where you're driving?' She sounded like a prim schoolmistress.

Rafaele eventually looked away, but not before purring with seductive arrogance, '*Cara*, I could drive blindfolded and not crash.'

This was what she remembered. Rafaele's easy and lethal brand of charm. Disgusted with herself, Sam faced forward and crossed her arms.

When he had parked and they'd got out, Milo clearly didn't know what to do first: stand and looking lovingly at the car, or go and see the animals. For a second he looked genuinely upset, overwhelmed with all these exciting choices. It made guilt lance Sam—fresh guilt—because the local park or swimming pool was about as exciting as it had got so far for Milo.

To Sam's surprise, before she could intervene, Rafaele bent down to Milo's level and said, '*Piccolino*, the car will still be here when we get back...so why don't we see the animals first, hmm?'

Milo's face cleared like a cloud passing over the sun and he smiled, showing his white baby teeth. 'Okey-dokey, horsies first.' And then he put his hand in Rafaele's and started pulling him the direction he wanted to go.

Sam caught the unguarded moment of emotion in Rafaele's eyes and her chest tightened at its significance. It was the first time Milo had reached out to touch him.

She followed them, doing up her slimline parka jacket and tried not to be affected by the image of the tall, powerful man, alongside the tiny, sturdy figure with identical dark hair.

Within a few hours Sam could see the beginnings of the hero-worship situation she'd predicted unfolding before her eyes. Milo had barely let go of Rafaele's hand and was now in his arms, pointing at the pigs in a mucky pen.

She was watching Rafaele for signs that this situation was getting old very quickly—she knew how demanding and energetic Milo could be—but she couldn't find any. Again she was stunned at his apparent easing into this whole situation.

Rafaele looked at her then and Sam coloured, more affected by seeing him with Milo in his arms than she cared to admit.

He looked grim and said, 'I think now is a good time.'

Instantly Sam understood. He wanted to tell Milo who he was. Panic flooded Sam. Until Milo knew Rafaele was his father it was as if she still had a way out—the possibility that this wasn't real. It was all a dream. But it wasn't, and she knew she couldn't fight him. He deserved for his son to know. And Milo deserved it too.

Jerkily, feeling clammy, Sam nodded her head. 'Okay.'

So when Milo had finished inspecting all the animals exhaustively they found a quiet spot to eat the food they'd got from the house's café and Sam explained gently to Milo that Rafaele was his father.

She could sense Rafaele's tension and her heart ached for him. Her conscience lambasted her again.

With all the unpredictability of a three-year-old though, Milo just blinked and looked from her to Rafaele before saying, 'Can we look at the horsies again?'

To his credit, Rafaele didn't look too surprised but when Milo had clambered off his chair to go and look at something she said, 'It's probably a lot for him to take in—'

But Rafaele cut her off, saying coolly, 'I know he took it in. I remember how much three-year-olds see and understand.'

He got up to follow Milo before Sam could make sense of his words and what he'd meant by them.

When they were back in the car Milo began chattering incessantly in the back.

'Rafelli, did you see the pigs? Rafelli, did you see the horsies and the goats? And the chickens?'

Sam looked out of the window, overcome with a surge of emotion. It was done. Rafaele truly was his father now. No going back. Tears pricked her eyes as the enormity of everything set in. She'd kept Milo from his own father for so long. Guilt was hot and acrid in her gut.

Suddenly her hand was taken in a much bigger, warmer one and her heart stopped.

'Sam?'

Panicked that he'd see her distress, Sam took her hand from his and rubbed at her eye, avoiding looking at him. Breezily she said, 'I'm fine. It's just some dust or something in my eye.'

CHAPTER SIX

TWO WEEKS LATER Sam was trying to concentrate on test results and threw her pen down in disgust when her brain just refused to work. She got up from her desk in her decent-sized office at the factory and paced, rolling her head to ease out kinks as she did so.

It felt as if an age had passed since that day at the stately home. Within a few days Milo had been tentatively calling Rafaele *Daddy*, much to Bridie's beaming approval, Rafaele's delight and Sam's increasing sense of vulnerability.

Bridie had also paved the way for Sam to go to work with Rafaele every day, assuring her that she had nothing to worry about where Milo's care was concerned. So in the past two weeks a routine had developed where Rafaele took Milo to playschool, either with or without Sam, and then they left for work and returned in time for Milo's supper. Sam had put her foot down, though, and insisted that she still only do a half-day on Wednesdays as that had been her routine with Bridie.

And also she felt the need to establish some control when it felt as if Rafaele had comprehensively taken everything over. They'd even come home one evening to find a chef in the kitchen and Rafaele saying defensively something about it being unfair to expect Bridie to cook for them as well as taking care of Milo.

Needless to say Sam could see that Bridie was not far

behind Milo in the hero-worship stakes. Most evenings now Rafaele tucked Milo into bed and read him a story, making Sam feel redundant for the first time in a long time.

In the middle of all this change and turmoil was the sheer joy Sam felt at being back working on research within an environment where the actual cars and engines were only a short walk away. The scale of Rafaele's English factory had taken her breath away. It proved just how far he'd come even in three and a half years. Professionally she would have given her right arm to be part of this process, and now she was overseeing a group of mechanics and engineers, focusing their expertise on the most exciting developments in automotive technology, thanks to Rafaele's unlimited investment.

But overshadowing everything was the fact that she was working for Rafaele. Back in a place where she'd never expected or wanted to be. She felt as if she was that girl all over again—that naive student, obsessed with her boss. Watching out for him. Aware of him. Blushing when their gazes met. It was galling and humiliating. Especially when Rafaele appeared so cool and seemed to be making every effort to steer well clear of Sam. Only addressing her in groups of people. Never seeking her out alone.

Even on their car rides to the factory and back their conversation centred mainly around Milo or work.

Her hands clenched to fists now, even as her whole body seemed to ache. She was glad. She *was*. She didn't want history to repeat itself. Not in a million years. It had almost been easier when Rafaele had hated her; now that they were in this uneasy truce it was so much more confusing to deal with.

Sam noticed the clock on the wall then, and saw how late it was. Normally Rafaele's assistant would have rung to inform her that he was leaving by now. Giving up any pretence that she could continue to work while waiting,

Sam decided to pack up and find him herself. She would inform him she was going home. He'd offered her one of the cars if she wished, so now perhaps it was time to assert some more independence from him.

Heading for his office, she saw it was quiet all around, most of the other staff and the main engineers and mechanics having left. His own secretary's desk was clear and empty in the plush anteroom of his office.

She hesitated for a second outside his door and then knocked. After a few seconds she heard him call abruptly, 'Come in.'

Rafaele glanced up from his phone call, frowning slightly at the interruption, and then when Sam walked in his whole body reacted, making a complete mockery of any illusion of control over his rogue hormones. She stopped in her tracks and made a motion to leave again, seeing he was on the phone, but everything within him rejected that and he held up his finger, indicating for her to wait.

She closed the door behind her and he couldn't stop the anticipation spiking in his blood. For two weeks now Rafaele had thought he was doing a good job of avoiding her. But it didn't matter how much space he put between them; he saw her everywhere. Worst of all was in the house at night—that cosy, domestic house, with his son sleeping just down the hall—when all he could think about doing was going into Sam's room, stripping her bare and sinking deep between her long legs.

His body was hardening even now, shaming him with his lack of control. The person on the other end of the phone continued talking but they might as well have been talking the language of the Dodo for all Rafaele heard. His gaze travelled down Sam's back and legs hungrily, taking in her slim build and the sweet lush curve of her buttocks as she turned away to look at a model of one of the first cars he'd designed.

When she turned back slightly he could see the profile swell of her breasts and immediately a memory came back, of spilling drops of Prosecco onto one pebbled nipple, making it grow hard— Sweat broke out on Rafaele's upper lip. This was untenable.

Abruptly he terminated the phone conversation, giving up any pretence of control. Sam had turned around to face him and he asked, more curtly than he'd intended, 'What do you want?'

Her face flushed and Rafaele pushed down the lurch of his conscience. Damn her and the way she did that, making him feel like a heel.

'I just…it's after six. We usually leave before now.'

The *we* struck him somewhere forcibly. He stood up and saw how Sam's eyes widened. His body reacted to that look and he cursed her again.

He reacted viscerally. 'I think this is a mistake.'

She frowned. 'What's a mistake?'

'You…here.' Dammit, he couldn't even string a coherent sentence together. The longer she stood there, the more he was imagining her naked, opening up to him, giving him the release he'd only ever found with her. Seeing her here at the factory these past two weeks had been giving him moments of severe *déjà vu*.

She was still frowning, but had gone still. 'Me…here… What exactly do you mean, Rafaele?'

Why was it that the way she said his name in that soft, low voice seemed to curl around his senses, making everything even more heightened?

He gritted out, through the waves of need assailing him, 'I shouldn't have insisted you work here. It was a bad idea.'

The unmistakable flare of hurt made her eyes glow

bright grey for a moment, reminding Rafaele uncomfortably of another day, in another office, four years before.

Stiffly she said, 'I thought I was doing everything you wanted—we set up the research facility here in one week. I know it still needs more work, but it's only been two weeks—'

Rafaele slashed a hand, making her stop. 'It's not that.'

Sounding wounded, she said, 'Well, what, then?'

Rafaele wanted to laugh. Could she not see how ravenous he was for her? He felt like a beast, panting for its prey.

He smiled grimly. 'It's you. Uniquely. I thought I could do this. But I can't. I think you should go back to the university...someone else can take over here.'

Sam straightened before him and her eyes flashed—but with anger and something more indefinable this time.

'You insisted on turning my world upside down, Rafaele, and now, just because you can't abide the sight of me, you think you can cast me out again? It seems as if you rather overestimated your desire for control, doesn't it? Well, if you've quite decided where it is you want me then don't worry. I'll be only too happy to get out of your way.'

Sam was quivering with impotent rage. She wanted to go over and slap Rafaele. Hard. It could be four years ago all over again. With nothing learned in the meantime. She was standing before Rafaele in his office and he was basically rejecting her. Again.

And, like before, Sam was terrified she'd crumple before him, so she fled for the door. But when she tried to open it with clammy hands it slammed shut again, and she squealed with shock when she felt a solid, hard presence behind her.

She whirled around to find her eye level at Rafaele's broad chest and looked up. Emotion was high in her throat. Her eyes were burning. 'Let me out of here, *now*.'

The hurt that had gripped her like a vice in her belly at hearing him say so starkly that he basically couldn't stand to see her every day was still like acid.

'You've got it wrong,' he gritted out, jaw tight, seemingly oblivious to what she'd just said. His hand was snaking around her neck under her hair, making her breath catch. His eyes were like green gems. Glittering.

Sam swallowed the pain, determined he wouldn't see it, but she was acutely aware of how close he was—almost close enough for his chest to touch her breasts. They tightened, growing heavy, the nipples pebbling into hard points.

'Got what wrong?' she spat out.

'I didn't overestimate my desire for control... I overestimated my ability to resist you.'

Sam blinked. But now Rafaele's chest was touching her breasts and she couldn't think straight. His hand tightened on her neck and his face was coming closer. Her lips tingled in anticipation. All the blood in her body was pooling between her legs, making her hot and ready.

Fighting the intense desire not to question this, Sam put her hands on Rafaele's chest. 'Wait...' she got out painfully. 'What are you doing?'

Rafaele's breath feathered over her mouth, making her fingers want to curl into his chest. She couldn't seem to take her eyes away from his, green boring into grey, making reality melt away.

Sam struggled to make sense of this, when only moments ago she'd believed he wanted her out of his sight because something about her repulsed him. 'But you don't... you don't really want me.'

He asked, almost bitterly, 'Don't I?'

Confusion filled Sam—and a very treacherous flame of hope. She fought it desperately, fearing exposure. She pushed against him but he was like steel. 'Let me *go*, Rafaele. I won't be your substitute lover just because you're turned on for five seconds. I don't like to repeat mistakes.'

Rafaele laughed again and it was unbearably harsh, scraping over Sam's sensitised skin like sandpaper.

'Five seconds? Try four years, Sam—four years of an ache that never went away, no matter how much I tried to deny it…no matter how many times I tried to eclipse it…'

His voice had become guttural, thick. Sam couldn't fully process his words, but somewhere deep inside her they did resonate, and she felt something break apart—some resistance she'd been clinging onto.

'I want you, Sam, and I know you want me too.'

And then his mouth was on hers and it was desperate, forceful. Like before, but *not*. Without the intense anger and recrimination behind it. And once again, like a lemming jumping over a cliff to certain death, Sam couldn't help but respond. And she couldn't deny the fierce burst of primal pleasure within her, deep inside where she'd locked it away.

But the kiss didn't stay forceful. Rafaele drew back, breathing harshly, and Sam followed him, too much on fire to be embarrassed by how much she wanted him. He wanted her, and the knowledge sang in her blood. She had nothing to be ashamed of.

Rafaele bent close again, and when he pressed a hot kiss to her neck Sam felt his hand do something behind her. She heard the snick of the lock in the door. It should have made alarm bells ring in her head. It should have reminded her of similar heated moments in the past. But it didn't. Or she wouldn't let it. She was weak and she'd ached for this for too long. Long nights when Milo hadn't wanted to sleep and she'd walked up and down, breasts sore from breast-feeding, but aching, too, for another far more adult touch.

Rafaele straightened and with an enigmatic look took Sam by the hand. For a second she felt absurdly shy and bit her lip. Rafaele stopped and reached out, freeing her lip with his thumb.

He muttered, '*Dio*, I've missed that.' And Sam's insides combusted.

He drew her over towards the desk and then turned to take Sam's bag off her shoulder, along with her jacket. They fell to the floor. Sam felt the back of the desk against her buttocks. Her legs were wobbly.

Rafaele cupped her face and jaw with his hands and then his mouth was on hers again, hot and hard, firm but soft. Demanding and getting a response that she had no control over. Her tongue stroked along his. She was desperate to taste every inch of him, revelling in the spiralling heat inside her. She was vaguely aware of her questing hands going to his chest, exulting in the feel of rock-hard muscle, her fingers finding buttons and opening them so that she could reach in and explore, feel that hair-roughened skin.

Rafaele's hands moved down, coming to her buttocks, kneading them, and then lifting her so that she rested on the desk. He came closer, wedging himself between her legs so that his belt buckle was hard against her belly. Below, the most potent part of his anatomy was also hard, right there between her legs, constrained by their clothes and making her want to strip everything between them away.

One of his hands clasped her head, tilting it so that he had deeper access. His tongue was mimicking another part of his anatomy now, and his hips were moving against her, making her squirm and whimper softly as the fever of desire rose within her.

Suddenly Rafaele pulled away and Sam looked up through a heat haze, aware of her heart pounding and her ragged breath. Rafaele's shirt hung half open.

'I need to see you,' he said thickly, and began to undo the buttons on her shirt.

As the backs of his hands brushed against her breasts she shivered minutely at the exquisite sensation, already imagining him touching them with his hands...his mouth and tongue.

Her shirt was drawn off and her bra dispensed with in an economy of movement, and then he just looked at her for a long moment, with an enigmatic expression that made butterflies erupt in Sam's belly. About to scream with the mounting tension, she felt Rafaele's hand finally cup her breast and shards of sensation rushed through her body. She tensed and arched her back, subconsciously begging him...and he needed no encouragement.

Cupping the full mound of firm flesh, Rafaele bent his head and surrounded that tight peak in moist heat. The feel of his intense hot sucking made Sam cry out.

Blindly, while Rafaele's mouth was on her breast, Sam reached for his belt and undid it, her hands and fingers clumsy. She pulled it free of his trousers and it dropped to the floor, but before she could put her hands to his fly he was standing up again and helping her, pushing his trousers down, leaving him bared to her hungry gaze. *Dear Lord.* He was as magnificent as she remembered. Thick and long and hard. For *her.*

Sam felt hot, as if she was on fire. She moved her numb fingers to Rafaele's shirt buttons, wanting to finish undressing him. Her breath was loud in the quiet of the office. All that mattered to Sam was getting Rafaele bared to her, and when she finally pushed his shirt open and off his shoulders she breathed in deeply, her hands smoothing over hard musculature roughened with dark hair, nipples erect and hard.

Unable to resist the lure, Sam explored with her tongue around those hard pieces of puckered flesh, aware of Rafaele's hand on her head. He sucked in a breath, making his broad chest swell. He was so sensitive there. Sam moved her mouth up now, stretching her whole body, trailing kisses and tasting with her tongue along his throat, discovering the hard resoluteness of his stubbled jaw grazing her delicate skin.

Her hands on his head drew him down. She was searching for his mouth again, like a blind person looking for water in a desert. Sucking him deep into her own mouth, Sam could feel his erection strain against her, and she dropped one hand to put it around him, feeling him jerk with tension.

'Sam...'

She almost didn't recognise his voice. It sounded so tortured. Sam tore her mouth away from his to look up and she was dizzy with need and lust. It was just them and this insane desire. He was so firm in her hand, so strong, and her mouth watered when she remembered how she'd tasted him before, how she'd sucked that head into her mouth, her tongue swirling and exploring around the tip, her hand pumping him the way he'd shown her...

She didn't even realise her hand was moving rythmically until he tipped up her chin with his fingers and said, 'I need to be inside you.'

Sam's sex throbbed. 'Yes,' she breathed, lifting her hips to help Rafaele when he went to pull her trousers and panties off. She was vaguely surprised she still had them on, that they hadn't melted off her before now.

Rafaele took himself in his hand—an unashamed and utterly masculine gesture. Sam was sitting on the desk naked, legs spread like a wanton, but she couldn't drum up any concern. She wanted him inside her so badly. Rafaele ran his hand down over her quivering body, teasing her until she bit her lip. He pushed her legs apart further and looked at her.

He stroked one hand up her inner thigh and let it rest for a moment at the tantalising juncture before his long fingers explored the wetness at her core—and then in one move he thrust them inside her.

Sam gasped and grabbed onto Rafaele's shoulders, unable to look away from that glittering, possessive green gaze. His fingers moved in and out, and her body started to clench around them, the anticipation building to fever-pitch.

On some level Sam rejected this. She didn't want to splinter apart while Rafaele looked on. She took his hand away from her and said roughly, 'No—not like this. I'll come when you come.'

Rafaele smiled and it was fierce. The smile of a warrior. He took her mouth in another devastating kiss and her wetness was on the fingers that he wrapped tight around her hips. Rafaele thrust deep inside her in one cataclysmic move and swallowed her scream of pleasure, his hand holding her steady when she went so taut with excitement that she thought she'd splinter apart there and then, despite her brave words.

But slowly, inexorably, expertly, Rafaele drew her back from that brink and then, with slow, measured, devastating thrusts of his body into hers he rewound that tension inside her until it built up higher and higher all over again.

Sam wrapped her legs around Rafaele's waist, her ankles crossed, her feet digging into his hard backside, urging him on, begging without words for him to go deeper, harder. Pushing her away from him slightly, but supporting her with an arm around her, he thrust harder and deeper.

Sam's head went back. Her eyes closed. She couldn't take it—couldn't articulate what she needed. She needed to come so badly, but Rafaele was relentless. She knew she was only seconds from begging. Overwhelmed, she felt tears prick her eyes—and then Rafaele thrust so deep it felt as if he touched her heart.

Eyes flying open, tendons going taut all over her body,

Sam came in a dizzying, blinding crescendo of pleasure so intense she couldn't breathe. She gasped and felt Rafaele thrust deep again, sending her spiralling into an even higher dimension of pleasure. His body jerked between her legs and she felt her endless pulsating orgasm milking him of his essence, which was a warm flood inside her.

In the aftermath of that shattering crescendo Sam barely knew which way was up. Her legs were still locked around his slim hips. Rafaele's head was buried in her neck and she had the strongest urge to reach out and touch his hair, but when she lifted a hand it was trembling too much.

His chest was heaving and damp against hers. Her breasts were tender. Rafaele was still hard inside her, his strength ebbing slowly. And then suddenly he reared back, eyes wild, making Sam wince as he broke the connection between their bodies.

'Protection. We didn't use protection.'

Sam looked at him and went icy, before reason and sanity broke through. Relief was tinged with something bittersweet. 'No,' she breathed, 'It's okay, I'm…safe.'

She bit her lip, suddenly acutely aware of how she was balancing precariously on the desk with Rafaele's eyes on her. She felt raw, as if a layer of skin had been stripped off her body. She clenched her hands.

'Are you sure?' he demanded.

Sam forced herself to look at Rafaele. Her mouth twisted. 'Yes. I'm sure. My period just finished.'

He sighed deeply. 'Okay.'

Sam couldn't keep the bitterness out of her voice. 'You believe me, then?'

He paused in reaching down to grab some clothes and looked at her. 'I believe you. I don't think you'd want to repeat history any more than I would.'

The words shouldn't have hurt her. Much as his earlier

words shouldn't have hurt her. But they did. Sam didn't want to question why.

Grimacing slightly when her muscles protested, she stood shakily from the desk and took her shirt and bra from Rafaele's outstretched hand.

She couldn't look at him. Face burning, she turned away to put on her clothes and castigated herself. She was repeating history right here, right now. Making love with him in his office exactly like she used to. She could remember what it had been like to go back onto the factory floor, feeling exhilarated and shamed all at once, as if a brand on her forehead marked her as some sort of fallen woman. The boss's concubine.

She pulled on her pants and trousers with clumsy fingers, aware of Rafaele just feet away, dressing himself, sheathing that amazing body again.

When she was dressed he said coolly from behind her, 'Shall we go?'

Sam steeled herself and turned around to see Rafaele looking hardly rumpled, his hair only slightly messy. She knew she must look as if she'd just been pulled through a hedge backwards. The tang of sex was in the air and it should have sickened her, but it didn't. It made her crave more.

'Yes,' she said quickly, before he could see how vulnerable she felt.

Rafaele burned with recrimination as he negotiated his car out of the factory in the dark with Sam beside him, tight-lipped. His recrimination was not for what had happened; he'd do that again right now if he could. His recrimination was for the way it had happened. He'd behaved like a teenage boy, drooling over his first lay with finesse the last thing on his mind.

When she'd asked him just now if he believed her, his

reaction had been knee-jerk and not fair. He was already repeating history with bells on, and he knew he wouldn't have the strength to resist her even if he wanted to.

It had been a miracle that he'd had the control to make sure Sam had come first—but then he recalled how ready to explode she'd been when he'd just touched her with his fingers. Just like that he was rewarded with a fresh, raging erection and had to shift to cover it in the gloom of the interior of the car.

He'd taken Sam *on his desk*. He'd only ever let one other woman get to him at work—the same woman. Until he'd met Sam his life had been strictly compartmentalised into work and pleasure. That pleasure had been fleeting and completely within his control. As soon as he'd laid eyes on her, though, the lines had blurred into one.

He could still remember the cold, clammy panic that last weekend four years ago at finding himself waking in his own bed with Sam wrapped around him like a vine. Far from precipitating repugnance, he'd felt curiously at peace. Until he'd realised the significance of that and that peace had been shattered. He'd postponed an important meeting that weekend to spend it with Sam. He'd even turned off his phone. Had not checked e-mails. He'd gone incommunicado. For the first time. For a woman.

It had been that which had made something go cold in his chest. Realising how far off his own strict path he'd gone.

Even now he was aware of that, but also aware of Sam's slim supple thighs in her black trousers next to him. Albeit slanted away, as if she was avoiding coming any closer than she had to in the small, intimate space.

Dio. If she was his he'd make her wear skirts and dresses all the time, so that all he'd have to do would be to slide his hand— *If she was his.* Rafaele let the car swerve momentarily and very uncharacteristically as that thought slid home with all the devastation of a stealth bomb.

He could feel Sam's quick glance of concern and imagine her frowning.

'Sorry,' he muttered, and regained control of himself. He could see from the corner of his eye that Sam had crossed her arms over her breasts. She was so tense he fancied she might crack in two if he touched her.

Her silence was getting to him, making his nerves wind tight inside him. He wanted to provoke her—get her to acknowledge what had just happened. What it possibly meant to her. Was the same round of unwelcome memories dominating *her* head?

Injecting his voice with an insouciance he didn't feel, Rafaele asked, 'Don't tell me you're already regretting what happened, *cara*.'

She snapped at him, 'Is it that obvious?'

Rafaele's mouth tightened in rejection of that, despite his recent thoughts. 'It was inevitable and you know it. It's been building between us from the moment we saw each other again.'

He glanced at Sam and their eyes met. A jolt of electricity shot straight to Rafaele's groin.

She hissed at him, 'It was *not* inevitable. It was a momentary piece of very bad judgment. You were obviously feeling frustrated—maybe it's because you've been forced to move to the suburbs so you can't entertain your mistress.'

Rage was building inside Rafaele and he responded with a snarl, 'I don't have a mistress at the moment.'

Sam sniffed. 'Maybe not, but I'm sure there's been a number in the last four years.'

And not one of them Rafaele could remember right now. But if he was a painter he could paint Sam's naked body with his eyes closed. He recalled seeing Sam bite her lip and how he'd let slip *'I've missed this.'* He'd also told her that no one had come close to her in four years. Then he'd all but admitted that he'd used other women to try and forget her. His belly curdled.

He ground out, 'Are you expecting me to believe that you've been celibate for four years?' He glanced at her and saw her go pale in the gloom. 'Well? Have you?'

Sam stared straight ahead. Stonily. 'Of course not. There was someone…a while ago.'

For a second Rafaele only heard a roaring in his ears. He saw red. He almost gave in to the impulse to swerve the car to the kerb. He'd fully expected her to say *of course not*, and his own hypocrisy mocked him. But, he told himself savagely, *he* hadn't given birth to a baby.

He was aware that irrational emotions were clouding his normally perfectly liberal views and it was not something Rafaele welcomed.

'Who was he?' he bit out, knuckles white under the skin of his fingers on the wheel. Just the thought of Sam even kissing someone else was making him incandescent.

'He was a colleague. He's a single parent too…we bonded over that.'

Rafaele felt as if a red-hot poker had been stabbed into his belly. In a calm voice, belying the strength of his emotions, Rafaele said, 'You were a single parent by choice, Samantha. You are *not* a single parent any more.'

Rafaele struggled to control himself. He wanted to demand Sam tell him more—how many times? Where? When?

As if sensing his intense interest, Sam blurted out, 'It didn't amount to anything. It was just one time. We went to a hotel for an afternoon and to be perfectly honest it was horrible. It felt…sordid.'

She clamped her mouth shut again and Rafaele realised he was holding his breath. He let it out in one long shuddery breath. His hands relaxed. Even though he still wanted to find this faceless, nameless person and throw him up against a wall.

From the moment Sam had stepped into his office earlier he'd been on fire. The culmination of weeks of build-up. The inferno inside him had been too strong to ignore. Feeling Sam in his arms, her mouth under his, opening up to him, pressing herself against him... He'd been thrusting into the tight, slick heat that he'd never forgotten right there on his desk before he'd even really acknowledged what was happening. He'd been in the grip of something more powerful than his rational mind.

They hadn't even used protection. Sam was the only woman that had ever happened with, and the result of that was probably being put to bed right now. He looked at Sam again and saw that she was still pale, a pulse throbbing at the base of her neck. She'd uncrossed her arms finally and her breasts rose and fell a little too quickly, giving her away. They were stopped in traffic and he reached over and took her hand, gripping it when she would have pulled away.

He forced her to look at him and her eyes were huge. Rafaele saw something unguarded in their depths for a split second, but then it was gone and he crushed down the feeling of something resonating deep inside him. The jealousy he felt still burned in his gut.

He wanted to hate Sam for ever appearing in his life to disrupt his ordered and well-run world. A world where nothing had mattered except rebuilding Falcone Industries and ensuring that he would never be ruined like his father. Sam had jeopardised that for a brief moment in time and now it was happening all over again. But he found that he couldn't hate her for that any more because Milo existed. And because he wanted her.

'Let me go, Rafaele,' Sam breathed.

Never resounded in his head before he could stop it. He kept his gaze on hers, slightly discomfited that it wasn't harder to do so. Usually he avoided women's probing looks. But not this one. Something solidified within him. He couldn't *not* have Sam again after that passionate interlude. It was an impossible prospect.

'No, Sam.'

He lifted her resisting hand and brought it to his mouth, pressed his lips to her palm. Her scent made him harder. His tongue flicked out and he tasted her skin, fancying he could distinguish her musky heat—or was that just her arousal he could smell?

Frustration at the prospect of the weekend ahead gripped him. He couldn't make love to her in the house. Not while his son lay sleeping. The thought of Milo waking and witnessing how feral Rafaele felt around Sam was anathema after his own experience of being that small and witnessing his father's breakdown.

Sam's eyes grew wide. Glittering. Pupils dilating. They were distracting him. Making him regret that he couldn't make love with her again for at least a few days. It would not happen in his office again. Never again. But they weren't done—not by a long shot.

'I'm not letting you go. Not until this is well and truly burnt out between us. I let you go too soon once before and I won't make that mistake again.'

The lights went green and Rafaele let Sam's hand go. He turned his attention to the road again and the car moved smoothly forward.

Sam clasped her tingling hand and turned her head, staring straight in front of her. Her whole body was still deeply sensitised after what had happened and yet she already felt ravenous for more. His words sank in: *I let you go too soon.*

He'd said something earlier about trying to eclipse her memory… His admission made her heart race pathetically.

And why on earth had she spilled her guts about her one very sad attempt at another relationship? To score points? To try and convince Rafaele that he hadn't dominated her life so totally?

But that was what she *had* attempted to do with the perfectly nice and normal Max. He'd caught her at a particularly vulnerable moment one day. Sam had seen a random newspaper report documenting the launch of a new Falcone car and there had been a picture of Rafaele with his arm around some gorgeous blonde model.

More than upset, and disturbed that she was still affected by him and the memories which would not abate after so much time, Sam had recklessly taken Max up on his offer of dinner. After a few weeks of pleasant but not earth-shattering dating Sam had felt a need to try and prove to herself that her memory of Rafaele was a mirage. That surely any other man could match him in bed and then she would not feel such a sense of loss, that she'd never experience such heights again.

It had been her suggestion to meet in a hotel one afternoon. As if they were both married and having an affair. But she'd thought it practical, considering their children were in their own homes, being minded. And Sam hadn't felt at all comfortable with introducing Max to Milo…even though he'd been hinting that the time to do so had come.

The afternoon had been awkward and horrendous from the first moment. Completely underwhelming. Disgusted with herself, because she had known that she'd acted out of weakness, Sam had called it off there and then.

Something very dangerous and fragile fluttered in the vicinity of her heart, where she'd blocked off any emotions for Rafaele a long time ago. Sam had fancied for a second that he had appeared jealous when she'd mentioned Max…which was ridiculous. What right had he to be jealous? He'd given up that right when he'd been with a woman less than a week after letting her go.

Sam took a deep breath and tried to crush the nebulous and very dangerous feeling growing within her. She would be the biggest fool on this planet if she was to read anything into Rafaele's possessive gesture and demeanour just now. As he'd said himself, he was only interested in whatever this was between them until it burnt out.

As Sam knew to her cost it was far more likely to burn out for him than for her, and she'd be left picking up the pieces again—except this time it would be so much worse because they were forever bound together now through Milo, and she had a very sick feeling that she was in danger of falling for him all over again. Or, more accurately, that she'd never stopped.

She went cold inside to think that perhaps part of her reluctance to tell him about Milo had been to avoid this very selfish scenario.

Rafaele smoothly drove the car into the space outside her front door and Sam blinked. She hadn't even been aware of the journey. Just then a curtain moved and Sam saw Milo's small face appear, wearing a huge grin. Her heart clenched hard. She could imagine him declaring excitedly, *'Daddy's home!'* as he'd been doing for the past few days according to an approving Bridie, who seemed to see nothing but good in Rafaele's appearance in their lives.

It was Friday. They had a weekend to get through now, and Sam had no expectation that Rafaele would be sneaking in through her bedroom door at night to pick up where they'd left off. She knew from experience that he liked to keep her a secret, on the periphery of his world.

Sam took a deep breath and schooled her features, hoping that Rafaele would never guess the extent of her turbulence around him, or that even now she ached between her legs for one of his hands to press against her and alleviate her mounting frustration.

The fact that she was back in a place she'd clawed her way out of four years before was not a welcome revelation. At all.

CHAPTER SEVEN

On Sunday Sam was folding laundry in the little utility room off the kitchen. Rafaele had taken Milo swimming on his own earlier, and since they'd come home they'd played with Milo's cars in the sitting room. Now he was putting him to bed.

She'd felt like a cat on a hot tin roof all weekend. Lying in bed at night, *aching* with frustration. Locking her muscles to avoid walking down the hall to Rafaele's room to beg him to make love to her. She refused to give herself away so spectacularly. And she'd been right. He'd treated her coolly all weekend, clearly reluctant to draw what had happened in his office into the domestic sphere.

Sam was only good enough within an environment which suited him. Nothing had changed. The bitterness that scored her shocked her with its intensity. Her emotions were see-sawing all over the place.

What *hadn't* helped was the little surprise Rafaele had had lined up when they'd woken that morning. The sleek supercar Rafaele had been using since he'd appeared in their lives had been replaced, probably by some hardworking minion, with a far more sedate *family* car.

'What's this?' Sam had asked faintly from the front door as Rafaele had deftly strapped Milo into his car seat to take him swimming.

He'd cast her a quick dry glance. 'It's a car, Sam. A more practical car, I think you'll agree, for a child...'

Sam had felt as if she'd just tipped over the edge of a precipice. All she'd been able to think about after they'd left, with an ecstatic Milo in the back, was of how Rafaele—one of the most Alpha male men she'd ever met, if not *the* most—had segued from playboy with a fast car into man with a child and a safety-conscious car without turning a hair. And somehow that had made Sam more nervous than anything else. She was too scared to look at all the implications and what they might mean...

She heard a noise then and tensed as she sensed Rafaele's presence behind her in the kitchen. She felt far too vulnerable to face him right now.

'I want you and Milo to come to Milan with me.'

Sam went very still for a moment, and then proceeded to fold a sheet as if he *hadn't* just dropped a bomb from a great height. Irritation with herself, with him, at the sexual frustration clawing at her insides, laced her voice. 'What are you talking about, Rafaele? We can't just go to Milan with you.'

Sounding impatient, Rafaele said, 'Sam, I can't talk to your back.' His voice changed and grew rougher. 'As delectable as it is. And your bottom in those jeans... *Dio*, do you know how hard it's been not to touch you all weekend?'

That made Sam whirl around, her blood heating instantaneously and rushing to every erogenous zone she had. She dropped the sheet from nerveless hands.

Despite her own craving need all weekend she hissed, 'Stop it. You can't talk to me like that. Not here, with Milo in the house.'

Rafaele was leaning against the doorjamb, far too close. His eyes narrowed on her, taking in her jeans and shirt. Grimly he admitted, 'I know. That's precisely why I restrained myself.'

Something gave way inside Sam at hearing him admit that his concern for Milo had been uppermost. It made her feel exposed, vulnerable. Between her legs she throbbed almost painfully.

Sam picked up the sheet and thrust it at Rafaele's chest. 'Here's some fresh linen for your bed.'

Rafaele caught the linen when it would have dropped to the ground again. His mouth had gone flat and tight.

'Well? Did you hear what I said about Milan? I want you and Milo to come with me this week.'

The thought of going back to the scene of the crime made Sam's emotions seesaw even more. She turned around again and blurted out, 'It's not practical, Rafaele. You can't just announce—'

'*Dio*, Sam.'

Sam let out a small squeak of surprise at Rafaele's guttural voice and saw the linen she'd just shoved at him sail over her head to land back on the pile haphazardly. Then she felt big hands swing her round until she was looking up in his grim face.

'Sam, I—' He stopped. His eyes went to her mouth and then he just said, *'Dio!'* again, before muttering something else in Italian and then pulling her into him.

His mouth was on hers, branding her, and she was up in flames in an instant, every point of her body straining to be closer to his hard form.

With a moan of helpless need and self-derision Sam submitted to the practised and expert ministrations of Rafaele's wicked mouth and tongue. Some tiny morsel of self-preservation eventually impinged on the heat and gave Sam the strength to pull free. She looked up into Rafaele's face and almost melted there and then at the sight of the feral look in his eyes. She put a hand to his chest, but that was worse when she felt his heart pounding.

'We can't. Not here…'

Rafaele smiled, but it was humourless. 'Maybe we'll have to book a hotel as you're partial to that kind of thing.'

That gave Sam the impetus to move, and she scooted out of the small space and rounded on Rafaele, arms crossed over the betraying throb of her breasts. Her voice was low with anger. 'You have no right to judge me when you were jumping into bed with someone new barely a week after I left Italy.'

Rafaele frowned. He looked volcanic. 'What the hell are you talking about? I wasn't with anyone.'

Sam emitted a curt laugh and tried to hide the flare of something pathetic within her. *Hope.* 'Well, that's not what it looked like—you were photographed all over the place with some Italian TV personality.'

Rafaele opened his mouth to speak but Sam put up a hand, stopping him.

Fiercely, she said, 'I don't care, Rafaele.' *Liar.*

Irrational guilt over her own liaison made her even angrier.

'Even if I had told you about Milo, it wasn't as if we were going to become some happy family. You told me what you thought of marriage and how you never wanted it in your life.'

Sam stopped, breathing heavily, and saw how Rafaele's face had become shuttered. Clearly he didn't like to be reminded of that.

'I seem to recall you agreeing fervently, Sam. Something about how seeing your father weep over your mother's picture had made you dread ever investing so much in one person only to lose them and be lonely for the rest of your life?'

Sam's insides contracted. She felt dizzy for a second and then mortification rushed through her like a shameful tide. She'd been so *open* with him. Had told him every little thing. As if he'd even been interested! Wasn't that exactly what she'd done, though? After a mere month in this man's bed she'd been ready to invest everything in him, only to realise how far off-base she'd been.

Panicking, she said the first thing she could think of to try and get them off this topic. 'What did you mean... about Milan?'

Rafaele's jaw clenched, but to her intense relief he appeared prepared to let it go.

'I want to take Milo to meet his grandfather—my father. It's going to come out sooner or later in the press that I have a son and I'd like Umberto to meet him before that happens. Also, he is old and frail...I'm conscious of his mortality.'

The words were delivered dispassionately enough to shock Sam slightly. Rafaele had never spoken of his father much before, except to say that he lived in a place called Bergamo, not far from Milan, and that he'd moved away after the family business had disintegrated and they'd lost everything. Sam knew that one of the first things Rafaele had done was to buy back the Falcone *palazzo* just outside Milan, as that was where he'd lived four years ago.

She hadn't met Umberto Falcone during the time she'd been with Rafaele, and against her better judgment her interest was piqued at the thought of seeing this tantalising glimpse of another aspect of Rafaele's life. And also to acknowledge that Milo had one grandparent still alive.

Rafaele continued, 'He's coming to Milan next week for a routine medical check-up and he's staying at the family *palazzo* just outside the city. I have to go back for a few days to attend a board meeting and drop in on the factory there. It would be a perfect opportunity to do this.'

She still resisted, despite being intrigued. 'Perfect for you, maybe... Milo has playschool, a routine. And what about my work?'

Rafaele's lip curled. 'Please—do you really expect me

to believe that Milo will be irreparably damaged by missing a few days of playschool? And...' those laser-like eyes narrowed on her '...I think that your boss would be very amenable to you taking the time off.'

Looking smug, Rafaele delivered the final nail in the coffin of Sam's hopes to escape.

'I spoke with Bridie about it when we met her outside just a while ago and she said she'd be only too happy to come to Italy with us and help watch Milo. She confided that as a devout Catholic she's always wanted to visit Rome, and I promised her we could make a stop there on the way back...'

Sam clenched her hands into fists at her sides. 'That's low-down and dirty manipulation, Rafaele.'

He shrugged lightly. 'Call it what you want, Sam, but I believe I'm entitled to a little "manipulation". You, Milo and Bridie are coming to Italy with me in two days' time so you'd better get prepared.'

Sam watched Rafaele turn and walk out and welcomed the rush of anger. No doubt he'd been planning this all along, lulling her into a false sense of security by moving into the house, demonstrating his capacity to compromise for his son's sake. Rafaele was just showing his true colours now: his desire to dominate.

But worse, much worse than that, was the prospect of how hard it would be to return to the place where it had all started. If she was barely holding it together here, how would she manage when she was face to face with the past?

Two days later, in accordance with Rafaele's autocratic decree, they were on a private plane belonging to Rafaele's younger half-brother, the Greek aviation and travel billionaire Alexio Christakos.

Bridie was in silent raptures over the plush luxuriousness of it all and Milo was like a bottle of shaken-up lemonade—about to fizz over at any moment. Every day for him at the moment seemed to bring nothing but untold treasures, and Sam looked at him kneeling on the seat beside her now, watching the world get smaller and smaller beneath them.

It was his first time on a plane and Milo automatically looked for his new favourite person on the planet: Rafaele. Pointing with a chubby finger, he said, 'Look, Daddy, *look!*'

Sam's heart squeezed so tight she had to put a hand there, as if that could assuage the bittersweet pain and the anxiety. How could she trust that Rafaele wouldn't grow bored and disappear from their lives, leaving Milo bereft? *And her...* Sam didn't even want to go there.

They were cruising now, and Rafaele stood up and managed to dwarf the very comfortable ten-seater plane. He held out a hand to Milo. 'Do you want to see the cockpit?'

He'd barely stopped talking before Milo had leapt off the seat and run to him. Rafaele picked him up. Milo didn't even look to Sam for reassurance.

Sam felt silly tears prick her eyes and turned away, but she heard Bridie saying quietly from across the small aisle, 'He's a good man. He'll take care of you both.'

Sam fought valiantly for control and looked at Bridie, gave her a watery smile. She couldn't hide anything from this woman who had seen her devastation when she'd come home from Italy. Her father hadn't even noticed, and had barely acknowledged her pregnancy in his sheer self-absorption. When Milo had appeared her father had merely raised an eyebrow and proceeded to behave as if he'd always been there.

Sam reached out and took Bridie's hand, squeezing it. 'I'm glad you're here.'

'So am I, love,' Bridie said, and then with obvious glee, 'I'm going to meet the Pope!'

Sam laughed, 'I know Rafaele can do most things, but I'm not sure his influence extends to that.'

'Not sure my influence extends to what?'

Sam tensed and looked up to catch Rafaele's green gaze. She blushed and said, 'Nothing... Milo should eat now. He'll be hungry.'

Bridie stood up and took Milo from Rafaele. 'I'll have a word with the stewardess and we'll get him sorted.'

Rafaele sat down in Bridie's vacant seat when they were gone and extended his long legs into the aisle. He was the epitome of Italian masculine elegance today, in a dark grey suit, white shirt and tie. But all Sam could think of was the raw magnetism lurking under the surface of that urbanity.

'It's rude to talk about people behind their backs, you know,' he observed without rancour.

Sam was immediately suspicious of this more civil Rafaele. He was undoubtedly happy to be returning to his own milieu.

She smiled tightly and avoided his gaze. 'Don't worry. Your number two fan only has good things to say about you.'

'Unlike you...'

In a bid to break the sudden tension Sam asked quickly, 'Your father...he knows about us coming?'

Rafaele sat back a little further. Milo could be heard chattering happily further up the plane.

The reserve that came over Rafaele's features at the mention of his father didn't go unnoticed by Sam.

'I spoke to him on the phone and explained.'

'How did he take the news of...of a grandson?'

Rafaele's mouth thinned. 'He's looking forward to meeting the next generation.'

'You're not close to him, are you?'

Rafaele looked at her and asked almost accusingly, 'How do you know?'

She shrugged minutely. 'You never spoke about him much…and I know you didn't grow up with him.'

'No,' he conceded. His mouth was even thinner, making Sam want to reach out and touch him. She curled her hands into fists in her lap.

With evident reluctance he said, 'My mother left him when I was three and took me with her. He was in no state to care for me even if she'd wanted to leave me behind.'

In an instant Sam remembered the day they'd told Milo who Rafaele was and Rafaele had made that enigmatic comment about being three years old. He must have been referring to this.

'Your mother wouldn't have done that, surely…?'

Rafaele arched a dark brow. 'No? So why did she abandon my older half-brother? Her firstborn son?'

Sam's mouth opened and closed. 'You have another brother?'

As if regretting saying anything, Rafaele said briskly, 'He turned up out of the blue at my mother's funeral. Alexio and I had no idea he even existed… Well, I had a memory of meeting him briefly when I was small but I thought it had been a dream.'

Half to herself, Sam said, 'So Milo has two uncles…'

Rafaele emitted a curt laugh. 'Don't worry, it's not likely we'll be getting together as one big happy family any time soon. Alexio is busy running his empire and Cesar wants nothing to do with us.'

Just then Milo came running down the aisle and grabbed Rafaele's hand, pulling him out of the seat. 'Lunch is ready!'

Rafaele let himself be pulled up and held out a hand to Sam.

She felt unsettled and a little vulnerable after their conversation. It was another snippet Rafaele hadn't revealed before. She put her hand into his and let him pull her out of the seat. He held it tightly all the way to the other end of the plane but Sam didn't feel as if the gesture was meant to be romantic. On the contrary—it was meant to remind her that they had unfinished business.

Rafaele's *palazzo* was as she remembered it: imposing, beautiful and impressive. The lush green gardens were stunningly landscaped. Its faintly crumbling grandeur hid opulent luxury inside. Four years ago Rafaele had still been in the process of doing it up and now it was finished.

As they approached up the grand steps Sam didn't even notice how tense she'd become until Milo said plaintively, 'Ow Mummy, too *tight*.' She immediately relaxed her grip on his hand.

A different housekeeper from the one Sam remembered met them at the door and Rafaele introduced her as Luisa. She was soon busy directing the driver with their bags. Bridie was open-mouthed with shock and awe, and Sam felt a semi-hysterical giggle rise up, but it faded fast when she saw the stooped figure of a man with a cane approach them.

He barked out something in Italian and Sam saw Rafaele tense just a few feet ahead of her. She had that disturbing urge again to touch him, to offer some comfort.

He said curtly, 'In English, Papa. They don't speak Italian.'

The old man snorted and came into view. His eyes were deep set and so dark they looked black, staring out from a strong face lined with age and disappointment.

Milo was clutching Sam now and she lifted him up.

'Well?' Umberto growled. 'Where is my grandson?'

Hesitantly Sam moved forward to stand beside Rafaele. She felt him snake an arm around her waist and didn't like the way something within her immediately welcomed and gravitated towards the support.

'Papa, this is Samantha Rourke, our son Milo, and Sam's friend Bridie.'

Our son.

Sam nodded in the man's direction. His black gaze seemed to be devouring them. He said nothing. Then, to Sam's complete surprise, Milo squirmed to be set free and she had to put him down.

Holding her breath, Sam watched as Milo started to walk towards his grandfather. She wanted to snatch him back, as if from the jaws of danger, and even moved. But Rafaele's hand stopped her, gripping her waist, making her *über*-aware of his hard body alongside hers. Even now...

Milo stopped in front of the man and asked with all the innocence of a child, 'Why do you have a stick?'

The man just looked at him for a long moment and then barked out a laugh. '*Dio*, Rafaele, it's like looking at you when you were that age. He's a Falcone—no doubt about it.'

Rafaele's hand gripped her waist so tightly now that Sam looked at him, but she could only see his hard jaw, a muscle twitching. Before she could do or say anything Rafaele had let her go and strode over to crouch down near Milo, who curled into him trustingly.

Huskily he was saying, 'This is your grandpapa, *piccolino.*'

Umberto Falcone held out a hand to his grandson. 'I am pleased to meet you.'

Milo grinned and took his hand, shaking it forcefully, making Umberto wince comically. Milo giggled and looked at Rafaele. 'Can we play now?'

Rafaele stood up, still holding onto Milo's hand, and something tense seemed to pass from him to his father. He said to Milo, 'Why don't we settle in first, hmm? We can play later.'

'Okey-dokey.' Milo took his hand from Rafaele's and came back to Sam, who picked him up again.

Rafaele was now drawing her and Bridie forward to introduce them to Umberto, but gone was the joking man of moments ago. He seemed to have retreated again.

Bridie was saying politely, 'You have a beautiful home here, Mr Falcone.'

The old man glanced at his son and said stiffly, 'It's not mine...it's Rafaele's. He bought it back after—'

'Papa,' Rafaele said warningly, and the man's mouth shut.

He looked at Bridie then and said, 'Come, let us take some refreshments and leave these young ones to settle in.'

Bridie looked at Sam, and Sam noticed that she was a bit pink in the cheeks. Sam pushed her gently in the direction where Umberto was setting off, surprisingly agile despite his cane and stooped figure. 'Go on—sit down and have a rest. We'll be fine.'

The housekeeper was despatching a younger woman in the direction of Umberto and Bridie with rapid Italian before leading them up the stairs herself. Sam was clinging onto Milo, afraid of the onslaught of memories lurking around each corner. She and Rafaele had made love all over this *palazzo*. He'd used to bring her here after work, apart from a couple of times when he'd taken her to her apartment, too impatient to wait, but she'd never spent a weekend here with him until that last weekend...

They were walking down a familiar corridor now, and Sam's heart thumped hard when she recognised Rafaele's bedroom door to the left. Thankfully they stopped at another door, just opposite.

'This is your room. Milo is in an adjoining one.'

Sam walked into the room indicated by Rafaele. The housekeeper disappeared. Milo wriggled to be free and she put him down so he could explore. The room was sumptuous without being over the top. Understated luxury. Lots of discreet flower designs and soft greys. Sam heard a squeal of excitement from Milo and followed him into his room.

It was a small boy's paradise. His bed was made in the shape of a car. The walls were bright. Books and toys covered almost every available surface. Sam looked at Rafaele helplessly as Milo found a toy train set.

He grabbed it up and went to Sam, 'Is this mine, Mummy?'

Sam shot Rafaele a censorious look. She bent down. 'Yes, it is, sweetie. But this is Rafaele's house. You'll have to leave it behind when we go home.'

Milo looked perturbed and turned to Rafaele. 'Will you mind it for me when we go home?'

Rafaele sounded gruff. 'Of course, *piccolino*.'

Milo's lip quivered. Sam could see that it was all too much.

'But…but what if another little boy comes and wants to play with it?'

Rafaele bent down and looked Milo in the eye. 'That won't happen. You are the only little boy who is allowed to play here, I promise.'

Instantly reassured, Milo spun away to start playing again.

Sam hissed at Rafaele. 'This is too much for him. You can't *buy* his affection, Rafaele.'

Rafaele stood up and took Sam's arm, leading her out of earshot. 'Damn you, Sam, I'm not trying to buy him… I want to spoil him—is that so bad?'

Sam looked into Rafaele's eyes and felt herself drowning. She knew instinctively that Rafaele had done this out of the generous good of his heart, *not* out of any manipulative desire. He might do that with her, but all along he'd been ultra-careful to take her lead on how to deal with Milo.

She crossed her arms and felt like a heel. She looked down. 'I'm sorry...that wasn't entirely fair.'

Rafaele tipped her chin up. 'No, it wasn't.'

All Rafaele could see were those swirling grey depths, sucking him down and down to a place he didn't want to investigate. Like Milo feeling overwhelmed, he suddenly felt the same. Letting go of Sam's chin, he stepped back. He needed space. Now.

'I'll have Luisa bring you up some refreshments. You and Milo should settle in and rest. We'll eat at seven.'

When he reached his study on the ground floor he closed the door and took a deep breath. He headed straight for his drinks cabinet and poured himself a shot of whisky, downing it in one. To his chagrin it wasn't even Milo and the fact that he had his son in this house that seemed to be featuring prominently in his head. It was Sam. Having Sam back here. Reminding him of the heated insanity he'd felt around her before. Of how badly he'd needed her, how insatiably.

How sweet she'd been—so innocent. So bright. So unlike any other woman he'd known, seducing him effortlessly into a tangled web of need from which he'd only extricated himself with great effort. And he had been relieved to do so, no matter what the dull ache he'd felt for four years might have told him.

The ache had disappeared as soon as he'd decided that he'd contact her in England. He'd told himself that it would be different, that he wouldn't still desire her. That he would be able to demonstrate how he'd moved on... But even at the first sound of her voice on the end of the phone his body had convulsed with need...

And then...*Milo*.

Rafaele felt pain lance his hand and looked down stupidly to see that he'd crushed the delicate glass. Cursing himself, he got a tissue and told himself he was being ridiculous. Seeing Sam here again, with his father too, in this *palazzo*…it was something he'd never expected to have to deal with. That was all.

The following morning when Sam woke up she was disorientated for a few long seconds, until the opulent surroundings and softer-than-soft bed registered. She sat up in a panic.

Milo.

Quickly she got out of bed and went to the open adjoining door. Milo's bed was tossed, his pyjamas were on the ground and he was nowhere to be seen.

Bridie must have taken him for breakfast. The previous evening had seen them all seated for dinner—Milo sitting on big books on a chair to elevate him, insisting on feeding himself like a big boy, wanting to impress his new grandpapa, who had looked on approvingly.

To Sam's relief, after dinner Rafaele, far too disturbing in jeans and a black top, had made his excuses and disappeared to his study. And then Bridie had insisted on taking Milo up to bed, as he'd been barely able to keep awake long enough to feed himself his new favourite dessert: *gelato.*

Sam had felt awkward, sitting with Umberto on her own, but the man had stood up and indicated for her to follow him and have some coffee, so she had. He'd led her to a small room off the dining room—comfortable, cosy.

Luisa had come and poured them coffee and Sam had felt she needed to break the ice. 'I'm sorry…that you didn't know about Milo before now.'

The old man had waved her words aside and admitted gruffly, 'I gave up any right to pry into Rafaele's life a long time ago.'

Not knowing how to respond, Sam had just taken a sip of coffee. She'd always loved the strength and potency of well-made Italian coffee.

'Milo is the same age as Rafaele was when he left here with his mother.'

Sam had looked at Umberto.

'He was very young.' The old man's face had darkened. 'Too young to witness what he did.'

Sam had frowned. 'I'm sorry… I don't know…'

Umberto had looked at her, his gaze shrewd. 'When my wife left me, Samantha, I was a broken man. I'd already lost everything. My house, the family legacy, the factory. My dignity. I begged her on my knees not to leave me but she did anyway. Rafaele witnessed my lowest moment and I don't think he's ever forgiven me for it.'

Sam had tried to take it in. She'd known Rafaele's mother had left, but not the extent of it. She wondered how traumatic it must have been for a child to see his mother turn her back on his father and it was as if something slid home inside her—she could see now where Rafaele's intensely commitment-phobic issues might stem from.

'It was a long time ago…' Umberto had said. 'It's good that you are here with Milo. This will be a challenge for my proud son, and perhaps that's not a bad thing.'

Sam blinked in the morning light of her bedroom, the memory fading. She remembered now that she'd had disjointed dreams all night of a man on his knees, begging, pleading, with Milo looking on, crying in distress… She pursed her lips. One thing she could guarantee pretty categorically was that Rafaele would never be reduced to begging on his knees to *anyone*.

Trying not to think of that vulnerable three-year-old Rafaele, when all she could see was Milo in her mind's eye, Sam washed and dressed and went to search for Milo and Bridie. She found them in the dining room with the sun pouring in.

Sam bent to kiss her son, aware of a cool green gaze on her from the head of the table. Umberto and Bridie broke off from their conversation to greet Sam and Rafaele stood up. Sam had to quell a dart of hurt. She felt as if the minute she entered a room he wanted to leave it.

'I've got to go to the factory this morning for my meeting... I've arranged for a driver to come and pick you all up in an hour. He will drop Umberto off at the doctor's and take you into Milan to sightsee. I'll join you there this afternoon for a late lunch.'

Umberto muttered something rude about doctors and Sam saw Bridie smile.

Milo was asking Sam, 'What's *sightsee?*'

Rafaele had pinned Sam with that unreadable gaze and instantly she felt breathless. 'I have to go to a function this evening. I'd like it if you accompanied me.'

Sam opened her mouth. 'I...'

Bridie chipped in quickly. 'Of course she will. You could do with a night out, Sam, love. I'll be here, and Milo can sleep with me so you won't have to worry about disturbing him.'

Sam glared at Bridie, who looked back at her with an innocence she didn't trust for a second. Umberto was unhelpfully silent.

Sam looked at Rafaele and was loath to let him see that she might not want to go for very personal reasons.

She shrugged a shoulder. 'Sure—why not?'

CHAPTER EIGHT

THAT EVENING SAM realised a fundamental flaw in her plan to join Rafaele for his function. She had no dress. She hadn't even thought about it earlier, while in Milan, too caught up in the whistlestop sightseeing tour Rafaele had arranged for Bridie and Milo, who obviously hadn't been there before. Then they'd picked Umberto up from the doctor's and met Rafaele for lunch.

Biting her lip and wondering what to do, Sam went to the wardrobe, fully expecting it to be empty. When she opened the door, though, she gasped and her heart stopped cold in her chest. There was a dress hanging up inside, and it was the dress Rafaele had bought her four years before. She remembered the big white box it had come in, along with the matching underwear, shoes and jewels. She'd left it all behind at the *palazzo* because she'd felt as if it had never really belonged to her.

About two months after Sam had returned to England the box containing the dress, shoes, underwear and jewellery had arrived via a courier company. As soon as she'd realised what it was and had read the accompanying note— *I bought this for you. Rafaele*—Sam had sent it back with the note torn in two pieces.

And now it was here.

Sam felt short of breath. She took the dress out of the wardrobe, its material heavy and slinky, and stalked out of her bedroom and across the hall to Rafaele's, not bothering to knock on the door.

Her eyes widened when she took in a naked Rafaele, strolling out of his bathroom and rubbing his hair with a towel. For a long moment he just stood there, and Sam's eyes were glued to that broad, magnificent chest. Instant heat bloomed in her belly.

With a strangled sound she lifted her eyes and held the dress out. 'What is the meaning of this?'

With supreme nonchalance Rafaele secured the towel around his waist and quirked his mouth sexily on one side. 'It's amazing how you can still blush, *cara*.'

Sam gritted out, 'Don't call me that. I'm not your *cara*. Why do you still have this dress?'

Rafaele's face was inscrutable. He shrugged. 'It seemed a shame to throw it away just because you didn't want it.'

Bile rose inside Sam. 'And how many lucky women have worn it since me?'

A muscle popped in Rafaele's jaw. 'None. I thought you'd appreciate blending in with the crowd tonight instead of appearing in your habitual tomboy uniform.'

To Sam's disgust she felt tears prick her eyes. 'I'll try not to disappoint you, Rafaele. After all, I know what an honour it is to be taken out in public with you, because you never deemed it appropriate before.'

She whirled around and left the room, slamming the door behind her.

Rafaele winced and put his hands on his hips. His chest was a tight ball of blackness. He cursed himself. He should have followed his head and thrown that dress out as soon as he'd realised she'd left it behind—instead of sending it to her, almost intrigued as to how she might respond when even then he'd known that he couldn't have anything more to do with her.

When it had arrived back with the torn note, *then* he

should have thrown it out. But instead he'd instructed his housekeeper to hang it up and had refused to analyse why he'd done such a thing.

It was just a dress.

Thoroughly disgruntled now, and regretting the impulse he'd had earlier to ask Sam to accompany him this evening, Rafaele got dressed.

Sam was still tight-lipped in the back of one of Rafaele's chauffeur-driven cars about an hour later. She was as far away from him as she could get without falling out of the door, and she hated the electric awareness that pulsed between them.

As they'd been leaving Milo had been holding Umberto's hand in the grand hallway of the *palazzo* and he'd gasped. 'Mummy, you look like a princess.'

Sam had gone red, and then grown even hotter when Rafaele had appeared, looking stupendously gorgeous in a classic tuxedo. Suddenly she'd been glad of the effort she'd made. She needed all the armour she could muster.

Her hair was up in a topknot, held in place with a jewelled pin loaned to her by Bridie. She'd put on more make-up than she'd normally wear, outlining her eyes and thickening her lashes. And wearing the vertiginous heels that had come with the dress Sam reached to Rafaele's shoulder.

He hadn't touched her while they were leaving. He'd merely indicated that she should precede him and, feeling horribly exposed under his cool gaze, Sam had walked out, praying she wouldn't fall over.

Now they were pulling up outside the glittering façade of a building with men in uniforms waiting to assist all the guests in their finery. Butterflies swarmed into Sam's belly.

She felt her arm being taken in a warm grip and showers of electric shocks seemed to spread through her body. Reluctantly she looked at Rafaele, and the momentarily unguarded look on his face took her by surprise.

'I should have told you earlier… You look beautiful.'

'I…' Sam's voice failed. 'Thank you.'

And just like that she felt the animosity drain away. She realised that as soon as she'd seen the dress hanging up she'd harboured a very treacherous wish that Rafaele had kept it for sentimental reasons, and that was the basis for her lashing out at him. It had been anger at herself for her own pathetic weakness.

Rafaele had let her go. Sam's door was being opened and someone was waiting for her to step out. When she did so, Rafaele was standing there, his face unreadable again. She wondered if she had imagined what he'd just said…

He took her arm and led her inside and Sam was glad he was supporting her, because nothing could have prepared her for the dazzling display of wealth and beauty as soon as they walked in.

She felt instantly gauche: both underdressed and overdressed. Rafaele got them drinks and almost immediately was surrounded by gushing acolytes—a mixture of men and women. As they stood there the number of women seemed to increase. They shot Sam glances ranging from the curious to the downright angry—as if he had no right to come here with a woman.

Clearly Rafaele was a prize to be fought over, and Sam really didn't like the way her own hackles rose and her blood started to boil in response. She felt a very disturbing primal urge rise up within her to claim him in some way. The fact that she had borne his child seemed to resonate deep within her, and she wanted to snarl at the women to back off.

With a lazy insouciance that did nothing to help cool her blood, Rafaele reached out and drew her to his side. The level of malevolence coming from the women increased exponentially.

He said to the people surrounding them, 'I'd like to introduce you to Samantha Rourke.'

Something in Sam went cold at this very bare introduction, which left her in some kind of limbo land—what exactly *was* she to him?

But what had she expected him to say? *Meet the mother of my child, who is such a pushover that she lets me sleep with her even though she knows I hate her...?*

Sam caught one or two smug looks from a couple of the women. As if to say, *She's no competition.* Her blood boiled over.

She managed to keep it together until they were alone again and then she rounded on him. 'If you brought me here just to deflect the attention from those man-eaters then I think I've done my bit. I'd prefer to be at home with Milo than to witness your simpering fan club line up to tell you how marvellous you are.'

Furious at herself for feeling so emotional, Sam stabbed Rafaele's chest with a finger. 'I'm the mother of your child—tell *that* to your next prospective mistress.'

Rafaele looked at Sam and felt something pierce his chest. Her words were lost to him for a second in the glare from those grey eyes. She looked so young, so stunning. Her neck was long and graceful, her skin so pale he could see the delicate veins underneath. The dress hugged and emphasised every curve, fitting her better now than it had four years ago. His eyes dropped down over the swell of her breasts and her words resounded within him: *I'm the mother of your child.*

Moments ago, when he'd reached out to pull her to him and introduce her, he'd felt a second of blind panic. The realisation had been immediate and stark: he'd just introduced his peers to Sam and when the news emerged of his son, and that she was his mother, they would assume that they were together. And that thought wasn't making him want to flee.

Rafaele had not even considered this prospect when he'd asked Sam to the function. He'd just looked at her that morning and the words had spilled out... Proving once again how she scrambled his thought processes. How she effortlessly tapped into something deep and instinctive within him that led to choices and decisions that his head might normally balk at.

He couldn't even blame her. It wasn't as if she'd inveigled her way to an invitation—if anything she'd looked horrified at the suggestion. Rafaele's blood simmered. He felt the imprint of Sam's finger in his chest. The rest of the room died away and he saw only her. Need and desire rose up to strangle him and magnified his feeling of exposure.

Reaching out a hand, he snaked it around her neck and brought her closer. Something triumphant moved through him when he saw those eyes flare with awareness. But the realisation of how comfortable he was with people knowing who Sam was, assuming they were together, was too raw, too new. He needed to push it back. Push *her* back.

'I have the only mistress I need right here, Sam. Why would I go looking when you've already proved yourself so amenable?'

Her cheeks went white and Rafaele felt the punch of something dirty and dark down low.

'You bastard.'

She pulled away from him and spun around, moving through the crowd. It was a long second before Rafaele could function again, and then he set off after her, a dense darkness expanding in his chest when he thought of those huge eyes and the pain in their depths that he'd just witnessed. That he'd just caused. Wilfully. From weakness.

* * *

Sam could barely drag enough oxygen into her lungs. She
was seething. Hurt and angry with herself for letting Rafaele get to her. For feeling so possessive and jealous around
those other women. For ever hoping even for a second
that his bringing her here tonight had meant something...

She raised a hand to get the doorman's attention, to ask
him to call her a cab, but just then it was caught by a firm
grip and she was whirled around.

'Where do you think you're going?'

Rafaele looked as livid as she felt, and he had no right
to be. Sam pulled her arm free. 'I'm going home, Rafaele.
I don't need to be reminded publicly how little you like to
acknowledge me in your life.'

She turned around again, but gave a gasp of dismay
when she saw Rafaele's chauffeur-driven car stopping at
the foot of the steps. He was marching her down to the
open door before she could do anything. The door was
quickly shut and he was sliding in the other side. Sam
had a perverse urge to open the door and jump out but
she curbed the childish desire. And also she realised she
didn't have enough money for a cab. She scowled at herself.
Being with Rafaele was eroding her very independence.

Rafaele issued a terse instruction to the driver and the
privacy window slid up noiselessly. His eyes glittered at
her in the gloom of the backseat but even now Sam's muscles clenched in her pelvis, and she felt the betraying heat
of desire getting her body ready for this man. *Her man.*
The stupid assertion flashed again. She could have growled
with frustration.

Eventually he bit out, 'I shouldn't have said what I did
back there. You didn't deserve that.'

It was the last thing Sam had expected to hear, and she
said faintly, 'No, I didn't.' And then, 'Why did you bring
me with you, Rafaele? People will only ask questions...

when they find out about Milo... We shouldn't be seen together. It doesn't help matters.'

Rafaele's face looked as if it was carved out of stone. 'You're the mother of my child, Samantha. It's inevitable that we'll be seen together, no matter what happens in the future.'

Sam had an image then of Rafaele, married to some cool blonde beauty, and of an older Milo heading off on a plane on his own to stay with his father and his new family. The image made her suck in a breath of pain and she scooted as far away from him in the back of the car as she could.

Mixed in with the pain she was feeling was the ever-present and building sexual frustration. She felt as if she was going mad. Heat burned her insides and made her skin prickle. All she could see in her peripheral vision was the huge dark shape of Rafaele and imagined that powerful body, naked and surging into hers, thrusting so deep that she'd finally feel some measure of peace.

She had to hold back a groan, and was aware of Rafaele's quick glance at her through the thick tension between them.

Lord. It had been a long time since Sam had had to pleasure herself, but if this need wasn't assuaged soon she'd go mad.

'Sam.'

Rafaele's voice was thick and Sam's heart palpitated. Reluctantly she looked at him and a pulse throbbed between her legs. She clamped her thighs together desperately.

He reached over and took her hand and Sam almost cried out at the sensation. She tried to pull back but he wouldn't release her.

'I want you.'

His face was in shadow but she could sense his desperation. It was little comfort. Inevitability rose up inside her. She could resist anything but this declaration. This promise that soon, if she allowed it, he would ease this ache that was inside her, tearing her apart. It transcended even what had just happened.

Helplessly, in a whisper of supplication that she hated, Sam just replied, 'Yes...'

Yes.

Rafaele felt primal satisfaction rush through him, hardening his body. He wanted to devour Sam, consume her, brand her. He wanted her *for ever*.

No!

Rafaele rejected that rogue assertion, which had slid into his mind before he'd even acknowledged it.

He couldn't let her hand go, though, even when she turned her head away to look out of the window. The rapid rise and fall of her breasts beneath the dress made him curl his other hand to a fist, just to stop himself reaching out to cup their heavy weight.

Sam was clearly aware of the same ramifications as he, of being seen together and how that might be construed. But the thought of her rejecting that suddenly made him want to claim her. In any way that he could. Publicly *and* in private.

But right now he couldn't really focus on what that meant. Right now he wanted the physical.

As the car swept gracefully through the *palazzo* gates anticipation spiked like a fever in his blood. When the car came to a halt he got out and strode around to Sam's door, helping her out himself. She looked up at him with those huge expressive eyes and desire was hot and urgent inside him—part of the tangled mess of emotions this woman inspired in him on a regular basis.

With one smooth move he picked her up into his arms. Her mouth was tight with a need that resonated within him.

He felt like a beast. He couldn't speak. What he needed right now was not something he could even articulate. It was visceral, physical. Urgent.

Sam was in Rafaele's arms and he was striding through the front door of the *palazzo*. All she could feel was her breasts crushed to the solid wall of his chest and the pulse of awareness between them, like a tangible forcefield of energy.

The house was quiet. He was striding up the stairs now and Sam bit her lip. Rafaele carried her straight into his bedroom. She tensed against the leap of her blood at the promise of satisfaction. A moment of sanity intruded, reminding her of the certain self-recrimination she would face in the aftermath and all the uncertainty about how he felt about her.

Weakly she seized on the first thing she thought of. 'Wait… Milo…'

Rafaele was putting her down, sliding her along the length of his hard body, one part of which in particular was very hard. He was already pulling down the strap of her dress and her skin tingled.

His voice was rough. 'Milo is with Bridie, as you well know.'

That sliver of sanity compelled her to try again, even though every part of her protested. 'Rafaele…'

'Stop talking, Sam. I want you. You want me. It's very simple.'

It *wasn't* that simple, though, and Sam opened her mouth to protest again. But then Rafaele was kissing her, and pulling the strap of her dress down further, and she felt the rising lust suck her under and weakly…she gave in. She wanted to forget sanity and take *this*.

Between her legs she was slick and throbbing. She didn't have a hope of resisting when Rafaele bared one breast and cupped it in his hand, squeezing the plump flesh, his thumb grazing her nipple.

Letting out a soft moan halfway between frustration at her own weakness and excitement at her building desire, Sam wound her arms around Rafaele's neck and pressed herself against him, trapping his hand on her breast.

Rafaele's other hand came down and cupped her buttocks, kneading the flesh, making Sam's hips roll against him impatiently. She could feel the thick length of his erection between them and fresh heat pulsed to her core.

Rafaele pulled back for a moment, breathing harshly, his eyes glittering fiercely. It was hard for Sam to open her eyes. She felt dazed. He'd always had this effect on her—one touch and she felt drugged.

He was dragging off his jacket, tie and shirt, dropping them to the ground, unbuckling his belt, undoing his trousers.

His voice was guttural. 'I want you naked *now*.'

Sam's flesh prickled with anticipation. Her hands felt stupid as she tried to pull down her strap and, issuing something that sounded like a curse, Rafaele took over, turning her around and finding the zip, pulling it down and peeling the heavy fabric from her body.

Sam kicked off her shoes. Now she wore only black lace panties. Rafaele turned her around again and that hot green gaze swept down her body, lingering on her breasts, which seemed to swell and tighten under his look.

'You're so beautiful.'

Sam ducked her head. 'No, I'm not.'

Rafaele tipped up her chin, forcing her to look at him. 'Yes, you are.'

He'd done this before—made her feel buoyant. Feminine. And it had all been ripped to pieces when he'd rejected her. But Sam couldn't focus on that now.

He pulled her into him again and Sam swayed towards

him like a magnet. He kissed her, tongue thrusting deep, fanning the flames of lust within her. He was naked now, and her hand instinctively sought to touch him, finding and encircling his erection, moving up and down, feeling the slip and slide of satin skin over all that steely strength.

His mouth not leaving hers, Rafaele skimmed his hand down from her breast over her belly, down to her panties and underneath, his fingers seeking and finding that sweet molten spot, making her legs part so that he could have more access.

As he stroked and explored Sam broke off the kiss. And then one of Rafaele's fingers thrust inside her and Sam's legs went weak with the sharp, spasming pleasure that gripped her.

With dextrous hands Rafaele pushed her panties down and lifted her, to deposit her on the bed. Sam could only look up at Rafaele and marvel at his sheer masculine magnificence. He was so broad and powerful. Narrow waist and hard-muscled thighs and between them... Her mouth watered.

She sat up and looked up at Rafaele. He was watching her almost warily and she felt a heady rush of power. She moved to the edge of the bed and reached for him, her hands going to his hips, pulling him towards her.

'Sam...'

She ignored him and drew his length into her hand, and then she took him into her mouth. The remembered taste and feel of him was like an explosion on her senses. She barely heard his deep moan of satisfaction as she swirled her tongue around the bulbous tip, relearning his shape and what made him tense. His hands were in her hair, gripping her head.

Her hand encircled him and her mouth and tongue licked and sucked. *He'd* taught her how to do this.

'*Dio*, Sam...'

Sam felt him tensing, the instinctive thrusting of his hips towards her, as if he couldn't help himself. His hands were trying to pull her back, but she knew it was against his will. He'd never let her go this far before but stubbornly Sam wanted to see him lose control because of *her* and she kept going, ignoring his rough entreaties, until finally she felt the heat of his climax gush into her mouth and throat, felt his hips jerking.

Sam kept her mouth on him for a long moment and then finally pulled back. She couldn't help a smile when she saw Rafaele's dazed-looking expression. Slowly that expression cleared and his eyes narrowed on her. She felt a shiver of trepidation mixed with anticipation go through her and recognised that he wasn't happy with the way she'd made him lose it like that. She felt more powerful in that moment than she'd ever felt...

Rafaele bent down and loomed over her on his hands, forcing her to move back onto the bed. She collapsed onto it.

'I think I'm going to have to restrain you...'

Sam looked at Rafaele blankly for a second, and then watched him stand up and go to a nearby cabinet. He pulled out two long slivers of silk and she realised they were ties. Something deep inside her quivered—but it wasn't with fear, it was excitement. She didn't know what he intended but secretly wanted to find out...

He took each hand and quietly wound a tie around each wrist, knotting it. Sam looked at him and bit her lip. Then Rafaele stretched her hands over her head, and Sam only realised what he'd done when she couldn't bring her hands down again...he'd tied them to one of the bed's four posts.

'Rafaele... What...?'

He came back down and over her. Not touching her, but letting her feel his body heat. 'I want you to know what it feels like to lose control...'

Sam could have laughed. She lost control every time she looked at this man! And there was something that felt so wickedly decadent about being restrained it overshadowed the sliver of discomfort. She trusted Rafaele above anything else, and that deep-seated knowledge shook her now. She hadn't realised just how much she trusted him till this moment.

He bent his head then, and his mouth was a hot brand on hers, opening her up to him, demanding a response which she gave unerringly. Already she felt the frustration of being bound. She wanted to touch him but couldn't. She moaned softly with it, and could have sworn she heard Rafaele chuckle darkly.

His mouth moved down, trailing over her jaw and neck. His hands were smoothing over her body, touching her but staying away from erogenous zones, making her grit her jaw to stop herself from begging. Her hands pulled ineffectually at the silken ties.

And then Rafaele's mouth was on her breast and her back arched. *Yes.* He lavished both taut peaks with attention until they were tingling and stinging. His hand had moved down to her belly and, like a wanton, Sam felt her legs part in mute appeal. Rafaele reared back for a moment and looked at her body. Sam gazed down to see his arousal already hard again, still glistening wetly from her mouth and tongue. She ached inside.

Rafaele's hand went to the juncture at her legs and then he was moving down, his mouth leaving little trails of fire as he pressed kisses under her breasts, to her abdomen and down. Sam's breath stopped when she felt him pull her legs wide apart. Her hands pulled at the ties. She'd never been so bared or so vulnerable.

Rafaele's mouth settled *there*, between her legs, and Sam's breath came back, choppy. She felt too hot, too tight, too…sensitive.

'Rafaele…'

But his tongue was on her now, exploring her sex, finding where she was so wet for him, opening her up, stabbing deep, making her moan uncontrollably, making her hips twitch. And then his tongue was replaced by his fingers, thrusting deep, and his other hand had found her breast, his thumb and forefinger pinching a nipple.

A broken scream emerged from Sam's mouth—a feral sound. Her hips were lifting off the bed, begging Rafaele for more, for him to drink from her as she came…as she'd done to him. And then the pleasure was peaking and spiralling out of all control, wresting her sane mind from her brain and leaving behind nothing but heat and deep, boneless satisfaction, with his mouth on her right to the end.

Rafaele slowly came up and over her body. He pressed a kiss to her mouth and Sam could taste the essence of her desire on him. Could he taste himself on her? The thought ignited new fires deep down, diminishing her need to curl up and cling onto the boneless feeling. Sam was barely aware of being restrained now. She didn't think she could have lifted her arms even if she'd wanted to.

And then Rafaele was sliding into her…deeply. Sam sucked in a breath, her eyes going wide. He looked down at her and all she could see was green. And heat. And broad shoulders damp with sweat. He moved back out… slowly. One arm came around her back, arching her into him, making one breast pout up towards him, so he bent his head and took it into his mouth, suckling fiercely as he thrust, going a little deeper, harder.

Sam gasped. It was too much. And now she *did* feel the restraints and she pulled against them. She needed to anchor herself to something. She felt as if Rafaele was going to drive her over the edge completely and she'd have nothing at all to hang onto.

But she couldn't articulate any words. Rafaele's chest against her breasts was delicious torture. The ruthless rhythm of his body in and out of hers drove her higher and higher. She could only look deep into his eyes, as if that alone could hold her to this earth.

Just at that moment something pierced her—*anger* at Rafaele, for reducing her to this mindless wanton, gasping and mute being. His powerful body was going so hard and deep now that Sam had to close her eyes, feeling as if a very secret part of herself was being bared to him in a way that she wasn't ready for.

Rafaele's voice was guttural. 'Sam, look at me.'

But she couldn't. He'd see it if she did. She'd never been laid so bare, made so vulnerable, and if she looked at him now he'd see how much she loved him—because she'd never stopped loving him. Even after all that had happened and the million reasons he'd given her for not loving him.

'No,' she said, equally guttural.

Sam heard his rough shout as he made his frustration clear, but both their bodies were locked in a primal dance now and they were equally unable to stop. They could only go on, until the tight grip of tension was shattered and they orgasmed moments after each other, Sam's body convulsing around Rafaele's thick length so hard that she could feel it. She was milking him, taking his very essence into her, and the feeling was so intense and powerful on top of this awful, excoriating vulnerability that tears pricked her eyes.

She turned her head away. Rafaele's body was still within her, pulsing, slowly diminishing. She felt a tear slip down one cheek and finally managed to find the words she hadn't been able to till now.

'Untie me Rafaele.'

She was trembling from an overload of pleasure and the revelation of just how deep her feelings for him were, still.

'Sam…'

'Just untie me.' Her voice sounded harsh to her own ears.

His hands reached up. She felt his arms and chest brush her body and she shivered convulsively against him. Even now. Deftly he undid the knots and Sam's arms were free again, her wrists sore after pulling against the restriction. Terrified that Rafaele would see her emotions bared, Sam scooted out from under him and off the bed. She grabbed the nearest covering she could find, which was his shirt, and pulled it on and walked to the door.

She heard Rafaele curse behind her and say, 'Sam, wait… Where are you—?'

But she was gone, walking blindly, on very wobbly legs, going anywhere that was away from his presence and his ability to reduce her to a melting mass of sensations and turbulent emotions. He'd wanted to dominate her and show her who was in control and he had done that beyond doubt. The eroticism of what she'd just been through felt tawdry now, as she imagined Rafaele coolly and clinically deciding how he would best show her who was boss. She had to get a grip before she faced him again.

Rafaele felt poleaxed. Self-recrimination rose upwards like bile. He would have an image burnt onto his retina for ever of Sam, with her hands bound above her head, her face turned away and a tear slipping down one cheek. He could still feel the strength of the pulsations of her body around his, and knew that it wasn't pain or discomfort that had made her turn away.

His last moment of semi-rational thought, he remembered, had been just before he'd come into Sam's mouth, his body thrusting against her, his hands holding her head so that he could— He cursed and got up off the bed, a restless jagged energy filling his body.

She'd always pushed him further than any other woman. He'd looked down at her when she'd taken her mouth from him—that wicked device of a torture more pleasurable than he could ever remember. She'd smiled at him and it had been full of something inherently feminine and mysterious... Rafaele's first insidious thought had been...Did she do that with *him?* The lover she'd taken? Had *he* been the first to experience her mouth around him, taking him in so deep that he'd not been able to pull back but had gone to the brink and over it... Had she milked him the same way?

The thought had made him see red. He'd felt exposed—far more exposed than just being naked in front of her. Vulnerable in a way he hadn't felt in a long time. It had had echoes of the past, when he recalled his mother looking at his father so dispassionately, even though he was broken, at her feet.

And suddenly Rafaele had wanted to regain control of a situation that was careening out of all control. He'd been losing it. So he'd bound her...so she couldn't touch him and make him forget again...but he'd still lost it anyway. Tying her up had only heightened the experience, making it even more erotic, compelling...and it had done nothing but highlight the fact that even while restrained she exerted a power over him that he couldn't deny.

He grabbed some clothes and pulled them on perfunctorily. Rafaele's gut felt sick as he left his room. She'd been crying. He looked in her room first, but it was dark and the bed was untouched. Then he went downstairs.

He found her in the drawing room, standing at the window through which he could see a full moon hanging low in the sky. On Sam his shirt reached down to the backs of her thighs. Her legs were long and slim underneath. She looked incredibly fragile in the voluminous white material.

'Sam...'

CHAPTER NINE

SAM'S SHOULDERS TENSED. Rafaele padded silently towards her on bare feet and she turned around, as if afraid he'd come too close. He saw a tumbler in her hand with a dark golden liquid.

She smiled and it was tight, lifted the glass towards him. 'Chin-chin.' And then she took a deep gulp, draining the glass.

He saw her cheeks flush but she made no sound. The evidence of tears was gone but her eyes looked huge, bruised.

'Sam...' He spoke through a sudden constriction in his throat. 'I'm sorry. I didn't mean to hurt you...'

'You didn't hurt me, Rafaele, I enjoyed it. You've obviously developed a kinkier side since I knew you... Was it any mistress in particular? Or is it just a sign of the times—routine sex is too boring?'

Rafaele gritted his jaw. He knew that Sam had been with him all the way because he'd felt the excitement in her body pushing him on...her distress had come afterwards...

'I've never done that with another woman,' he admitted reluctantly. He'd never felt the need to.

Sam emitted a curt laugh and raised a dark brow. 'So it's just me? I should feel flattered that I made you so angry you felt you had to restrain me...?'

Rafaele frowned, losing the thread. 'Angry?' Had it been that obvious? His fit of jealousy and vulnerability?

But Sam was continuing. 'I know you're angry about Milo, Rafaele, but you can't take it out on me like this.'

Half without thinking, Rafaele said, 'But I'm not angry about Milo.'

He realised in that moment that he truly didn't feel angry about that—not any more. It had faded and been replaced by a much darker anger...stemming from this woman's unique ability to make him lose his self-control and lose sight of what was important to him. Anger that he felt so vulnerable around her.

But Sam seemed not to have heard him. She came closer to put the empty glass down and Rafaele could see the tantalising curve of her breast through the haphazardly tied shirt. Instantly his lower body was on fire, reacting. He had a momentary revelation: *he was never going to get enough of this woman, not even in a lifetime. It would never burn out between them, only grow brighter.*

Rafaele was stunned, his head expanding with the terrifying knowledge that he would never be free of this insatiable need. He was barely aware of Sam walking out of the room. His brain was working overtime, trying to take in the knowledge that had come to him earlier, before he'd really been ready to deal with it, that he couldn't let her go. And now it was the most obvious thing in the world.

Sam gripped the bannister as she went up the stairs. Rafaele might have just said that he wasn't angry about Milo... but he *was* still angry with her. It was as clear as day. Maybe it was because he wanted her and resented himself for it?

Any control she'd clawed back before Rafaele had appeared and during that brief conversation had drained away again, leaving her feeling shaky. Somehow she got to her room, closed the door behind her and sagged against it. Tears pricked her eyes. Again. More tears for the man downstairs whom she would probably never be able to read.

Sam was too drained to deal with buttons. Her body was made weak from pleasure and sensation. She ripped Rafaele's shirt, making buttons pop and fall silently to the ground, and crawled into bed. In the morning she would shower and wash the scent of sex off her skin, but right now—treacherously—she didn't want to. In spite of what had happened.

'Rafaele said that we'll be leaving in an hour for Rome.'

Sam looked up with a studied air of nonchalance at Bridie, who had just come into the dining room. 'Oh?'

Bridie had Milo by the hand and he ran over to Sam, who picked him up and hugged him close, revelling in his sturdy body and sweet baby scent.

Bridie helped herself to some coffee and asked, 'How was the function last night?'

When Sam had woken that morning and come downstairs Bridie, Milo and Umberto had evidently already eaten, because the detritus of breakfast had been at the table but they had not. To her intense relief it appeared as if Rafaele had eaten also, as his place at the head of the table had already been used.

'It was...very swish,' Sam replied, knowing Bridie would love to hear about all the gowns and luxury. She took the cowardly way out and detailed to Bridie all of those things, while trying to ignore the disturbing memories threatening to spill into her mind at any given moment.

It took less than an hour to get from Milan to Rome and they arrived by lunchtime. Rafaele had arranged for one of his assistants to meet them at the airport with a car, and Bridie was whisked off in it to the Vatican, for the private tour Rafaele had arranged for her—much to her delight.

Another car was waiting for them, and Sam saw that Rafaele was going to drive them himself as he deftly secured Milo into the child's car seat installed in the back. It made Sam think once again of how seamlessly Rafaele had incorporated Milo into his life and her heart ached to think of what might have happened if she had told Rafaele from the start about her pregnancy.

Sam got into the car and her heart thudded heavily when Rafaele settled his powerful body behind the wheel. So far this morning she'd managed to avoid saying anything more than yes or no.

He glanced at her now and she had to acknowledge him. She turned and his gaze on her was intent. Her face grew hot as lurid images from the previous night came back.

'Okay?' he asked, disconcerting her because there was a quality to his voice she hadn't heard before. It sounded intimate. Concerned.

Sam was sure she'd imagined it so nodded quickly and looked back at Milo, who smiled, showing his small teeth. He was clutching a floppy teddy bear that Umberto had gifted him on their departure. Sam had been surprised to see what had looked suspiciously like tears in the old man's eyes as they'd left, and also a lingering glance or two at Bridie, who had looked a bit more flustered than she usually did.

As Rafaele negotiated their way out of the private airfield Sam said, 'Your father...was not what I expected.'

Rafaele's mouth tightened, but he said, 'No...I was surprised at how he welcomed Milo so instantaneously.'

'It was nice,' Sam admitted. 'After all, he's his only living grandparent now. My father was only alive to see Milo as a baby, so they didn't really connect and Milo won't remember him. Bridie is like a granny to Milo, but it's different when it's blood...'

Rafaele looked at her, his face inscrutable. 'Yes,' he agreed. 'It is.'

For the first time Sam didn't feel that Rafaele was getting in a dig. He was sounding almost as if he was realising the same thing himself.

'We should...' Sam blushed and stopped. 'That is, I should make sure to try and let Milo see Umberto as much as possible. Do you think he'd come to England?'

Rafaele's mouth quirked and he slid another glance to Sam. 'I think he could be persuaded—especially if Bridie is going to be there.'

Sam smiled, rare lightness filling her chest. 'You noticed it too, then?'

Rafaele looked at her and grew serious. He took her hand from her lap and held it. Immediately Sam's body reacted. She tried to pull away but he wouldn't let her. Memories of the bondage of last night came back. Arousing her. Disturbing her.

He said something crude in Italian and had to let Sam's hand go to navigate some hairy traffic. When it was clear again he said, 'Sam, we need to talk...'

'No,' Sam said fiercely, panicked at the thought of dissecting what had happened last night. She looked back at Milo, who was still happily playing with the toy, and then back to Rafaele. 'There's nothing to discuss.'

'Yes, there is, Sam,' he asserted, 'whether you like it or not. Tonight we'll go out for dinner.'

'Rafaele—'

But he cut her off with a stern look.

Sam shut her mouth and sat back, feeling mutinous. But deep down she knew Rafaele was right. They had to talk, but she would make sure that it would centre around the future and what would happen with Milo and also on the fact that she didn't want to sleep with him again. *Liar*, a voice mocked her. But she quashed it. Last night had almost broken her. She'd nearly revealed just how much Rafaele made her feel. And if they slept together again… she wouldn't be able to keep it in.

'I'll drop you and Milo off at the apartment and show you around, and then I'm afraid I have to go into the office for a couple of hours.'

'Okay,' Sam said, too quickly, seizing on the fact that she'd have a few hours' respite from Rafaele's disturbing presence. Maybe then these memories would abate and give her some peace.

Rafaele's Rome apartment was situated in a beautiful crumbling building just streets away from the famous Piazza Barberini, right in the heart of Rome's bustling centre. A smiling housekeeper met them and conversed easily in English for Sam's benefit. Rafaele showed Sam to her room, which was stunning, with parquet floors and delicate Rococo furnishings. There was another door which Milo was already reaching up to try and open, but the handle was too high.

He turned around, comically frustrated, and Rafaele scooped him up. 'First you have to grow a little more, *piccolino.*'

Rafaele opened the door and walked through, leaving Sam to follow them. It was a room for Milo, and once again Rafaele had obviously given instructions for it to be decked out for a three-year-old. It was a kiddie's paradise, and Milo was already jumping out of Rafaele's arms to explore all the treasures.

Rafaele looked at Sam, as if expecting another diatribe, but she could only smile ruefully and shrug her shoulders as if to say, *What can I do?*

He came closer then, blocking out Milo behind him, and cupped her jaw with a hand, his thumb rubbing her lower lip, tugging at it. Instantly Sam craved his mouth there, kissing her hard, pressing his body against hers.

Heat flooded her and she had to pull away with an effort. She shook her head, warning him off.

He said silkily, 'Tonight, Sam. We'll talk then.' He turned back to Milo. '*Ciao, piccolino.* I have to go to work now.'

Milo stopped what he was doing and for the first time since Rafaele had entered their lives, ran to him and gave him a kiss when Rafaele bent down to hug him.

'Bye, Daddy.'

Milo's easy and rapid acceptance of this whole situation made Sam's chest ache, and that emotion threatened to bubble over. She'd never in a million years envisaged that it could be this easy...or this cataclysmic.

Rafaele left and a long, shuddering breath emerged from her mouth. In truth, she'd not known what to expect if she'd ever plucked up the courage to tell Rafaele about Milo, but it had ranged from complete uninterest to his storming into their lives to take over, demand to take control.

It had definitely veered towards the latter end of the scale, but also *not.* For one thing she hadn't expected Rafaele still to want her. Or to admit that he had thought about her—that he'd never *stopped* wanting her.

Questions made her head hurt... So why had he let her go, then? If he'd wanted her...? She knew instinctively that she'd got too close. Was that why he'd pushed her away?

'Mummy, play with me!' came the imperious demand that sounded suspiciously like someone else.

Sam looked at her son and smiled. She got down on the floor beside him and devoted herself to the fantastical world of a bright, inquisitive three-year-old and welcomed the distraction.

That evening Bridie was still brimming over after her trip to St Peter's and the Vatican. 'I was the only one looking at the Sistine Chapel—the only one! And I think I saw the Pope walking in a private garden, but I couldn't be sure... A lovely priest said Mass in Latin. Oh, Sam, it was gorgeous.'

Sam smiled indulgently as she went to pick up her bag. Rafaele had called to say he was sending a car to pick her up and he'd meet her directly at the restaurant.

Suddenly Bridie broke off from her raptures and said in a shocked voice, 'You're not going out like *that?*'

Sam looked down at her outfit of jeans and a plaid shirt. Trainers. Suddenly she felt gauche. Of course Rafaele would have probably booked somewhere extremely fancy and expensive. She should have realised.

Bridie was bustling off. 'I know you packed that black dress, Sam. You have to change.'

Sam followed Bridie, knowing that she couldn't leave without changing now. Bridie seemed determined to throw her and Rafaele together, clearly believing that a fairytale ending was in the making.

When Sam walked into the bedroom Bridie was shaking out the plain black dress that Sam had packed just in case.

'Now, put this on and do your make-up. I'll let you know when the car gets here.'

Milo came barrelling down the hallway. Bridie caught him and said, 'Right, dinnertime for you, young man, and then an early night. We have to go home tomorrow so you need to be fresh.'

Sam quickly changed clothes and grimaced at her reflection, finally putting on some foundation to take away the pallor of her cheeks and then some mascara.

Home tomorrow. No wonder Rafaele wanted to talk now. He would have strong ideas about how they would proceed from here, she didn't doubt it, and she felt a shiver of trepidation that he would want to change their routine utterly.

This was all an exciting holiday to Milo now, but it couldn't continue like this. He needed routine and stability, and his life—*their* lives—were in England.

Sam heard Bridie call out, 'Sam, the car is here!'

Taking a deep breath and slipping on the one pair of low-heeled shoes she'd brought, Sam went to meet her fate.

The restaurant was nothing like Sam had expected. The car had taken her across the river to the very hip and bustling Trastevere area and the building looked small and rustic, with tables outside despite the cool early February air. Golden light spilled onto the pavement and the smells coming out of the door were mouth-watering.

Sam went in and immediately her eye was drawn to the tall man who'd stood up. Her heart kicked betrayingly, as if she hadn't seen him just hours ago. She felt ridiculously shy all of a sudden too—which was crazy, considering what had taken place in Rafaele's bedroom last night.

By the time a solicitous waiter had taken her coat and she'd made her way through the small tables to Rafaele her face was burning.

He held a chair out for her and Sam felt self-conscious in her dress, hoping that Rafaele wouldn't think she'd gone to any extra-special effort.

In a bid to deflect his attention she said quickly, 'Bridie thought I should dress up a bit…' She looked around the restaurant. 'But I don't think I needed to. I thought you might choose somewhere more upmarket.'

'Disappointed?' Rafaele's voice sounded tight.

Sam looked at him quickly and felt her hair slide over her shoulder. 'Oh, no! I love it. It's just…I never expected you to like a place like this.'

Something relaxed in Rafaele's face and seeing the faint stubbling on his jaw made Sam feel hot for a second as she imagined the abrasive rub of it between her legs. She pressed them together tightly under the table, disgusted with herself.

'This is my favourite restaurant. They specialise in cuisine from the north and they're world renowned. But they've remained humble and haven't sold out...'

Just then a man with a huge barrel chest came over and greeted Rafaele effusively, before taking Sam's hand in his and lifting it to his mouth to kiss. She couldn't help smiling, even though she couldn't understand a word he was saying. She caught *'bellissima'* and blushed, which only made him gush some more.

Eventually he left, and Rafaele indicated after him with his head. 'That's Francisco—the manager... I've known him since my student days when I used to work here.'

Sam's eyes widened as she recalled Rafaele telling her about his working three jobs to get through college. 'You worked *here?*'

He nodded and broke some bread to dip into oil and balsamic vinegar. Sam took some bread too, a little blindsided at imagining a younger, driven Rafaele working here, with women drooling over him in his waiter's uniform of white shirt and black trousers.

She admitted wryly, 'That's a little hard to believe.'

Rafaele arched a brow, mock affronted. 'You don't think I'm capable of taking orders and clearing tables?'

Sam felt a flutter near her heart and looked away, embarrassed. This was so reminiscent of before, when Rafaele had been intent on wooing her.

She looked at him. 'You never...talked about this stuff before...'

Immediately his expression closed in and Sam wanted to reach out and touch him. Her hands curled to fists.

'Before was different...'

Sam's mouth twisted and old bitterness rose up. 'I know. You didn't want to be seen in public with me.'

Rafaele looked at her, his jaw tense. 'It wasn't like that—'

A waiter interrupted them then and asked for their orders.

Another couple entered the restaurant, hand in hand, and Sam felt a bittersweet yearning rise up within her. Damn Bridie for making her wish for something that would never exist. She'd been foolish enough to hope for it in the past. She wouldn't make the same mistake again.

When the waiter had left with their menus Sam sat back and looked at Rafaele. 'What *was* it like, then?'

For a second he looked so like Milo did when he was reluctant to do something that he took her breath away and she felt tenderness fill her.

'I didn't want to share you…that's the truth. I wanted to lock you away in my *palazzo*. It used to drive me crazy that you worked all day surrounded by men who would look at you and want you.'

Sam had to bite back a strangled laugh and ignore a very treacherous swooping of her belly to hear the evident jealousy in Rafaele's voice. 'No, they didn't!'

'They did,' Rafaele growled. 'You didn't notice, though—oblivious to your effect on them. I'd never met another woman like you, and certainly not one who could match any man around her for knowledge and expertise. One who managed to turn me on more than I'd thought was possible.'

The swooping sensation intensified and Sam felt increasingly out of her depth—as if the rules had changed and she wasn't sure where she stood any more. Their starter arrived and Sam concentrated on it as if it was the most interesting thing in the world. She was in uncharted waters with Rafaele, and not sure where this conversation was headed.

After the starter was cleared Rafaele sat back and took his wineglass in his hand. Sam sensed the interest coming from a couple of women who had come in a few minutes before and, like last night, felt the rush of jealousy in her blood.

Slowly he said, 'Sam…last night at the function…'

She tensed. She really didn't want to talk about it. That acrid jealousy was all too recent and current.

'I didn't mean what I said…about you becoming my mistress. I know you're not that kind of woman.'

Sam emitted a small laugh and felt a dart of hurt. 'You can say that again.'

He leant forward and put his wine down, '*Dio*, Sam, stop putting words in my mouth. I meant that you're worth more than any other woman who was there last night.'

She looked at him and her heart jumped into her throat. His eyes were intense on hers.

With imperfect timing the waiter appeared again with their food, and Sam looked at the fish she'd evidently ordered but couldn't remember selecting now. *You're worth more than any other woman who was there.*

She looked at Rafaele and whispered, 'What do you mean?'

'Eat…then we'll talk.'

Sam felt as if she could no more eat than walk over hot coals, but she forced some of the succulent food down her throat and wished she could enjoy it more. She was sure it was delicious.

When the dishes were cleared away Sam felt very on edge. Rafaele regarded her steadily and her nerves felt as if they were being stretched taut.

Finally he clarified, 'I should have thought more about it before taking you with me last night.'

He obviously saw something Sam was unaware of on her expressive face because he put up a hand and went on, '*Not* because I don't want to be seen with you in public but because you were right. We need to know what…we are.'

Sam frowned. 'What *we* are?'

Rafaele reached out and took her hand. Sam looked at her much smaller pale hand in his dark one and her insides liquefied.

'Sam…I think we should get married.'

Sam raised her eyes to his. Shocked. 'What did you just say?'

'I said, I think we should get married.'

Sam was barely aware of Rafaele letting her hand go so that the waiter could put down coffee and dessert in front of them. She was stunned. Blindsided.

She shook her head, as if that might rearrange her brain cells into some order so that she could understand what Rafaele had just said. She had to be sure. 'Did you just say that you think we should get married?'

He nodded, looking at her carefully, as if she was made of something explosive and volatile.

'I… Why on earth would you say that?'

Now that the words were sinking in, a reaction was moving up through Sam's body, making her skin prickle. Four years ago, in the time between finding out she was pregnant and seeing Rafaele again, she'd daydreamed of such a moment—except in her dream Rafaele had been on one knee before her, not sitting across a table looking as if he'd just commented on the weather.

The most galling thing of all was that she had grown up vowing never to marry, terrified of the way her father had effectively gone to pieces after losing her mother. But she'd forgotten all about that when she'd met Rafaele, weaving dreams and fantasies around him that had had no place in reality.

'Why?' she repeated again, stronger now. Almost angry. Definitely angry, in fact. 'Do you think that I'm some kind of charity case and I'll be only too delighted to say yes because you can take care of me and Milo?'

She couldn't stop now.

'Decorating a few bedrooms doesn't a father and husband make, Rafaele. So I don't know where you're getting this notion from. It's just another way to control us, isn't it?'

His eyes flashed at her outburst. 'No, Sam. Think about it. Why *shouldn't* we get married? I've been thinking about buying a home in London. We could live there. Bridie could come too… We could look for a good school for Milo. A lot of my work for the foreseeable future will be in England, and my commutes to Europe shouldn't take me away too much…'

He had it all figured out. Square Sam and Milo away in a convenient box and tick them off the list. On the one hand the image he presented tugged at a very deep and secret part of her—a fantasy she'd once had. She only had to think of last night and how close she'd come to baring herself utterly. She didn't doubt that he hadn't factored in the reality that she would want to be a wife for *real*.

Terrified at the strength of emotion she was feeling, Sam stood up and walked quickly out of the restaurant.

Rafaele watched Sam leave. Not the first time he'd provoked her into walking away from him. She'd looked horrified. Not the reaction a man wanted when he proposed. He grimaced and acknowledged that he hadn't exactly *proposed*. But since when had Sam wanted hearts and flowers? *Did* she want that? What he was suggesting was eminently practical. Logical. Unfortunately Sam plus any attempt on his part to apply logic always ended up in disaster.

Rafaele stood up. His friend Francisco was waving him

out of the restaurant to go after his lover. The old romantic. Rafaele just smiled tightly.

When he emerged into the street it was quiet. This time of year it was mainly locals. But in a few months the place would be warm and sultry and heaving. Sam was stalking away, and when he called her she only seemed to speed up.

Cursing softly, Rafaele followed her and caught up. 'Your coat and bag, Sam.'

She stopped and turned around, arms crossed mutinously across her breasts. She reached out and grabbed for them, pulling the coat on, hitching her bag over her shoulder.

She looked at him and her eyes were huge in the gloom. 'I don't know why you would even suggest such a thing.'

Rafaele curbed his irritation. Did she really have to sound so repulsed at the idea?

He dug his hands into his pockets to stop himself from reaching for her—he didn't know if he wanted to shake her right now or kiss her. Actually, that was a lie. He'd always want to kiss her, no matter what. That thought sent shards of panic into his bloodstream.

'I happen to think it's a very good idea. There are far more reasons why you should consider this than not. We have a history. We get on well. We have a child together... And there's the physical chemistry. You can't deny that, *cara*.'

'The chemistry will burn out.'

That was said with a desperately hopeful edge that resonated within Rafaele.

He had to make her see what he'd realised last night— that marriage was the solution... *To this tangled mess of emotions you don't want to deal with*, his conscience sneered. He ignored his conscience. Surely by marrying her he would no longer experience this wildness around her? This need to devour, consume? This loss of all reason? It would negate this completely alien need to possess her... It would publicly brand her as *his*, and maybe then he'd feel some equanimity again.

'We have a child. Is that not enough of a reason? I want Milo to have my name. He is heir to a vast industry and fortune.'

'No, Rafaele,' she said in a small voice. 'It's not enough. I might have thought it would be at one time, but not any more. I want more for me and Milo. He deserves to have two parents who love each other.'

Rafaele responded with a sneering edge to his voice. 'You and I both know that fairytale doesn't exist. What we have is better than that, Sam. We can depend on each other. We respect each other.'

She lifted her chin. 'How do I know you've forgiven me for keeping Milo from you? That you won't use it in the future? That it won't be a reason for resentment when you think about it?'

Rafaele slashed a hand through the air. 'Sam, it's not about that any more. I appreciate that you had your reasons, and I admit that I didn't give you any indication to believe that I would welcome a child into my life. We can't change the past, but we can make sure we go into the future right.'

For a long moment Sam just looked at him, and then she said, 'I won't marry you. Not just to make things nice and tidy. To make things easier for you. I want more...' She shrugged her shoulder in a gesture of apology.

Rafaele felt the red mist of rage rising when he thought of some other man moving into that cosy house in the quiet suburbs, waking up next to Sam, having lazy early-morning sex...

'Do you really think someone like your ex-lover can give you a happy-ever-after? When it doesn't even exist?'

Sam started to back away. 'I'm not talking about this

any more, Rafaele. I don't want to marry you. It's plain and simple.'

Rafaele felt his chest tighten and an awful cold feeling seeped into his veins. 'Well, then…' He almost didn't recognise his own voice. 'It would appear that you're giving me no option but to take the legal route to establish custody of my son.'

Sam stopped and crossed her arms. She whispered, 'It doesn't have to come to that, Rafaele. We can come to an arrangement.'

Rafaele felt as hard inside as granite. 'I want my son, Sam, and I want him to have my name.'

'I can't fight you in a court, Rafaele. I don't have those kinds of resources.'

Rafaele pushed down his conscience. He was full of darkness—a darkness that had clung to him all his life. He was standing in front of this woman and for one second, when she'd said she didn't want to marry him, he'd been tempted to go down on one knee to convince her. It had been fleeting, but there. And it had been like a slap in the face. Had he learnt *nothing?*

Sam would not reduce him to that. No woman would. All that mattered was his son. He would not walk away from him and leave him to fend for himself as his own father had done with him.

Rafaele's voice was as cold as he felt inside. 'You're the one who started this, Samantha.'

Sam's arms tightened and Rafaele could see her knuckles turn white against the skin of her fingers.

'You were stringing us along all this time, lulling me into a false sense of security. We're leaving here tomorrow to go home. Do your worst—see if I care.'

Rafaele felt impervious to anything in that moment. He was numb. He saw Sam spot a taxi driving slowly alongside them. A very rare Rome taxi. She hailed it and jumped in. When she passed him, her profile was stony through the window. Rafaele felt something trying to break through, to pierce this numbness that had settled over him, but he pushed it down ruthlessly and tried to ignore the feeling that something very precious had just shattered into pieces.

CHAPTER TEN

THE FOLLOWING DAY Rafaele saw them off at the airport. They had been booked onto a scheduled flight home, albeit first class.

Milo was confused and kept saying, 'Why is Daddy not coming too, Mummy?'

Sam repeated for the umpteenth time, praying that she wouldn't start crying, 'Because he has to work. We'll see him again soon.' *Probably in a courtroom!* she thought half hysterically.

She'd gone straight to her bedroom last night when she'd got in, and locked the door. Not that Rafaele would be banging it down to get in. Rafaele's cold proposal had shown her that nothing had changed. He wanted Milo and he merely saw her as a way to get to him.

Once she'd said no to him he'd revealed his true colours. She felt sick to think that perhaps even the physical side of things had been a monumental act for him. Going through the motions so that he could use that as one more thing to bind them together.

Sam caught a worried glance from Bridie and forced a smile. She couldn't take Bridie's maternal inquisitiveness now. Better that she think nothing was wrong and everything was as per schedule—Rafaele had told them on the flight over that he would be staying on in Rome for work. Sam's head hurt when she thought of what would happen in the immediate future, with regard to Rafaele staying in her house.

Rafaele had Milo in his arms and was saying in a low, husky voice that managed to pluck at Sam's weak and treacherous heartstrings, '*Ciao, piccolino*. I'll see you very soon.'

Milo threw his small chubby arms around Rafaele's neck and Rafaele's eyes met Sam's over Milo's shoulder. His green gaze was as cold as ice and it flayed Sam. Their flight was called and she put her hands out for Milo. After a long moment he handed him over.

Then Bridie was saying goodbye to Rafaele, and gushing again over her trip to the Vatican, and Sam was walking away towards the gate, feeling as if her heart was being ripped to pieces.

'I thought I might stay on here for a while, if you don't mind?'

Rafaele curbed the urge to snarl at his father. It had been a week since Sam and Milo had returned home and an aching chasm of emptiness seemed to have taken up residence in his chest.

'Of course,' he said curtly. 'This is your home as much as mine.'

The old man smiled wryly. 'If it hadn't been for you it would have remained in ruins, owned by the bank.'

Rafaele said gruffly, 'That's not important. Everything is different now.'

'Yes,' Umberto said. 'Milo is…a gift. And Sam is a good woman. She is a good woman for *you*, Rafaele. Real. Honest.'

Rafaele emitted a curt laugh and said, 'Don't speak of what you don't know, Papa. She kept my son from me for nearly four years.'

Rafaele stood up from the dining table then and paced

to the window. He'd only come back to Milan to check on the factory and now he felt rootless. He wanted to go back to England to see Milo but was reluctant because... *Sam*. She brought up so many things for him.

'She must have had good reason to do so.'

Yes, she did. You gave her every reason to believe you couldn't wait to see the back of her.

Rafaele's conscience slapped him. It slapped him even harder when he thought of the resolve that had sat so heavily in his belly when he'd decided that he would have to let her go. Of her face when he'd confirmed that he didn't want to see her any more. It was the same feeling he'd had in his chest the other night in the street.

His jaw was tight as he answered his father. 'Once again, it's none of your business.'

He heard his father's chair move behind him but stayed looking out the window, feeling rigid. Feeling that old, old anger rise up even now.

'I'm sorry, Rafaele...'

Rafaele tensed all over and turned around slowly. 'Sorry for what?'

Umberto was looking at him, his dark gaze sad. 'For everything. For being so stupid as to lose control of myself, for gambling away our fortune, for losing the business. For begging your mother not to leave in front of you... I know seeing that must have had an effect...'

Rafaele smiled and it was grim, mirthless. It hid the awful tightening in his chest, which made him feel as if he couldn't draw enough breath in. 'Why did you do it? Why didn't you just let her go? Why did you have to beg like that?'

His father shrugged one shoulder. 'Because I thought I loved her. But I didn't really love her. I just didn't know it then. I wanted her because she was beautiful and emotionally aloof. By then I'd lost it all. She was the one thing left and I felt that if she went too then I'd become vapour. Nothing.'

Rafaele recalled his words as if it was yesterday. *'How can you leave me? If you leave I'm nothing. I have nothing.'*

'I wanted you, you know,' he said now in a low voice. 'I wanted to take you back when I got a job and was making a modest living. But your mother wouldn't let me near you. I was only allowed to see you on those visits to Athens.'

Rafaele remembered those painfully tense and stilted meetings. His mother had been vitriolic in her disgust at the man who had once had a fortune and had lost it, compounding Rafaele's sense of his father as a failure and compounding his own ambition to succeed at all costs.

'Why are you telling me this now?' Rafaele demanded, suddenly angry that his father was bringing this up.

'Because I can see the fear in you, Rafaele. I know that it's driven you to become successful, to build Falcone Industries from the ground up again. But you don't have to be afraid. You're not like me. You're far stronger than I ever was. And you won't do to Milo what I did to you. He will never see you weak and humiliated.'

Rafaele felt dizzy now, because he knew that he did have the capacity to repeat exactly what his father had done. He'd almost done it the other evening, albeit not in front of his son. *Thank God.*

Umberto wasn't finished, though. 'Don't let fear ruin your chance of happiness, Rafaele. I lived with bitterness for a long time and it makes a cold bedfellow. You have proved yourself. You will never be destitute… Don't be afraid to want more.'

Rafaele saw his father then, slightly hunched, his face lined with a sadness he'd never truly appreciated before.

'I'm not afraid,' he said, half defiantly. But he knew it was a lie. He realised he was terrified.

* * *

'Come on, you, it's time for bed.'

'No. Don't want to go to bed.'

Sam sighed. Milo had been acting up ever since they'd got home, and every single day he asked for Rafaele.

'Where's my daddy? When is he coming back in the car? Why can't we have a car? Where is Grandpapa?'

Sam shared a look with Bridie, who was helping to clear up Milo's things, just as the doorbell rang. They looked at each other and immediately Milo ran for the door, shrieking, *'Daddy, Daddy!'*

Sam went after him, her heart twisting. 'Milo, it won't be him…'

She pulled him back from the door and opened it, fully expecting to see just a neighbour or a door-to-door religious tout. But it wasn't either of those.

'Daddy!' Milo's small clear voice declared exactly who it was.

He was jumping up and down, endearingly still too shy to throw himself at the man who had only so recently come into his life. But when Rafaele bent down and opened his arms Milo ran straight into them and Sam's heart squeezed so tight it hurt. She heard Bridie behind her exclaim and usher Rafaele in.

Sam could see that he was holding something in his hand, and when he put Milo down he handed it to him. It was a mechanical car.

Milo seized it with inelegant haste. 'Wow!'

Sam chided him automatically through a fog of shock. 'Milo, what do you say?'

'Thank you!'

Sam was so tense she could crack. She avoided looking at Rafaele, dreading seeing that ice-cold green again.

Bridie was taking Milo by the hand and saying, 'Come

on, you promised you'd help me to find my spectacles in
my flat earlier—'

Milo started protesting, and Sam felt like doing the
same, but Bridie had lifted Milo up and was quelling his
protests by promising him a DVD. And then they were
gone before Sam could get a word out, and she was alone
in the hall with Rafaele.

She still hadn't really looked him in the eye as he
reached out and pushed the front door closed. Finally she
looked at him and her eyes widened. He looked terrible.
Well, as terrible as a gorgeous Italian alpha male *could*
look—which was not terrible at all. But Rafaele looked
tired, drawn, pale. Older. Somehow diminished.

Immediately Sam was concerned and said, 'What is
it? Your father?'

Rafaele shook his head. 'No, it's not my father. He is
fine. Asking after you all.'

'Well…what is it, then? You look…' *As bad as I feel.*

Rafaele smiled, but it was tight, and then it faded again
and he'd never looked more serious.

Sam crossed her arms and started babbling out of nervousness. 'Are you here ahead of your team of lawyers?
Because if you are you could have saved yourself the
bother, Rafaele…'

He shook his head and looked pained. For an awful moment Sam thought there might be something wrong with
him and she felt weak.

'No. I should never have said that to you. I'm sorry. Of
course there won't be a team of lawyers…'

Sam wanted to sit down. Relief swept through her like
a cleansing balm. 'But why did you say it then?'

Rafaele gave out a curt laugh. 'Because you threaten
me on so many levels and I thought I could control it…
control *you*.'

His words sank in. *You threaten me.* And then, as if

feeling constricted, Rafaele took off his battered leather jacket and draped it over the bottom of the stairs. He was wearing a light sweater and worn jeans and Sam could feel her blood heating. Already.

Suddenly Rafaele asked, 'Do you mind if I have a drink?'

Sam shook her head and stood back. He walked into the front room and, bemused, she uncrossed her arms and followed him. Rafaele was at the sideboard, pouring himself a shot of her father's whisky. He looked around and held up a glass in a question but she shook her head. She stood tensely inside the door. Half ready to flee.

Her voice felt rusty, unused. 'Rafaele, why are you here?'

He turned around to face her. 'Because we need to talk. Properly talk.'

Sam tensed even more, and as if sensing she was about to say something Rafaele put up a hand to quell her.

'I told you that I was about Milo's age when my mother left my father and took me with her?' he began.

Sam nodded carefully.

Rafaele's mouth became a thin line. 'Unfortunately that day I was subjected to a vision of my father prostrating himself at my mother's feet…begging her not to go. Crying, snivelling. I saw a broken man that day…and I believed for a long time—erroneously—that it had been my mother's fault, that she had done it to him. When, of course, it was much more complicated than that… It didn't help that he blamed her for most of his life, refusing to acknowledge his own part in his downfall.'

Sam took a breath. 'Your father told me a bit…'

Even now her heart ached, because she thought of Milo's pain and distress if he were to witness something like that. How would a scene like that affect a vulnerable, impressionable three-year-old?

But Rafaele didn't seem to hear her. He was looking at the liquid in the glass, swirling it gently. 'And then my stepfather… He was another piece of work. I'd gone from the example of a broken man who had lost everything to living with a man who *had* everything. What they had in common was my mother. They were both obsessed with her, wanted her above all. And she…?' Rafaele smiled grimly. 'She was aloof with them both, but she chose my stepfather over my father because he could provide her with the status and security she'd come to enjoy…'

Rafaele looked at her and his smile became bleak.

'For a long time I never wanted to think about why she did those things…but since I've discovered my older brother and learned she abandoned him I have to realise that perhaps for her, security had become the thing she needed most—above warmth and emotion. Above anything. God knows what happened with her first husband to make her do such a drastic thing as to leave her son, leave his father…'

His mouth twisted.

'From an early age I believed instinctively that women could ruin you *even* if you had money and success. I believed that to succeed *I* had to hold women at the same distance my mother had always done with the men around her. I wouldn't ever be weak like my father or stepfather, and never lose control.'

Rafaele smiled again but it was impossibly bleak.

'And then you came along and slid so deeply under my skin that I didn't realise I'd lost all that precious control until it was too late.'

Sam's heart was beating like a drum now. She felt light-headed. 'I don't… What are you saying, Rafaele?'

He looked at her and his gaze seemed to bore into her. 'I still want us to get married, Sam…'

Something cold settled into her belly. He wasn't going

to let this go. He'd basically just told her how he viewed the women in his life and that only the fact that she'd proved herself to be completely different had merited her this place in his life. She backed away to the door and saw him put down his glass and frown...

'Sam?'

Sam walked out through the door and went to the front door and opened it. Rafaele appeared in the hallway, still frowning.

She shook her head. 'Rafaele, I'm really sorry that you had to see so much at a young age, and that it skewed your views of women... And I can see how Milo is at an age where he must have pushed your buttons... But I can't marry you.'

She forced herself to keep looking at him even though she felt as if a knife was lacerating her insides. 'I want more, Rafaele... Despite what I told you about my views on marriage I've always secretly hoped I'd meet someone and fall in love. I thought I could protect myself too, but I can't...none of us can.'

Rafaele saw Sam backlit in her porch and even in such a domestic banal setting she'd never looked more beautiful. His heart splintered apart into pieces and he knew that he had no choice now but to step out and into the chasm of nothing—*and possibly everything.*

He walked into the middle of the hall and looked at Sam. And then very deliberately he got down on his knees in front of her. For a terrifying moment Rafaele felt the surge of the past threatening to rise up and strangle him, heard voices about to hound him, tell him he was no better than his father... But it didn't happen. What he did feel was a heady feeling of *peace* for the first time in a long time.

Sam was looking at him, horrified. She quickly shut the

door again and leant against it. 'Rafaele, get up... What are you doing?'

Somehow Rafaele found the ability to speak. 'This has been my nightmare scenario for so long, Sam, and I'm tired of it. The truth is that I want more too. I want it all. And I am willing to beg for it—just like my father. Except I know that this is different. I'm not him.'

Sam shook her head and Rafaele could see her eyes grow suspiciously bright.

Her voice sounded thick. 'You don't have to do this just to prove a point. Get *up*, Rafaele...'

He shook his head. The view from down here wasn't bad at all, Rafaele realised. Prostrating himself in front of the woman he loved was something he'd do over and over again if he had to.

Almost gently now, he said, 'Sam...don't you realise it yet?'

She shook her head faintly. 'Realise what?'

Rafaele took a deep breath. 'That I am so madly and deeply and crazily in love with you that I've made a complete mess of everything...'

He looked down for a moment and then back up, steeling himself.

'I know you don't feel the same way...how could you when I've treated you so badly in the past? But... I truly hope that we might have enough to work with...and in time you might feel something. We have Milo...'

Sam just looked at him for a long moment, and then she whispered, 'Did you just say you love me?'

Rafaele nodded, sensing her shock, feeling icicles of pain start to settle around his heart despite his brave words. Humiliation started to make his skin prickle. The demons weren't so far away after all.

Sam closed her eyes and he heard her long, shuddering breath. When she opened them again they overflowed with tears.

'Sam...' he said hoarsely, and went to stand up.

But before he could move she'd launched herself at him and they landed in a tangle of limbs on the floor. The breath was knocked out of Rafaele's chest for a second, and then he saw Sam's face above his own, felt her tears splash onto his cheeks. And he couldn't resist pulling her head down so that he could kiss her. Even in the midst of not knowing, he had to touch her.

The kiss was desperate and salty and wet, and then Sam drew back, breathing hard. She put her hands around his face and said again, 'You love me?'

She was lying on his body, they touched at every point, and Rafaele could feel himself stirring to life. He nodded. 'Yes. I love you, Sam. I want you in my life for ever...you and Milo. I want us to be a family. I can't live without you. When you left last week...I died inside.'

A sob escaped Sam's mouth and Rafaele felt her chest heaving against his.

Finally she managed to get out, 'I love you, Rafaele. I fell for you four years ago, and when you let me go I thought I'd die...but then there was Milo...and I thought I'd stopped loving you and started hating you. But I hadn't. I've always loved you and I will always love you.'

Rafaele sat up and Sam spread her legs around his hips so they faced each other. She sat in the cradle of his lap, where his erection was distractingly full, but he forced himself to look at her, sinking willingly into those grey depths and wondering how on earth he'd not let himself do this before now. It was the easiest thing.

His chest expanded as her words sank in and he felt a very fledgling burgeoning sense of trust take root within him and hold...

'I fell for you too...but it was so terrifying that I ran.

You got too close, Sam—closer than I'd ever let anyone get—and when I realised it I couldn't handle it. Like a coward I left you alone to deal with your trauma…'

Sam smoothed his jaw with a tender hand. She looked at him, her eyes wounded. 'I punished you…in the most heinous way. You were right. I was hurt and upset, heartbroken that you didn't want me… I kept Milo from you, and you didn't deserve that.'

Rafaele tucked some hair behind Sam's ear. He was very serious. 'I understand why you did it. You sensed my reluctance, Sam, my need to escape. But it wasn't from you, it was from myself… You never really left me. You haunted me.'

Sam's eyes flashed. 'Not enough to stop you going to bed with another woman almost immediately.'

Rafaele struggled to comprehend, and then he recalled her accusing him of being with another woman a week after he'd left. He shook his head and smiled wryly, knowing that she was going to demand every inch of him for the rest of his life and not wanting it any other way.

'Would it help you to know that, despite appearances to the contrary I didn't sleep with anyone for a year after you left?' He grimaced. 'I couldn't…perform.'

Sam's eyes widened with obvious feminine satisfaction. 'You were impotent?'

Rafaele scowled. 'I'm not impotent.'

Sam wriggled on his lap, feeling for herself just how potent he was. 'You're not impotent with me.'

Rafaele groaned softly, his hands touching her face, thumb pressing her lower lip. 'I could never be impotent with you. I just have to look at you and I'm turned on.'

Sounding serious, Sam said, 'Me too…'

'Sam…that night when I tied you up…'

A dark flush highlighted those cheekbones and something inside Sam melted anew at seeing him so unlike his usual confident, cocky self. He was avoiding her eye and she tipped his chin towards her.

'I liked it…' she whispered, blushing.

'But you cried afterwards…'

Her eyes softened. 'Because I had just realised how much I still loved you. I felt so vulnerable, and I thought you were still punishing me for Milo.'

Rafaele groaned. 'I *was* angry, but it was because you were under my skin again and I didn't want you there. You brought up too many feelings, made me feel out of control…so I needed to control *you.*'

A wicked glint came into Sam's eyes. 'We can call it quits if you let me tie you up next time.'

Sam felt Rafaele's body jerk underneath hers.

He quirked a brow at her. 'Bridie has Milo…'

Needing no further encouragement, Sam scrambled inelegantly off Rafaele's lap and stood up. She looked down at him and held out a hand. Rafaele felt his heart squeeze so much that it hurt. The symbolism of the moment was huge as he put his hand in Sam's to let her help him up, but just before he came up all the way, he stopped on one knee.

'Wait…there's one more thing.'

Rafaele's heart beat fast at the way Sam bit her lip. He gripped her hand like a lifeline and with his other hand pulled out the small but precious cargo from his pocket.

He held up the vintage diamond ring and looked at her. 'Samantha, will you marry me? Because I love you more than life itself—you and Milo.'

She looked at the ring and her eyes glittered again with the onset of fresh tears. 'It's beautiful…'

He could see the final struggle in her face, the fear of believing that this was *real*…but then she smiled and it bathed him in a warmth he'd never known before.

'Yes, I'll marry you, Rafaele.'

She held out her hand and it trembled.

With a none too steady hand himself, Rafaele pushed the sparkling ring onto her finger. And then, with his other hand still in her firm grip, she pulled him up out of the painful past and into a brighter future.

A month later...

Sam took a deep breath and started her walk down the aisle of the small church in the grounds of Rafaele's Milan *palazzo*. Umberto was giving her away and he wasn't even using his cane. He was walking taller and stronger almost every day...especially on the days when Bridie was around...

Milo walked ahead of them in a suit, throwing rose petals with chaotic random abandon. He'd look back every now and then with a huge smile and Sam would have to prompt him to keep going. The small church was filled with people, but Sam was oblivious. She saw only the tall figure of the man waiting for her at the top of the aisle. And then he turned around, as if unable to help himself, and he smiled. Sam smiled back.

Umberto handed her over with due deference and then Rafaele was claiming her, pulling her into him. The priest's words washed over and through Sam. She would never have said she was a religious person, but something in the ritual seemed to complete the process she and Rafaele had embarked on a month before, cleansing away any vague residual painful pieces of the past.

There was only now and the future, and the heavy weight of the wedding band on her finger, and Rafaele bending to kiss her with such a look of reverence on his face that she could have wept. In fact she did weep, and he wiped her tears away with his fingers.

Later, as they danced at their reception, which had been

set up in a marquee in the grounds of the *palazzo*, Rafaele said, 'Have I told you yet how beautiful you look?'

Sam smiled. 'About a hundred times, but I don't mind.'

And Sam *felt* beautiful, truly, for the first time in her life. Even though her dress was simple and her hair hadn't been styled by a professional and she'd done her own make-up. She felt confident, and sexy, and most importantly *loved*.

Milo appeared at their feet and Rafaele lifted him up and that was how they finished their wedding dance—in a circle of love, the three of them.

Over in a corner of the marquee stood Alexio Christakos, Rafaele's half-brother. He'd been best man, done his duty and given his speech, made everyone laugh. Made the women giggle and look at him covetously. Even now they surrounded him, waiting for their moment to strike, for the slightest gesture of encouragement.

Alexio grimaced. He was starting to feel claustrophobic. *Hell*. Who was he kidding? He'd been feeling claustrophobic on his brother's behalf ever since Rafaele had told him that he was getting married and had a *son!*

He shook his head again and grimaced when he saw Rafaele kiss his bride for the umpteenth time. Alexio looked at her. He guessed she was pretty enough, in a subtle and unassuming way, but he couldn't see how she made Rafaele turn almost feral whenever another man came close. Even Alexio had been sent none too subtle hands-off signals from the moment he'd met her.

Alexio wondered how it was possible that Rafaele couldn't see that she *must* be marrying him only for his security and wealth. Had he become so duped by good sex that he'd forgotten one of the most important lessons they'd learnt from their dear departed mother? That a woman's main aim in life was to feather her nest and seek the security of a rich man?

Alexio mentally saluted his brother and wished him well. He told himself he'd try not to say *I told you so* when it all fell apart. Mind you, he had to concede the kid was cute. *His nephew.* He'd actually had quite an entertaining time with him earlier, when he'd looked after him for a bit between the wedding and the reception. Still… He shuddered lightly. He had no intention of embarking on that path any time soon, if ever…

Alexio stopped focusing on his brother and his new wife and son for a minute and took in the crowd around him. From nearby, a gorgeous brunette caught his eye. She was tall and lissom, with curves in all the right places. She looked at him with sexy confidence and smiled the smile of a practised seductress.

Alexio felt his body stir, his blood move southwards. It wasn't the most compelling spark of attraction he'd ever felt…*but when was the last time that had happened…?* Alexio ignored that voice and smiled back. When he saw the light of triumph in her eyes at catching the attention of the most eligible bachelor in the room, Alexio forced down the feeling of emptiness inside him and moved towards her.

* * * * *

WHEN CHRISTAKOS MEETS HIS MATCH

I'd like to dedicate this book to all the fabulous Mills & Boon readers and fans who make my job so much easier, especially on the days when the task can seem impossible!

ALEXIO CHRISTAKOS HAD always known his mother had had affairs all through her marriage to his father. He just hadn't expected to see such a public display of it at her funeral. Her coffin was strewn with lone flowers and there were displays of wet eyes from a handful of men he'd never met before in his life.

His father had stomped away with a glower on his face a short while before. He couldn't exactly claim the moral high ground as he too had had numerous affairs.

It had been a constant war of attrition between them. His father always seeking to make his mother as jealous as he felt. And she…? Alexio had the feeling that nothing would have ever made her truly happy, even though she had lived her life in the lap of luxury, surrounded by people to cater to her every whim.

She'd had a sadness, a deep melancholy about her, and they'd never been emotionally close. A vivid memory assailed him at that moment—a memory he hadn't allowed to surface for a long time. He'd been about nine, and his throat had ached with the effort it had taken not to cry. He'd just witnessed his parents having a bitter row.

His mother had caught him standing behind the door and he'd blurted out, 'Why do you hate each other so much? Why can't you be in love like you're supposed to be?'

She'd looked at him coldly and the lack of emotion in

her eyes had made him shiver. She'd bent down to his level and taken his chin in her hand. 'Love's a fairytale, Alexio, and it doesn't exist. Remember this: I married your father because he could give me what I needed. *That's* what is important. Success. Security. Power. Don't ever concern yourself with emotions. They make you weak. Especially love.'

Alexio would never forget the excoriating feeling of exposure and shame in that moment...

He felt a hand on his shoulder then and looked to his older half-brother, Rafaele, who stood beside him and smiled tightly. They'd always shared the same conflicted relationship with their mother. Rafaele's Italian father had gone to pieces after their mother had walked out on him when he had lost his entire fortune—an unpalatable reminder of their mother's ruthless nature so soon after that disturbing childhood memory of his own.

For years Alexio and his brother had communicated with habitual boyish rough-housing and rivalry, but since Rafaele had left home to make his way when Alexio had been about fourteen their relationship had become less fractious. Even if Alexio had never quite been able to let go of his envy that Rafaele hadn't had to endure the almost suffocating attention he'd received from his father. The heavy weight of expectation. The disappointment when Alexio had been determined to prove himself and not accept his inheritance.

They turned to walk away from the grave, engrossed in their own thoughts. They were of a similar build and height, both a few inches over six feet, drop-dead gorgeous, dark-haired. Alexio's hair was darker, cut close to his skull. Their mother had bequeathed to them both her distinctive green eyes, but Alexio's were lighter—more golden.

When they came to a stop near the cars Alexio decided to rib his brother gently, seeking to assuage the suddenly bleak feeling inside him. He observed his brother's stubbled jaw. 'You couldn't even clean up for the funeral?'

'I got out of bed too late,' Rafaele drawled with a glint in his eye.

Alexio smiled wryly. 'Unbelievable. You've only been in Athens for two days—no wonder you wanted to stay at a hotel and not at my apartment...'

Rafaele was about to respond when Alexio saw his face close up and his eyes narrow on something or someone behind him. He turned to look too and saw a tall, stern-faced stranger staring at them from a few feet away. Something struck him in the gut: recognition. Crazy. But the man's eyes were a distinctive green...and that gut feeling intensified.

The stranger flicked a glance at the grave behind them and then his lip curled. 'Are there any more of us?'

Alexio bristled at his belligerent tone and frowned, '*Us*? What are you talking about?'

The man just looked at Rafaele. 'You don't remember, do you?'

Alexio saw Rafaele go pale. Hoarsely he asked, 'Who are you?'

The man smiled, but it was cold, 'I'm your older brother—*half-brother*. My name is Cesar da Silva. I came today to pay my respects to the woman who gave me life... not that she deserved it.'

He was still talking but a roaring was sounding in Alexio's ears. *Older half-brother? Cesar da Silva.* He'd heard of the man. Who hadn't? He was the owner of a vast global conglomerate encompassing real estate, finance— myriad businesses. Famously private and reclusive.

Something rose up inside Alexio and he issued an abrupt, 'What the *hell*?'

The man looked at him coldly and Alexio could now see the fraternal similarities that had led to that prickle of awareness. Even though da Silva was dark blond in colouring, they could be non-identical triplets.

Da Silva was saying coldly, 'Three brothers by three fathers...and yet she didn't abandon either of *you* to the wolves.'

He stepped forward and Alexio immediately stepped up too, feeling rage building inside him in the face of this shocking revelation. His half-brother topped him only by an inch at most. They stood chest to chest.

Cesar gritted out, 'I didn't come here to fight you, brother. I have no issue with either of you.'

A fierce well of protectiveness that Alexio had felt once before for his mother, before she'd rejected it, rose up within him. 'Only with our dead mother—*if* what you say is true.'

Cesar smiled, but it was bleak, and it threw Alexio off slightly, making the rage diminish.

'Oh, it's true—more's the pity.'

He stepped around him then and Alexio and Rafaele turned to watch him walk to the open grave, where he stood for a few long moments before taking something from his pocket and throwing it into the black space, where it landed with a dull thud.

Eventually he turned and came back. After a long, silent but charged moment, during which he looked at both brothers, he turned and walked swiftly to a waiting car. He got into the back. It drove off smoothly.

Rafaele turned towards Alexio and looked at him. Gobsmacked. Shock reverberated through his body. Adrenalin made him feel keyed up.

'What the...?'

Rafaele just shook his head. 'I don't know...'

Alexio looked back at the empty space where the car had been and something cold settled into his belly. He felt exposed, remembering that time when he'd thought his mother would allow him to protect her. She hadn't. Ever elusive, she was now managing to reach out from beyond the grave and demonstrate with dramatic timing just how a woman couldn't be trusted to tell the truth and reveal her secrets. She would always hold something back. Something that might have the power to shatter your world.

CHAPTER ONE

Five months later...

'*CARA*...DO YOU have to leave so soon?'

The voice oozed sultry sex appeal. Alexio stalled for a second in the act of buttoning up his shirt—not because he was tempted to stay but because, if anything, he felt even more eager to leave.

He schooled his features and turned to face the woman in the bed. She was all honeyed limbs and artfully tumbled glossy brown hair. Huge dark eyes, a pouting mouth and the absence of a sheet were doing little to help Alexio forget why he'd chosen to take her to his hotel suite in Milan after his brother Rafaele's wedding reception last night.

She was stunning. Perfect.

Even so, he felt no resurgence of desire. And Alexio didn't like to acknowledge the fact that the sex had been wholly underwhelming. On the surface it had been fine; but on some deeper level it had left him cold. He switched on the charm he was famed for, though, and smiled.

'Sorry, *bellissima*, I have to fly to Paris this morning for work.'

The woman, whose name he all of a sudden wasn't entirely sure of—Carmela?—leant back and stretched seductively, displaying her perfectly cosmetically enhanced naked breasts to their best advantage, and pouted even more. 'You have to leave *right now*?'

Alexio kept his smile in place and when he'd finished dressing bent down and pressed a light kiss to her mouth, escaping before she could twine her arms around his neck. Claustrophobia was rising within him.

'We had fun, *cara*…I'll call you.'

Now the seductive pout was gone, and the woman's real nature shone through as her eyes turned hard. She knew when she was being blown off and clearly did not like it when the man in question was as sought-after as Alexio Christakos.

She stood up from the bed naked and flounced off to the bathroom, issuing a stream of Italian petulance. Alexio winced slightly but let out a sigh of relief as soon as she'd disappeared behind a slamming door.

He shook his head as he made his way out of the suite and towards the lobby of the plush hotel in the private lift reserved for VIP guests. *Women*. He loved them, but he loved them at a distance. In his bed when it suited him and then out of it for as long as he cared to indulge them—which invariably wasn't for long.

After years of witnessing his mother's cold behaviour towards his father, who had remained in slavish thrall to her beauty and eternal elusiveness, Alexio had developed a very keen sense of self-protection around women. He could handle cold and aloof because he was used to that, and he preferred it.

His father, thwarted by his emotionally unavailable wife, had turned to his son, making him the centre of his world. It had been too much. From an early age Alexio had chafed against the claustrophobia of his father's over-attention. And now when anyone—especially a woman—became even remotely over-emotional, or expected too much, he shut down inside.

Brief encounters were his forté. Witnessing his half-brother's wedding the day before had inevitably brought up questions of his own destiny, but Alexio, at the age of thirty, felt no compelling need to settle down yet.

He did envisage a wife and family at some stage…far in the future. When the time came his wife would be perfect. Beautiful, accommodating. Undemanding of Alexio's emotions. Above all, Alexio would not fall into the same trap as his father: tortured for life because he'd coveted a woman who didn't covet him. He'd been disabused at an early age of the notion that love might be involved.

He thought of his older brother turning up at his mother's funeral and all the accompanying unwelcome emotions he'd felt that day: shock, anger, hurt, betrayal.

Used to blocking out emotions, Alexio had relegated the incident to the back of his mind. He hadn't sought Cesar da Silva out, hadn't mentioned it again to Rafaele—even though he knew Rafaele had invited their half-brother to his wedding. Predictably enough, after that first and last terse meeting, he hadn't turned up.

Emotions were messy, unpredictable. They tripped you up. Look at Rafaele! His life had just been turned upside down by a woman who had kept his son from him for four years. And yet two months after meeting her again he was getting married, looking foolishly in love and blithely forgetting the lessons his own father had taught him about the fickle nature of women.

As far as Alexio was concerned—even if Rafaele appeared to be happily embarking on wedded bliss, and no matter how cute his three-and-a-half-year-old nephew was—his brother had been played for a fool by his new wife. Why *wouldn't* she now want to marry Rafaele Falcone, *wunderkind* of the worldwide automobile industry, with an estimated wealth running into the billions? Especially if she had a son to support?

No, Alexio was steering well clear of similar scenarios and he would never allow himself to be caught as his brother had been. He would never forgive a woman who kept a child from him. Still, a sliver of unease went down his spine. His brother, whom he'd considered to share a similar philosophy, had managed to get caught...

Alexio's mouth firmed and he pushed such rogue notions down deep. He put on a pair of shades as his driver brought the car around to the front entrance and was oblivious to the double-take stares of a group of women as they walked into the hotel.

As soon as the car pulled away Alexio was already focusing on the next thing on his agenda, the introspection his brother's wedding had precipitated along with his recent unsatisfactory bed partner already relegated to the back of his mind.

Sidonie Fitzgerald buckled her seatbelt on the plane and took a deep breath. But she was unable to shift the ball of tension sitting in her belly. For once her habitual fear of flying was being eclipsed by something else, and Sidonie couldn't even really enjoy that fact.

All she could see in her mind's eye was her beloved Tante Josephine's round, eternally childish and worried face and hear her quavering voice: *'Sidonie, what does it mean? Will they take my home from me? All these bills... where did they come from?'*

Sidonie's aunt was fifty-four and had spent a lifetime locked in a world of innocence. She'd been deprived of oxygen as a baby and as a result had been mildly brain-damaged. She'd always functioned at a slightly lesser and slower level than everyone around her, but had managed to get through school and find a job. She still worked in the grocer's shop around the corner from where she'd lived for years, giving her precious independence.

Sidonie pursed her lips. She had loved her self-absorbed and endlessly vain mother, who had passed away only a couple of months before, but how could her mother have done this to her sweet and innocent younger sister?

The never forgotten sting of shame reminded Sidonie all too uncomfortably of *exactly* how her mother could have done such a thing—as if she could ever really forget. Ruthlessly she quashed it.

When Sidonie's father had died a few years before, their comfortable lives had crashed around their ears, leaving them with nothing. Sidonie had been forced to leave her university degree before the start of her final year in order to find work and save money to go back.

Moving to Paris to live with Tante Josephine had been her mother Cecile's only option to avoid becoming homeless or—even worse—having to find *work*. Cecile had not been happy. She'd been used to a life of comfort, relative luxury and security, courtesy of her hard-working husband who had wanted nothing more than to make his wife happy.

It would appear now, though, as if Sidonie's mother's selfish ways had risen to the fore again. She'd encouraged her sister to take out a mortgage on the apartment that had been bought and paid for by her husband because he'd cared for his vulnerable sister-in-law's welfare. Cecile had used this fact as leverage to persuade Tante Josephine to agree to the remortgage. She'd then used that money, and credit cards in both their names, to spend a small fortune. Tante Josephine now found herself liable for the astronomical bills as the remaining living account-holder.

Sidonie had to figure out the best way forward to help her aunt—she had no intention of leaving her to fend for herself. The start of the process had been taking on the burden of the debts into her own name. She hadn't thought twice about doing it—ever since her childhood innocence had been ripped away Sidonie had developed a well-ingrained instinct to cover up for her mother—even now, when she was gone.

Sidonie was facing the prospect of moving to Paris to help her aunt get out of this crisis. She staved off the sense of panic. She was young and healthy. Surely she could get work? Even if it was menial?

In a sick way events had conspired to help her—she'd lost her waitressing job in Dublin just before she'd left for Paris to meet with a solicitor to discuss her aunt's situation. Her restaurant boss had explained miserably that they had gone into liquidation, like so many others. Sidonie was going back to Dublin now—just to tie up loose ends and collect the deposit owed to her on her flat when she moved out.

Her hands clenched into fists at the thought of how her mother had only ever thought about herself, oblivious to the repercussions of her—

'Here is your seat, sir.'

'Thank you.'

Sidonie's thoughts scattered as she heard the exchange above her head, and she looked up and saw a man. She blinked. And blinked again. He was very tall and broad. Slim hips at her eye level. He was taking off an overcoat and folding it up to place it in the overheard locker, revealing a lean, muscular build under a fine silk shirt and jacket. Sidonie was vaguely aware of the way the air hostess was hovering attentively.

The man said in English, with a seductive foreign accent, 'I've got it, thank you.'

The air hostess looked comically deflated and turned away. The man was now taking off his suit jacket, and Sidonie realised she was staring—no better than the gaping air hostess. Quickly she averted her head and looked out of the window, seeing nothing of the pewter-grey Parisian spring skies and the fluorescent-jacket-clad ground staff preparing the plane for take-off.

His image was burned onto her brain. It didn't help when she felt him take the seat beside her and all the air around them seemed to disappear. And it *really* didn't help when his scent teased her nostrils; musky and masculine.

He was quite simply the most gorgeous man she'd ever seen in her life. Dark olive complexion, high cheekbones, strong jaw. Short dark brown hair. Firmly sculpted masculine mouth. He should have been pretty. But Sidonie's impression was not of *pretty*. It was of hard and uncompromising sexuality. *Heat*. The last kind of person she'd have expected to sit in an economy seat beside her.

And then he spoke. 'Excuse me.'

His voice was so deep that she felt it reverberate in the pit of her belly. She swallowed and told herself she was being ridiculous—he couldn't possibly be *that* gorgeous. She turned her head and her heart stopped. His face was inches away. He *was*…that gorgeous. And more. He looked vaguely familiar and she wondered if he was a famous male model. Or a French movie star?

Something funny was happening to Sidonie's brain and body. They didn't seem to be connected any more. She felt a hysterical giggle rise up and had to stifle it. She didn't giggle. What was wrong with her?

One dark brow moved upwards over the most startling pair of green eyes she'd ever seen. Gold and green. Like a lion. She had green eyes too, but they were more blue than green.

'I think you're sitting on my seatbelt?'

It took a few seconds for the words to compute, and when they did Sidonie jumped up as if scalded, hands flapping. 'I'm so sorry… Excuse me… Just let me… It must be here somewhere…'

Sounding irritated, the man said, 'Stay still and I'll get it.'

Sidonie closed her eyes in mortification, her hands gripping the seat-back in front of her, and she hovered, contorted in the small space, as the man coolly retrieved his seatbelt and buckled it.

Sidonie sat down again and attended to her own belt. Feeling breathless, and avoiding looking at him again, she said, 'I'm sorry. I—'

He cut her off. 'It's fine, don't worry about it.'

A flare of something hot lanced Sidonie's belly. Did he *have* to sound so curt? And why was she suddenly so aware of the fact that her hair was scraped up into a messy bun, that she had no make-up on, that she was wearing jeans that were so worn there was a frayed hole at her knee and an equally worn university sweatshirt. And her glasses. If Central Casting had been looking for 'messy grunge student type' she would have been hired on the spot.

She was disgusted at herself for letting a man—albeit a man as gorgeous as this one—make her feel so self-conscious. She forced herself to take a deep breath and looked resolutely forward. Out of the corner of her eye, though, she was aware of big, strong-looking hands opening up a tablet computer. Her belly clenched.

The seconds stretched to minutes and she heard him sigh volubly when the plane still wasn't moving. His arm nearest to her reached up to push something, and she realised it must have been the call button when the stewardess arrived with indecent haste.

'Yes, sir?'

Sidonie heard the irritation in his voice. 'Is there a reason why we're not moving yet?'

She looked over and saw only his strong profile and jaw, and even though she couldn't see it she could imagine the kind of expression he'd be using: imperious. She glanced at the woman and felt sorry for her because she looked so embarrassed.

'I'm not sure, sir. I'll check right away.' She rushed off again.

Sidonie let out a faint snort of derision. Even the stewardess was treating him as if he was some sort of overlord.

He looked at her then. 'I'm sorry… Did you say something?'

Sidonie tried not to be affected by his overwhelming presence. She shrugged minutely. 'I'm sure we're just waiting in line to take our slot on the runway.'

He turned to face her more fully and Sidonie cursed herself. The last thing she needed was his undivided attention on her.

'Oh, really? And what if I have an important meeting to attend in London?'

Something hot flashed into Sidonie's veins and she told herself it was anger at his insufferable arrogance. She crossed her arms in an unconsciously defensive move and said in a low voice, 'Well, in case it's escaped your attention, there are approximately two hundred people on this plane. I'm sure more than one other person has a meeting to make, and I don't see them complaining.'

His eyes flashed and momentarily stopped her breath. They were so unusual and stark against his dark skin. He was like a specimen from some exotic planet.

'There's two hundred and ten, actually, and I don't doubt that there are many others who have important appointments lined up—which makes my question even more relevant.'

Sidonie barely registered the fact that he knew exactly how many were on board and bristled at the way his eyes had done that quick sweep up and down her body, clearly deducing that she *wasn't* on her way to an important meeting.

'For your information,' she said frigidly, 'I have a connecting flight to Dublin from London and I'll be very inconvenienced if we're late. But that's just life, isn't it?'

He leant back a little and looked at her. 'I wondered where your accent was from. It's intriguing.'

Sidonie wasn't sure if that was a compliment or not, so she clamped her mouth shut. Just then someone dressed in uniform with a cap came alongside their seats and coughed slightly to get the man's attention.

Releasing Sidonie from his compelling gaze, the man turned, and the pilot bent down and said discreetly, 'Mr Christakos, sorry about this delay. It's beyond our control, I'm afraid… They've got a backlog of planes waiting to take off. It shouldn't be much longer, but we can get your private jet ready if you'd prefer?'

Sidonie knew her eyes had gone wide as she took in this exchange.

After a few moments the man said, 'No, I'll stay, Pierre. But thank you for thinking of it.'

The captain inclined his head deferentially and left again and Sidonie realised that her mouth was open. Abruptly she shut it and looked out of the window before the man could see. In her line of vision was a similar plane to theirs, standing nearby, with the distinctive Christakos logo emblazoned on the side, along with a quote from a Greek philosopher. All of Alexio Christakos's planes sported quotes.

Alexio Christakos.

Sidonie shook her head minutely, in disbelief. The man next to her—now on his phone, with that deep voice speaking in a language that sounded like Greek—could *not* be the owner of Christakos Freight and Travel. That man was a legend. And he would certainly not be sitting beside her, with his long legs constricted by the confines of economy class seating.

He'd been a case study in their business class at college before she'd had to leave. Astonishingly successful while still disgustingly young, he'd made headlines when he'd cut himself off from his father's inheritance to go his own way, never revealing to anyone his reasons for doing so.

He'd then grafted and worked his way up, starting up an online freight company that had blown all of the competition out of the water, and when he'd sold it after only two years he'd made a fortune. It was that early success that had given him the finances to branch out into air travel, and within the space of five years he'd been competing with and beating the best budget airlines in Europe. He had a reputation for treating customers like people and not like herded cattle, which was a trademark of a lot of Christakos's competition.

He was also one of the most eligible bachelors in Europe, if not the world. Sidonie was not a gossip magazine aficionado, but after they'd studied his entrepreneurial methods in college she'd had to listen to her fellow classmates wax lyrical about the man, drooling over copious pictures of him, for weeks. With a sinking feeling in her chest, she realised why he looked vaguely familiar. Even though she'd not shared in their collective drooling she'd glanced at a couple of pictures, dismissing him as a pretty boy.

Now she knew: pretty he was *not*. He was all male. Virile and potent. She felt like squirming, and she wanted to change seats. She was suddenly acutely uncomfortable and didn't like to analyse why that might be. She wasn't used to someone having such an immediate physical effect on her.

The woman in the seat next to Alexio was starting to fidget. He had to curb the urge to put his hand on her thigh to stop her and curled that hand into a fist. She was clearly a nervy sort from the way she'd reacted when she discovered she was sitting on his seatbelt.

It was intensely irritating to him that he was aware of her at all. That he'd done a minor double-take on hearing

her challenge him. He chafed at being in such close confines with another person after years of the luxury of private air travel, but if he wasn't so damned conscientious…
and controlling… His mouth quirked at the thought of the
insult that had been hurled his way more than once.

On the phone, his assistant was informing him of his
schedule in London, but Alexio caught sight of a sliver of
pale knee peeping out of torn jeans beside him and stifled
a snort. Could she be *any* messier? He'd taken in an impression after exchanging those few words—light-coloured
hair, a slim body, pale face, glasses. Voluminous sweatshirt
that hid any trace of femininity. And a surprisingly husky
voice with that intriguing accent.

Alexio did not take notice of women who did not dress
like women. He had high standards after being brought
up by one of the world's foremost models. His mother had
always been impeccably turned out. He frowned. He was
thinking of her *again*.

Realising the novel fact that he was not actually taking
in a word his assistant was saying, Alexio terminated the
conversation abruptly. The woman went still beside him
and something tensed inside him. He could be on his way
to his private jet right now but he'd refused. Again, not like
him. But something had stopped him. Something in his gut.

He glanced over to see that the woman had a capacious
grey bag on her lap and was pulling things out of the seat
pocket in front of her to put them in haphazardly. Another
strike against her. Alexio was a neat freak. She'd pushed
her black-framed glasses on her head and his eye was drawn
to her hair.

It was actually strawberry blonde. An intriguing colour. It looked to be wavy and unruly if let loose, and he
found himself wondering how long it was when it wasn't
confined in that high bun, with wisps curling against her
neck and face.

Something tightened inside him, down low. Her face, too, was not as unremarkable as he'd first thought. Heart-shaped and pale. He could see a faint smattering of freckles across her small straight nose and it shocked him slightly. It had been so long since he'd been this close to a face without make-up. It felt curiously intimate.

Her hands were small and quick. Deft. Short, practical nails. And just like that Alexio felt a punch of desire bloom in his gut. It was hot and immediate as he imagined how small and pale those hands would look on his body, caressing him, touching him, stroking him. The images were so incendiary that Alexio's breath stopped for a moment.

The girl seemed to have restored her belongings to her bag and now, almost as an afterthought, she took her glasses off her head and put them in too.

She must be aware of his scrutiny—he could see a flood of red stain her cheeks. And that stunned him anew. When was the last time he'd seen a woman blush?

Alexio leant back slightly, noting that her mouth in profile looked full and soft. Kissable.

'Going somewhere?' he asked, slightly perturbed that his voice sounded so rough.

The woman took a breath, making her sweatshirt rise and fall, drawing his eye to the flesh it concealed. He had a sudden hunger to *see* her. And he wondered about her breasts. That desire increased, shocking him slightly with its force. He'd just left a woman in his hotel suite—what was wrong with him?

She looked at him and Alexio's eyes met hers. He sucked in a breath. Without the black-framed glasses they were stunning. Almond-shaped. Aquamarine. Like the sea around the islands in Greece. Sparkling green one second and blue the next. Long dark lashes were a contrast against her pale colouring, and her eyebrows the same strawberry blonde tone as her hair.

She looked resolute, her hands gripping her bag, that soft mouth tight now, eyes avoiding his. 'I'll move seats.'

Alexio frowned. Everything in his body was rejecting the notion with a force he didn't like to acknowledge. 'Why on earth do you want to move?'

This was another novel experience—a woman trying to get away from him!

Alexio settled back further in his seat. The woman opened her mouth again and he saw small, even white teeth. Her two front teeth had a slight gap in the middle. He had the uncanny feeling that he could just sit there and stare at her for hours.

Now she was blushing in earnest.

'Well, you're obviously…you know…' she looked at him now, slightly agonised.

He quirked a brow. 'What am I?'

Her cheeks went an even brighter red and Alexio had to curb the desire to reach out and touch them to see if they felt as hot as they looked.

She huffed now, impatiently. 'Well, you're obviously *you*, and you have things to do, people to talk to. You need space.'

Something cold settled into Alexio's belly and his eyes narrowed. Of course. She'd heard that exchange with the pilot and would have deduced who he was. Still…in his experience once people knew who he was they didn't try to get away—the opposite, in fact.

'I have all the space I need. You don't need to go anywhere. I'll feel insulted if you move.'

Sidonie had to force herself to calm down. What on earth was wrong with her? So what if he was Alexio Christakos, one of the most powerful entrepreneurs of his time? So what if he was more gorgeous than any man she'd ever seen? Since when had she become a walking hormone, anyway? The flight was only an hour. She could handle anything for an hour. Even sitting beside Alexio Christakos.

She forced herself to relax her grip on her bag and said, in as calm a voice as she could muster, 'Fine. I just thought that in light of…who you are…you might appreciate some more space. I mean physically. You're not exactly…' Sidonie stopped and bit her lip, slid her gaze from his uncomfortably.

In an effort to distract him she started to take stuff out of her bag again: a book, papers…

'I'm not exactly what?'

Sidonie could hear the barely suppressed smile in his voice and it made her prickle at being such an object of humour for him.

'You know very well what I mean…' She waved a hand in his general direction. 'You're not exactly designed to fit into economy class, are you?'

She could have sworn she heard a muffled snort but refused to look, thrusting her bag back down under the seat in front. She hated to acknowledge the zinging sensation in her blood, as if she'd been plugged into a mild electric current.

She sat back and crossed her arms, and looked at him to find him regarding her with a small smile playing around his mouth. *Lord.* Almost accusingly she asked, 'Why are you here anyway? Apparently you could be on a private jet rather than waiting here like the rest of us.'

That green gaze was steady, unsettling.

'It's a spot-check. I like to do them from time to time, to make sure things are running smoothly.'

Sidonie breathed out as something clicked in her brain. 'Of course. I read about that.'

He frowned and she clarified reluctantly, feeling hot and self-conscious. 'You were a case study in my business module at college.'

That information didn't appear to be news to him. 'What else did you study at college?'

Embarrassed now, Sidonie admitted, 'Technically I'm still in college… I had to leave before the start of my final year just over a year ago, due to personal events. I'm saving money to try and complete my course… My degree is in Business and French.'

'What happened?'

Sidonie looked at him. On some level she was shocked at his directness, but it was also curiously refreshing. She couldn't seem to remove her gaze from his. The small space they occupied felt strangely intimate, cocoon-like.

'I… Well, my father lost his construction business when the property boom crashed in Ireland. He struggled for a while but it was useless. He only managed to get himself into debt.' Sidonie went cold inside. 'He passed away not long afterwards. Everything was gone—the business, the house… College was paid for up to a point, but then the money ran out. I had to leave and work.'

Sidonie felt uncomfortable under his gaze. It was intense, unsettling.

'And why were you in Paris?'

Sidonie arched a brow. 'What is this? Twenty questions? What were *you* doing in Paris?'

Alexio crossed his arms and Sidonie's belly clenched when she saw how the muscles in his arm bunched under the thin silk of his shirt. She gulped and looked back into that hypnotising gaze.

'I was in Milan yesterday at my brother's wedding, he said. 'Then I flew to Paris this morning to catch this flight, so that I could do my check while en route to London.'

'Are you not concerned about missing your meeting?'

Alexio smiled and the bottom dropped out of Sidonie's belly.

'It's not ideal, but they'll wait for me.'

Of course they would, she thought faintly. Who wouldn't wait for this man?

'So,' he said patiently, 'now will you tell me why *you* were in Paris?'

Sidonie looked at him and unbidden a lump came to her throat for her wayward. selfish mother and her poor Tante Josephine who was so worried. She swallowed it down.

'I was here to meet with a solicitor to deal with my mother's affairs. She passed away in Paris a couple of months ago. She'd been living with my aunt; she's from here originally.' She corrected herself. '*Was* from here, I mean. She moved back after my father died.'

Alexio uncrossed his arms and his expression sobered. 'That's rough—to lose both parents in such a short space of time. I lost my mother too—five months ago.'

Sidonie's chest tightened. A moment of empathy. Union. 'I'm sorry... It's hard, isn't it?'

His mouth twisted. 'I have to admit that we weren't that close—but, yes, it was still a shock.'

That feeling intensified in Sidonie's chest. She revealed huskily, 'I did love my mum, and I know she loved me, but we weren't that close either. She was very... self-absorbed.'

Suddenly the plane lurched into movement and Sidonie's hands went to grab the armrests automatically as she looked out of the window. 'Oh, God, we're moving.'

A dry voice came from her left. 'That's generally what a plane does before it takes off.'

'Very funny,' muttered Sidonie, and their recent conversation was wiped from her mind as she battled with the habitual fear of flying she faced.

'Hey, are you okay? You look terrible.'

'No,' Sidonie got out painfully, knowing she'd probably gone ashen. Her eyes were closed. 'I'm not okay, but I will be if you just leave me alone. Ignore me.'

'You're scared of flying? And you're taking two flights to Dublin? Why didn't you just take a direct flight?' Now he sounded censorious.

'Because,' Sidonie gritted out, 'it worked out cheaper to do it this way, and the direct flights were all full anyway. It was short notice.'

The familiar nausea started to rise and she clamped her mouth shut, feeling cold and clammy. She tried not to think back to the huge breakfast her Tante Josephine had insisted on them both having before they'd left on their respective journeys. It sat heavily in her belly now.

The plane was moving in earnest; this was always the worst part—and the take-off. And the landing. And sometimes in between if there was turbulence.

'Did something happen to make you scared?'

Sidonie wished he would just ignore her, but bit out, 'What? You mean apart from the fact that I'm miles above the earth, surrounded by nothing but a bit of tin and fibreglass or whatever planes are made of?'

'They're actually made mainly of aluminium, although sometimes a composite of metals is used, and in newer technology they're looking at carbon fibre. My brother designs and builds cars, so we're actually looking into new technologies together.'

Sidonie cracked open one eye and cast Alexio a baleful glance. 'Why are you telling me this?'

'Because your fears are irrational. You *do* know that air travel is the safest form of travel in the world?'

Sidonie opened both eyes now and tried to avoid seeing outside the plane. She looked at Alexio. That didn't really help, she had to admit.

She said somewhat churlishly, 'I suppose that the likelihood of the plane going down while its owner is on board is not very high.'

He looked smug. 'See?'

Then he leant closer, making her pulse jump out of control.

'And did you know that of all the seats on the plane these are the safest ones to be in—in the event of a crash?'

Sidonie's eyes widened. 'Really?'

She saw humour dancing in those golden depths and clamped her eyes shut again while something swooped precariously in her belly.

'Very funny.'

Then the plane jerked and Sidonie's hands tightened on the armrests. She heard a deep sigh from beside her and then felt her left hand being taken by a much bigger one. Instantly she was short of breath which she could ill afford to lose.

'What are you doing?' she squeaked, very aware of how tiny her hand felt in his.

'If it's all right with you, I'd prefer it if you abused me rather than my armrests.'

Sidonie opened her eyes again and glanced left. Alexio was looking stern, but with a twitch of a smile playing around his mouth. *Lord, oh, Lord.* She said, a little breathlessly, 'I think somehow that your armrests can withstand my feeble attempts to bend them out of shape.'

'Nevertheless,' Alexio replied easily, 'I won't let it be said that I couldn't offer support to a valued customer in her hour of need.'

CHAPTER TWO

SOMETHING HOT AND shivery went through Sidonie's body. He was flirting with her. She felt as if she was teetering on the edge of a huge canyon, with the exhilaration of the fall reaching out to beckon her into the unknown. He was so utterly gorgeous, and so charming when he turned it on. It was smooth, practised. And she was no match for a man like him.

With her body screaming resistance, Sidonie pulled her hand free from his grip and smiled tightly. 'I'll be fine. But, thanks.'

His eyes flashed for a second, as if he were taken aback or surprised. The regret in Sidonie's body was like a sharp pang.

She clasped her hands in her lap, well out of reach, and turned her head, closing her eyes so that she didn't have to look out of the window. Her battle with fear as the plane took off was being eclipsed by her need not to show it to the man beside her.

More than once she wished that he'd take her hand again. His palm had felt ever so slightly callused. The hands of a working man, not a pampered man.

'You can open your eyes now. The seatbelt sign is about to go off.'

Sidonie took a deep breath and opened her eyes, releasing her hands from their death grip on each other. Alexio was looking at her. She had the impression that he'd been looking at her the whole time. She felt clammy. Hot.

He held out his hand then, and said, 'I believe you already know who I am, but I don't know who you are…'

He wasn't backing off. Butterflies erupted in Sidonie's belly again. She couldn't ignore him. She put her hand in his, unable to help a small smile which was only in part to do with the trauma of take-off being over.

'Sidonie Fitzgerald—pleased to meet you.'

He clasped her hand and once again an electric current seemed to thrum through her blood.

'Sidonie…' he mused. 'It sounds French.'

'It is. My mother chose it. I told you she was French.'

'That's right…you did.'

He was still holding her hand and Sidonie felt as if she was overheating. 'Did they just turn the heating up?'

'You do look hot. Maybe you should take your sweat-shirt off.'

He finally released her hand and it tingled. Faintly, Sidonie said, 'I'm sure I'll be fine…' She had no intention of baring herself to this man's far too assessing gaze.

It was then that Sidonie remembered what they'd been talking about. The fact that they'd both lost their mothers recently. That feeling of kinship. Feeling exposed now, she looked away and reached for her book. She held it for a minute and then turned to Alexio again. He had put his head back against the seat, closed his eyes. She felt ridiculously deflated for a moment.

But then she realised she could drink him in unobserved. His profile was patrician. His eyes deep-set, with long dark lashes. His cheekbones would have made a woman weep with envy, but the stark lines of his face took away any pretty edges.

His jaw was firm, even in repose, and she could see the faint stubbling of fresh beard growth. A spasm of lust gripped her between her legs, taking her by surprise. She'd never experienced such raw *desire*. She'd had a couple of boyfriends at college and had had sex, but it had all been a bit...bland. A lot of fuss over nothing. Mildly excruciating. The guys had certainly seemed to enjoy it more than she had.

She could imagine, though, that this man knew exactly what to do...how to make a woman feel exactly as she should. Especially a man with a mouth like his...sensual and wicked. Hard lines but soft contours... Sidonie pressed her legs together to stop the betraying throb between them. She hadn't even known she had a pulse there, but she could feel it now, like a beacon.

'It's rude to stare, you know.'

Sidonie sprang back. Cheeks flaming. One lazy eye had opened and was focused on her, seeing her mortification.

She spluttered, 'How did you know?'

Before she could feel any more embarrassed he bent down and his head of thick dark hair, closely cropped to his skull, came dangerously near to her thighs. Heat bloomed from Sidonie's groin.

Then he straightened up, holding her book in his hand. He took a quick glance at the title before handing it back to her and commenting dryly, '*Techniques for Analysing Successful Business Structures*? That's bound to send you to sleep.'

Sidonie scowled and took the book from him jerkily. 'I'm trying to keep up with my course so that when I go back I won't be too rusty.'

Alexio dipped his head. 'Very commendable.'

Sidonie felt defensive and wasn't even sure why. 'Some of us have to study the subject. We don't have the natural ability or the support to be able to launch a stratospherically successful business first time.'

His mouth tightened and Sidonie knew she'd raised his hackles.

'I didn't have any support—or did your case study not cover that?'

Sidonie flushed and looked down, inspecting a spot of dirt on her jeans. She looked up again. 'I didn't mean it to sound like that… It's common knowledge that you turned your back on your inheritance… However, you can't deny that your background must have given you confidence and an anticipation of success that most mere mortals mightn't feel or experience.'

His face relaxed somewhat and Sidonie felt herself relax too. Weird.

'You're right,' he surprised her by admitting. 'After all, I grew up absorbing my father's business nous whether I want to admit it or not. And I had the best education money could buy… My brother is also a successful entrepreneur, so I learnt from him too.'

Sidonie was itching to ask him why he'd turned his back on his inheritance, but just then the stewardess turned up with a trolley, smiling winsomely at Alexio. Sidonie felt the most bizarre rise of something hot and visceral. Possessiveness. It shocked her so much that she shrank back.

Her sweatshirt felt hot and constricting, even more so now, and Sidonie longed to feel cool. While Alexio was distracted, ordering some coffee from the woman, Sidonie whipped it over her head—only to emerge seconds later to find two pairs of eyes on her. The distinctly cold blue of the stewardess and a green gaze, intent and disturbing.

'What…?' She looked from Alexio to the woman, who now spoke to her in tones even cooler than her arctic gaze.

'Would you like some tea or coffee, madam?'

In fluent French Sidonie replied that she would love some tea. She could sense the small smile playing around Alexio's mouth without even looking. Her skin prickled as she put down her table and accepted the steaming tea. She felt exposed now, in her loose singlet top, even though it was layered over another one.

Before she could reach for her purse Alexio had paid for her drink as well as his. Not a welcome move, according to the pursed lips of the stewardess who moved on with barely disguised huffiness.

Alexio seemed oblivious, though.

'Thank you,' Sidonie said. 'You didn't have to do that.'

He shrugged. 'It's nothing—my pleasure.'

Sidonie shivered a little to think of *his pleasure*.

To get away from such carnal imaginings, she remarked, 'How is it beneficial to do a spot-check on one of your planes if everyone knows who you are?' He quirked a brow at her as he took a sip of coffee and Sidonie blustered a bit. 'Well, you know what I mean. That stewardess will obviously be doing her best to impress.'

'True,' he conceded, and put his cup down.

Sidonie was acutely aware of how dark his hands looked against the cup, how large.

'But I never inform them when I'm coming, and I'm not just interested in the behaviour of my staff—it's everything. I can overhear the passengers' observations too.'

Sidonie frowned. 'But don't you have people who work for you who can do this sort of thing and report back?'

Alexio shrugged minutely. 'I have to go to London today—why not take one of my own commercial flights? If I expect others to do it then I should be able to, too. I am aware of my carbon footprint. I have a responsibility.'

Sidonie could see unimstakable pride in his business on his face. She nodded her head. 'It's smart. Because if anyone ever criticises you you can say that you know first-hand what it's like to fly on your budget flights. And,' she added, warming to her theme, turning more towards

Alexio, 'it gives the customer a sense of kinship with you. You're one of the people.'

He smiled. 'That too. Very good, business student. It's a pity you had to drop out.'

Sidonie glanced away, uncomfortable again under that gaze. It was as if he could see right through her to a place she wasn't even aware of herself. Some secret part she'd not explored yet.

'So your mother was French…and your father?'

Sidonie rolled her eyes and said lightly, 'Back to twenty questions again?'

She sat back and tried not to notice how confined the space was. Their elbows kept touching lightly when they moved. Their thighs would be touching if she shifted hers towards him by about an inch. His legs were so long he had to spread them wide.

Instantly warm again, Sidonie answered before he could comment. 'My father was Irish. My mother went to Dublin many years ago…she met my father and stayed in Dublin and they got married.'

Sidonie slid her gaze from Alexio's, afraid he might see something of her very deep shame revealed. It wasn't exactly the way things had happened, but near enough. He didn't need to know the darker secrets of her parents' relationship and her origins. Or about subsequent shattering events.

She looked at him. 'And you?'

His expression became veiled, piquing her interest.

'My mother was Spanish and my father is Greek. But you probably knew that.'

Sidonie answered, 'I didn't realise your mother was Spanish…'

'I presume your fluent French is from your mother?'

Sidonie nodded and took another sip of tea. She realised

then that if only she wasn't so *aware* of Alexio it would actually be quite nice talking to him.

'She spoke French to me all the time, and my father encouraged it. He knew it would come in handy at some stage.'

'You were close to your father?'

She nodded. 'Why do you ask?'

Alexio reached out and to Sidonie's shock touched her cheek with the backs of his fingers for a fleeting second.

'Because your face softened when you mentioned him.'

Sidonie touched her cheek where he had touched her and felt embarrassed. She ducked her face again, wishing her hair was down so she could hide. 'I loved him. He was a wonderful man.'

'You're lucky to have had that... My father...we don't exactly see eye to eye.'

Sidonie glanced back at him, grateful for the attention to be off her, and laughed slightly. 'Surely he must be one of the proudest fathers in the world?'

Alexio smiled, but it was grim. 'Ah, but my success didn't come through him. I fought for my own piece of the pie and he's never forgiven me for it.'

Just then they were interrupted again, when a different stewardess came along to clear up their rubbish. It gave Alexio a reality check and he balked inwardly.

What on earth was he doing? Blithely spilling his guts to a complete stranger because he was momentarily mesmerised by pale skin, beautiful eyes and a very supple, slim body?

When the stewardess had gone and Alexio was still berating himself he saw Sidonie undo her seatbelt buckle.

She looked at him expectantly before saying, 'I need to go to the bathroom. Please.'

Relieved to have a chance to gather his completely scattered senses, Alexio undid his own seatbelt and stood up. Deliberately he didn't move out into the aisle completely, so that Sidonie had to brush past him. He saw the flash in her eyes, making them sparkle a brilliant blue-green, and felt that punch to his gut again.

As she went past him he saw that she was doing her best not to touch him, but even the most fleeting glance of her hip against his thigh sent shards of desire into his belly. He couldn't help but smell her scent—cool and crisp, with a hint of something floral. That was what she was like— one minute spiky, the next as soft as a fresh rose. And as alluring.

She was taller than he had expected—about five foot seven...

When he'd sat down again, and she'd moved down the aisle to the bathroom, Alexio stuck his head out to watch her, his blood heating through every vein and artery at the way her skinny jeans hugged her slim, shapely legs and cupped her surprisingly lush derriere. To Alexio's consternation he saw more than one other male head dip out to take a look too as she passed.

It felt as if he hadn't taken a proper breath since he'd seen her take off that horrific sweatshirt. He'd happened to look at her for her response when the stewardess had asked if she wanted something, only to find her in the act of taking it off. He'd been unable to look away as Sidonie had fought with the voluminous material, gradually showing tantalising glimpses of pale flesh, slim arms, tiny wrists, delicate shoulders and collarbone.

She'd emerged flushed, and Alexio's libido had been suddenly ravenous. She was wearing a vest top, with a loose singlet over it, so she was showing nothing that wasn't completely respectable. But she might as well have been naked, the effect within Alexio was so violent. He felt like a Victorian man seeing bared arms for the first time; they were almost provocative in their slim, delicately muscled definition.

He'd sat there with a raging erection, trying in vain to concentrate on the conversation and those flashing expressive eyes and not let his gaze drift down to where her small but lush cleavage was revealed under those two tops. The hint of a bright pink bra strap every now and then had enflamed him more than the most expensive lingerie modelled by any of his previous lovers. The memory of his Latin lover of last night was being comprehensively eclipsed.

Alexio wanted to see her—*all of her*—with a hunger that might ordinarily cause him to stop and think. He could already imagine her perfectly formed breasts, made to fit a man's hands like plump fruits. Would her nipples be small and peaked? Or large and succulent? He hadn't been able to resist touching her hot cheek for a second. Her skin was as soft and unblemished as a peach.

This was the kind of desire he'd missed for so long. The kind he'd lamented not feeling last night. Urgent and hot. Utterly compelling. As if he couldn't envisage *not* getting off this plane and taking Sidonie with him so that he could taste her all over. And Alexio had to wonder in that moment if he'd ever really felt like this. Or had it just been a figment of his imagination till now?

The revelation sent him reeling, and he wasn't prepared at all when a soft voice said hesitantly, 'Er...excuse me, Mr Christakos?'

He looked up and there she was, and just like that any semblance of clear-headedness was gone. He was reduced to animal lust again. Her breasts were in his eyeline and he could see the thrust of her nipples against the thin fabric of her two tops, like berries. He had to get up and let her back in, cursing his body, which would not obey his head.

One thing he was sure of as she brushed past him in the small space again and her scent tantalised him: he wanted this Sidonie Fitzgerald with her husky voice with a hunger he'd not known before. And he would have her. Because Alexio Christakos always got what he wanted. Especially women.

Sidonie sat down again and tried to hang on to the control she'd struggled to find in the tiny bathroom space just moments before. She'd splashed cold water on her face, as if that might wake her from the trance she seemed to be in.

Any return of her equilibrium had been short-lived. As soon as she'd got back Alexio Christakos had looked at her—that molten green gaze travelling up from her breasts to her face—and it had been so intense...almost predatory. Her whole body had reacted to it, igniting like a flame. Even the air seemed to be crackling between them now, as if something had been turned up a notch.

He's a playboy, he's a playboy, she repeated like a mantra in her head. *He's programmed to go after anything with a pulse.* But Sidonie grimaced at that. Alexio Christakos, according to her fellow enamoured students, was discerning—only choosing the most stunning models and actresses. The beauties of this era. And Sidonie, with her fair colouring, freckles and wayward hair, did not fall into that category. Not by a long shot. This crazy desire...whatever it was she was feeling...she had to be imagining it.

A wave of mortification rushed up through her body, sending her hot and cold. Was she projecting her own pathetic subconscious fantasies onto this man who had the misfortune to be paired with her for the flight?

She heard him clear his throat beside her and was almost scared to look. She could sense his gaze on her—or could she? With a sick desire to know how badly she'd been deluding herself Sidonie turned her head and met that green gaze head-on. Slamming into it, almost. The breath left her mouth in a little sigh. Her belly swooped and her skin tingled all over. Her nipples drew so tight she could feel them like stinging points, chafing against her lace bra.

'Don't...' he growled softly, intimately. 'Don't call me Mr Christakos again. It makes me feel like an old man. It's Alexio.'

Sidonie could feel the plane dip in altitude. Somehow she found her voice. 'We're landing soon. I won't see you ever again, so it doesn't really matter what I call you.'

'Don't be so sure about that.'

Sidonie blinked. Her heart spasmed in her chest. 'What's that supposed to mean?'

'I'm taking you out to dinner tonight.'

Sidonie had two contradictory reactions. Head and heart/body. Her heart/body leapt and sizzled. Her head said *Danger! Danger!* He was definitely arrogant, and she was loath to let him see that even a small part of her was tempted. A man like this? He would chew her up over dinner and a one-night stand and then cast her out with little or no second thought.

She was a fleeting interest.

Maybe the lack of air and the confines of economy class had gone to his head. Maybe he was bored, jaded, and something about her intrigued him because she was so different from his usual women.

Sidonie crossed her arms and narrowed her eyes. She saw Alexio's jaw clench, as if he was priming himself for a fight, and something deep within her quivered and then went soft and molten. She fought it. They were both oblivious to the stewardess, who had come to check their seatbelts for landing.

'That sounded remarkably like an order and not an invitation. I'm catching a connecting flight to Dublin—or didn't you hear that part earlier?'

Sidonie wasn't sure exactly why she felt so threatened

by his advance, but she did. Even though she knew she was probably right in her suspicions about why a man like Alexio was flirting with her, a very large part of her wanted to leap into his arms and say *yes*.

She would bet that not many women turned him down—if any. But she wouldn't be able to live with herself if she gave in to him for what she had no doubt would amount to one night. She told herself it was because she valued herself too highly, but she knew, treacherously, that she was afraid of how strongly this man affected her. One night would never be enough. She felt it deep in the pit of her belly. And that freaked her out. She was a naturally responsible and cautious person, not given to spontaneous acts like this.

He cast his glance to the very sexy platinum watch on his wrist, and then back to her. 'I'd say you've missed that connecting flight, and as I'm the owner of the airline company the least you can do is allow me to make it up to you. By taking you for dinner.'

Sidonie snorted inelegantly and quashed the swooping sensation in her belly. 'I don't see you offering everyone on this plane dinner to recompense them for missing their connecting flights.'

That formidable jaw clenched again. 'That's probably because I don't *want* to take them for dinner. However, I would like to take *you* for dinner. *Please.*'

Sidonie's chin lifted, but she quivered inwardly at his *please*. 'I'm a terrible dinner companion. I'm a fussy eater and I'm a vegetarian. Vegan, actually.'

That wasn't true, but some devil inside her was working now. Sparking.

Alexio smiled. 'I'm sure you are a scintillating dinner companion, and I know a fabulous vegetarian restaurant—all the eggplant you can eat.'

That humour danced in his eyes again, transporting him from downright gorgeous to downright irresistible.

Sidonie scowled. He didn't believe her for a second. His eyes dropped down her body and then came back up again. A wickedly sexy slow smile tipped up his mouth, telling her better than any words that dinner and conversation were not the only things on his mind. As if she couldn't feel it vibrating between them. This awareness she'd never felt before.

Sidonie glared at him and tried to will down the heat in her body that mocked her with the realisation that dinner wasn't exactly foremost in *her* mind either. Very belatedly she remembered she had taken off her sweatshirt and scrabbled around to find it and pull it back on.

She heard a sound beside her and looked to see Alexio making a face.

'That thing should be burnt.'

Sidonie gasped, affronted. 'It's my favourite.'

'It's a crime to hide your body underneath that shapeless thing.'

Suddenly there was a sharp thudding and crashing sensation and Sidonie's heart stopped. She felt all her blood drain south.

Instantly Alexio had her hands in his and he was saying soothingly, 'We've just landed, that's all.'

Sidonie's heart was still palpitating. Her ears popped. She could see the ground through the window across the aisle and felt the powerful throttle of the plane as it pulled back.

She looked at Alexio, shocked. 'I've never not noticed landing before.' She'd been distracted. By *him*.

Her hands were still in his and she looked down to see them, so much smaller and paler next to his. As she watched he entwined his fingers with hers and between her legs she throbbed. He exerted pressure on her hands and Sidonie looked up, her head feeling heavy, her blood hot.

For a long, taut moment they just looked at one another. Sidonie's breath grew choppy. Alexio pulled one hand free and brought it up to cup her jaw, his thumb moving back and forth as if learning the shape of her cheek.

His eyes were on her mouth now. She wanted him to kiss her so badly. The air sizzled. And then his eyes met hers again and he emitted a guttural sound like a curse. His jaw clenched. He took his hand away. Sidonie had to bite the inside of her lip to stop herself from crying out.

As if she'd been drugged just by that look Sidonie slowly came back to her senses, and mortification gripped her innards when she realised how she must have looked: like some love-starved groupie.

She jerked back. Thank goodness he hadn't kissed her, because she knew that she would have put up no fight whatsoever. And she hated the part of her that felt *bereft* of the experience. She looked away.

'Sidonie.'

The fact that his voice was rough didn't give her any comfort.

'What?' she snapped, reaching for her bag and putting it on her lap so that she could put her stuff back into it.

She found her glasses and stuck them on, even though she only needed them for reading. They felt like the armour she needed. She looked at him and then wished she hadn't. His face was all stark, lean lines. Nostrils flaring. Eyes dangerous.

People around them were starting to stand up, unbuckling seatbelts, reaching for bags.

Sidonie forgot for a moment that he'd even asked her for dinner. She felt ridiculously vulnerable. Exposed.

'I'm sure you have an assistant waiting nearby to fast-track you off the plane and out of the airport.'

Alexio's mouth firmed. She was right. Even now he could see a uniformed official saying, 'Excuse me...' as he fought his way through the crush to get to Alexio.

He grabbed for her hand and Sidonie glanced around

them, but no one was looking. All eager to get on with their journeys.

'Sidonie, I meant what I said. Come for dinner with me tonight.'

She looked at him and still felt that awful sting of rejection because he hadn't actually kissed her. She hated that it made her feel vulnerable. 'I'm going to Dublin. I can't stay in London just on your…whim.'

His eyes flashed. 'It's not a whim. If you stay I'll take care of you—get you home.'

Sidonie pulled her hand free. She shook her head. 'No… I'm sorry, but I can't.'

The uniformed person was at their seats now and he bent down to say something to Alexio, who made a curt reply. He stood up and reached for his jacket and coat. He looked down at Sidonie, whose eyes had been glued to that magnificent torso as he'd stretched up.

'Come with me. At least let me try to help you make your flight.'

Sidonie looked at him and gulped. Now he was distant, unreadable. A shiver went down her spine and she knew in that moment that she would hate to cross him. He would be a formidable enemy.

Stiffly she said, 'You don't have to do this. I can find my own way and wait for another flight if I have to.'

He sighed deeply. 'Just…don't argue, okay? Come with me—please.'

He held out his hand and Sidonie looked from him to it. This was probably the last time she'd ever see him. On some level she realised with a jolt that she felt as if she could trust this man who was all but a total stranger. Even though she was fighting it.

That revelation stunned her. She'd never trusted easily after the cataclysmic events of her childhood. And losing both parents within such a short space of time, together with the recent revelations about her mother's nefarious actions, had made the world feel increasingly fragile around her. As if nothing she knew was solid any more. Yet being in the company of this man had made Sidonie feel more solid than she'd ever felt. Protected. Which was crazy.

Even more crazy, though, was the fact that Sidonie couldn't resist the lure of a few more minutes with this man. Her hand slipped into his almost of its own volition and it was disconcerting how familiar it felt—and yet how deliciously terrifying, as if she were stepping off a ledge.

She was out of her seat and Alexio was leading her towards the back of the plane, guided by the man who had come to fetch him. The back door was open just for them, with the frosty stewardess saying goodbye, sending Sidonie daggers on seeing her hand clasped tightly in Alexio's.

Hating herself for how much she liked the way her hand felt in his, Sidonie followed him down the steps to where another official and a car were waiting. She heard Alexio give her name to the person and instruct him that her luggage should be brought to meet them on the other side. A VIP customs official inspected her Irish passport.

And then they were in a chauffeur-driven car and speeding towards the terminal Sidonie needed to get to for her connecting flight.

CHAPTER THREE

ALEXIO WAS LOOKING at his smartphone but not seeing anything. He was incandescent with rage…and lust. Angry with himself that he'd not taken the opportunity to kiss Sidonie when he'd wanted to. But something had held him back—something that had whispered to him that she wasn't like the women he knew. That the strength of what he was feeling was off the charts.

He prided himself on being a civilised man. With very select tastes. Not a man given to random outbursts or to passionately kissing a woman an hour after meeting her. And yet he'd come within seconds of doing just that.

Yet still…had he let her go? No. He'd all but hauled her off the plane. Sidonie was a tense figure beside him now, her bag on her lap, her hands clasping it.

Unable to help himself, Alexio reached out and touched a finger to her jaw, trailing it over the delicate line. Even that made his body scream with hunger. She tensed even more, but she turned to look at him. Alexio marvelled to himself. One wayward curling strand of hair had come loose and coiled over her shoulder like a burst of silken sunrise. Her cheeks were flushed. No make-up, and those ridiculous black-framed glasses. Her shapeless sweatshirt and those worn jeans. He shouldn't want her. But he did.

He couldn't explain it, but in that moment she was the most beautiful woman he'd ever seen in his life. And suddenly that need was back, even more urgent than before. The realisation hit him: he might never see her again.

Rationality dissolved to be replaced by raw hunger and need. Sidonie obviously saw something on his face, in his eyes, and her own eyes widened, her cheeks getting pinker. Alexio couldn't have stopped himself now if a thousand men had tried to hold him back.

He pulled her into him and slanted his mouth over hers.

That first sweet taste of her soft lips crushed under his made his brain go white with heat. She fell against him, hands pressed to his chest, and Alexio hauled her even closer, his mouth moving over hers, coaxing her to open up to him...

One of his hands moved up her arm to her neck, his thumb angling her chin, cupping her head...and then, after an infinitesimal moment, she opened her mouth on a sigh. He deepened the kiss and all that hunger he'd been holding in exploded in a dizzying rush of desire.

Sidonie was still in shock. Alexio's mouth was on hers, his tongue seeking, thrusting, tasting... She couldn't breathe, couldn't think. And didn't want to. All she knew was that as soon as he'd looked at her so hungrily and then reached for her she'd been ready to throw herself into his arms. The evidence that he did want her was like balm to her ravaged spirit.

There was nothing gentle about his kiss, and she wanted it with every fibre of her being. It was passionate, hotter than anything she'd experienced before. He was tasting and plundering, both hands on her head now, his fingers in her hair, making it loose. Sidonie felt as if she was breaking apart into a million tiny pieces, but it was so delicious...so drugging...that she never wanted it to stop.

A ravenous beast she'd never known before woke inside her and she felt herself matching the passion of Alexio's kiss. Matching it and seeking for more. Now *she* was the one who wanted to taste, nipping at his lower lip with her teeth, feeling the hard resilience of that sensual contour... her tongue automatically soothing where she'd nipped.

She heard a faint sound coming from a long way away. And then Alexio was stopping, pulling back. Sidonie went with him, loath to release him even for a second.

Some sliver of sanity intruded and Sidonie realised that she was clinging to Alexio. And that he'd just been kissing her to distraction in the back of his car. She found the strength to pull herself out of the whirlpool and broke free, breathing harshly. Dazed. Eyes unfocused for a second.

She realised two things at once: the car had come to a halt outside the terminal and it must have been the driver who had made the noise to get their attention.

Alexio's hands were still on her arms, as if she needed support, and his face was still close, those eyes looking heavy-lidded and glittering with all sorts of decadent promises. All she wanted to do was pull him back to her and kiss him again and never stop.

Almost violently she pulled free completely. Her cheeks burned. Her hair was loose and coming down. Quickly she scrabbled with trembling hands to put it back up.

She couldn't look at him. What the hell had just happened? Mutual combustion? And she'd leapt into the fire without a second's hesitation. As much as she'd been a willing participant in what had just happened, it scared Sidonie how quickly she'd lost control.

'We're here,' Alexio said, somewhat redundantly. He was trying to control the clamour of his blood. He felt altered after that kiss. Disorientated.

Sidonie was avoiding his eye, breathing fast. He saw her throat work. She opened her mouth and already he wanted to cover it with his, taste that sweetness again.

There was something so unexpected about her—something that pierced him right through to where he'd never been touched, smashing aside his cynical jaded shell. If he could think for a moment he might even feel suspicious, but right now he was too hot for her to feel anything but carnal hunger.

She glanced at him and all he could see were the swirling blue and green depths of those luminous eyes. She was still wearing those glasses. Then he saw her hand reaching for the door handle, and everything in him rejected the notion that she was going to leave. But before he could stop her she'd looked away, opened the door and was stepping out.

Alexio moved so fast that she was only just straightening up when he reached her side of the car. Her eyes were huge and wary. Someone rushed up with her bag on a trolley and Alexio took it, only just restraining himself from snarling at the completely innocent staff member to leave them alone.

Alexio looked at Sidonie for a long moment, feeling as if he was tipping over a precipice he'd never let himself near before.

'Are you sure I can't change your mind?'

For a second he thought she was about to capitulate, and the blood thundered in his head, but then she bit her lip and shook her head. 'I can't. I need to get back.'

Alexio didn't want to move. 'You have a job?'

She avoided his eye. 'I did… But the restaurant closed down.'

Alexio's body grew tight. 'So there's nothing to rush home for…?' Something very unpalatable occurred to him and he bit out, 'Unless you have a boyfriend?'

Sidonie shook her head quickly and at the same time shot him an insulted look. 'No… I would never do…what we just did…if I had…'

She stopped for a moment, then focused on him again and looked tortured, but it was little comfort to Alexio.

'I just...can't do this. With you.' Her chin lifted. 'I'm not easy, Alexio. I won't just fall into bed with you because you click your fingers and expect me to.'

Alexio wanted to smash aside the trolley, rip off those glasses and grab her, kiss her into submission. Kiss her *again*. Instead he bit out, lying admirably, 'I asked you for dinner, Sidonie, not for sex.'

She blanched and avoided his gaze again, slinging her bag across her body. It did little to douse his desire—the strap coming between her breasts made them stand out, defining their pert shape. *Theos*, what was *wrong* with him? Had he lost all reason in the past hour?

Sidonie took the trolley and said, 'Look...thanks, okay? If I lived in London maybe I'd go out with you, but I don't, and I have to go home.'

She was pulling away, taking the trolley with her case on it, and something like panic gripped Alexio's chest, constricting his breathing. He thrust a hand into his jacket pocket and pulled out a card, handed it to her.

She took it reluctantly and he wanted to push it into her hand, wrap her fingers around it. 'Those are my private numbers. If anything changes...call me.'

After a few torturous seconds she just nodded and said, 'It was nice to meet you...'

And then she pulled the trolley round, disappeared into the departures hall and was swallowed up by a thousand faceless, nameless people.

Alexio did not like this feeling of being out of control. *At all*. It was something he'd fought against his whole life— every time his father had tried to mould him into the son and heir he'd wanted. Every time his father had suffocated him with the weight of his expectations. And most all every time he'd seen his father lose it because he couldn't control his emotions around his cold wife.

And yet this wisp of a woman had managed to slide control out from under his feet without him even noticing.

He cursed volubly.

Twenty minutes later Sidonie was about to scream with frustration. Her body was still sensitive, tingling with an overload of sexual awareness. All she could see in her mind's eye was Alexio Christakos's hard-boned gorgeous face and that mouth-wateringly perfect body, but all she could hear was the airline official saying again, 'Look, miss, I'm sorry. This is the weekend of the England versus Ireland rugby final. There is no way you are going to get a ticket to Dublin today or tomorrow. So unless you want to try swimming the Irish Sea...'

Sidonie felt the press of people behind her, all looking to get home, and felt despair. The official was already dealing with the next person and, despondent, Sidonie turned away. She went back out through the main doors, half expecting to see Alexio still standing there with an imperious look on his face, but he and his car were gone and Sidonie felt absurdly like crying.

Why had she been so hell-bent on denying herself an evening with the most charismatic man she'd ever met? The ghost of her mother whispered to her, reminding Sidonie of her strong instinct to deny anything that was just for herself. She always had to work for it.

She'd vowed long ago not to be grasping like her mother, who had been oblivious to the pain of others around her—especially that of her husband, who had devoted his life to her in spite of the fact that she'd humiliated him publicly. In spite of the fact that he'd always known that Sidonie wasn't even his biological daughter.

And now she had a huge responsibility: Tante Josephine

needed her support. She didn't have the luxury of just thinking about herself. A small voice taunted her. *But you could have had tonight. One night.*

Sidonie felt a lurch as she thought of how for one second she'd almost given in to Alexio and said *yes* when he'd asked if she would change her mind.

The one thing that should have held her back was her aunt—but she had gone on her annual two-week holiday with a local charity group. Sidonie had encouraged her to go, knowing it would take her aunt's mind off things while she sorted herself out in Dublin. For an exhilarating second Sidonie had remembered this and thought it might be possible...but she hadn't seized the moment. Too afraid to throw caution to the wind and trust completely.

And it was too late now anyway. She looked down and saw her hand clenched around his card. Her belly flipped. She had an image of him on his way into London to his important meeting. He would have forgotten about her already. An aberration. She'd missed her chance. Maybe she'd even dreamt him up?

A hollow feeling made her ache inside. She turned around again and faced the door, steeling herself to go back into that throng. She would buy a seat on the next available flight and then she would find somewhere to stay—

'Sidonie.'

Her heart slammed to a stop and the blood rushed from her head to her feet. *It couldn't be.*

Sidonie forgot about the trolley and whirled around. Alexio was standing there, as gorgeous as she remembered. Not a dream. Shock mixed with relief and joy jumped in her belly.

'What are you doing here? You were gone,' she breathed, half afraid she was hallucinating.

Alexio's mouth tightened as if he didn't like admitting it. 'I doubled back...just in case.'

Sidonie made a gesture behind her. 'All the flights are full. A rugby match is on between England and Ireland. I can't get home till the day after tomorrow at the earliest...'

'So you're stuck here at the airport? That's unfortunate.' His eyes were glinting with that dark humour again.

Incredible joy was bubbling up inside Sidonie. He'd come back. *For her.* He hadn't forgotten about her.

She fought back the goofy grin threatening to erupt. 'I was going to rebook my flight and then I was going to find somewhere to stay.'

Alexio put one hand in the pocket of his trousers. His jacket hung open. He was stunning, blinding. Mesmerising.

'I happen to have a very spacious apartment here in London. If you were to agree to accompany me to dinner this evening I'd let you stay. And then I'd make sure you got home at the earliest opportunity.'

Warning bells went off in Sidonie's head again but she ignored them. She was getting a second chance. She'd never thought she'd see this man again, because she would never have had the nerve to call him.

She made a mental decision and took a step into the terrifying and exhilarating unknown.

'I'll accept your offer.'

Something within her leapt to see his eyes flare and his cheeks darken with colour.

She held up a hand. 'On one condition.'

'What?' he bit out, clearly impatient now.

'That you allow *me* to buy dinner...for letting me stay with you.'

Sidonie had a mental image of her bank account and her already close to maxed-out credit card after the flights she'd had to take back and forth to Paris in recent months. She bit her lip.

'Except I hope you like cheap Italian, because that's about the best I can offer.'

Alexio stepped up to her and reached around to get her trolley, taking her small case off it as if it weighed nothing. He took her elbow in his hand and looked down at her, taking her breath away.

'I'll tell you what. We'll eat in—that way we don't have to worry about who's paying.'

'But…' Sidonie spluttered ineffectually as he handed her into the back seat of his car.

He came around and got in the other side and then just looked at her, and it was so stern that she stopped.

'Okay—fine. I get it,' she said a little mutinously, 'but I just don't want you to think that I'm not grateful.'

Alexio issued a terse command in a guttural language and Sidonie saw the car's privacy window slide up silently. Then he was reaching for her and pulling her sweatshirt up and over her head before she had the wits to stop him. When she emerged he had his hands in her hair, taking it out of its confines and making it fall down around her shoulders.

Then he plucked off her glasses—which weren't doing much for her sight anyway.

She slapped at his hands ineffectually. 'What do you think you're doing?'

Sidonie hated that her whole body sizzled at his masterful actions, knowing she should be objecting vociferously.

He took her face in his hands, holding her still. Sidonie's heart skipped and her breath stopped.

'Much better,' Alexio breathed approvingly, just before his head bent and his mouth met hers.

Sidonie groaned deeply, because from the moment she'd pulled away from that first kiss she'd craved this again. In her mind she ordered herself to stop thinking and gave herself up to the dark fantasy of Alexio Christakos, who had just turned her world upside down and inside out.

By the time they pulled up outside a huge, impressive building Sidonie felt completely flustered, aching and undone. Alexio's tie was loose and he looked as feverish as Sidonie felt.

'Come in with me. Wait for me.'

Sidonie's mouth felt swollen. She wasn't sure if her vocal cords worked any more. She just nodded her head. It was as if in the space of the back of that car, in the space of the increasingly passionate kisses they'd shared, some indelible link had been forged between them. She was loath to let him out of her sight.

He held her hand walking in, but Sidonie caught sight of her reflection and balked. She jerked in his grip and he looked down at her and raised a brow.

Sidonie blushed. 'I don't look exactly *corporate*.'

His hot gaze swept her up and down and he said throatily, 'You look perfect.'

But Sidonie knew she was out of place in her chain-store tops, jeans and sneakers the moment the immaculate blonde receptionist sent her a look that could have frozen the Sahara.

When they emerged from the lift there was a veritable entourage of people waiting for Alexio. Someone took his jacket and coat; someone else handed him a folder. Someone else was on the phone. And then someone approached her and said, solicitously, 'Miss Fitzgerald? If you'd like to follow me I can show you where you can wait…'

Sidonie was looking helplessly at Alexio, who glanced at her and then waved her off in the direction of her guide. He was already being spirited away in the opposite direction.

Sidonie was led down plush carpeted hallways. She saw the distinctive Christakos logo on the walls and blanched when she realised that this entire building must be *his*.

The young woman in a pristine trouser suit with her dark hair clipped back showed Sidonie into a palatial office with huge windows looking out over what seemed to be the whole of London. This had to be Alexio's office, with its massive desk near the window.

The woman spoke with an accent that Sidonie guessed must be Greek. 'Can I get you anything, Miss Fitzgerald?'

Sidonie looked at her and felt even more mussed up. 'Er...maybe some tea would be nice?'

'Of course. I'll be right back.' And she left and pulled the heavy door behind her.

Alexio's scent was in the air, faint and tantalising. Exclusive. Masculine. *Sexy*. Sidonie took a deep breath in and walked over to the window to take in the view. It was spectacular, breathtaking.

She could see doors leading out to a terrace and opened them. She went out and was confronted with the real vista—not behind a plane of glass. It was in that moment that she had the full, gut-churning sense of the man she'd met only a few short hours before. He was one of the kings of the world.

'Miss Fitzgerald?'

Sidonie whirled around to see the assistant hovering with a tray. She rushed forward, aghast, and took the tray from the startled woman. 'I can look after it myself. Thank you so much.'

The woman backed away. 'If you need anything else I'm just down the hall. Mr Christakos shouldn't be too long, I heard him say he wanted to keep the meeting short.'

Sidonie's belly somersaulted. Was that because of *her*? She nodded her head and the woman left. Sidonie put down the tray. She didn't want to sit at Alexio's desk so she sat at a small coffee table on the other side of the room. She noticed that her hand was trembling when she poured the tea.

Lord. What was she *doing* here? Sitting in Alexio Christakos's palatial office, waiting for him. He'd picked her up on a *plane*.

Sidonie blushed. She'd engaged him in conversation in

the first place. If she'd buried her head in her book he probably wouldn't have looked twice at her. Sidonie put down her teacup. She knew she could walk out of there right now, get her bag out of his car and melt into the crowds in London and quite possibly never see Alexio again... But, treacherously, she didn't want to.

The novel sensation of putting herself first was uncomfortable. It felt like a coat she'd never worn. Tante Josephine's face popped into her mind...but even Tante Josephine was okay for the moment, on holiday with her friends. There was no reason why Sidonie couldn't be here, doing this.

Sidonie felt a sense of lightness, freedom, and it was heady. Dinner tonight. A place to stay. A chance to get to know this amazing man a little better. She breathed deeply and tried to quell her rapid heartbeat. That was all. And that was all she wanted. No matter what her body might be screaming for. She would emerge from this adventure with her emotions intact.

When Alexio could finally get away from his meeting, which he'd cut ruthlessly and uncharacteristically short, he headed for his office, pulling at his tie impatiently as he did so. *Sidonie.* When he'd ordered his driver to turn around before they'd hit the main motorway into London he'd felt like an abject fool. But the compulsion to go back and see her again had been too great. To find her, persuade her to stay.

And then she'd been standing there, like a lost waif, looking at his card, and the sheer relief that had rushed through him had eclipsed any niggling concerns about his uncharacteristic behaviour.

And now she was here, waiting for him. Alexio gritted his jaw to stop his body reacting. He had to get it together. It had been hard enough to concentrate in the meeting.

When he went into his office he didn't see her and his blood turned to ice.

She'd left.

But then he saw the open terrace doors and his heart started beating again. He went forward and saw her slimly curvaceous form, that plump bottom, as she leant against the railing, taking in the view.

He went right up behind her and put his arms next to hers on the railing.

She started for a moment. 'You scared me.'

Alexio imagined that he felt her heart pick up pace— or was it his? Her lush derriere pressed against him *right there*. And Alexio didn't have a hope in hell of controlling his body.

She was tense in the circle of his arms. 'Your meeting wasn't very long.'

Alexio put out his hand and pulled her long, rippling hair over one shoulder, baring her neck. It was a crime to confine such hair. He bent his head and pressed his mouth to the soft skin just under her ear. Immediately she quivered and her bottom moved against him. His other arm came down and wrapped around her midriff, dragging her in tighter.

Theos. He would take her right here and now if he could.

He drew back slightly, dragging in breath, control. 'I told them I had urgent business to attend to.'

Sidonie turned around in his arms and that was worse— because now Alexio's steel-hard erection was pressed against her soft belly and the hard tips of her breasts were visible through her sleeveless vest tops.

'Alexio...'

Alexio dragged his gaze up and met two pools of aquamarine.

'Hmm?'

'If I stay with you tonight...that doesn't mean I'm going

to sleep with you...' She bit her lip. 'I'm not saying I don't want to, but I'm not like that.' She winced. 'I mean...I won't sleep with you as some sort of payment. I would prefer to stay in a hostel or something.'

Alexio cupped her jaw. She *would* sleep with him. They both knew it.

'I think you've already made your morals clear, and I respect that. Firstly, you are *not* staying in a hostel or anywhere else.' His voice was rough. 'Secondly, I do not expect you to sleep with me to pay me for the room. *If* you sleep with me it will be because you want to. Not for any other reason. We're two consenting adults, Sidonie, not bound by any ties. Free to do as we wish...'

She was breathless now. He could feel her chest moving against him and he wanted to groan.

'Yes...but after tonight we won't see each other again... I don't do one-night stands. We barely know each other.'

Alexio bent his head and feathered a kiss at the corner of one succulent pouting lip. He could feel her yielding against him.

'I already know more about you than I do about my own secretary. And I thought you said you couldn't get a flight for at least a couple of days...so that's two nights... And you know what? You think too much. Tomorrow is a long way away. We have tonight, and that's all that matters right now.'

Alexio's apartment was not as Sidonie had expected. She'd anticipated some kind of penthouse apartment in a sleek building, but his loft-style apartment was in an old converted redbrick building on the Thames, with stunning views.

It had huge windows and exposed brick walls. Sleek and modern furnishings married well with the old shell of the building. Abstract art and compelling black and white photos hung on the walls. The furnishings were unmistakably masculine, but not in an off-putting way. It was comfortable.

Alexio was standing with his arms crossed, watching her. Sidonie blushed and answered his look. She shrugged slightly. 'I'd expected something a bit more...'

'Generic? Without taste?' Alexio put a hand to his chest. 'You wound me...although maybe when you see this your suspicions will be proved right.'

He took her hand and led her to an alcove off the main open-plan living area. It was a dark nook, decorated like an opulent private gentlemen's club, with a pool table and a fully stocked antique bar. A huge mirror behind the bar made the whole space glitter with decadence.

Sidonie smiled. 'Now, this is more like it.'

Alexio let her go and moved to the bar. He disappeared behind the counter to re-emerge holding a chilled bottle of champagne and two glasses.

Sidonie's skin prickled.

He arched a brow. 'Can I tempt you with an aperitif?'

Sidonie saw then how the light was lengthening outside the huge stunning windows and over London. London Bridge was in view—an iconic landmark. She hadn't even noticed that the day had almost flown by.

Vowing to stop thinking so much and just to enjoy, she went and perched herself on one of the velvet-covered stools.

'I'd love one, thank you.'

Alexio expertly popped the cork with only the smallest, most sibilant hiss, and poured them both a glass of the sparkling golden liquid. Sidonie tried not to notice the label, which proclaimed it to be one of the most expensive brands in the world.

Don't think. Enjoy.

He handed her a glass and then came around the counter to stand in front of her. If she widened her legs Alexio could step right between them. Sidonie's pulse leapt.

But he merely clinked his glass to hers and said, 'To us, Sidonie Fitzgerald. Thank you for coming with me today.'

Sidonie couldn't look away from that green gaze. 'Cheers…and thank you for your hospitality.'

They both took a sip and Sidonie blinked at the effervescent bubbles rushing down her throat. She felt buoyed up, heady. Alexio took her hand again and something within her loved the way he did it.

He tugged her gently from the stool. 'Let me give you the tour.'

Carrying their glasses, Alexio brought her through the living area and showed her the sleek kitchen, which again had a lived-in look about it.

'Do you cook?' she asked curiously.

He shrugged minutely. 'I can cook enough for me. I wouldn't put it to the test of a dinner party, though.'

Sidonie teased him to hide her nervousness. 'So what have you lined up for tonight? Beans on toast?'

He looked back at her. 'A chef from one of London's best restaurants. He'll be arriving to serve us in about an hour.'

'Oh…' That shut Sidonie up. For a second she'd almost forgotten who she was with…

Alexio was leading her up some wooden stairs now, with brass railing banisters. There was glass everywhere, all the spaces blending into one another seamlessly as only the best architecture could.

This upper level was like a mezzanine. Alexio was leading her to a room on the left, and Sidonie could see her bag on a huge white-covered bed. A window looked out over the Thames, and the *en suite* bathroom was rustic and yet delightfully modern, with two sinks and an enormous wet-room-style shower. A huge antique bath stood alone.

'It's gorgeous,' she breathed, her hand tightening unconsciously around Alexio's fingers.

He exerted pressure back and she looked at him.

'This is your room, Sidonie. Like I said, I don't expect you to sleep with me…but I won't deny that I want you.'

Just that. Stark. No games. No false seduction. He wanted her. It was devastating in its simplicity.

Feeling shaky, Sidonie just replied, 'Okay…thank you…'

Before they left he showed her how to pull the huge white curtains across the windows that were both walls and door for privacy.

Then he was leading her out along the corridor to another room. This one had to be his. Much larger. Bare but for some choice furniture. An enormous bed, a chair, a wardrobe and a chest of drawers. And again that amazing view.

His *en suite* bathroom was black-tiled, undeniably masculine.

They came back out and Alexio showed her two other guest rooms and an office that looked to be equipped with enough technology to make a space rocket take off.

'London is my next main base after Athens,' he explained. 'I spend most of my time between here and there.'

He led her back down to the bar and Sidonie perched on the stool again. Alexio refilled her glass and then produced a bowl of fresh strawberries from somewhere. Sidonie almost groaned when he dipped one in champagne and handed it to her. The taste of the sweetly tart fruit exploded in her mouth. She wasn't unaware of his intent look at her mouth and she melted inside. She knew that at some point she would have to make things very clear to herself about how far she was prepared to go, because Alexio was waiting for the barest sign of encouragement. And yet she believed him when he said he'd leave it up to her. He wouldn't put pressure on her. He wouldn't have to!

Speaking of inconsequential things as the light outside Alexio's apartment faded into dusk, Sidonie felt herself being more and more seduced. That line she didn't want to cross was blurring and becoming something she wanted to leap over. The sparkling wine did little to help her keep her inhibitions raised.

After a while Alexio glanced at his watch and made a face. 'I don't know about you but I'd like to freshen up—and the chef will be here soon.'

Immediately he said that Sidonie felt sticky after the long day. She nodded. 'I'd love to have a shower...if that's okay.'

Alexio looked at her, and she was shocked and thrilled at the explicitness of it.

'Meet you back down here in twenty minutes?'

'Okay.' Sidonie slid off the stool.

She relished the opportunity to get some space, even for a few minutes. Alexio was so all-encompassing. She still couldn't really believe she was here, with him.

When she let herself into her bedroom she pulled the drapes over the door and windows, marvelling again at the genius design. She went to the main windows overlooking the view and opened one, breathing in the late spring London air.

London Bridge was teeming with traffic, but Sidonie felt deliciously cut off from everything. The real world was fading, being held at bay. With Tante Josephine safe, and away from her own worries, Sidonie could fool herself into thinking she had no responsibilities. She could just...*indulge*.

Realising that she was standing mooning at the view, she galvanised herself into action, unpacked some things and took her shower.

Afterwards, wrapped in a towel, she bit her lip as she looked at her pathetic clothes options. Jeans and more jeans. T-shirts. She had one smart outfit that she'd brought over for the meeting with the solicitor, but that was a black skirt she'd worn for work as a waitress and a black shirt. She'd look as if she was going to a funeral.

Clothes had become a luxury a long time ago, when she'd sold most of her more expensive items to help pay for college while her father had been struggling.

She felt absurdly gauche right then, knowing that Alexio must be used to women who dressed like...*women*. Not impoverished students. Which was what she was. But what she wouldn't give right now for some sleek little black number...

Sighing deeply, Sidonie reached for a pair of dark denims that might be construed as smart and selected a grey T-shirt with a glittery sequin design on the shoulders. She slipped on the slingback heels she'd worn for the meeting and, after inspecting herself in the mirror and balking at her freshly scrubbed pink face, applied some make-up to try and make up for her woefully inappropriate outfit.

She was tempted to put her hair up again, but recalled Alexio taking it down earlier. The thought of those hands and long fingers touching her made her leave it alone. She didn't want to tempt him in any way unless she was competely prepared for his response. But then, she didn't think she'd ever be prepared for the response of a man like Alexio.

Sidonie took a deep breath, as if that might ease the tumult in her breast and in her blood. The ease with which this relative stranger seemed to have sneaked under her skin scared her and exhilarated her in equal measure. It was like being on a rollercoaster ride with no one at the controls.

CHAPTER FOUR

ALEXIO CAUGHT A movement out of the corner of his eye and looked up from where he was pouring some wine into two glasses. His heart stopped in his chest.

Sidonie stood at the bottom of the stairs, her hands clasped together. She was in black figure-hugging denims and pointy shoes. She wore a grey T-shirt with something that sparkled on its shoulders. She hadn't put her hair up—*because she knew he'd just take it down?*—and it tumbled over her shoulders, glowing with an inner fire that flared under certain lights.

Despite the obvious cheapness of her clothes, once again he was struck by her natural beauty, and he wondered how on earth he'd ever dismissed her. The jeans he'd put on felt restrictive, and he gritted his jaw against his newly rampant libido. He had been mourning its dysfunction only twenty-four hours ago. The irony was not lost on him.

He put down the wine bottle and walked over. He saw her cheeks flush as he got nearer. His blood leapt in response. It was as if they were linked. Attuned to exactly the same rhythms. Making love with this woman… Alexio knew instinctively that one night would not be enough, but he pushed that revelation down rather than deal with the skin-prickling awareness of something dangerous that accompanied it.

She looked nervous and gestured to her clothes, clearly

self-conscious, making Alexio feel as if he wanted to re-assure her in a way that no other woman of his acquaintance ever needed.

'I didn't come prepared for a fancy dinner. You'll have to excuse me.'

Alexio took her hand. His voice was gruff. 'I want you to be comfortable. I didn't make much effort either.'

He saw her eyes drop to take in his plain white shirt and faded jeans. Bare feet. She looked back up again and her eyes had grown wider, their pupils dilated. Her cheeks were more flushed. *She wanted him.*

She obviously heard movement in the kitchen and said, 'Was I longer than twenty minutes?'

He smiled. 'About forty...but I allowed for that. It seems a safe bet where a woman is concerned.'

He immediately saw the aquamarine fire in her eyes, the way her small chin tipped up, and expected a tart reply. But he wouldn't let her hand go when she tried to pull away. He had to keep touching her. It was like a compulsive need.

'You've known a lot of women, then, to make this empirical study of their time-keeping on a general level?'

Alexio's smile faded. He could see past the bluster to where there was a hint of genuine insecurity. He touched her jaw and saw her mouth firm, as if warding off his effect on her.

'I'm no monk, *glikia mou*. But neither am I half as promiscuous as the press would like to paint me. When I take lovers I'm always up front. I don't offer anything more than mutual satisfaction. I'm not into relationships right now.'

Sidonie looked at him with that incredibly direct gaze that seemed to sear straight through him.

'Okay...' she said, and smiled, showing that gap between her teeth.

Alexio wanted to throw her over his shoulder so that he could take her upstairs right now and to hell with dinner.

She grinned then in earnest, and bent down to do something. Alexio saw her shoes being kicked off on the floor and her height dropped by an inch.

'Well, seeing as you're not making an effort to wear shoes,' she clarified, 'I don't see why I have to go through the pain.'

Before he did something to inadvertently demonstrate how off-centre she made him feel, Alexio tugged her towards the dining area, where a table had been laid for two, complete with lit candles. It was by the window, with a view of London lit up by night beyond the river and the bridge.

The chef's assistant was setting out their starters and Alexio said, 'Thanks, Jonathan. I think we can take it from here. Say thank you to Michel for me.'

The young man exited swiftly.

Alexio had done this many times before—for business meals in his apartment as well as for women—but tonight it felt different. Sidonie was looking at everything with such wide eyes.

'I presumed you were joking earlier about being a vegetarian.'

Alexio lifted the platter's lid to reveal *confit* duck dumplings and saw Sidonie's eyes gleam with anticipation. It had a direct effect on his body, and he wondered if she would have that same hungry look when they made love.

She had the grace to glance at him sheepishly. 'I had you figured for a chest-beating carnivore who would be horrified at the thought of watching me chew a lettuce leaf for half an hour.'

Alexio held Sidonie's chair out for her so she could sit down, and said in a low, throaty voice as she did so, 'I had a vegetarian option lined up just in case…but don't you know by now that nothing you could have said would have put me off?'

He was rewarded by pink cheeks when he took his own

seat opposite her. He raised his glass of white wine and she took hers. *'Yiamas.'*

Sidonie repeated the Greek phrase. They both took a sip of their drinks and Alexio dished out the starter.

'Don't you know by now that nothing you could have said would have put me off?' Alexio's softly delivered words still echoed in Sidonie's head. The steel behind them…

He had just taken their dessert plates into the kitchen and Sidonie was standing on the small terrace which hugged the side of the building, leaning on the railing, with the Thames moving beneath her feet somewhere in the dark.

In all honesty she couldn't have recalled, if asked, what they'd just eaten except to know that it had been exquisite. She'd been too mesmerised by her charismatic dinner companion and how easily the conversation had flowed. Like on the plane, once they'd started they hadn't stopped. Every now and then a tiny jolt of electric shock had run through her at the realisation of where she was and with whom… She'd met him only hours before… She should be back in Dublin, reorganising her life…

She still wanted to cringe when she thought of the way Alexio had looked her up and down when she'd arrived downstairs in her jeans and T-shirt, acutely conscious of how tatty she must look. The fact that he was equally dressed down had been little comfort, because she'd almost melted on the spot at seeing him in the faded hip-hugging jeans and white shirt. He epitomised cool, laid-back elegance.

To give him credit, he hadn't made her feel uncomfortable. Just hot and bothered…

She heard a noise in the kitchen and turned round to see Alexio putting plates in a dishwasher. She shook her head wryly. Who would have believed it?

She walked back in to help. He stood up tall.

'Coffee? An after-dinner liqueur?'

Sidonie put the last plate in the dishwasher and closed the door. She'd made a decision during dinner—a momentous one. It had been helped by the direct way he'd informed her earlier that he wasn't *'into relationships'*. Well, neither was she. Not when she faced such a huge upheaval in her life, and not when she had responsibilities. And certainly not when the man was Alexio Christakos and so far out of her league it wasn't funny.

During dinner Sidonie had recalled the name of a favourite perfume of her mother's: *Ce Soir ou Jamais.* Tonight or never. This evening felt all too ephemeral. She wanted to seize the moment, live it fully. She wanted this man with a hunger she knew was rare. Once in a lifetime.

She turned and put her hands behind her against the counter and looked up. *Was she really going to do this?* Her sex spasmed in response. *Yes.* She wanted one night with this man, just one night of decadent escapism, and then she would walk away knowing what it was like to be truly made love to.

Having no idea how to go about letting a man like Alexio know what she wanted, without declaring baldly that she wanted to have sex with him, Sidonie seized on an idea. 'I'd like a liqueur, please…and did I mention that I'm a mean pool-player?'

Alexio went still and shook his head. 'No, you did not. I believe we touched on many subjects over dinner, including favourite films and music, and you tried to trick me into telling you the secrets of my success, but there was no mention of your pool abilities.'

Sidonie bit back a grin. And a sigh. This man should come with a warning label: *Approach with caution! You are liable to get burnt if you stand too close.* It was too late for her. She would burn for ever in the tormenting hell of regret if she didn't allow herself to indulge in this fantasy.

'Well, I happened to be something of a local champion in college. And I would like to challenge you to a game, Mr Christakos.'

Alexio leant back against the opposite counter and crossed his arms. 'Interesting, Miss Fitzgerald. Tell me... are there terms for this challenge?'

Sidonie crossed her arms too and tried to look mock serious—not as far out of her depth as she felt. 'Of course. My terms are simple: whoever wins gets to decide what we do for the rest of the night.'

Sidonie's heart was beating so hard now she felt light-headed. Alexio looked serious, but his eyes had darkened.

'I take it that if you win your choice will be...?'

Sidonie affected an air of piety. 'To go to bed with a good book, of course.'

His eyes flashed. 'And if I win...and I ask you nicely to come to bed with me...?'

Sidonie shrugged minutely. 'Then I guess I'll have to suffer the consequences.' She straightened up and dropped her arms. 'But you won't win, so maybe I should just leave now...'

She made to walk off and like lightning Alexio grabbed her hand and hauled her into him. Sidonie gasped. His body was hard all over, pressed against hers. Her legs promptly turned to jelly.

'Not so fast.' His voice was low, seductive. 'I believe you challenged me to a game, and in light of the fact that I'm doomed to failure I'd like to raise the stakes a little... For every shot lost, we also lose a piece of clothing.'

Sidonie's blood rushed to her every erogenous zone at the thought of seeing Alexio bared. 'There's no such game,' she said breathlessly as Alexio pulled her in the direction of the bar and games room.

'There is now, sweetheart.'

Alexio let Sidonie go when they got into the darkened

room. After he had poured them both drinks—a liqueur for her and a whisky for him—he took out two cues and handed her one. Sidonie made a big show of chalking it up while Alexio put out the balls.

When they were laid out he flourished an arm. 'Please, ladies first.'

Sidonie moved around the table, deliciously aware of Alexio's eyes on her, and yet still a little terrified. She wasn't sure what demon had made her come up with this idea—as if she thought she could make it look as if her decision *wasn't* fuelled with the desperate need she really felt. As if she played these kinds of games with men all the time.

Eventually she settled on a point to start and positioned herself, drawing back the cue. She was on the opposite side of the room to Alexio and he sat with his hip was hitched against a stool, his legs long, thighs powerful underneath the denim. Distracting her already.

'Take as long as you like,' he said, in a patronising tone which enflamed Sidonie enough for her to scatter the balls masterfully, potting her first one.

She stood up and smiled. 'You were saying…?'

Alexio scowled. 'Beginner's luck.'

Sidonie walked around the table again, aware of the tension in the small room thickening. As she took her next shot she realised too late that her palms were sweaty and the cue slipped slightly, throwing her off and making her lose her aim. She missed.

Alexio tsked and stood up. Sidonie's heart thumped hard. *For every shot lost, we also lose a piece of clothing.* Alexio smiled and it was the smile of the devil.

'I don't mind what goes, but I'd suggest your T-shirt or your trousers.'

Now Sidonie scowled. She'd thought she'd have a little more time. She'd also thought she'd have him almost naked before her, giving her time to get used to it. Then she thought of something and smiled sweetly, executing a nimble move so that she undid her bra, pulled its strap down one arm and then pulled it out neatly from the armhole of her T-shirt. An old boarding school trick.

Alexio's face darkened ominously. 'That's cheating.'

Sidonie grinned. 'Not at all. I took your suggestion on board and ignored it.'

She tossed her bright pink bra onto the seat beside her and saw Alexio's eyes follow the movement and then come back to linger on her braless chest. Her breasts felt tight and heavy, their tips pushing against the cotton of her top. Alexio's cheeks flushed and it had a direct effect on the pulse in her groin.

Slowly he put down his drink and stood up. Sidonie crossed her arms and then quickly thought better of it when Alexio's eyes widened and she realised she was only making things worse.

He took his eyes off her with visible effort. Despite all their play, Sidonie's blood was infused with a heady feminine energy at having this man look at her with such naked desire. But she got distracted when he came close and bent over the pool table right in front of her, and her eye was drawn helplessly to his taut, muscular buttocks.

She couldn't see exactly what he was doing, but he'd hit the ball and nothing was pocketed.

He turned around and said, 'Whoops…' and started undoing his shirt.

Sidonie's mouth went dry at seeing his torso revealed bit by bit. And when he shrugged the shirt off completely she went weak at the knees.

He was stunning. Beautifully muscled. Not an ounce of fat. Broad and powerful. Very masculine whorls of hair dusted his chest, leading down to that tantalising line which disappeared into his jeans. They clung precariously to his hips and Sidonie had to clench her hands to fists to stop herself reaching out to undo that top button. She gulped when she saw the bulge pushing insistently against the denim.

His rough voice cut through the heat in her brain. 'Your turn, I think.'

He turned to walk away and Sidonie felt as if someone had just hit her. His back was as beautiful as his front. Wide and smooth. He turned around at the bar and leant on it nonchalantly, arched a brow.

Sidonie forced herself to move and looked at the table. She couldn't seem to compute what to do any more. She hadn't been boasting—she knew she could play and quite possibly beat Alexio on a good day. But right now…she was useless. Eventually she saw the shot she needed to take. But she couldn't get that torso out of her mind, those muscles rippling under silken flesh. *Hard.*

Predictably, Sidonie missed the shot—because just as she moved so did Alexio. She stood up and glared across at him, feeling hot. 'Now, *that's* cheating.'

He arched a brow, all innocence wrapped up in the devil—*again.* 'I don't know what you're talking about…'

And then his look changed to one so carnal her toes curled.

'Shirt or trousers, Sidonie—unless you've got some very cute way to take off your panties from under your jeans without removing them.'

Of course she didn't. Sidonie huffed. She only had one choice, really. She wasn't about to bare herself completely to the sexiest man she'd ever met. So off came the jeans. She wriggled out of them, deliberately avoiding his gaze, self-conscious in her very plain white panties decorated with flowers.

Alexio watched with a heavy-lidded gaze as Sidonie carefully folded her jeans and put them to the side, near the bright pink splash of her bra. The same pink bra that had been tantalising him all day. The way she folded her jeans made him feel weak inside. There was something curiously vulnerable about it.

Now she looked at him, and her chin was up. *Brave*. She wasn't half as confident as she was letting on. Alexio hid the way that made him feel by focusing on her gently swaying breasts beneath her T-shirt. They were beautifully rounded and pert. Their tips hard. His mouth watered. His erection got harder. He had to shift on the stool.

Her hips were slim, but womanly. Her panties looked positively virginal with their cute flowers. Yet the way she was looking at him now as he caught her gaze again was anything but virginal. *Good*. Because when they came together Alexio knew he wouldn't have the patience to go slowly.

Aware that he couldn't actually stand up without revealing how turned on he was, Alexio said, 'I'm feeling generous. You can have another shot.'

Sidonie looked determined this time. 'That's the last piece of clothing I'll be removing.'

She picked up the cue and moved around the table again, clad only in her T-shirt and panties. The soft white cotton hugged her bottom, revealed in all its lushness now.

Alexio had to admit that his jaded palate was well and truly *un*jaded now. He'd never been so turned on in his life. He'd never been brought so close to the edge without even touching a woman before.

And then Sidonie stopped right in front of him, her back to him. He saw a sliver of pale skin, the gentle curve of her lower back just over the band of her panties. He saw the two dimples of Venus above her buttocks and nearly groaned out loud.

When she bent over the table and widened her legs to get a better aim the tiny thread holding his control together snapped completely. With a feral sound Alexio wrapped an arm around her bare midriff and deftly scooped Sidonie back against him, ignoring her soft squeal of surprise. He took the cue out of her hands, throwing it to one side.

She was breathing heavily. 'That's not fair. That's blatantly against the rules. Obstruction.'

'Damn the rules,' Alexio growled, turning Sidonie around to face him. Her eyes were dark blue now, the pupils huge.

'You win. I forfeit the game,' he said.

Sidonie couldn't hide the crestfallen expression on her face as she obviously considered for a second that she had been hoist by her own petard. Alexio wanted to howl in triumph, but he played it out.

'So I guess this means you're going to bed with a book then?'

Sidonie looked sheepish. 'I don't have one with me apart from my textbook.'

Alexio made a face. 'Too bad…maybe I can change your mind?'

'How are you going to do that?'

Sidonie's breath was getting choppier. Her breasts under their thin cotton covering were teasing his bare skin now, making him harder.

'Like this…'

Alexio picked her up and sat her on the edge of the pool table, then came to stand between her spread legs. He cupped her face and her jaw in his hands and did what he'd been aching to do all evening: he covered her mouth with his and sank into dark, sweet, urgent oblivion.

Sidonie clutched Alexio's wide shoulders, her fingers digging into smooth hot skin. The question had been asked and answered. He knew she wanted this.

He felt so good between her legs—so big. Instinctively her bare thighs tightened around him, and the friction of her skin against the tough denim was exquisite. Their tongues met and duelled fiercely, stroking, sucking. Between Sidonie's legs she spasmed and squirmed, seeking more contact with Alexio.

She was barely aware of one of his big hands leaving her face and going to the bottom of her T-shirt, tugging it up, urging her to lift her arms so he could lift it off completely, breaking the contact between their mouths to do so.

She opened her eyes and felt dizzy. Her T-shirt was a blur of grey behind Alexio, hanging precariously on the stool. Now she only wore her panties.

He looked down between their bodies and his hot gaze rested on her bared breasts. Sidonie had been naked in front of a man before…but it had never felt like this. As if she was on fire from the inside out. Her breasts literally throbbed for his touch. Aching…

He cupped them, making her flesh tingle. His thumbs rubbed back and forth across her tight, sensitised nipples and Sidonie dragged in a painful breath. Her heart was beating so loudly she thought it had to be audible.

'You're beautiful…'

Sidonie shook her head, about to deny his compliment, but he took the words out of her mouth as he pushed her back slightly and bent to take one straining peak into his mouth, sucking hard. Sidonie gasped. One hand went to his head, fingers tangling in short silky hair, the other moved behind her, balancing.

It was as if a wire of need was linked directly to the pulse between her legs, tightening the tension inside her, making her arch her back towards him. She felt desperate, wanton. When he moved to her other breast his hand cupped her intimately between her legs, and Sidonie moaned as he pressed against her where every nerve seemed to be screaming out for release.

One of Alexio's fingers slipped behind her underwear

and stroked her where she ached most. Sidonie's breath stopped completely. His mouth was on her breast and that wicked finger was circling, exploring...

She was approaching her peak... She could sense it... The rhythmic pulsations of her body were gathering force—and then Alexio abruptly pulled back and stood up. Sidonie had to put her hands on his hips to stay upright. Everything had turned molten inside her.

'Not here...' he said roughly, his breath uneven.

'Wh—?'

But Sidonie's question was halted as she was scooped up into Alexio's arms and he strode through the apartment to the stairs. Her arms had gone around his neck automatically and the friction of his chest against her deeply sensitised breasts was almost excruciating.

She looked at his face and his jaw was tight. He glanced down at her and that sexy mouth tipped up at one corner. Butterflies danced with the lava in her belly.

He said, 'I refuse to take you on a pool table for the first time. I've been fantasising all day about laying you out and tasting every inch of you, and for that we need a bed.'

The heat inside Sidonie shot to boiling point at the thought of him *fantasising* about this, and at the thought of being spreadeagled, naked, for this man to explore. And that this would be their *first* time, not their only time.

'Oh...' was all she could manage as Alexio shouldered his way into his room, which was dark apart from one low light in the corner and the glittering lights of the city outside.

When he got to the bed he laid Sidonie down and stood back. She was breathless. Her body was still hovering on the edge of fulfilment and she ached for completion. But she sensed that Alexio wasn't about to allow either of them a quick release.

As if reading her mind, he said throatily, 'I want you so

much that I'm tempted to take you now, hard and fast... I want to...'

She'd never experienced hard and fast. She'd experienced mundane and underwhelming. Feeling unaccountably shy, although she was all but naked and panting for the man, Sidonie said in a small voice, 'I don't mind...'

Alexio shook his head and looked grim, his hands going to his jeans, where Sidonie's eyes dropped to watch with mounting fascination.

'No, you don't get off that easily—not after that little sideshow back there.'

Sidonie couldn't drag her gaze back up. She could only watch, helpless, as Alexio opened his buttons and then pushed his jeans down, taking his underwear with them. Her eyes widened and she went even hotter, if that was possible. He was...*magnificent*. And *big*.

A shiver of trepidation ran through her and finally she managed to look at him.

He almost grimaced at her wide eyes. 'Another reason why this won't be hard and fast... I need to make sure you're ready... I don't want to hurt you.'

His concern made Sidonie's chest constrict, and even through the heat haze engulfing her she was aware of a little voice: *danger...danger...*

But then Alexio was bending over her, his big hands making quick work of her underwear, tugging it off her hips and down her legs.

He stood back and looked at her again. Sidonie wanted to turn away and hide herself. Instantly self-conscious. Was he measuring her up against his last lover? Finding her wanting? A disappointment? Did the fact that she wasn't shaved everywhere turn him off?

She brought her arm over her breasts and turned her head, unable to watch him looking at her so intently. And then the bed dipped and his long, powerful body was beside her, legs touching hers, his erection between them, his arms coming around her.

'Don't feel shy…' His hand tipped her chin towards him so she had to meet his gaze. 'You're beautiful…and I want you more than I've ever wanted anyone.'

Sidonie looked into those gorgeous exotic eyes and searched for some hint of insincerity. She couldn't see it. She could see something, though—something unguarded for a moment, as if he was surprised by what he'd said. She was afraid of the tug of emotion in the pit of her being.

Suddenly Sidonie was aware of thinking too much again, and she put her hand up to touch his jaw, reached up to kiss him. All she knew was that she wanted him too—more than anything she'd ever experienced.

When he drew her into his body so that they were touching length to length a wave of intense desire washed through her, brushing aside any doubts and questions. She wanted Alexio to slide into her right then, couldn't bear the thought of the drawn-out torture he'd promised to inflict, and as if reading her mind—*again*—he stopped and pulled back for a moment.

His voice was guttural. 'I don't think I can wait—as much as I want to…'

Sidonie moved so that his leg slid between hers. She could feel how wet she was, ready for him, and she moved against his thigh. His eyes flared.

'I don't want you to wait… I need you too.'

It was a primal, urgent request. Alexio reached behind him to a small cabinet by the bed and took something out. Sidonie realised what it was when he ripped open the foil packet and stroked the condom onto his thick length.

Pressing her down, Alexio came over her, pushing her legs apart. He reached between them and touched her with his fingers, stroking her, entering her. She bent her knees on either side of him and had to bite the inside of her cheek to stop herself from begging him to stop...to go on.

And then he took his hand away and he was guiding the thickness of his erection to her soft folds, pushing in gently, stretching her. Pushing deeper. He was awe-inspiring as he loomed over her. Shoulders broad and powerful, chest sheened with sweat. He pushed her knees further apart, baring her to him completely. Demanding she open up to him.

Something was happening inside Sidonie—some awakening. She'd had sex before, but this felt different. Infinitely different. Slowly, inch by torturous inch, Alexio slid into her, giving her time to adapt and take him, his eyes never leaving hers. She saw sweat break out on his brow, felt the tension in his big body.

'*Moro mou*...you're so tight...'

Instinctively Sidonie tilted her hips, forcing Alexio to thrust deeper, and the movement made her gasp. He filled her now completely.

'Are you okay?' he asked.

Sidonie was speechless. But she nodded. She *was* okay. More than okay. She felt whole, joined to him like this. She moved her hips again experimentally and Alexio drew out a little. Her body clasped at him as he went, already relishing the moment when he would slide back in again, seeking for that delicious friction.

With slow, deliberate thrusts Alexio moved in and out, and the storm grew again inside Sidonie, increasing in its strength and power. With every move of Alexio's body within hers something tightened inside her. He thrust a little harder and Sidonie welcomed it, feeling it burn but not noticing because she ached for it too much.

The tempo changed, became more desperate. Sidonie was aware of small sounds coming from her mouth— moans and laboured breathing, incoherent words. Alexio's body moved faster within hers now, gathering pace. He came closer, hands cupping her face, tangling in her hair, as his mouth met hers and his body thrust powerfully over and over again.

His tongue stabbed deep and she stroked him fiercely, teeth nipping, holding him to her with a desperation as they raced together, hearts thumping in unison.

Sidonie's arms were around his neck, her breasts pressed flat against his chest. She wrapped her legs around his hips. The crescendo was building, leaving her no control over anything. She was part of something huge, magical. Their mouths clung, their kisses became more desperate, biting, and then, just when she thought her body would break in two with the building tension, it broke apart into a million tiny pieces on a wave of orgasmic pleasure, robbing Sidonie of every rational thought. She was flung high into a place she'd never dreamed existed.

Alexio's powerful body thrust one more time and he broke free of their kiss and shouted out as his release swept him up too, seconds behind her.

Sidonie realised she was trembling in the aftermath and was horrified. She tried to pull away from Alexio but he only dragged her closer, wrapping his arms around her until the tremors ceased. She felt more than a little over-whelmed. Alexio pulled his head back and looked at her. She was almost afraid to look at him—afraid he might see something she wasn't ready to expose yet.

'Sidonie…?'

Reluctantly she looked at him and his eyes were molten, still. It had an instant effect on her body. Already. She felt ashamed. How could she want him again so soon?

He was frowning now, pulling away from her, and she tried not to be acutely aware of her nakedness, of feeling vulnerable.

He rested on one elbow. 'Did I hurt you? You weren't innocent?'

Sidonie came up on one elbow too. She shook her head, her hair falling forward. Alexio brushed it back and something about that small gesture heartened her. 'No,' she admitted huskily. 'I've been with a couple of guys. In college. But…it was never like that…I didn't…'

She stopped and went puce, looked down at the sheet. Predictably Alexio tipped her chin up again, not letting her escape.

'You didn't…what? Come like that?'

Sidonie shook her head, mortified to be talking about this when she imagined that his usual post-coital repartee must be far more sophisticated. Still, she was stuck now.

'No,' she got out. 'I mean, I've…*come*…before, but not during sex. Not with a guy.'

Alexio's voice seemed to drop an octave and it sent shivers of sensation right to her core. 'You mean you've experienced it when you've…?'

'Done it to myself. Yes…'

Sidonie glared at him now, beyond embarrassed, and not remotely mollified by the way his eyes had darkened suspiciously. 'Can we stop talking about this now?'

Sidonie reached for the sheet, trying to tuck it around her, but Alexio swatted her hands away and pulled her into him, making her gasp when tender flesh came into contact with his fast reviving arousal.

'I'm glad you told me,' he said gruffly. 'And those guys were idiots.'

The embarrassment drained away, leaving Sidonie feeling the effects of their lovemaking again. Her body was sensitive all over, but sated in a way that was truly wicked.

With awe-inspiring strength Alexio scooped her up and took her into the bathroom with its black-tiled shower. He put her down, keeping an arm around her, and leaned in to turn on the powerful spray. Then he walked her into the shower, following right behind her.

It was pure bliss to have steaming water pounding her skin and then Alexio's big hands, soapy, running all over her body. Over her breasts and belly, down between her legs, across her buttocks. His touch wasn't overtly sexual, but she could see his erection and her body hummed with satisfaction, ready to flare fully back to life if only she wasn't feeling equally ready to crawl into a small space and sleep.

She could only sag against the wall and look at him, so huge and dark in the hot mist, like some kind of pagan warrior. She was boneless, and as if he could sense the lethargy rolling through her body he turned off the spray and wrapped her in a towel, rubbing her brusquely before scooping up her long hair and wrapping it up turban-style.

Then he picked her up again and Sidonie protested weakly. 'I *can* walk, you know.' But even as she said the words she doubted that she could walk right now.

Alexio pulled back the covers and laid her gently on the bed. Sidonie's eyes were already closing and she fought to keep them open, aware of the towel on her head.

'My hair will be frizzy...' she protested sleepily.

Alexio pulled a cover over her, still naked and damp from the shower himself. Sidonie was very aware of that.

'Shh, it'll be fine. You need to rest now. I'll be back in a minute.' He pressed his mouth to her forehead.

Sidonie cracked her eyes open enough to see Alexio drag on his jeans, leaving them tantalisingly open, before he walked out of the room. And then it was too much to fight. She slid into sweet oblivion.

CHAPTER FIVE

WHEN ALEXIO POURED whisky into the glass his hand was shaking. He'd had to get away from Sidonie and he cursed himself for thinking it would be a good idea to take her into the shower. Washing her supple body, seeing her delicate skin marked after their making love and knowing he couldn't touch her again so soon, had been a torture he wouldn't inflict on an enemy.

He'd barely been able to walk away from her in bed, even though her eyes had been closing.

Sex. It had been sex. Alexio knew all about sex. He'd been having it and excelling at it pretty much since he'd been seduced by the sister of a friend of his older brother at the age of fifteen.

But what he'd just experienced up there in his bedroom, with someone he'd met mere hours before, had not been any kind of sex he knew. It had blown his mind. And yet they'd done nothing kinky... Apart from that little strip-tease downstairs it had been perfectly straightforward. Sidonie obviously wasn't experienced.

Alexio's brain struggled to grapple with this anomaly. Was it that? That she was a little gauche? Was his palate so jaded that the sheer novelty of an inexperienced lover turned him on?

But he knew in his gut it was more than that. Deeper. And he hated to admit it. Alexio threw the whisky down his throat as if it could burn away the hunger that was already building again, which had abated only for mere seconds after his orgasm. He prided himself on his stamina, but this was ridiculous.

When he went back into his room Sidonie had shifted to lie on her front. The sheet clung precariously to her bottom, barely hiding its voluptuous swell, and those dimples were making his mouth water. Her hair had come out of the towel, which had been flung aside haphazardly, and the damp strawberry golden tresses were spread out around her head like glowing halo.

Alexio curled his hands into fists. No way could he go near her on that bed and not rouse her and make love to her again. Silently he turned and took his aching body to his office, where he tried to distract himself with some work.

After staring at the computer screen for a while and seeing nothing but the memory of Sidonie's face as he'd slid into her tight body for the first time, he sat back and rubbed his hands over his face. This was crazy. He was useless. He needed Sidonie again. *Now.*

When he padded back into the bedroom she had moved again and now lay on her back, the sheet pulled up, just about covering her breasts. She moved minutely, as if sensing him. He came close to the bed and saw those dark lashes flutter on pale cheeks scored with pink. Her mouth moved and he wanted to cover it with his. His gaze was riveted to its lush lines and he wondered again how he'd dismissed her at first glance.

'Hey...'

Her husky voice startled him. Her eyes were open, slumberous. Shy. Something punched him in the gut. He had the bizarre feeling that everything in his life up till now had been a bit of a blur and he quashed it ruthlessly. This was no different from anything he'd done before. It was a little more intense, maybe...good chemistry. That was it.

'Hey, yourself…mind if I join you?'

Sidonie shook her head and Alexio undid his jeans, taking them off. When he got into bed he couldn't *not* reach for Sidonie and she came willingly, her arms sliding around him like missing pieces of a jigsaw fitting together. Their mouths found each other and before Alexio could articulate another word he was giving up any attempt to rationalise what was happening because the urge not to think and just to *act* was stronger than anything he could resist.

'I want you to come to Greece with me.'

Sidonie was in paradise. A paradise where she felt at peace and sated and in a state of bliss she'd only ever read about. And that gorgeous voice…

'Sid…wake up.'

Sid. No one had ever called her that before. She liked it. A mouth brushed hers and Sidonie instinctively followed it, seeking more. The by now familiar spurt of desire and awareness was rousing her. *Arousing* her.

She opened her eyes to see Alexio's hard-boned stunning face and bare torso. She was aware of light flooding the big sparse room. Daylight. She blinked. Alexio hovered over her on one arm. His jaw was dark with stubble and she recalled feeling the delicious abrasion on her skin, her thighs. Her belly swooped alarmingly. A jumble of X-rated images tumbled through her mind and she had to breathe to try and not let them overwhelm her.

She remembered him waking her last night…making love to her again. Showing her that the first time, as spectacular as it had been, had only been a precursor. She'd never known it could be like that—so intensely, violently pleasurable. So altering. She felt different.

Alexio was looking at her, waiting for her to say something. Her voice felt rusty, hoarse from crying out over and over again. 'What did you say?'

His hand was on her bare belly under the sheet now and it quivered. Instantly Sidonie's body came to life, nerves tingling, skin tightening. As if well aware of his effect on her, Alexio moved his hand up with exquisite slowness until he cupped her breast, trapping her nipple between his fingers, tightening it gently, enough to pinch.

Sidonie sucked in a breath, wide awake now.

'I said,' he repeated, 'I want you to come to Greece with me. I have a place on Santorini. I've decided to take a few days' break…'

Sidonie automatically went to shake her head but Alexio's hand left her breast and swept up to cup her chin.

Softly he said, 'We've been here before, Sid…you know what happens if you say no to me.'

Sid. The way he said it made her feel as if she were drowning—as if she'd known this man for aeons when it had been a mere twenty-four hours. All she could see were those amazing golden-green eyes, hypnotising her. Drugging her.

'You said yourself you don't have a job to go back to…so why not extend your trip for a few days? Come with me… and I'll show you paradise.'

He bent his head to kiss Sidonie and she felt like letting out a short, shocked laugh. He'd already unwittingly shown her paradise. But then his mouth was on hers and she couldn't think. She struggled to try and focus. She knew that her aunt was safe and secure for a couple of weeks. All that responsibility hovered in the wings, but it didn't have to be dealt with right at this moment—could she stretch one night into a few days? She wanted to, with a fierceness that surprised her.

As Alexio moved over her body, sinking his hips between her thighs, his erection hard and ready, Sidonie was melting, weakening. She wasn't ready to walk away yet…

she wanted more of this man. More of this fantasy. More of this wicked self-indulgence.

She wrapped her arms around his neck and opened her legs to him and then, when he stopped kissing her for a few seconds, just before he joined their bodies, Sidonie looked up at him and said huskily, 'Okay...I'll come with you.'

Alexio Christakos was a magician. A sexy, devilish magician. Just over twenty-four hours after meeting him he had magicked her to an island in another country. Where everything was painted blue and white, where the sun sparkled overhead, and where the glittering sea stretched as far as the eye could see. There was nothing but the hazy shapes of more islands in the distance to break the horizon line.

Her hand was wrapped tightly in his as he showed her around his stupendously gorgeous villa near Oia, on the north-west coast of Santorini. Sidonie could feel the faint burn of secret muscles after the long hours of intense lovemaking the previous night. If she stopped to think about it all for a second she might explode...so she bit her lip and tried not to gape as he showed her into the master suite, which led directly out to a terrace featuring an infinity pool.

He glanced back at her, saying, 'I know you didn't exactly come prepared...there are some clothes here for your use.'

Sidonie watched as he let her hand go to open double doors which led into a walk-in closet. His clothes were hung up and laid out on the left hand side and the right hand side was bursting with a glorious kaleidoscope of colours and textures.

A funny pain lanced her chest. Of *course* he had a wardrobe stocked with women's clothes. This had to be a frequent pitstop for him with his lovers/mistresses. He was a generous man. She was sure many of the garments must still be unworn.

To buy time, and hide her reaction, Sidonie reached out and fingered a piece of silk which felt as delicate as air in her hands.

This whole experience was transitory and all this was doing was driving the point home. She had to *not* think about things like how attentive he'd been on the flight to Athens on his private jet—distracting her from her fear of flying with drugging kisses. Or the revelation on the helicopter flight to the island that instead of feeling her fear increasing she'd felt exhilarated.

Sidonie forced herself to smile and said with bright joviality, 'Well, at least I won't have to worry about washing my knickers out in the sink. I'm sure your housekeeper would be horrified.'

She looked at him and her smile slipped a little as she saw something hard in his eyes—something she hadn't seen before. But before she could dwell on it he'd stabbed his fingers deep in her hair and tipped her face up to his, distracting her with a mind-altering kiss.

When he finally pulled away they were breathing harshly and Sidonie's body trembled all over. She still wasn't used to this unprecedented physical reaction—as if she were some kind of a puppet and he could control her responses at will. It made her feel intensely vulnerable.

'Get changed and let's go for a swim.'

Sidonie burned at the thought of seeing Alexio's semi-naked body just for her private pleasure.

She managed a rough-sounding, 'Okay.'

And when he gently turned her around and pushed her in the direction of that wall of clothes again Sidonie tried in vain to stem the flood of emotions that made her hands shake as she searched for the relevant garments.

Sidonie wrapped her legs around Alexio's waist and her arms around his neck. His back was broad, strong and smooth between her legs and against her chest. They were both wet and salty after swimming in the sea at the bottom of a precipitious set of stone steps leading directly down from the villa. His arms were looped under her thighs as he carried her piggyback-style back up.

The sun was hot on Sidonie's back and Alexio grumbled good-naturedly, 'I'm not a mule, you know.'

She grinned and pressed a kiss to Alexio's neck, feeling his arms tighten under her legs. 'I know. You're much, much better-looking than a mule, and far more comfortable.'

She rested her head on his shoulder for a moment, squinting her eyes at the glittering endless azure blue of the sea. Three days had passed since they'd arrived at his villa. Three days of sun, sea and... She blushed at the thought of all the mind-blowing sex.

They'd only left the villa once. Yesterday evening Alexio had taken her out on a small boat into the Caldera where he'd surprised her with a light supper complete with wine. They'd had prime position for watching the famous Santorini sunset and Sidonie had never seen anything so stunning or special.

She'd felt absurdly emotional at the beauty of everything...at the experience that this man was unwittingly giving her when her life was about to change so dramatically. She was storing up every moment—morsels she would take out at a later date and comfort herself with.

An all but invisible housekeeper at the villa left out food at strategic times, so she and Alexio had done little but eat and sleep and make love. Sidonie felt sated on a level she'd never known before. Sated...but curiously unfulfilled too.

Conversation with Alexio never went beyond the superficial. It felt almost as if the level of closeness and intimacy she'd experienced when they'd first met had been closed off.

But then what had she expected? This was transient.

Alexio didn't do relationships, and neither was she in any position to cleave herself to a man.

Sidonie had realised that the only way she could get through this and remain in any way protected was to try and fool Alexio into believing that this wasn't half as special for her as it really was. So she was doing her best to project an air of vague nonchalance. Every time her mouth wanted to drop open in awe, or she wanted to squeal with excitement, she reined it in.

Because if she let her guard slip for a second Sidonie was terrified he would read the depth of her emotions—and as she wasn't even prepared to inspect them herself she certainly wasn't ready for his laser-like gaze to see them.

'I want to take you out tonight.'

Sidonie murmured something indistinct. Her cheek rested on Alexio's chest and one of her legs was thrown over his thighs. He could feel his body stir against her and despite the sated languor of his body he could have groaned. When would it end? This ever-present hunger?

His fingers trailed up and down Sidonie's spine. After carrying her up the steps from the sea earlier he'd walked her straight underneath the outdoor shower on his terrace, near the glittering infinity pool. The cool spray had done little to stem hisdesire. Within seconds Sidonie had been in his arms, her body pressed against his, and they'd inevitably ended up in bed.

Alexio forced his mind from the memory because it made him uncomfortable. 'Did you hear me, Sid? I want to take you out tonight...'

Sidonie eventually lifted her head and looked at Alexio with slumberous eyes and deliciously tousled hair. 'You might have to give me a piggyback again.'

Alexio tipped her chin up, averting her hungry gaze

from his mouth to his eyes. 'No. You're not going to tempt me again. We'll pretend we're civilised if it kills us.'

Sidonie shifted slightly so that she was moving on top of Alexio. His blood started to sizzle all over again. She spread her thighs either side of him and her breasts touched his chest, the hard nipples scraping against his chest hair, making him thicken with need.

He could see something in her eyes—something innately feminine and full of wicked mystery. She wriggled her bottom so that his erection pressed against her body, where she was already damp, ready for him again. And just like that Alexio had to give up any pretence that he could be civilised.

He took her hips in his hands, pushing her back so that he could thrust up and into her. Sidonie gasped at the intrusion and then sighed voluptuously as her body began to move against him, the delicious dance of desire starting all over again.

'Witch...' Alexio muttered as their movements became more urgent and they gave themselves up to the inexorable ride into ecstasy.

Alexio was waiting for Sidonie to emerge from the villa after her shower late that evening. The sun had set a while ago. They'd watched it from a lounger by the pool, both languid after their intense lovemaking. The spectacular sky was now fading into a faint orange and pink hue and the famous lights of Santorini's west coast were coming on.

Alexio was oblivious to it, though. He was feeling more and more off-balance. Exposed. And, even worse, vulnerable. The last time he'd felt like this had been in front of his mother as a child, when she'd coldly infected him with her cynicism. From then till now it had formed a part of his protective armour. It had become a second skin, and everything in his life had merely compounded his world view.

As soon as he'd turned his back on his inheritance so publicly his coterie of so-called friends and hangers-on had left him—apart from one or two people and his brother. Then, as soon as he'd shown signs of making a fortune, they'd come back in their droves.

Nothing much had surprised him after that telling experiment in human nature—as if he hadn't had enough lessons from his parents. *Until Sidonie.* She surprised him. She was like a whirling dervish, smashing everything in her path and taking him with her. He'd had no intention of taking a few days' holiday until he'd woken up beside her in London the morning after that night and felt the insistent throb of hunger in his blood and his body.

No way could he have let her go.

He'd known one night wouldn't be enough, but he'd felt then as if a month wouldn't be long enough to sate himself with her. Feeling slightly panicked, Alexio had decided that the best thing to do would be to take her away, so that he could indulge this desire day and night and let it burn out.

However, this was the third night, and he felt as if a lifetime wouldn't be enough to sate himself with Sidonie. He'd done his best to hold her at a distance, deliberately curbing the way she made him want to relax and speak whatever was on his mind. But it was hard. And getting harder.

When she'd leapt onto his back earlier, to be carried up the steps, Alexio's chest had swelled with an emotion that had made him shake. No woman he knew was so impulsive, so tactile, so effortlessly affectionate.

Yet despite her easy affection she wasn't suffocating him with emotion—far from it. She was holding back—exuding an air of nonchalance.

Something dark inside him had raised its ugly head. *Suspicion.* He remembered showing her the closet full of clothes on that first day. He'd expected shock, awe, gushing gratitude. Even his most cynical lovers never failed to put on an act when he presented them with gifts. But Sidonie, whom he would never have put in their category, had been completely blasé, and since then he hadn't been able to push down a niggle of disquiet.

One minute she was like an open book, her expressions as unguarded as a child's and equally disarming. The next she was as mysterious as the Sphinx, exhibiting an age-old feminine mystique that made him wonder if he was being completely naïve.

Alexio didn't like the reminder that from the moment he'd met Sidonie on that plane he'd been acting out of character. He *never* encouraged a woman to stay overnight in his apartment, even if they'd had dinner there. And he certainly never took off at a moment's notice, throwing his normally rigid schedule out of the window.

The growing doubt had prompted Alexio to put in a call to his most trusted employee and personal friend—his solicitor—just a short while before. He was one of the few who had stuck by Alexio's side through his lean times. Pushing down a feeling of guilt, he had instructed him to engage someone to do a background check into Sidonie.

His friend had chuckled. 'I thought you only did this when you wanted to take over another company or find an adversary's weak points? Now you're including your lovers?'

He'd answered far more curtly than he'd intended. 'Just do it, Demetrius. I don't expect a discussion about it.'

Despite the guilt he'd felt at taking such action, when Alexio had put the phone down he'd felt some semblance of equilibrium return. Sidonie hadn't scrambled his head so badly that he wasn't still aware of protecting himself. He *was* in control.

That control was about to be shot to pieces, though, as he heard a sound and turned around. Sidonie had emerged onto the terrace and for a long second Alexio literally lost his breath. All he could feel was his heart pounding as it struggled without oxygen.

The dress was a burnt orange colour and silk. Looped over one shoulder, and strapless on the other side, It had a big hole cut out over one hip, showing off the naked indentation of Sidonie's waist. A hint of one breast was visible just above the top of the dress as it swooped over her chest, hugging the delicious curve. The silk fell to her knees, but one leg peeped out of a thigh-high slit.

She was wearing nothing that he hadn't already seen on other lovers. He'd seen far less. But Alexio had to battle the very strong urge to tell her to go back and change, like an over-protective father. Or a mindlessly jealous lover, imagining the effect she'd have on other men. That thought alone made him stop and take in a breath. His chest swelled painfully.

'Is it okay?'

Sidonie was frowning, plucking at the dress. She looked at Alexio and this was one of those moments when she looked endearingly exposed, reminding him of the woman he'd met on the plane—all at once spiky and yet vulnerable.

'Come here,' he husked.

Sidonie moved towards him and Alexio had to bite back a groan of need. One long, slender leg was displayed in all its provocative glory as she walked towards him, her dainty feet encased in gold peeptoe heels.

She stopped before him and looked up. Her hair lay loose and long around her shoulders, glinting like golden fire in the dusky light. Her skin had already taken on a golden glow from the sun, despite the copious amounts of factor fifty he'd insisted she keep putting on—much to her disgust. Her freckles had exploded and magnified across her nose and cheeks. And her shoulders.

When Alexio finally felt able to touch her without tipping her over his shoulder and taking her back inside, he slid a hand around the back of her neck. That silky fall of hair against his hand made his body throb.

'You look…stunning.'

The vulnerability he'd seen dissipated and Sidonie smiled. 'Thank you…so do you.'

Alexio was used to compliments and they always felt empty. Except when she said it. He took his hand away, because he knew if he did something like kiss her now he'd never stop. Instead he took her hand and led her out of the villa to a nearby hidden garage which housed a sports car— one of his brother's new models.

It was a convertible, and Sidonie whistled in appreciation as she got in. Alexio held the door open for her, trying his best not to look at her exposed leg. Dammit, maybe he *should* get her to change?

Gritting his jaw, and wondering why on earth he'd thought taking her out would be a good idea, he got in the other side and soon they were driving along the coast, towards the bustling night-life of Fira.

As Alexio's car swept them along the coast of the island, and the sky became darker over the expanse of the sea, the lights of the houses and dwellings and the approaching town of Fira made everything look like a fairytale. Alexio was driving relatively slowly on the narrow roads and the cool evening air was delicious on Sidonie's sun-heated skin.

She shivered when she thought about how gorgeous Alexio had looked on the terrace against the setting sun, dressed in a dark suit with a dark shirt. The more time she spent with him, the more gorgeous he seemed to get. She felt weak inside when she thought of how protective he was, too, making sure she wore a high-factor cream in the sun.

'But I want to get *some* colour!' Sidonie had protested earlier.

Alexio had held her down easily on the lounger and proceeded to slather her with cream, saying sternly, 'You are *not* damaging your skin.'

Then she'd got so distracted by where his hands were going that she hadn't had the strength to fight him...

'Are you cold?'

Sidonie blushed in the darkening light and shook her head. 'No, I'm fine. I like the freshness.'

Alexio looked back to the road. 'I should have made you bring a jacket. It still gets cool at night this time of year.'

Sidonie smiled. 'You can't help yourself, can you?'

'Can't help what?'

'Being protective. I bet you were like that with your mother.'

Alexio made a noise then. It sounded like something between a snort and a cough and Sidonie looked at him. After a minute he glanced at her and she could see that his jaw was tense. The air was definitely cooler now.

'Believe me...' his tone was icy '...my mother did not need a protector. Anything but.'

Sidonie frowned, 'Why do you say that? What was she like?'

Alexio's jaw got even tighter. Sidonie could see it reflected in the lights of the dashboard.

'She was self-contained. Aloof. And she didn't need anyone.'

Sidonie held in a gasp at his stark words. 'Everyone needs someone—even if they don't want to admit it. You make her sound lonely.'

Eventually Alexio responded, just as the town of Fira came into view. 'Maybe she was... But I don't really want to discuss my mother when we have far more exciting things to talk about—like where I'm going to take you clubbing.'

Sidonie felt the door slam in her face with his terse delivery. His personal life was obviously a no-go area. She thought of the darkness in her own past, and how she'd hate for Alexio to know about it, and figured maybe it was for the best that he wasn't inviting this kind of intimacy.

She turned and faced the front and saw the stunning cavalcade of lights in the town as it seemed to drop precipitously to the gaping black of the sea. Momentarily distracted, Sidonie breathed, 'This is beautiful.'

Alexio was parking the car outside an upmarket-looking hotel and a young man was rushing out. 'We have to walk from here; the streets are pedestrianised,' Alexio explained as he got out.

He threw the keys to the young man, who was all but drooling at the sight of the stunning car, then came around to Sidonie's door and opened it for her, giving her his hand to help her out. Sidonie felt shaky and insecure at the thought of being seen in public with Alexio.

He kept her hand in his and said a few words in Greek to the man, whose face went pale. Then they walked away.

'What did you say to him?' Sidonie asked curiously.

Alexio smiled. 'I told him that if I came back to find one mark on the car I'd break his legs.'

'Oh…' Sidonie held in a giggle when she thought of the man paling so dramatically. 'Well, that makes things clear for him.' Her fingers tightened around his hand and she looked up. 'You wouldn't, though, would you? Break his legs?'

Alexio stopped and looked down, horrified, 'Of course not—what do you take me for? I just told him he'd be paying me out of his wages for the rest of his life.'

Sidonie tucked her other arm around Alexio's and said with mock relief, 'Okay—that's so much better than broken legs.'

Alexio looked down. He could see the smile playing around Sidonie's mouth, and that tantalising glimpse of long and slender leg. He could feel her breast against his arm and had to grit his jaw. It still felt tight after her questions about his mother... *'You make her sound lonely.'*

The truth was that Alexio had always had the impression that his mother *had* been lonely, and he didn't like the way Sidonie's innocent comments had brought him back to a time when it had been all too apparent that he couldn't protect his mother simply because she would not allow it. Not even when she needed it.

He forced his train of thought away from that unwelcome memory. They were approaching a narrow street with a glittering array of jewellery shops and Sidonie had stopped, enthralled, outside the first one.

She sighed deeply and sent a quick rueful glance to Alexio. 'I have to admit to a deeply unattractive trait: a love for glittery objects. My father used to say I was like a magpie, obsessed with shiny things. I used to collect the most random objects and put them in a box in my room and then take them out to look at them.'

Sidonie looked at the display again and Alexio couldn't stop the prickle of something across the back of his neck. The sensation of exposure was strong, along with something like disappointment. A feeling of inevitability. This was what he was used to. Women cajoling, seeking something. And even though Sidonie wasn't going about it in a way he was used to wasn't it the same thing? She was hinting that she loved jewellery and that she expected him to spoil her with some.

She looked up at him then and must have seen something in his expression. She frowned. 'What is it?'

Quickly he schooled his features. 'Nothing.' His voice was tight. 'The club is just down here.'

CHAPTER SIX

SIDONIE FELT AS if she'd done something wrong. The look
on Alexio's face just now had been almost...*disgusted*. She
felt stupid for blurting out that she'd always loved glittery
things. It was a trait that she'd inherited from her mother
and Sidonie didn't like to be reminded of that. Especially
when she knew deep down that it wasn't like her mother's
love for real jewels. When she'd found her childhood jewellery box during the clearing of the house after her father had
died she could almost have laughed, because it was full of
ten-cent pieces, buttons and tin foil. Hardly a treasure trove.

Sidonie tried to push down the sense of disquiet and
followed Alexio into a very mysterious-looking doorway
with no name on it. A man in a black suit with an earpiece
let them in with a deferential nod to Alexio.

Determined to put his reaction out of her mind, Sidonie
tightened her hand reflexively in Alexio's and he looked
down at her. She was relieved to see that the tightness in
his expression was gone and that the lazy, sexy insouciance was back.

Another entrance was just ahead, with billowing white
curtains wafting in the breeze. A stunning glamazon of a
woman stepped out, dressed in a tiny black dress which
showcased her astounding body.

Sidonie nearly tripped over her heels and Alexio stead-
ied her, looking down. 'Okay?'

Sidonie nodded, still struck dumb by the dark-haired Greek beauty who was now greeting Alexio *very warmly* with kisses on each cheek—far too close to his mouth for Sidonie's liking. She felt something rise within her—something hot and acrid. *Jealousy.*

The woman turned her gaze on Sidonie and dismissed her with a cool glance before turning back to Alexio. She pouted ruby-red lips and proceeded to talk to Alexio in Greek, which Sidonie of course couldn't follow.

Alexio replied in English, though, saying, 'I've been too busy to come back. This is Sidonie—Sidonie, this is Elettra.'

Sidonie smiled, but the other women barely smiled back at all. It was like the air hostess all over again. Far from making Sidonie feel triumphant that she had the man everyone wanted, it only made her feel insecure. Was Alexio even now looking at this woman and wishing he was availing himself of her charms instead of gauche, inexperienced Sidonie's?

But then the sight of the interior of the club took every thought out of Sidonie's head. It was a massive, cavernous, breathtaking space. Dark and dimly lit with what seemed to be a thousand lanterns. A huge bar took up one entire wall. There was a dance floor with glowing boxes of neon lights in the old Studio 54 style. There were booths and private tables dotted around the place, and then there was a whole other level down below which was already heaving with people.

Beautiful people were everywhere. Funky music throbbed from the sound system. It was achingly hip and exclusive.

Elettra was leading them to a booth, her hips swaying sinuously in her teeny-tiny dress. When they got there Sidonie could see that they had a bird's eye view of the entire place, and almost immediately after Elettra left—with clear reluctance—an equally stunning-looking waitress was there to take their orders. She was dressed in tiny shorts and a white shirt with very low-cut buttons. She had a pinafore-style apron that did little to detract from the sexiness of the outfit—if anything it fetishised it slightly.

Sidonie felt seriously out of her depth.

After Alexio had given an order he leant back and looked at her. She knew she must look like some wide-eyed hick.

'Well? What do you think?'

Sidonie sat back, overwhelmed, and gave a little laugh. 'I think that we're not in Kansas any more, Toto.'

Alexio frowned and Sidonie explained with a wave of her hand. 'When Dorothy ends up in Oz...' She shook her head. 'This is out of this world. I've never seen anything like it. I'm used to grimy college student bars.'

The waitress came back with small plates of finger food and a bottle of champagne. Sidonie groaned softly. She hadn't realised she was hungry and she stole a glance at Alexio, who was watching her with amusement.

'My appetite is just one big joke to you, isn't it?'

He shrugged and prepared some pitta bread and tzatziki, handing it to her. She ate it with relish and took a sip of the sparkling wine.

Joking, she said, 'I could get used to this, you know.'

She missed Alexio's enigmatic look as she plucked an olive from a bowl. When she did look at him he was lounging back, regarding her with an expression that had her blood heating up. It was *that* look. The one that made him look hungry and made her feel hungry. But not for food.

'I want to dance with you.'

Sidonie swallowed what she was eating. The mere thought of dancing with this man made any appetite she did have flee. A slow, sexy hip-hop song was playing, its beat sending tremors of sexual awareness through Sidonie's body.

'Okay…'

Moving out of the booth seat, Alexio stood and held out his hand. He looked so young in that moment, and so breathtakingly gorgeous, that Sidonie had to relegate it like a snapshot to the back of her mind because it was too much to deal with.

His hand in hers, Alexio led her to the dance floor, which was filling up with similarly minded couples. He drew her into his arms, close to his body, and it was the most natural thing to loop her hands and arms around his neck.

His hands were possessive on her, sexual. One hand rested over her buttocks. The other slid under the gaping hole at the side of her dress to splay across her naked back. *Lord.* How was she expected to stay standing when he touched her like that? As Sidonie looked into his eyes the infectious beat of the music throbbed through every vein and made her tingle. She realised, not for the first time, how far under her skin he'd sneaked.

There was something so…so up-front and unashamed about him. He was too confident to play games. Too assured. She knew exactly where she stood. And even though that brought misgivings about how cool she was with that— which was a lot less cool than she pretended—she couldn't blame him for her growing confusing emotions. Her attachment.

The fact that she trusted him was huge. She'd never trusted anyone, really…not since those awful days when her mother had exposed a very ugly side of reality and herself. Sidonie suspected now that her highly developed reticence had influenced her experiences with her first two brief relationships. No wonder they'd been unsatisfactory; she hadn't let either of them get too close.

But Alexio… Alexio had smashed through a wall she'd been barely aware of building around herself and now all that remained was rubble. And her exposed beating heart.

It hit her then, as she looked up into those golden compelling eyes...she was falling for him. And it was too late to stop herself.

Her arms tightened around Alexio's neck in automatic rejection of her thought, as if she could ward it off if she squashed it right away. But Alexio couldn't read the stricken nature of her revelation. He saw only those wide aquamarine eyes and felt Sidonie's arms tighten around him and he pulled her even closer.

Her breasts pressed against him, her hips welded to his, and his arousal was urgent and insistent. Damn her. He *never* lost it like this.

Wanting to punish her for something he wasn't even sure of, Alexio cupped the back of her head and, as the throbbing beat of the music changed and got faster, bent his head and took her mouth in a bruising passionate kiss.

As if something was holding her back, Sidonie didn't respond for a moment. Incensed by this, Alexio used every skill in his arsenal to make her respond—and when she did his blood ignited.

After long, drugging moments, Alexio struggled to drag himself from Sidonie's mouth. He felt dazed. The music was faster now. People were dancing around him. They were the only ones standing still. She was slow to open her eyes. They looked slumberous, filled with hidden depths. Filled with...emotion. Instantly Alexio waited for that cold feeling to infect him, but it didn't.

Before he could feel any more disjointed he all but dragged Sidonie off the dance floor and back to the booth. The food had been cleared away. They sat down and Alexio took a swig of champagne. But it was no good. He couldn't feel civilised sitting next to Sidonie with that provocative dress testing his control every time she moved.

He took her hand and she looked at him. Her mouth was swollen. Her eyes were huge, pupils dilated.

'Let's get out of here…'

She opened her mouth, paling slightly, as if she saw something in his expression that frightened her slightly. He felt feral.

'But we only just got here.'

Alexio forced himself to calm down and tried not to think about the fact that when he usually came to a club with a woman it was a very different experience. He was usually a lot more in control.

Tightly he said, 'If you don't want to go we can stay…'

'Why do you want to go?' she asked, surprising him. Most women would have pouted or sidled up to him, trying to distract him, cajole him.

'Because,' he offered with brutal honesty, 'I'm afraid if we don't leave that I'll get arrested for making love to you in front of an audience, and the last time I checked this wasn't a sex club.'

'Oh…' Sidonie said, in a small voice barely audible above the music. She took a swift sip of her drink and then looked at him. She was all at once shy and confident—again that intriguing mix. 'In that case maybe we should go…'

Relief and anticipation swept through Alexio as he grabbed for her hand and led her out of the booth—this time back to the VIP exit.

The return journey to Alexio's villa in the car was torturous. Sidonie was acutely aware of the thick sexual tension that enveloped them. Alexio had looked so…*primal* back at the club. She hadn't had a chance of pretending everything was normal after that dance and after his bald declaration. She'd wanted them to be alone as badly as he had.

Alexio looked at her now and lifted his arm for her to come close to his side. Sidonie didn't hesitate. She slid her arms around his hard-muscled torso and rested her head on his chest. Alexio's hand found the hole in the side of her dress and sneaked underneath, climbing up until he could cup her breast, his fingers pinching a nipple.

Sidonie's breath grew choppy. Between her legs she was embarrassingly wet.

By the time they reached the garage and he stopped the car Sidonie had to peel herself off Alexio.

He growled softly, 'Where do you think you're going?'

Sidonie stopped and looked at him. He had that look again, and it sent tremors of excitement into her blood. 'Inside?' she said hopefully, already imagining the huge bed.

Alexio shook his head and as he did so moved his seat back. 'No time. I can't wait. Take off your knickers.'

Sidonie's eyes went very big when she saw Alexio's hands go to his belt. He started undoing it. They were going to do it here. Right now. Heat washed up through Sidonie and her hands shook with need as she did as she was bid, sliding her panties off and down her legs.

When they hit the floor of the car Alexio reached for her and brought her over to straddle his lap. Sidonie's heart was out of control as Alexio dragged her dress down to bare one creamy white breast, its nipple already hard and pouting flagrantly for his mouth and tongue.

She groaned out loud when he surrounded it in sucking heat and clasped his head. Her hips were already grinding gently against his lap and the hard bulge she could feel there, still constrained by his trousers. Feeling frustration build, Sidonie reached down, lifting up slightly, and almost wept with relief when she could feel Alexio's naked arousal pushing against her where she ached.

When he thrust up and into her their mingled breaths were harsh in the quiet of the small space. Sidonie could feel the steering wheel digging into her back, the gearshift against her knee, but she didn't care. Her body rose and fell against Alexio's. They were both so turned on and ready that their mutual completion shattered around them in minutes. Sidonie could only sag against him afterwards, her mind a blissful blank of nothingness.

As dawn broke over the eastern side of the island and bathed the western edges in a pink glow Sidonie lay awake, with her cheek resting on Alexio's chest. Despite their frantic coupling in the car as soon as they'd got back, their hunger for one another hadn't been dented.

She knew he was awake too because she could feel the tension in his body. The master bedroom of the villa, despite its vast airiness, felt like a cocoon around them. Sidonie never wanted to leave this place, or this man. For a second she resented the inevitable intrusion of reality and *responsibility*—and then felt immediately guilty when she thought of Tante Josephine. Of course she couldn't expect her aunt to deal with the debts incurred by her mother.

Sighing deeply, Sidonie snuggled closer to Alexio, hating how a shiver went down her spine, as if someone had just walked over her grave.

'What's wrong?'

Sidonie shook her head against him and whispered, 'Nothing.' *Everything*, she didn't say.

A question she'd wanted to ask him for days rose up within her and, longing for a diversion from her own thoughts, she lifted her head and rested her chin on her hand against his chest.

He looked at her and she almost smiled at the wariness of him. As if she were some kind of unexploded device.

'Can I ask you something?'

A small smile played around that gorgeous sexy mouth. 'Do I have a choice?'

'Not really,' Sidonie said cheerfully, and then, 'Why did you turn your back on your inheritance to make your own way?'

She'd asked him the question that first evening in his

apartment but he'd deflected it easily. Now his face became inscrutable, and Sidonie prepared herself for another brush-off, but to her surprise his chest rose and fell in a deep sigh. As if he was giving in.

He said carefully, 'You *do* know that if I tell you I'll have to kill you?'

Sidonie nodded with mock seriousness. 'I know. However, I feel like I've packed a lot into my twenty-three years, so I'm prepared to go if I have to.'

Alexio took some of her hair between his fingers and caressed it, saying, 'Such a pity…but if you're positive…?'

Mock resolute, Sidonie said, 'I'm positive.'

Joking aside, Alexio lifted one shoulder and said, 'It's really not that exciting.'

'I'm intrigued. It's not many people who would turn their back on an Onassis-sized inheritance.'

Alexio grimaced. 'The size of the inheritance was vastly exaggerated…'

Sidonie stayed quiet.

With clear reluctance Alexio told her, 'I am my father's only son. Even though my half-brother grew up with us, my father used to taunt him every day that he would not receive a cent from him. I always resented my father's lack of generosity and the way he wielded his power over everyone else. But I saw how it forged in my brother a will to succeed and prosper on his own. I envied him because he wasn't constrained like I was. Bound to my father's expectations. My father used to pit us against each other all the time, me and my brother.'

Alexio grimaced.

'Obviously this didn't do our relationship much good, and by the time my brother left home it's safe to say we hated each other's guts. My father just assumed I would be joining him in his empire. He never listened to me long enough to know that I had no interest in his shipping business. I rebelled against that expectation. The business wasn't even his—not rightfully. He was the second son and his brother had died at a young age, leaving him in line to take over. His own father hadn't wanted it for him, but my father grabbed it with both hands and ousted my grandfather as soon as he could.'

Sidonie's eyes grew wide. 'But that's so…'

'Ruthless?' Alexio interjected with a grim smile.

Sidonie nodded.

'That's my father's way. To grab at things. Take them. He wanted me to inherit and join him—but not as an equal, as someone he could control.' He sighed. 'In the meantime I saw Rafaele, my brother, single-handedly resurrecting his own family name and business out of the ashes. All those years of rivalry were still in my blood—if he could do it so could I.'

Sidonie spoke softly. 'So when your father expected you to follow in his footsteps you said no?'

Alexio looked into Sidonie's clear eyes and felt in that moment as if he could just spill all the secrets in his guts and keep spilling. It was dangerous. Too dangerous. He stifled the impulse with effort.

'I said no. And walked away. He disinherited me and now here I am.'

'Probably more successful than he is…'

Alexio was surprised that she'd surmised that but it was true. What he didn't tell her, though, was how his success hadn't given him any measure of satisfaction where his father was concerned. It had never been about besting his father. It had been about distancing himself from a man who had made him fear *he* had the same lack of emotional control in his own make-up. Fear that he might be similarly greedy and never experience the thrill of making it on his own as his brother had. Fear that he'd never get away from that sterile house full of tension and hatred. *Violence.*

He felt cold inside all of a sudden.

Just then Alexio's mobile phone beeped on the nearby bedside cabinet. He reached for it and saw the text message icon winking. He opened it and saw it was from his solicitor.

I have information about your Miss Fitzgerald. Call when you get a chance. D.

Instantly something cold slithered into Alexio's gut.

'What is it?' Sidonie asked with obvious concern.

Alexio put the phone back, face down, and looked at her. 'Nothing important.'

Guilt warred with something much deeper inside him. Superstitiously he wanted to pretend he hadn't just seen that text and that there wasn't something dark lurking in the wings.

He came up and hovered over her, feeling that familiar heady rush of desire when he looked at her body, breasts bared and tempting. Her mouth was enticing him ever downwards, where he wouldn't have to think about anything...for a little longer.

'What did you just say?' Alexio asked faintly.

He was stunned. The sun was high outside his villa's office. His body was still humming in the aftermath of seriously pleasurable lovemaking and he couldn't really compute this information.

His solicitor repeated himself. 'Her mother went to jail for two years.'

Alexio went cold all over. 'Jail? Why?'

Demetrius sighed. 'I really wish I didn't have to tell you this. Her mother was prosecuted for stalking and blackmailing her married lover. She'd been doing it for years, in ever increasing amounts. It would appear that her husband, Miss

Fitzgerald's father, wasn't making enough to keep her in the style to which she wanted to be accustomed. Even though it also appears he did his best to try and keep both his wife and daughter in comfort and relative luxury.'

Alexio struggled against the shock. This information was not pleasant, but it hardly condemned Sidonie.

His friend continued, 'When her mother was released they moved to another part of the country to avoid the scandal and Miss Fitzgerald's father's business started to boom. Sidonie went to one of the best local schools, had a pony…the works. Her mother was a regular on the social scene…designer clothes and jewellery. They managed to keep her past a secret for the most part. When the property market collapsed so did her father's business and they lost everything.'

Alexio was feeling increasingly uncomfortable. 'Demetrius, is that it? I think I've heard enough.'

'Well, not quite. I think you should hear the rest. After Mr Fitzgerald died his wife went back to Paris to move in with her younger sister.'

'Demetrius—'

The man butted in. 'Alexio, I did some more digging via some colleagues in Paris and you need to hear this… Sidonie's mother persuaded her sister to take out a mortgage on a flat her husband had bought and paid for years before. She also maxed out credit cards in her sister's name. She died leaving the woman in so much debt that she'll never recover.'

Alexio felt angry now and gritted out, 'What does this have to do with Sidonie?'

'You met her when she was on her way home from Paris?'

'Yes,' Alexio agreed curtly, regretting having ever involved his friend like this.

'She'd just signed an agreement to accept responsibility for all those debts on her aunt's behalf. Now, let me ask you this—has she given any hint at all that she's a woman with a huge financial burden on her shoulders? If not,' his friend went on heavily, 'you have to ask yourself why she's acting as if nothing is wrong.'

When Sidonie woke again she was alone in the bed and for some reason her belly went into a ball of tension. Something was wrong. She could feel it.

She lifted her head and looked around. No sign of Alexio. Maybe he'd gone for a swim? He was a powerful swimmer and liked the sea as opposed to the pool.

Muscles protesting pleasurably as she sat up, Sidonie got out of bed and went to the bathroom, tying her hair up so that it wouldn't get wet in the shower.

When she came out again she rubbed her body dry with a towel and looked at the vast array of clothes hanging in the walk-in wardrobe. Something bitter struck her again to think of his other women, but Sidonie shoved it down. She didn't have the right to feel jealous, possessive.

She found some shorts and a green halterneck top and stuck them on and then went to find Alexio, still with that odd feeling of foreboding in her belly. Before she could leave the bedroom, though, she heard the sound of her phone ringing. She kept it on mainly in case Tante Josephine was looking for her, and when she located it at the bottom of her bag she saw that it *was* her aunt.

Expecting nothing more than her aunt wanting to chat, Sidonie sat on the edge of the bed and answered warmly in French. Her smile faded in an instant, though, when all she could hear were racking sobs from the other end of the phone.

Instantly Sidonie stood up. 'Tante Josephine, what is it? Please try to stop crying…'

Eventually her aunt was able to calm down enough to

start talking, after Sidonie had encouraged her to breathe slowly. Her aunt was prone to panic attacks and Sidonie didn't want one to happen before she could find out what was wrong.

Through fits and starts it transpired that someone on her *vacances* had heard about Tante Josephine's financial woes and put the fear of God into her by telling her all sorts of horror stories about repossessions and jail sentences for not paying debts. No wonder her aunt was hysterical.

But no matter what Sidonie said it didn't seem to have any effect. Her aunt was working herself up into another bout of hysterics. Desperate, Sidonie racked her brains for what she could say that might calm her down. Tante Josephine didn't understand nuances, and Sidonie knew that if she tried to placate her with reassurances that the debts were now in *her* name it would have no effect. Her aunt still believed the debts were hers.

Her aunt only understood *right now*—and right now, she was panicking. Sidonie knew that in her aunt's mind the threat was as real as if *gendarmes* had just turned up to arrest her.

Tante Josephine needed to hear something concrete, even if it was a white lie. 'Okay, look, Jojo—are you listening to me? I need you to listen because I'm going to tell you why you don't have to worry about a thing.'

To Sidonie's relief her aunt stopped crying abruptly at the use of the nickname that had come about when, as a toddler, Sidonie hadn't been able to pronounce Josephine. She hiccuped softly. Sidonie's heart ached for this poor, sweet and innocent woman who did not deserve this stress.

'Jojo, everything is going to be fine...I promise you.'

Unbeknownst to Sidonie, who stood facing away from the view and the open terrace doors, a tall dark shape had approached and stopped.

'But Sidonie...*how*?'

Sidonie could hear the hysteria approaching again and cursed the distance between them. 'I'm not going to let you go through this alone, Jojo, do you hear me? Didn't I promise to do everything in my power to get us out of this mess?'

Her aunt sniffled and Sidonie pressed on, seizing the advantage, knowing how fragile her aunt was mentally.

'You don't have to worry about a thing because I've...'

Sidonie faltered. She'd been about to say she had everything in hand, but she knew that would sound vague to her aunt, so she mentally crossed her fingers, squeezed her eyes shut and said, 'I've met someone, Jojo...and he's really, really rich. One of the richest men in the world. And you won't believe how we met—it was on a plane, and he *owned* the plane.'

Immediately her aunt, who was always enthralled by stories like this, perked up. 'Really, Sidonie? Truly? Is he your boyfriend?'

Sidonie opened her eyes. 'Yes, he is. He's crazy about me. And I've told him all about you and he's promised to take care of everything.'

As much as Sidonie hated using Alexio like this, she knew it would resonate with her aunt, who was simplistically old-fashioned. After her father had bought the apartment for Tante Josephine she'd believed all men had the power to sweep in and make magic happen.

Her aunt's voice quavered, but this time it sounded like relief. 'Oh, Sidonie...I'm so happy... I was so worried—and then when Marcel told me those things and—'

Sidonie cut her off before she could work herself up again and behind her the tall, dark shadow melted away, unnoticed.

'Jojo, don't talk about this to anyone again—and if Marcel says anything just know that you have nothing to worry about.'

Sidonie felt awful, lying like this, but she knew that her

physical presence would reassure her aunt when she got back to Paris. She could then tell her that something had happened with the *'boyfriend'*. The idea was laughable. Alexio was no boyfriend.

'Oh, Sidonie…is he handsome?'

Sidonie felt ashamed, but she was relieved to hear her aunt's natural effervescence return—she loved stories about people meeting and falling in love. Sidonie tried to gloss over the details about Alexio as much as possible, and before her aunt terminated the conversation she made sure to have a chat with one of the supervisors, to warn them that she was particularly vulnerable at the moment. She castigated herself for not thinking of doing it before the holiday.

When she put her phone down she felt drained, but at least happier that Tante Josephine should be okay until the end of her holiday. The supervisor had promised to keep a close watch over her.

Sidonie turned round and her eyes widened when she saw the tall figure of Alexio, standing with his back to her at the railing of the terrace outside. He was dressed in faded jeans and a T-shirt. That feeling of foreboding was back but Sidonie tried to shake it off. And also the sudden fear that he might have heard some of her conversation.

She padded out on bare feet and went to stand beside Alexio at the railing. He didn't look at her. Sidonie forced her voice to be bright. 'Hey, you…I was wondering where you'd got to.'

Alexio was trying to hold in the cold rage that had filled his belly when he'd overheard her poisonous words: *'He's crazy about me…he'll take care of things…'*

Here was the very unpalatable proof that his solicitor had been right to make Alexio question why Sidonie hadn't told him about this before.

Forcing his voice to sound neutral, he asked, 'Who were you on the phone to just now?'

He couldn't look at her. His hands tightened on the railings.

Sidonie was evasive. 'Er…just my aunt. She's away at the moment, on holiday…'

Alexio felt a hard weight settle into his belly. Everything from the moment he'd met her unspooled like a bad film in his mind. All the little moments when she'd appeared shy, naïve, mocked him now.

So this was how she was going to do it: she was going to bide her time, wait to catch him in a weak moment and then launch into her sob story, seducing money out of him. And maybe even more. Maybe he'd be so weak by then he'd offer to buy her a place, set up her and her aunt completely? He felt dizzy at the thought.

He thought of how weak he'd felt in the aftermath of their lovemaking—how he'd blithely allowed himself to spill his guts, how he'd almost spilled *more*, telling her everything. How close he'd come to making a complete fool of himself.

Thank goodness he'd had the sense to investigate her. When he thought of how guilty he'd felt to have instigated such a thing, the conversation he'd heard just now taunted him. Where had his cynical shell gone?

Sidonie touched his arm. 'What is it, Alexio? You're scaring me.'

Alexio jerked his arm from her as if burnt and stepped back, finally looking at her. He saw her go pale and welcomed it. He couldn't hide his disgust and despised the way his body reacted to seeing her in short shorts and that sexy halterneck top.

'You really think I'm that stupid?' he sneered.

Sidonie looked at him and blinked. He could see something like fear flash in her eyes.

'What did you hear?'

Alexio felt murderous now, because her guilt was obvious.

'Enough,' he spat out. 'Enough to know that you and your aunt think that you can use *me* to clear your debts.'

Sidonie just stood there, looking a little shell-shocked. No doubt because she'd been found out.

She said faintly, 'You speak French.'

'Of course I speak French—along with two or three other European languages.'

He was dismissive.

Sidonie's eyes seemed to clear and she reached out with a hand that Alexio stepped back from. 'You don't understand. I didn't mean a word of it. I was just saying what I could to reassure her—she was upset.'

Alexio could have laughed at her earnest expression, which was a travesty now that he knew everything was twisted and black and nothing had been real. He felt betrayed, and that made him even more incandescent with rage. He *never* let women get close enough to do this to him.

'You expect me to believe a single word from the daughter of a criminal? You obviously learnt well from her— but not well enough. If you had had the decency to *tell* me about this—come to me and merely asked me for help—I might have given it. Instead you insisted on this elaborate charade. Maybe you got off on the drama?'

CHAPTER SEVEN

FOR AN AWFUL second Sidonie thought she might faint. She couldn't actually believe that Alexio had just said those words...*daughter of a criminal.*

She went icy cold, despite the heat, and forced words out through numb lips. 'What do you mean, the daughter of a criminal?'

His voice flat, he admitted, 'I know all about your mother, Sidonie. I know that she blackmailed her married lover and went to jail.'

The words fell like shattered glass all over her. The old shame rose up to grip her vocal cords so she couldn't speak, much in the same way as had happened when she'd been eight years old in the schoolyard and her classmates had surrounded her, jeering, *'Your mother's going to jail...your mother's going to jail...'*

Sidonie could not believe she was hearing this. It had to be a nightmare. Perhaps any minute now she'd wake up to Alexio saying, *Sid...wake up. I want you.*

She blinked. But nothing changed. Alexio was still standing there. A stranger. Cold and remote. Condemnatory. She felt dazed, confused.

Somehow she managed to get out, 'How on earth do you know about that?' Something else struck her. 'And how do you know about my aunt's debts?'

Alexio crossed his arms and now he looked completely forbidding. 'I had you investigated.'

This information made Sidonie literally reel. She had to put her hands behind her on the railing just to hold onto something or she was afraid she'd fall down.

'You had me *investigated*?' she whispered incredulously, looking at him, at this complete stranger.

Alexio lifted one shoulder minutely and didn't look remotely ashamed or sheepish. 'I can't be too careful… Someone, a complete stranger, comes into my life… I got suspicious.'

'My God,' Sidonie breathed, horrified. 'Who *are* you?'

She felt sick. And then angry. It was a huge surge of emotion, rising up within her. She stood up straight, let go of the railing. She was shaking.

'And how *dare* you pry into my private life? What my mother did has got absolutely nothing to do with you.'

Sidonie had lived with that shame all her life but had finally come to terms with what her mother had done—not least because she understood a little of why she'd acted the way she had. Something that she could never explain to this cold stranger. She hadn't even let her guard down enough with him to tell him of her deep private secrets. He'd gone looking for them.

Sidonie was aware of parts of herself breaking off inside, shattering. She knew she had to hold it together.

Alexio spoke again, his voice as cutting as a knife. 'But it wasn't just that, was it? She put your aunt into severe debt, to fund her own expensive tastes.'

Shame heaped on top of shame. Sidonie felt horribly exposed. From somewhere deep inside, and far too late, she reached for and pulled up an icy shield.

'That is none of your concern.' Because she'd never intended to tell him about it. It was part of the real world, which *wasn't* part of this fantasy world.

Alexio's mouth twisted. 'But it would have been, wouldn't it? You were waiting for the right moment, when enough intimacy had been established, and then you were going to make your move. I just wonder if you were going to ask only for enough to cover the debts or more...based on how many nights we'd spent together? Based on how duped you thought I was by then?'

'Theos.' He was lashing out now, making Sidonie flinch. He narrowed wild-looking eyes on her.

'You were good. I'll give you that. But there were a few signs... The way you were so blasé with the clothes, as if you had expected nothing less. That little wistful moment outside the jewellery shop... Were you hoping to wake up and find a diamond bracelet winking at you on the pillow?'

Sidonie desperately tried not to let the awful insidious insecurity take hold, telling her that despite everything she *was* her mother's daughter. Had something about the sheer level of Alexio's wealth called to her? More than the man himself? Suddenly she doubted herself. She had to take deep breaths to avoid throwing up right there on the terrace.

The sheer depth and evidence of Alexio's cynicism was astounding, shocking. The lengths he'd gone to because he hadn't really trusted her... Because he'd *suspected* something.

The things he'd found out... The fact that she had so fatally misread this man. *How* had she not seen an inkling of this? Only those most fleeting moments when a look would cross his face...hardly enough to make her wonder.

Nevertheless, a small, tender part of Sidonie not lashed by this terrible revelation was making her say, 'You have it all wrong. I was only telling my aunt something to re-assure her. She was hysterical. I didn't mean it. You were never meant to hear that and I had no intention of asking you for money.'

To Sidonie's own ears it sounded flat. Didn't sound convincing. She couldn't seem to drum up the necessary passion to convince him. She was too stunned, too shocked... too wounded.

Predictably, Alexio didn't believe her. His eyes were a dead, emotionless void.

'I do not wish to discuss this any further. We're done here. I am going back to Athens within the hour. If you come with me I will ensure you get a flight home.'

Sidonie felt devoid of all feeling except one: she hated this man. And she couldn't believe how gullible she'd been—how naïve not to have assumed that a man as powerful as him would, of course, be suspicious and cynical by nature.

She said flatly, 'I would prefer to swim home.'

Alexio shrugged minutely, as if he couldn't care less. 'As you wish. There's a boat leaving for Piraeus this evening. My housekeeper's husband will take you to the port.'

Sidonie welcomed that. Because right now she hated herself for automatically thinking about what it would be like to get on a plane again without this man distracting her from her fear with his charming sexy smile. With that wicked mouth.

He turned away and then turned back abruptly, his eyes dark. Something in his voice was a bit wild, but Sidonie was too traumatised to notice it.

'Tell me...was it on the plane, when you knew who I was? Did you decide then to try and hook me by making me believe you were different from every other woman I've ever met?'

Sidonie just looked at him. Words of defence were stuck in her throat. She had no defence—not when this man had proved that he had suspected her of something long before he'd even had a reason to. And he still had no reason to. She had trusted him, blindly, right from the start, never suspecting for a moment how dark he was inside. How he could so easily condemn her.

She never wanted to see him again because he had just proved that she would never be free of the past. He had broken her heart into a million pieces and she'd never forgive herself for that weakness. Or him.

His condemnation would be her defence, so she said, 'Yes. On the plane. As soon as I knew who you were.'

Alexio looked at her for a taut moment and then he turned and strode away, leaving her standing there. As soon as he was out of sight Sidonie blindly made her way into the *en suite* bathroom of the bedroom where they'd made love too many times to count and was violently ill.

Afterwards, when Alexio's helicopter had left and she'd changed into her own clothes and packed her bag, Sidonie sat on a lounger outside with the glorious view unnoticed in front of her. She was still numb. Devoid of any substantial feeling. She knew it was the protection of shock.

One thing impinged, though: disgust at herself for having indulged in this fantasy. She'd wanted one night and had then grabbed for more... Had she on some level hoped that Alexio would want her for longer? Deeper? Had she ignored her own usually healthy self-protective cautious nature because she'd been blinded by opulence? The thought made her feel sick again.

Bitterly she surmised that she should have listened to him more closely when he'd told her his reasons for turning his back on his inheritance. He was driven and ruthless—had dashed his own father's expectations and dreams to fuel his own desires.

She'd believed his reasons were justified when she'd heard them at first—she'd heard the way his voice had constricted when he'd talked about his father, as if even now he felt the unbearable yoke of expectation. She'd admired him.

But now she saw him for what he really was: an amoral, ambitious, greedy man who would step over his nearest and dearest to get ahead. She hadn't stood a chance. He might have heard her damning conversation with her aunt, but he'd already investigated her at that stage and had clearly believed her worthy of judgement because of her mother's criminal record.

Those two years of her mother's incarceration were etched like an invisible tatoo into Sidonie's skin. A stain of shame that would never be gone, but which had faded over time...until now.

Sidonie's well-ingrained sense of responsibility rose up. She should never have indulged herself like this. She had her aunt to worry about now, and clearing the debts.

She heard a car pull up somewhere nearby. It would be the housekeeper's husband. She stood up and tried not to let the emotion brewing within her break free. She couldn't let it. She was afraid of its awesome power. Of how much it would tell her about a hurt that shouldn't be so deep—not after just a few days with a man she hadn't even known.

A man appeared, old and bent, with a weathered face and black eyes. His dour expression gave Sidonie some sense of relief. If he'd been kind she might have broken apart altogether. He took her bag and at the same time handed her a white envelope with nothing written on it.

Sidonie opened it and saw a cheque with her name on it inside. It was for an amount of money that took her breath away. Enough to halve her aunt's debts at least. The signature at the bottom was bold and arrogant. Reeking of condemnation and disgust.

Fire filled Sidonie's belly. She stalked straight back into the villa and went to Alexio's office.

She took the cheque out of the envelope and ripped it

up into tiny pieces. Then she put them back in the envelope and wrote on the outside.

It was never about the money.

And then she left.

Four months later...

Alexio looked down at the craggy dark island below him with its distinctive white and blue roofs. The helipad on his own villa loomed into view and tension made his gut hard. Alexio grimaced as his solicitor's words came back to him. *'You're heading for burnout, man. I've never seen you like this before.'*

Alexio couldn't remember being like this before either—not even in the days when he'd been struggling and working night and day to make a success of his business. But for the last four months he'd barely stopped to breathe. On automatic pilot.

His fortune had doubled. His acquisitions had extended to North America, making him the first European budget airline to secure such a lucrative contract. Now he was global, having taken half the time people had predicted.

But Alexio felt as if an essential fire inside him had been doused. He rejected the thought immediately. Nothing was different. He was still the same—held the same values and ambitions.

As the small aircraft circled lower and lower he fought *her* memory. This was precisely why he'd avoided coming back here before now. During daylight hours he had to make a concerted effort not to think of her; that was where work came in. But in the nights she haunted him. Stopped him from sleeping. Made his body ache so badly that he had to ease it like a horny teenager.

He wouldn't mind if he could alleviate his frustration with another woman, but he could barely look at a woman these days without feeling a measure of disgust. And a disturbingly flatlining libido.

He told himself it was because he'd come so close to being burnt. A vivid memory came into his mind as the glittering sun-kissed sea below the villa came into view—Sidonie launching herself onto his back as they'd walked up the steps from the sea, kissing his neck, joking, laughing. And all the time plotting to feather her nest.

Alexio felt sick, and he almost told the pilot to keep going…but they were landing now and Alexio refused to let a memory override his intellect.

He'd finally agreed to go somewhere for a few days' R&R after he and his brother had almost come to blows for the first time in years. Alexio had been closing a deal with Rafaele to create a joint company which would invest in research for future technologies in cars and aircraft. They'd been in Rafaele's *palazzo* outside Milan, where he was spending the summer with his family.

Alexio had been keen to keep working one day and Rafaele had looked at him incredulously. 'Are you crazy? We've been working all day—Sam is making dinner tonight and Milo's back from summer school in Milan. I haven't seen him since this morning. I have a family now, Alexio… things are different.'

Alexio had felt a completely irrational anger erupt at his brother's very valid reasons not to keep working. Since he'd arrived he'd found the domestic idyll of Rafaele's family almost too much to bear. The openly loving looks between him and his wife. His precocious and gorgeous nephew, who bathed everyone in his sunny charming nature. The way he was doted on by both Sam and Rafaele. The way Rafaele's relationship with his own father had clearly undergone a transformation for the better.

It had brought Alexio back to that dark place when he'd believed such things existed, only to find out that they didn't. It had brought back the resentment that he'd felt because he'd witnessed something ugly in his own family that Rafaele had never had to witness simply because he'd been free to get on with his own life, leaving Alexio behind in a toxic atmosphere.

He'd been caught in the grip of that darkness, emotions swirling in his gut, and he'd sneered, 'You're losing your touch, Rafaele, ever since you let that woman get to you—'

His brother had stepped right up to him, chest to chest, and Alexio had felt the heat of his anger.

Rafaele had blistered at him, 'Do not ever call Sam *that woman* again. Whatever is going on with you, Alexio, sort it out.'

Sam had come into the study then, smiling widely, oblivious to the tension at first. And then her grey eyes had grown wide and concerned as she'd immediately looked to her husband. Something in that look, something that had seemed so naked and *dangerous* to Alexio, had made him push past his brother.

He'd found the wherewithal to stop and say tightly, 'I'm sorry, Sam. I have to leave. Something's come up...' and then he'd left the *palazzo* as if hounds were at his heels. Running from that picture of domestic bliss which he wanted to believe was a sham...but which he knew deep down wasn't.

He'd avoided the repeated phone calls from his brother since then.

He was here now, so he'd get it together if it killed him. And maybe tonight he'd go to that nightclub and his libido *wouldn't* flatline in the presence of other women. Maybe it would surge back to life and he would finally be able to erase *her* image from his mind once and for all, claw back some sense of equilibrium.

* * *

Sidonie gave a groan of satisfaction as she slid into the steaming water of the cracked and discoloured bath. Tante Josephine had squirted in enough bubbles to hide Sidonie's body from view completely, but she didn't need it to be hidden to know what she'd see without the bubbles: a small bump protruding over the waterline, as it had started to do over the last week.

It seemed to be getting bigger by the day now as she became more noticeably pregnant.

Her boss at the café had pulled her aside earlier and said bluntly, 'I have five children. You're pregnant, aren't you?'

Sidonie had blanched, too shocked to deny it, and nodded her head.

Her boss had sighed. 'Okay, you can stay for a couple of months, but as soon as you start to get big you're gone—this is not work for a pregnant woman.'

Sidonie had gasped, but he'd walked away. She'd realised the irony of her boss being a chauvinistic Greek man but hadn't felt like laughing.

She bit her lip now with worry. So far she and Tante Josephine were doing okay. When Sidonie had got back to Paris and moved in with her aunt she'd gone to see a financial advisor who had helped them consolidate their debts to a monthly total. Now all Sidonie had to do was earn enough to make that payment. Every month. For a long, long time into the future.

They were just about managing, with Tante Josephine's job and Sidonie's two and sometimes three jobs. But now that a baby was in the mix…

Sidonie bit down on her lip hard and put her hand over the small swell. Since the moment she'd seen the first pregnancy test turn positive, and then the next and the next— five tests in all—she'd forged an indelible bond with the clump of cells growing inside her. She'd never consciously thought about having a baby—it was something she'd put off into the distant future, not really wanting to consider the huge responsibility, especially after her own damaging experiences—but crazily, in spite of everything, somehow it felt *right*. And Sidonie couldn't explain why, when she had every reason to feel the opposite.

Sometimes, though, panic gripped her so hard she had to stop and breathe. She fought it. She would get through this somehow.

It didn't help that Tante Josephine kept asking Sidonie, 'But where is your boyfriend? The one you told me about? Won't he want to take care of you? I thought he was going to make everything okay?'

Sidonie would take her aunt's face in her hands and say firmly, but lovingly, 'We don't need him, Jojo, we have each other. We're a team and we're invincible. I won't let anything happen to us, okay?'

Her aunt would sigh and then quickly get distracted by something—usually talk of the baby. She'd already decided that if it was a boy it would be called Sebastian and if it was a girl Belle, after a favourite cartoon character.

As Sidonie lay in the bath now, after a punishing day of work, she felt helpless tears spring into her eyes. Immediately she cut off the emotion ruthlessly, as she'd been doing for four months. Anger rose and she welcomed it. She cultivated it. It was the only thing that kept her sane, kept her going. And now the baby.

She would never contact *him* and she had to stop thinking about *him*. For a man who had accused her of being a gold-digger on the basis of conducting an investigation into her private life and overhearing an admittedly unfortunate conversation, news of a baby would consign her to the hell of his condemnation for good—and she would not give him the satisfaction.

Her anger rose, swift and bright, washing away those

dangerous tender feelings that hovered on the periphery and had no place after what he'd done to her.

Alexio returned to the villa feeling more disgruntled than ever. After sleeping for almost eight hours on a lounger on the terrace he'd gone to the club.

Elettra, encouraged by the fact that he was alone, had twined herself around him like a clinging vine, making him feel nothing but claustrophobia.

In a fit of darkness he'd taken the same booth as last time and had been bombarded with images and memories: Sidonie's dress, the way the silk had clung and moved with her body. How it had felt to dance close to her, sliding his hand under her dress to touch her naked back. The insistent throb of the music, with the same beat as the desire rushing through his blood. The way she'd looked at him, hungry and innocent.

Innocent.

Except she'd never been innocent. She'd been scheming the whole time, just reeling him in, waiting for an opportunity to secure her future, debt-free.

Bile had risen up inside Alexio after all these months, just as it had that awful day. Immediately he'd had to get out of there.

And now here he was, looking over the inky blackness of the sea. Thoroughly disgusted with himself, Alexio felt the lure of work—even though he meant to be avoiding it. But he knew he wouldn't sleep, and especially not in that bed. It had been a terrible idea to come here. He should have gone to the farthest corner of the world and he vowed to do so the next day. He'd wanted to check out the potential of setting up in South East Asia anyway...

When he went into the office and sat down heavily on the chair he saw an unexpected white envelope sitting squarely on the blotter. Saw the writing in a feminine scrawl.

It was never about the money.

Feeling something in his belly swoop and his skin prickle, Alexio picked up the envelope. As he did so something fluttered out. The torn pieces of the cheque he'd left for Sidonie in a fit of tumultuous anger and disgust. If she wanted the money so badly then he'd give her some. But now he felt dizzy. Disorientated. He opened the envelope and more and more pieces fell out. Nothing else.

It was never about the money.

He hadn't even checked to see if or when she'd cashed it. He'd just assumed that she had. He hadn't wanted to know. But she hadn't. She'd left that day and taken a torturous eleven-hour ferry to Piraeus. His last contact from her had been via a message relayed to him by one of his Greek assistants whom he'd instructed to meet her at the port with a plane ticket for a flight to Dublin.

She'd not taken the ticket and had said succinctly, *'Tell Alexio Christakos he can go to hell.'*

The message had been relayed with great trepidation by the employee after Alexio had instructed him to tell him her words *exactly.*

Alexio had put it down to anger that he'd thwarted her plans. He'd felt vindicated. But now he felt sick. Why hadn't she just taken the cheque?

Holding the jagged remains made a conflicting mix of things rush through him. Not least of which was the poisonous suspicion that this was a desperate ruse to pique his interest—make him go after her to find out *why.* So that ultimately she might get even more money.

Even now Alexio could feel anticipation spiking in his blood just at the thought of seeing her again, but…*damn her*…had she counted on this?

He felt something underneath him then, and shifted slightly to find that he was sitting on Sidonie's tatty university sweatshirt. She must have left it behind that day. Her pale face and wide, stricken eyes came back to him— the way she'd flatly agreed with him that, *yes*, she'd set out to seduce him on the plane. Something about that felt off now. His gut twisted…

She had protested her innocence. But he'd been so incensed he'd been unable to feel anything but the bitter sting of betrayal and anger at his own weakness for her.

Emotion, hot and impossible to push down, made his chest go tight. Without even thinking about what he was doing he brought the sweatshirt up to his nose and breathed deeply. Her scent, still faint but there, hit him like a steam train, that intriguing mix between floral and something spiky.

Galvanised by something that felt like a combination of panic and desperation, Alexio stood up and went into the bedroom. He hadn't opened the closet doors yet but now he did. All of the clothes were still hanging there. The clothes that he had ordered to be delivered for Sidonie before they'd arrived. She'd taken nothing. Not even the dress she'd worn to the club that night.

He could hear her voice as if she was there right now: *'Well, at least I won't have to worry about washing my knickers out in the sink. I'm sure your housekeeper would be horrified.'* This time Alexio heard and recognised the over-brightness of her voice and his sense of discomfort grew.

'You'll have to do it again. It's not good enough.'

Sidonie fought down the urge to scream and smiled as if her boss *wasn't* a sadistic control freak. There was nothing wrong with the way she'd made this bed in the five-star hotel where she worked for minimum wage three days a week.

'No problem.'

'And please hurry—the guest is due to arrive within the hour.'

Sidonie sighed deeply and stripped the bed in order to make it again. She ached all over and she longed for a hot bath like the one she'd had the other night. She hadn't had the time since then, because she'd taken on a full-time waitressing job in a Moroccan restaurant near the apartment six evenings a week. Her boss there had no qualms about hiring a pregnant woman, unlike the boss of the café where she worked the other two days a week when she wasn't at the hotel.

Finally her shift was over and she stretched out her back, instinctively putting a hand over her small bump, feeling the prickle of guilt. She knew she shouldn't be working so hard but she had no choice. A small voice taunted her. *You could contact him.* But she slammed her locker door shut in the staff changing room.

No way. Not going there. The thought of crawling to Alexio for help was anathema. She never wanted to see his cold, judgmental face again.

But when she emerged from the staff entrance at the side of the hotel and walked to the top of the lane his was the first face she saw. Shock held her immobile. He was leaning nonchalantly against the bonnet of a gleaming sports car, with his hands in his trouser pockets and his legs crossed at the ankles. Then he saw her and tensed, straightened up.

She blinked, but he didn't disappear. He was looking right at her with those golden-green eyes. For an awful treacherous second emotion rose in a dizzying sweep inside Sidonie. Her blood grew hot in her veins and her breath shortened. Her nipples tingled. All the signs of a woman in the throes of a lust that had lain dormant.

The oppressive, muggy August air seemed to seize the oxygen going into her lungs. For a second she felt so light-headed she thought she'd faint and she sucked in breath. It couldn't be him, she told herself, in spite of his not disappearing. It was a mirage. An apparition from her imagination torturing her.

In a bid to convince herself of that Sidonie turned and started to walk down the street. She heard a curse behind her and then her arm was taken in a strong grip. A familiar grip. Immediately Sidonie reacted violently to the effect it had on her body and soul and whirled around, ripping herself free.

She looked up and felt dizzy again. It was Alexio. In the flesh. That gorgeous flesh. He had no right to look so gorgeous. She frowned. Even if he did look leaner than when she'd last seen him and even if there were lines around his mouth and face. Lines she recognised, because she saw them in her own mirror every day. But he was still gorgeous, and she was still aware of the woman who had just walked past and done a double-take.

Anger flared and she seized it like a drowning person might seize a buoy.

'What do you want?' she spat out, her belly jumping with panic and a mix of other things she didn't want to investigate.

Sidonie vaguely noticed his open-necked light blue shirt and dark trousers and became very belatedly aware of her own woeful state of dress. Skinny jeans which she had to wear with the button open, flip-flops and a loose sleeveless smock shirt. Panic gripped her and then she reassured herself. He wouldn't notice the bump.

The fact that he hadn't come looking for her sooner stung her more than she liked to admit. She was pathetic.

That hatred burned bright within her, giving her strength. 'Well? What do you want? As far as I recall I didn't take anything on my way out of the villa.'

'No,' Alexio said heavily, 'it's what you left behind.'

Sidonie went blank for a moment, and then she saw that cheque in her mind's eye and felt fury all over again. Suddenly it made sense and she said out loud, 'You went back to the villa and discovered I hadn't cashed your precious cheque?'

'Yes,' he admitted.

Sidonie didn't like the way that made the fury diminish slightly. She'd assumed that he'd known all along that she hadn't taken his money and that it had made no difference. But all this time he'd thought she'd cashed in. Still, that didn't change anything.

'And this...'

Sidonie looked to see him holding out her university sweatshirt and was immediately bombarded with memories of meeting him on that plane, feeling like a hick.

She took it from him and said cuttingly, 'You came all this way to deliver my sweatshirt?'

A muscle in his jaw popped and Sidonie felt increasingly vulnerable.

She looked at her watch, and then at him, and injected her voice with false sweetness. 'Look, I'd love to stay and chat, but I have work to get to—so if you don't mind...'

She turned to walk away but he caught her arm again and Sidonie's blood leapt. She stopped and turned around and said in a low voice, 'Let me go, Christakos. We have nothing to say to each other.'

Except for the fact that he's the father of the baby growing in your belly.

Sidonie ignored her conscience. She needed to get away from him before her composure slipped.

Alexio battled to control the lust that had almost felled him the second he'd laid eyes on Sidonie again. His libido was back with a vengeance. He felt the fragility of Sidonie's arm under his hand. She'd lost weight—weight

she could ill afford to lose. Her face was more angular...
giving it a haunting beauty. Her eyes looked huge and
there were shadows underneath. She was exhausted. He
recognised it well.

He frowned. 'Aren't you just leaving work?'

She tried to pull her arm out of his grip but he had an
almost visceral fear that if he let her go he'd never see her
again. That glorious light golden hair was duller than he
remembered, and scooped up into a bun much as it had
been when they'd first met. Her neck looked long and
vulnerable.

'I have two jobs—daytime and evening. Now, if you
don't mind, I don't want to be late.'

'I'll give you a lift,' Alexio said impulsively.

He was still trying to get his head around seeing her
again. His conscience pricked hard. She hadn't taken the
money and she was working two jobs. To pay off the debts.
Debts that weren't even hers. Because she had never wanted
the money from him in the first place. The ramifications
of this, if it were true, made Alexio reel.

This time Sidonie wrenched her arm free. She glared
at Alexio and her eyes spat blue and green sparks at him.
'No, thank you. I do not want a lift or anything else from
you. Now, please, go back to where you came from and
leave me be.'

She turned and hurried away, her bag slung over her
body. She looked very young. Alexio was grim. No way
was he going to walk away until he knew what she was up
to. The fact that he was clearly the last person she wanted
to see only made him more determined.

As Alexio battled not to go and grab her again, and
watched her disappear down the steps of a nearby metro
station, he took out his mobile phone and made a terse call.

CHAPTER EIGHT

THAT NIGHT WHEN Sidonie left the Moroccan restaurant she felt so weary she could have cried. It wasn't helped by the state of agitation she'd been in all day after seeing Alexio. She'd kept expecting him to pop up out of nowhere again and she couldn't forget how he'd looked so drawn. Intense. He hadn't looked like the carefree playboy she remembered.

Still… She firmed her mouth. She'd done the right thing by sending him away. He had no right to come barging into her life again just because he wanted to solve the riddle of the mysterious uncashed cheque.

She would never forgive him for delving into her private life, seeking out her most painful memory and then throwing it in her face as an accusation. He hadn't been remotely interested in listening to her protest her innocence because he'd been all too ready to believe she was just as guilty as her mother. Although Sidonie winced slightly when she thought of the misfortune of him hearing that phone call when he had.

As Sidonie approached Tante Josephine's apartment she saw a familiar low-slung vehicle parked outside. Clearly out of place in this run-down area of Paris.

Her heart thumped erratically. The car was empty. Sidonie looked up and could see the first-floor apartment's lights blazing. Tante Josephine was usually in bed by now. Sidonie had a horrific image of her beloved Jojo being confronted by a tall, dark, intimidating Alexio and stumbled in her haste to get in.

When she almost fell in the front door she saw an idyllic scene of domesticity. Her Tante Josephine was perched on the edge of a chair, holding a cup of tea, and Alexio was seated opposite her on the couch, drinking a cup of coffee.

Tante Josephine put down her cup and stood up, her small matronly bosom quivering with obvious excitement. Her cheeks were bright pink. Sidonie could have rolled her eyes in disgust. The Alexio charm offensive had struck again.

Her aunt took her hands as she came in and Sidonie shot an accusing look at Alexio, whose face was unreadable. But something in his eyes made her heart jump. It was dark. Hard. As it had been on that day.

'Oh, Sidonie, your friend called by earlier. I told him he could wait here for you and we've been having the most pleasant chat.'

Alexio stood up then and made the small apartment laughably smaller. He looked pointedly at her belly and said, in perfect accentless French, 'I believe congratulations are in order?'

Sidonie went cold. *No*. Her aunt couldn't have… But she was notoriously indiscreet—especially with strangers…

Sidonie looked at her with horrified eyes but Tante Josephine, having the nous to suspect that something had just gone very wrong, fluttered nervously and said, 'Well, it's past my bedtime. I'll leave you young people to catch up.'

And then she was gone, leaving Sidonie facing her nemesis. The air was thick with tension.

Sidonie lifted her chin and waited. It didn't take long.

'You're pregnant?'

She tried not to be intimidated by the murderous look on Alexio's face. She'd never allowed herself the indulgence of daydreaming about this scenario, but for a man who didn't even want *a relationship*, this was pretty close to what she might have imagined.

'Yes,' she confirmed starkly, reluctantly. 'I'm pregnant.'

Alexio went pale under his olive skin. His voice sounded rough. 'Whose is it?'

Sidonie gaped at him. She'd also never envisaged that he would doubt the baby was his. She started to speak but a flash of anger rendered her speechless again. Incensed, she stalked over to him and planted her hands on her hips, looked up into that remote hard-boned face.

'Well,' she said, her voice dripping with sarcasm, 'I *did* have a threesome shortly after you cast me out of your life like a piece of unwanted luggage, so it could be Tom, Dick or Harry's baby. But we won't know until it's born and we can see who she or *he* looks like.' She was breathing hard.

Alexio just looked at her.

Growing even more incensed, Sidonie stabbed at his chest with her finger and tried to ignore how hard it felt.

'It's yours, you arrogant jerk,' she hissed, mindful of Tante Josephine. 'Cold-bloodedly seducing another billionaire hasn't exactly been high on my priority list lately.'

Alexio looked down into that furious face and felt numb. He welcomed it. His solicitor had failed to mention the very poignant fact that Sidonie's aunt had mild mental health issues.

And now…now *the baby*. *His* baby. Ever since Tante Josephine had excitedly informed him that Sidonie was expecting a baby, Alexio had felt as if he'd swallowed nails.

At first he'd told himself it couldn't possibly be his: they'd used protection every time. He'd been fanatical about it. Except for when they'd come home from the club and made love in the car, unable even to walk the few steps into the villa. That night was almost sixteen weeks ago now. Sixteen weeks of living in a blur. And now suddenly everything was in focus again.

Disgust at the memory of his lack of control that night had curdled his insides as Sidonie's aunt had chattered on, blithely unaware of the bomb she'd dropped. And then Sidonie had come in, looking panicked. Guilty.

The knowledge that she was telling the truth sank into him like a stone, casting huge ripples outward. He wanted to walk out through the door and keep walking. The sum of all his fears was manifesting itself right now in this room. He wasn't anywhere near ready to contemplate bringing a child into the world. Not after the childhood he'd endured.

A child had perhaps existed in his future life—far in the distant future—along with his perfect blonde wife. He had vowed long ago to make sure that no child of his would see the ugly reality of marriage, because any union *he* would have would be a union of respect and affection—not one punctuated by cold silences, bitter rows, possessive jealousy and violence.

'Well?' Sidonie demanded, hands on hips. 'Aren't you going to say something?'

Alexio's gaze narrowed on her and he realised he wanted to say plenty—but most of it involved his mouth being on Sidonie's. And then his gaze travelled down and he saw the small proud bump evident under her light jacket and the black clingy top she wore. Something within him seemed to break apart. Crumble.

Her hand went there automatically, as if to protect the child, and Alexio felt incensed at that. He thought of the recent revelation of the existence of his oldest half-brother and how his mother had kept him a dirty secret. After abandoning him. Would Sidonie have kept this child from him?

Finally he found his voice, and it was accusing. 'Why didn't you come to me?'

* * *

Sidonie let out a small mirthless laugh and backed away a step. Standing this close to Alexio was hazardous to her mental health and to her libido, which had decided to come out of its ice-like state.

She'd been dreadfully sick for the first trimester of her pregnancy but thankfully that had stopped and she was finally beginning to feel human again. She did not welcome this resurgence of a desire she had no control over.

Alexio was looking increasingly explosive as the news sank in and Sidonie felt a twinge of conscience. She recalled her own shock at finding out about the pregnancy, four weeks after she'd come back to Paris and with no sign of her period.

She crossed her arms tightly. 'You really think I would come to you with this news after you accused me of being a gold-digger? After you judged and tried me—after you had me *investigated* like a common criminal?'

Alexio flushed. 'Why did you agree with me, then, and let me believe that you set out to seduce me?'

Sidonie's arms tightened. 'I told you the truth, but you weren't interested in listening. Would you have believed me if I'd insisted on protesting my innocence?'

Remembering the excoriating feeling of betrayal was acute. Sidonie's emotions were rising and she knew she was too tired to hide them. She stood back and gestured to the door.

'I'd like you to leave now, please. I have to be up early.'

Alexio's eyes widened; his nostrils flared. He looked huge and intimidating, and Sidonie hated the impulse she had to run into his arms and beg him to hold her. She gritted her jaw and avoided his eyes.

Silkily he said, 'You expect me to just walk away?'

Sidonie nodded. 'Yes, please. We have nothing to discuss. You found me, I'm pregnant—end of story. You have nothing else to do here. Please go.'

Alexio's voice was tight with anger. 'We have plenty to discuss if I am your child's father. And you still haven't told me why you didn't take the money.'

Sidonie rounded on him again, eyes blazing, two spots of pink in each cheek. 'I didn't take your damn money, Christakos, because I wasn't interested in your money. I wasn't then and I'm not now.'

Emotion was getting the better of Sidonie, rising, making her shake.

'I will never forgive you for going behind my back and prying into my life. You had no right to judge me on the basis of something my mother did years ago. She paid that due, *I* paid that due, and so did my father. I want nothing to do with you and I wish I'd never laid eyes on you.'

She turned and went to the door, opened it.

Without looking at Alexio she said, 'I have to be up in five hours. Get out or I'll call the police and tell them you're harassing me.'

Alexio made some sort of sound—half anger, half frustration. To Sidonie's everlasting relief, though, he came to the door. She didn't look at him.

He said, with deadly precision, 'This isn't over, Sidonie. We need to talk.'

'Get out, Alexio.' Sidonie's voice had an edge of pleading to it that she hated. But finally he left.

For three days Sidonie had refused to talk to Alexio. She stonewalled him if he was waiting for her to come out of the hotel. She walked in the opposite direction if he was there when she emerged from the café. And at night she was tight-lipped if he offered her a lift for the short distance to the apartment after finishing her shift in the Moroccan restaurant.

Alexio seethed with frustration. He was getting her message loud and clear. She wanted nothing to do with him. She preferred working herself into a lather doing menial jobs rather than turn to him for help. But Alexio had had enough. He'd already set things in motion. Sidonie was pregnant with his child and that changed everything. As he'd watched her for the past three days the knowledge had sunk in more and more.

He needed to talk to her, though. And even though she looked half dead with exhaustion Alexio's body burned for her. Even now, from his car, where he was parked outside the restaurant, he let his gaze rake her up and down, taking in the black skirt, sheer tights and black top. The apron that barely disguised the growing swell of her belly. *His baby.*

In the past few days he'd had time for the news of the baby to sink in, and much to his surprise he'd found himself *not* feeling as trapped as he might have expected. Instead he felt a fledgling sense of excitement, wonder.

He thought of his nephew Milo and wondered if he'd have a son too—precocious and cute like him. Or a daughter, like Sidonie, with golden hair? When he imagined that he felt a tightening sensation in his chest so strong he had to take deep breaths to ease it.

She was serving a big table of men now, and she plucked the pen out from where she'd stuck it into the bun on the top of her head. She looked tired and harassed. Pale.

Alexio saw one of the men put a fleshy hand on her arm and a red mist came over his vision. Before he'd even realised what he was doing he was out of the car and pushing open the door of the small tatty restaurant.

'Sir,' Sidonie gritted out, 'please take your hand off me.'

'Don't tell me what to do. You're serving *me*.'

Sidonie felt a frisson of fear cutting through her hazy exhaustion, but even that didn't give her enough adrenalin to pull free. Just then a blast of warm evening air hit Sidonie's back and she looked around automatically to see Alexio, bearing down on her, his face tight with anger, his eyes fixed on where the man still held her.

Her heart thumped unevenly. For three days he'd dogged her heels and she'd ignored him. She'd seen his car outside and had hated to admit to herself that a part of her liked knowing he was there. She'd told herself stoutly that she hoped he was bored to tears and that she'd irritate him so much that he'd leave and never come back.

Alexio was right behind her now, and treacherously she wanted to lean back, to sink against him. That kept her rigid, fighting the waves of weariness which seemed to be gathering force.

His voice came low and threatening over her head.

'Let her go.'

The heavyset man was drunk and belligerent. He tightened his grip on Sidonie's arm, making her gasp out loud. Alexio reached around her and prised the man's fingers off her arm. He drew her back against him, his other hand going around her midriff, where her belly was round.

It was his touch that did it. It burned like a physical brand. It was too much. Alexio was turning her around now, looking down at her, asking something, but she couldn't hear it because a white noise was making her head fuzzy.

As if standing apart from herself, observing, Sidonie saw herself looking utterly fragile and helpless, with Alexio's hands huge on her arms, and she felt a moment of disgust at herself before everything went black.

Sidonie was in a dark, peaceful place with a soft regular *beep-beep* sound coming from somewhere nearby. Slowly, though, as her consciousness returned so did her memory, and she remembered looking up into Alexio's face and seeing him frown.

Alexio.

The baby.

Tante Josephine.

Sidonie's eyes opened and she winced at the bright light and the stark whiteness of the room. She went to move her arm and something pulled. She looked down to see a tube coming out of the back of her hand.

Her head felt slightly woolly. She noticed a movement out of the corner of her eye—something big—and then Alexio loomed into her vision. Tall and dark. His shirt open at the neck, looking crumpled. Stubble on his jaw.

The faint *beep-beep* sound got faster.

Automatically Sidonie's free hand went to her midriff, where she felt the comforting swell of her baby. Even so, she looked at Alexio. 'The baby?'

He looked grim. 'The baby is fine.'

'Tante Josephine?'

'Is fine too. She's been here all night. I sent her home a while ago.'

'All night?'

'You collapsed in the restaurant. I brought you straight to A and E in my car. You've been on a drip since you arrived and unconscious for nearly eight hours.'

'Am I okay?'

Some of the obvious tension left Alexio's jaw. 'The doctor said you're suffering from a mixture of exhaustion and stress and are generally run down.'

'Oh.'

Alexio started to look grim again, making flutters erupt in Sidonie's belly.

'You've run yourself completely into the ground…'

Something dangerous welled up inside her at his obvious censure and she looked away, terrified of the way her throat was starting to hurt and of the emotion which wouldn't go down.

In a voice that was far too high and tight she said, 'Thank you for bringing me here. You can go now.'

Alexio merely walked around the bed until he was in her eyeline again and folded his arms. Succinctly he said, 'No way.'

Just then the door opened and Sidonie turned her head to see a doctor and a nurse come in.

The doctor declared in French, 'You're awake! You gave us a bit of a scare, young lady...'

While he and the nurse did some tests and elaborated on what Alexio had told her Sidonie was busy trying to block out his presence in the room.

The doctor was soon sitting on the side of the bed and saying, 'You're due for your twenty-week scan in a few weeks, but after what's happened I'd like to do a scan now, just so we can double-check everything is okay.'

He must have seen something on her face because he said quickly, 'I've no reason not to believe everything is fine, but we'd like to be sure.'

Within a few minutes Sidonie was being wheeled in her bed to another part of the hospital. Alexio was by her side. She felt panicky. She was about to have a scan with Alexio looking on. She'd never envisaged *this* happening.

After they were wheeled into the room it all happened very fast. Sidonie's belly was bared and they were smoothing cold gel over it. She felt acutely self-conscious all of a sudden—which was crazy considering Alexio had seen more of her naked body than she probably had herself.

When the doctor put the ultrasound device over her belly a rapid sound filled the room. The baby's heartbeat. Immediately Sidonie's focus went to the screen, which was showing a fuzzy grey image. Her heart thumped as emotion climbed upwards again—but this time it was a different kind of emotion.

After a few minutes the doctor smiled and said, 'Everything looks absolutely normal. You have a fine, healthy baby, Sidonie—a little small, but developing well.'

Then he looked at her and at Alexio.

'Would you like to know the sex?' he asked. 'It's quite clear at the moment.'

Sidonie looked at Alexio, mortified that the doctor had assumed they were together. Even if Alexio *was* the father.

Alexio looked inscrutable and then said, 'It's up to you.'

Sidonie wrenched her gaze away from his with more effort than she liked and looked at the doctor again. She said hesitantly, 'I...I think so.' And then more firmly, as a sense of excitement took hold, 'Yes. I'd like to know.'

The doctor beamed at them. 'I'm very pleased to tell you you're having a baby girl.'

Sidonie felt something joyous erupt in her chest and heard a slightly choked sound coming from beside her. She looked up to see Alexio's eyes fixed on the screen, and there was an expression on his face that she'd never seen before. A kind of wonder.

Her belly swooped. She'd never allowed herself to imagine this kind of scenario. She'd expected to have the baby and then see how she felt about informing him, making sure she did it in such a way that he knew she wasn't telling him in order to get his money.

The thought of being likened to her grasping mother again had made her feel sick. But now that had all been taken out of her hands and she had the very uncomfortable sensation that Alexio was about to get a lot more prominent in her life.

Especially when the doctor wiped the gel off her belly, rearranged her clothes and said, 'We'll keep you in for one more night to help you get your strength back, and then I've been assured that your partner here will be getting you the best care and attention until you're back on your feet.'

Sidonie's head swivelled from Alexio's determined expression to the doctor's equally stern-looking face. *Her partner.* The words sent more flutters into her belly. After three days of being followed, she knew the likelihood of shaking Alexio off when she was feeling weak and vulnerable was extremely unlikely.

She looked at Alexio and said, 'I don't have much choice, do I?'

'No,' he agreed equably.

And that was that.

A week later

'You've done *what*?' Sidonie's mind was hot with rage and she felt her heart-rate zooming skyward, the flutters increasing in her belly. She even put a hand there unconsciously, barely noticing how Alexio's eyes dropped to take in the movement. She was too incensed.

Alexio faced her across the expanse of the beautiful first-floor apartment living room, overlooking the Jardin du Luxembourg. He was dressed in a steel-grey shirt and black trousers and Sidonie didn't like the way she was so *aware* of his physicality. The way she became even more aware of it each day as she grew stronger.

Alexio's voice was low, deep, 'I should have known Tante Josephine couldn't keep it quiet. I asked her not to say anything until you'd had a few more days' rest. But I didn't want her to be worried with you out of work.'

Sidonie struggled to take this in—along with the reminder that Alexio and Tante Josephine seemed to have forged a mutual admiration society.

Sidonie had been in this apartment, which Alexio was renting, for almost a week now. A week of Alexio being cool and solicitous. The consummate host. Paying for a nurse to come every day to check on Sidonie. Taking her outside to the Jardin du Luxembourg across the road to get some air. He was seemingly unperturbed by her continued campaign of obdurate silence, which was more due to her wish to avoid this reckoning and his probing gaze than to anything else. Her searing anger had been proving hard to hang onto, as if merely being in his presence on a daily basis was wearing away at it.

Except now it was back, and Sidonie welcomed it.

Her aunt had just left, to be taken home by Alexio's driver, but before she'd gone she'd spilled her secret.

Sidonie had marched straight into Alexio's office without knocking and declared, 'We need to talk.'

He'd looked up from his papers and sat back, arching a brow. '*Now* you're ready to talk?'

Before she'd had time to regret her impetuous action Sidonie had turned on her heel and walked into the vast living room, not liking how intimate the office space had felt. She had also been very aware that his assistant, who was there every day, had left. Until now she'd been a master at staying out of Alexio's way in the spacious apartment.

Sidonie crossed her arms over her chest and almost winced at how sensitive her breasts were. They had grown bigger. That awareness made her voice curt.

'Answer my question.'

Alexio looked as immovable as a rock, tall and intimidating. At that very moment Sidonie had a vivid memory of lying naked beneath him, spreading her legs wide to accommodate his body, feeling the bold thrust of his arousal against her slick body. Her legs wobbled alarmingly but she held firm.

Thankfully Alexio spoke before Sidonie's wayward memory could take over completely.

'I have paid off all of the debts and ensured that your aunt's mortgage has been paid in full.'

The sheer ease with which he'd been able to magic their debts away made her feel disorientated.

'How dare you?'

Sidonie was trembling. But she was afraid it was more to do with his proximity than her anger.

Alexio's eyes narrowed on her. 'I dare because you are carrying my child and we are now family. Tante Josephine is as much my responsibility as you are—and the baby.'

Sidonie's arms grew so tight she could feel her nails digging into her skin. She spoke from a deep well of hurt and rejection at this attempt to muscle into their lives. 'We are not your responsibility. I never came to you. I want nothing from you. As soon as I'm feeling better I will go and find work again and pay you back what we owe.'

Alexio's mouth went into a bitter line. 'I think you've more than proved your point, Sid. You'd prefer to put our child's health in jeopardy in order to save your pride.'

A lurch of hurt emotion rose up, strangling Sidonie for a moment. Then his words *our child* and *Sid* impacted.

When she'd gathered herself she said with quiet ferocity, 'Do not call me that. My name is Sidonie. And the last thing I want to do is put *my* child in danger. I will keep working because, in case you've forgotten, you called me a hustler and I would prefer to work than to be accused of being that again.'

To her horror, Sidonie's voice had cracked on the last words and she turned now, facing blindly away from Alexio, breathing harshly, emotion getting the better of her.

She heard him move behind her and said rawly, 'Don't come near me.'

He stopped. Tears stung at Sidonie's eyes; her throat ached. She hated him. And she repeated this to herself as she struggled to regain her equilibrium.

His voice came from behind her, tight. 'Sidonie, we need to talk about this… I recognise that I was too hasty that day. I didn't give you a chance to explain.'

Sidonie let out a half-choked laugh at that understatement and said bitterly, 'No, you'd obviously made up your mind and couldn't wait to see the back of me.'

She heard him sigh. The shadows outside were lengthening into dusk. His voice was gruffer now. 'The chef has left some food for us. Let's eat and then we can talk…okay?'

Like a coward, she felt herself wanting to make up some excuse, say that she was too tired, but in truth she felt fine. She turned round, arms still crossed, and faced him. His eyes were intense and her skin prickled. She couldn't keep putting off the conversation.

'Okay, fine.'

Within minutes Alexio was serving them both a light chicken casserole in the dining room off the kitchen area. They ate in silence, but tension was mounting inside Sidonie as she tried to avoid looking at Alexio's large hands and remembering how they'd felt on her skin.

Sitting here eating like this was bringing back memories of that first night in London. The sheer fizzing exhilaration of anticipation. And as if her body was some dumb appendage—an assortment of limbs that wasn't attached to her brain—that same fizzing anticipation was rushing through her right now. Gathering force.

She was uncomfortably aware of every erogenous zone. Her breasts felt tender, sensitive. Swollen. She couldn't stop imagining Alexio's mouth lowering towards one thrusting, naked peak…

With a spurt of agitation, Sidonie let her knife drop with a clatter to the plate. Alexio looked up, that gaze narrowed on her flushed face.

Sidonie stood up, feeling feverish. 'I've had enough. Food.' *God.* She couldn't even articulate a sentence.

Alexio looked as cool as a cucumber while Sidonie felt a bead of sweat trickle between her breasts.

He wiped his mouth with his napkin and said, 'Coffee?'

Sidonie seized on the chance to escape that incisive gaze

and nodded her head. 'Some herbal tea, maybe…the house-keeper brought some today.'

Alexio got up and left the room. Cursing herself for this very unwelcome resurgence of desire, Sidonie went back into the drawing room to stand at the window. Praying for control. Praying that the butterflies in her belly would cease.

She put her hand on her belly and was half frowning at how strong the sensation was when she suddenly realised something. She gasped out loud.

A voice came from behind her, concerned. 'What is it?'

Sidonie whirled around, alight with her discovery for a moment, forgetting everything else. 'For a few days I've been feeling butterflies, but I thought it was—'

She stopped dead, because she'd been about to blurt out *just your effect on me.*

She blushed and said, 'It's the baby. I can feel the baby moving…'

Alexio was holding out a cup towards her and she grabbed it before she could see the effect of her words on his face.

She had a sudden image of one of his hands splayed across her belly and said quickly, 'It's not strong enough yet for anyone else to feel…'

Sidonie took the cup and moved away, taking a sip to hide her burning face.

Alexio gritted his jaw at how Sidonie moved so skittishly away from him, that golden hair looking so much shinier and thicker now, down and shielding her face from him. In the space of only a few days of rest and being well fed she was already looking so much better. The hollows of her cheeks were filling out.

He felt as if he was going to snap soon with the tension building inside him. With every second that passed he wanted to turn into a feral animal and strip Sidonie bare and take her, sating himself and drowning out the recriminatory voices in his head.

But he couldn't. She was pregnant. And she hated his guts.

She looked incredibly young now, in leggings and a loose T-shirt. Of course she'd refused his offers to get her some clothes, so her Tante Josephine had brought her some.

When he could finally move his gaze up from those slim shapely legs and over her belly, hidden under the loose material, to her face, she was looking at him with that aquamarine gaze, something determined in their depths.

'Why did you have me investigated?'

Alexio put down his coffee cup onto a nearby table. Sidonie had her hands wrapped tightly around her own mug.

He looked into her eyes. He owed her this.

'Because what happened between us made me nervous. Because I'd never taken a woman to Santorini before. Because for my whole life I've been cynical and when I was with you I forgot to be. And it freaked me out enough to think that by investigating you I'd still be in control.'

CHAPTER NINE

SIDONIE BLINKED. SHE tried to take his words in. Her belly felt as if it was dropping from a height, and she felt unsteady. 'I'm…you hadn't taken a woman there before?'

He shook his head, eyes intent on her reaction.

She couldn't even hide it. She thought of something. 'But…the clothes…I assumed they had belonged to other women…' Sidonie felt very gauche now.

Alexio frowned and then emitted a disgusted, '*Theos.* You think I would do that? Buy a wardrobe full of clothes and just hope that they would fit a stream of women?'

Sidonie glared back at him, stung with embarrassment. 'Well, how would I know? I thought that was some lovers' bolthole.'

Alexio ran a hand through his hair and said, half to himself, 'No wonder you sounded funny…and yet you didn't say anything.'

Now Sidonie was squirming. 'I didn't want to look stupid…or naïve. If you'd had lovers who were used to that kind of thing…'

The clothes had been bought for her alone. The knowledge made her reel. They hadn't been cast-offs. Sidonie felt increasingly as if she wanted to claim fatigue and run away. But Alexio had a familiar stern look on his face now.

Sidonie went and sat down on a nearby couch, placing

her cup on a table. She clasped her hands on her lap to stop them trembling.

Alexio walked away and stood at the window with his back to her for a long moment, as if he too had to gather himself. When he turned around he looked bleak.

'My solicitor had rung me with what he'd learned about your past that day... I told him it had nothing to do with you. But then he told me about the fact that you'd taken on your aunt's debts, and that put a question in my head as to why you hadn't mentioned this—why you were acting as if you didn't have this huge thing hanging over you.'

Sidonie replied, with a trace of bitterness, 'Because I was escaping from it. I never had any intention of telling you about it. What did it have to do with anything? I knew we were only going to be together for a few days...it was only meant to be one night.'

That last came out almost accusingly as Sidonie recalled how persuasive he'd been and how easily she'd capitulated.

'I knew my aunt was okay—she was on holiday with a group she travels with every year...'

Alexio's voice was hard. 'My solicitor put the seed of suspicion in my head. I refused to believe the worst, though. I told him that. I was angry with myself for even asking him to investigate you.' He sighed heavily. 'I went looking for you. I was going to confess what I'd done and ask you about it...and that's when I overheard part of your conversation.'

Sidonie felt as if the wind had been knocked out of her for a moment at hearing this. When she could speak she admitted, 'I can appreciate how damning that conversation must have been to hear, but my aunt was in hysterics. Someone had fed her with horror stories of being repossessed and worse. I knew she wouldn't feel placated with any reassurances that I'd be there to take her burden. You've met her—you can see for yourself what she's like. I knew she'd only understand something emphatic like someone else saving us. She wouldn't have believed that I could get jobs and pay off the debts over time unless I was physically there to reassure her.'

Sidonie cringed when she thought of how she'd told her aunt *He's crazy about me* and looked down.

'I panicked and said the first thing I thought of.'

She looked up and Alexio's face was unreadable. Sidonie hated the suspicion that he still didn't fully believe her. But then he came and sat down on a chair near the couch and looked at her.

'Will you tell me what happened with your mother?'

Sidonie was about to blurt out that it was none of his business and then she felt those delicate flutters in her abdomen again. *Their daughter*. He had a right to the full story.

She sighed deeply. She'd never told anyone about this before. Feeling it might be easier to talk without Alexio's cool gaze on her, Sidonie stood up and went to the window, arms hugging her midriff.

'She was born in the suburbs. She and my aunt had an extremely impoverished upbringing. Their father ran out on my grandmother, leaving her to raise two daughters on her own—one with special needs My grandmother had drink problems…mental health issues…depression. Neglect was a feature of their lives. She died when my mother was about seventeen. She had to look after Tante Josephine full-time then…which she resented. She was young and bright. Beautiful. She craved opportunities beyond the grim reality of the suburbs.'

Sidonie turned round.

'My mother never told me much, but Tante Josephine's told me enough for me to know that it was pretty tough. When my mother was twenty she won a local beauty competition. Part of the prize was a trip to Dublin for the next round. She went and never came back, leaving my aunt to fend for herself on social protection in their mother's flat.

That's why my father bought her the apartment when he could. He always felt sorry for her—for how my mother had treated her...'

Shame rose up within Sidonie but she forced it down and kept looking at Alexio, determined not to allow her mother's shame to be *her* shame.

'My father was the married man my mother had the affair with—*not* the man she ended up marrying. He owned the language school where she'd signed up to do an English course with the prize money from the competition. When he found out she was pregnant he dumped her. She never forgave him for it. My stepfather met my mother around the same time. He was crazy about her and stepped in and offered to marry her.'

Sidonie's chin lifted imperceptibly.

'She was avaricious and selfish. No one knows that better than me and my aunt. And my stepfather, who stood by her despite the public humiliation she put him through. She put us all through hell when she ended up being prosecuted, and yet my stepfather never once let me feel anything less than his own child. She was put in jail for two years when I was eight years old. I had to endure taunts at school every day, because we couldn't afford to move until she was released from prison.'

Sidonie's voice shook with passion.

'I spent my whole life dreading someone finding out about her past. That's why I don't talk about it. But I am *not* her, and you had no right to assume I was like her—no matter what evidence you thought you had...'

She recalled one of the things he'd hurled at her. 'Not even the fact that I told you I liked jewellery. I'm a woman, Alexio. A lot of women like glittery shiny things. It doesn't mean we're all inveterate gold-diggers.'

Alexio stood up too, and immediately a flare of awareness made Sidonie take a step back. His eyes flashed at her movement and something tightened between them.

His mouth was a grim line. 'I'm sorry that I didn't give you the chance to tell me this, for misjudging you and for leaving you to go through what you have for the past few months. You should never have had to deal with this on your own...'

The lines of his face grew stark and his voice roughened.

'But I'm not sorry you're pregnant. I want this baby too.'

He came closer and everything in Sidonie tightened with anticipation. She tried to ignore it.

Heavily, Alexio continued, 'I should tell you why I jumped to such conclusions. My mother was the most cynical person I've ever known. She taught me not to trust at an early age, and the world and my peers have only confirmed her lesson. I'm used to lovers as cynical as I have become. You were so different from anyone I've ever met before...'

His words resounded in Sidonie's head, shocking her. She felt weakened by this mutual confessional. The hard knot of tension and pain inside her felt as if it was dissolving, treacherously.

Alexio went on. 'My parents' marriage was not happy. It was sterile, loveless. I told you why I decided to break with my father...but there's more to it than that. Once he beat my mother. I rushed in to stop him, to protect her, but she put me out of the room and went back in and closed the door, shutting me out.'

Alexio's mouth twisted.

'She didn't want or need my protection—not even then... And that's why I wanted nothing more to do with my father.'

Sidonie's heart clenched. She felt increasingly vulnerable and was aware that only inches separated them now. When had they even moved that close?

Alexio's hand closed around one upper arm, warm against her bare skin, setting off a chain reaction.

'I'm sorry, Sidonie. Truly.'

Something moved between them. Something fragile and yet something very earthy too.

But Sidonie was reeling. It was too much. She pulled her arm free and said weakly, 'I'm tired now. I should go to bed.'

Alexio just looked at her in the soft glow of the lamps. 'Yes.'

Sidonie knew she should move, but for a second she couldn't seem to. All she could see was that mouth, and all she could think about was how she wanted to feel it on hers right now. She had to get out of there before she did something stupid. Exposed herself.

Backing away, eyes huge, as if she was afraid he might pounce on her, Sidonie left the room and shut herself inside her bedroom. Her heart was beating as rapidly as if she'd just run a mile. Alexio's words swirled in her head and every cell in her body was protesting at being out of his proximity.

Trying her best to ignore the insistent throbbing of her blood and pulse, Sidonie washed herself and put on her nightshirt, got into bed. But as soon as she lay down she knew sleep was an impossibility.

She clenched her hands into fists. It was as if his words had unlocked something tight and painful inside her and replaced it with pure desire. She needed Alexio with an almost physical pain. Hunger for him made her grit her jaw. Hormones were flooding her body, stronger than anything she'd felt before.

Almost without thinking, operating on some very base level, Sidonie got out of bed and opened the door of her bedroom. She went back into the drawing room and saw Alexio standing at the window, looking like a remote fig-

ure. For a second she hesitated, but then he turned round…
and she was no more capable of going back than she was
of ceasing breathing.

Rawly, she blurted out, 'I need you to make love to me.'

Alexio thought he was dreaming. He saw Sidonie silhou-
etted in the light of a nearby lamp. Her flimsy nightshirt
clearly showed the shape of her body and the fact that she
wore no underwear. His blood boiled, blanking his brain
of everything he'd been thinking about. Lust surged, making him so hard it hurt.

Her breasts looked bigger, he could see the swell of her
belly, and something deeply primal within him exulted
fiercely. *His* seed in her belly. After their conversation he'd
been feeling ridiculously exposed, but that was incinerated
by the heat he felt right now.

Fearing she might disappear, Alexio instructed her
throatily, 'Come here.'

Sidonie moved with endearing jerkiness, and then she
was in his arms and Alexio's mouth was on hers. Her body
was pressing into him so hard it felt as if he'd be branded
with her shape for ever and he was devouring her…and
wondering dimly how he'd survived for as long as he had
without this.

Sidonie groaned deep in her throat as sheer wanton pleasure
burned up inside her at the feel of Alexio's arms around her
again, his mouth on hers, his tongue stroking hers.

She barely noticed him lifting her up into his arms, feeling weightless as she wrapped her arms around his neck
and sank deeper and deeper into the kiss. They only broke
apart so that Alexio could lay Sidonie down on his bed,
and she looked up at him as he pulled off his shirt, revealing the hard-muscled perfection of his torso. He looked
leaner, harder than she remembered, and everything feminine within her sighed voluptuously.

He took off his trousers and underwear and he was unashamedly naked and aroused. The dusky light from outside bathed him in a golden glow.

'I need to see you.' His voice was hoarse.

Sidonie's body was on fire. She couldn't remember feeling so desperate, so sensitised. Her breasts were literally throbbing, aching with need. And between her legs she felt damp and hot.

She sat up slightly and pulled her nightshirt off, but her hands were awkward.

Alexio said roughly, 'I'll do it.'

He reached down and pulled it up and then all the way off. She was naked but she couldn't drum up any embarrassment. She needed him too badly.

She could see Alexio's jaw tighten as his eyes devoured her. And then his gaze moved down to the swell of her belly. She lay back on the bed, her breathing tortured. Alexio moved between her legs, forcing them apart slightly, and then came down, resting over her on his hands. Sidonie put her hands on his arms and he bent his head again, kissing her deeply, intimately. His tongue stabbed deep, sliding along hers, making her moan with need.

When his mouth moved across her jaw and down further Sidonie's nipples tightened unbearably. Torturously slowly he came closer and closer to that distended hard tip, and when he drew it into his mouth and suckled she cried out. It hadn't been like this before. This intense.

His hand was cupping her other breast, kneading it gently, fingers pinching that peak. Sidonie's hands were in his hair, clasping him to her with a death grip. When his mouth left her breast and his head moved down Sidonie let out a gasp of disappointment which quickly turned to something else when he pressed a kiss to her belly. For a second her desire was eclipsed by something much more profound and dangerously tender.

Before she could dwell on it Alexio was moving lower, spreading her legs wide, his breath feathering across the incredibly sensitised nerves between her legs. She had to put her fist to her mouth to stop from crying out again when his mouth covered her. His tongue swirled and suckled with merciless and expert precision until she couldn't hold it back and a flood of ecstasy rushed through her in unstoppable waves.

The intensity of her orgasm left Sidonie trembling all over and she had a moment of *déjà vu*, remembering her first time with Alexio and how intense it had been. He loomed over her now, broad and awe-inspiring, and she wanted him deep inside her with a ferocious urgency that made her feel desperate.

Sidonie hooked her legs around his thighs, drawing him closer.

He emitted a guttural, 'I don't want to hurt you…the baby…'

'You won't,' she assured him breathlessly.

With a low groan, Alexio pressed closer, and then she felt the thick head of his erection sliding into her. So big.

Sidonie let out a sound of frustration, needing more, drawing him even closer, and then with one powerful thrust he sheathed himself deep within her tight, slick body. Tears of emotion sprang into Sidonie's eyes and she closed them fiercely in case Alexio might see the betraying glitter.

He was moving now—slowly, ruthlessly, in and out. The ride was slow and intense. Tension tightened inside Sidonie, making her moan and plead incoherently for Alexio to never stop.

When her climax approached Sidonie's eyes flew open. She could only see Alexio's green gaze boring into her. He held her suspended on the crest of the wave until he thrust one last time and her whole body convulsed with pleasure around his.

* * *

At some point, in the silvery glow of the moon, Sidonie woke up to feel Alexio behind her, pressing kisses to the back of her neck, making her shiver with renewed arousal. He bent over her, scooping her back against him, coming behind her, a hand reaching to find her breast and cup it, making her moan with sleepy and delicious desire.

He said softly beside her ear, 'Come up on your knees.'

Sidonie was wide awake now, and practically panting with need. Just like that—within seconds. She did as he asked and came up on her knees, her legs spread. Her upper body was on the bed, her elbows bent. Alexio stretched over her back and she could feel his steel-hard erection move against her. He took her arms and stretched them over her head. Her hands automatically gripped the pillow.

And then his thighs were behind hers, his legs moving hers even further apart. Like this, she felt unbelievably exposed and wanton. And yet never more aroused. He drew his hand down her spine, fingers tracing her bones, and then his hands spread around her hips, drawing her back and into him.

She turned her cheek to the bed. Her hands tightened to white knuckles when she felt one hand move between them to explore how ready she was. She could have wept when she felt the tremor run through his body on feeling the evidence of her desire.

Taking his hand away, he replaced it with his potent erection, and as he thrust deep and started the relentless slide of his body in and out of hers again Sidonie felt as if she was losing it completely. All that control she'd held on to for four months, the hatred... It was being washed away and leaving her vulnerable, defenceless. Raw.

Alexio's body moved with awesome power, wresting away Sidonie's ability to think rationally. When he bent close over her back and drew her hair aside, so that he could press a kiss to her exposed skin and cup her breast, she couldn't hold on any more and shattered to pieces for a third time.

When Alexio woke in the early dawn light he kept his eyes closed for a minute, relishing the hum of satisfaction in his body. Slowly, though, the satisfaction faded as memories took over.

Alexio opened his eyes and realised he was alone in his bed. If not for the crumpled sheets and that hum in his body he might have imagined that he'd had another night of dreams so vivid he woke up aching and aroused.

But sleeping with Sidonie had been no dream. It had surpassed any mere dream. She was more than he remembered—even more responsive.

Why had she left him? Suddenly irritated at the empty bed, Alexio threw back the covers and jumped out. He pulled on a pair of discarded jeans nearby, left them open, and prowled through the apartment to Sidonie's room. The door was shut. He opened it softly and went in. His heart clenched. She was in her nightshirt, lying on her side, with her legs pulled up. Long golden copper hair was spread out around her head. Lashes were long and dark against her flushed cheeks. Her breaths were deep and even.

He stood transfixed for a long moment and realised with a creeping sense of fatality that everything he'd ever known or believed in had spectacularly blown up in his face.

Yet even now he could hear his mother's cold voice in his head, mocking him: *'It's all an act, Alexio...she's fooling you even now, making you want her. Making you believe that she'd do anything but take your money when she has your baby in her belly, the best insurance a woman can get...'*

Alexio blocked out the voice with an effort. He couldn't believe he'd told Sidonie *everything* last night. The darkest, dirtiest secret of his father's violence. He'd never even told Rafaele about that. He'd never forget his mother's beautiful face, bruised and battered. But she hadn't cried out. She hadn't let him help. She'd put him from the room and closed the door and contained the incident. Always so cold, so frigid.

He could feel the remnants of the same rigidity that he'd learned from her in him, and also the desire to let it loosen. He thought of everything Sidonie had told him last night. He believed her. He *wanted* to believe her. But some deep part of him was clinging to the tentacles of the past like a drowning man clinging to a buoy.

One thing was for sure: there was no way she could not agree to the fact that Alexio was going to be an integral part of her life from now on—and his daughter's.

When Sidonie woke the following morning her whole body felt deliciously lethargic and sated. And then her eyes opened and horror coursed through her. *Alexio.* She'd begged him to make love to her last night like some kind of lust-crazed wanton.

She cringed. But then she recalled their conversation and that sensation of something giving way inside her, melting. In the cold light of day, and after what had happened last night, Sidonie couldn't keep pretending to herself that she hated Alexio. Far from it.

She'd fallen for him on Santorini—if not as early as that first night in London. *Who was she kidding?* she castigated herself. She'd probably fallen for him on that plane, before they'd even kissed. And, yes, she'd hated him for the way he'd treated her, but she'd really never stopped falling for him.

And after what he'd told her about his mother and his father… It didn't excuse him, but it made her weak heart want to empathise with how a man had become so cynical at such a young age and never had any experience to counteract that.

No wonder he'd checked himself and doubted what was going on between them if he'd never allowed a woman that close before…

Feeling dangerously dreamy all of a sudden, Sidonie got out of bed and took a shower, all at once eager to see Alexio and cursing herself for having left his bed because she'd felt so raw and exposed.

Since he'd come back into her life he'd done nothing but support her, and had taken the news of her pregnancy on board with admirable equanimity. And what had she done? Thrown everything back in his face…scared in case he got close enough to see how deep her feelings ran for him. Scared in case he'd see how flimsy that hatred was because she knew she still loved him and hated her own weakness.

He'd paid off the debts to ease her aunt's mind and to take the burden of pressure off *her*. And even though that still made Sidonie feel uncomfortable she knew that he'd undoubtedly done it out of concern for her health and the baby's.

Those debts were a drop in the ocean for him, But she was still concerned enough to make a case for paying him back. The thought of just letting him pay off debts her mother had been responsible for made Sidonie feel faintly ill.

But after last night—surely something had shifted between them? Maybe something of what they'd had before hadn't been irretrievably lost…?

Sidonie's heart beat fast at that. Maybe the lines of communication could be a little more open now. Surely he would respect her desire to pay him back?

When Sidonie went in search of Alexio and found him reading a newspaper at the breakfast table she had a smile on her face. It soon faded, though, when he looked at her with a cool expression, his face unreadable.

'Good morning.'

'Morning...' she said faintly, wondering if this clean-shaven epitome of elegance in a dark suit and shirt was the same man who had driven her to the brink of her endurance three times last night. Now she didn't feel so bad about leaving his bed. The sense of rawness and vulnerability was back with a vengeance.

The housekeeper who worked for a few hours every day, preparing meals and cleaning the apartment, bustled in with breakfast for Sidonie and she sat down silently. The doctor had recommended a diet full of nutrients to help her get back on her feet but she couldn't stomach anything now. She felt a little sick.

'Okay?' Alexio's question was cool.

Sidonie nodded and avoided his eye, picking at the food. It was as if nothing had happened.

He finished his coffee and put his paper down. 'We should talk...' he said.

Sidonie gave up pretending to try and eat and pushed her plate away slightly. She looked at him and wished she could block out the images from the previous night. The way he'd looked so intense... And she wished she could block out her feelings too, but it seemed as if now she'd admitted how she felt to herself she'd opened a dam.

'Talk about what?'

Alexio looked serious. 'About us...where we go from here.'

Something went cold inside Sidonie. She'd imagined a conversation like this, but not with Alexio sounding as if he was about to discuss profits and losses. Foolishly she'd imagined something altogether more passionate.

In her silence, he clarified, 'We can't go on in this state

of limbo... You're feeling better. I have to get back to work.
We need to figure out the logistics.'

Limbo. Was that what he thought last night had been
about? While Sidonie had been realising how much she
loved him?

She slid out of her chair and stood up. Alexio stood too,
instantly dwarfing her. She moved back.

'I don't think I'm quite getting your meaning.'

His hands curled around the back of his chair. 'What
I'm talking about is where we'll live—how we will proceed. I'll have to buy a new house, of course. The apartment isn't suitable for a baby... Or maybe you want to be
here? Near to your aunt?'

Sidonie's mouth had fallen open at the way he'd laid everything out so starkly. There was no emotion involved.
She recovered her wits and felt anger rising at his cool arrogance.

'This baby is not *logistics*—it's a baby. Our daughter.'

Those words pricked her heart. She put her hands on her
belly, the by now nearly constant fluttering comforting her.

'I don't expect *us* to *proceed* anywhere. I do expect *me*
to go on with *my* life, though.'

Alexio looked every inch the powerful tycoon in that
moment. 'This isn't up to you, Sidonie. You *will* allow me
to provide for you and the baby.'

Sidonie cursed herself for ever having cast him in the
role of benign benefactor. Emotions bubbled over. Enough
for the both of them.

'Her name is Belle. Not *the baby*. And I stupidly thought
that after last night something had changed...that—' She
stopped and cursed herself silently. She'd said too much.

Alexio looked disgusted. 'Our daughter is *not* going to
be called Belle—what kind of a name is that?'

Sidonie replied faintly, 'It's Tante Josephine's favourite name.'

She felt dazed at how naïve she'd been. *Again*. Nothing had changed.

That green gaze narrowed on her. 'You thought *what* had changed?'

Sidonie shook her head, feeling sick at how she'd almost given herself away. Disgusted with herself for allowing some confessional conversation and some hot sex to melt away her feelings of anger. She'd only ever been a transitory visitor through Alexio's bed. And now he was stuck with her.

'Nothing. I'm not doing this, Alexio—committing to some sterile arrangement just for your benefit.'

'We desire each other. Last night proved that beyond a doubt.'

Sidonie felt as exposed as if he'd just stripped her naked. A few hours ago he had.

Lifting her chin, she said tautly, 'That was hormones.'

Alexio looked comically confused for a moment. 'Hormones?'

Sidonie nodded, desperate to convince him that he had it wrong. 'It's in my pregnancy book—you can read about it. It's very common for pregnant women to feel more...' Sidonie faltered. In spite of her best efforts she blushed fiercely. 'More...amorous. It's because of all the extra blood.'

The confusion left Alexio's face and now he looked livid. A muscle throbbed in his temple. 'Hormones...? *Extra blood*? That was chemistry—pure and simple.' He was almost roaring now. 'Are you trying to tell me that any man would have done to satisfy your urges last night?'

Sidonie's face burned, but valiantly she affected as much insouciance as she could and with a small shrug reiterated, 'I'm just telling you what's in my pregnancy book.'

Alexio's face was rigid with rejection, and even she felt the sting of her conscience.

'You wanted me as much as I wanted you. There might have been extra hormones involved, but it was inevitable.'

Sidonie cursed silently. So much for hoping to convince Alexio that any man would have done. *As if.* Even now she wanted him, in spite of his being so arrogant that she wanted to hit him.

Sidonie clenched her hands into fists and glared at him for making her love him. For making her want him. For humiliating her.

'Nothing has changed, Alexio. We're exactly where we were when you arrived in Paris. The only difference now is that I owe *you* money instead of a bank.'

Alexio looked livid again. 'Stop saying that. You owe me nothing. I want to try and make this work, Sidonie.'

Sidonie felt bitter. '*This* is not a car, Alexio. And I can tell you that it's not working. Desire or no desire. That's not enough. I won't allow you to put me and our daughter up like some kind of discarded mistress and her child. I am not a sponger. I will work to pay my way for me and my child, like millions of other women around the world.'

Alexio's mouth was a tight line of displeasure. 'Millions of other women around the world haven't had the sense to fall pregnant by a billionaire.'

Sidonie gasped and went pale as his unspoken words throbbed silently between them: *So stop pretending that you don't want my support.*

Alexio immediately put out a hand. 'Sid…wait. I didn't mean it like—'

Sidonie cut him off with ice in her voice, even as her heart was breaking all over again. 'I've already told you *not* to call me that. My name is Sidonie. And you've said quite enough. You still don't trust me, do you?'

She saw the flare of guilt in his eyes and something inside her withered and died. She couldn't say another word.

She shook her head and backed away, and then turned and walked out of the room.

Alexio watched her go and then tunnelled his hands through his hair. He closed his eyes and repeated every curse he'd ever heard under the sun. Watching the way she'd gone pale just now... Something inside him had curdled and now he felt the acrid taste of panic. That hadn't gone at all the way he'd expected it to.

As if one moment of this relationship with this woman had *ever* gone the way he'd expected it to...

From the moment she'd appeared at breakfast with that shy smile Alexio had felt the dam of emotion inside him threatening to burst free. But he wasn't ready yet. It was too much.

When he came out of the dining room he saw Sidonie putting on her coat and lifting her bag. The panic escalated, making him feel constricted, rudderless. As if he were freefalling from a great height.

'Where are you going?'

Sidonie avoided his eye. 'I said I'd go over to Tante Josephine's this morning.'

She looked at him then, but there was no expression on her face or in her eyes. She was pale. The swell of her belly was visible under her top. Alexio had a sudden urge to beg Sidonie not to go, but something held him back. The memory of his mother's cold face when he'd blurted out, *Why can't you love each other?* Those tentacles were dragging him back, stronger than he could resist.

He assured himself he was overreacting. Sidonie would be back this afternoon and they would talk again. When he'd regained some sense of being in control. He was still shaking with rage at the insinuation that she would have slept with any willing red-blooded man last night because she'd just been horny.

'My car and driver are outside if you want to use them.'

Sidonie said a quiet, 'Okay.' And then she opened the door and left. Alexio had the awful sensation that even while he was so intent on retaining control he was losing it anyway.

Alexio spent the morning and early afternoon on the phone to his offices in London and Athens. But he couldn't get his poisonous words to Sidonie out of his head: *Millions of other women around the world haven't had the sense to fall pregnant by a billionaire.* Or how stricken she had looked after he'd said them. She'd looked that stricken on Santorini.

A cold fist seemed to be squeezing his heart.

His solicitor Demetrius rang and asked him, 'When are you going to stop playing nursemaid and come back to work?'

A volcanic rage erupted deep inside Alexio as he recalled how this man, *his friend,* had unwittingly fed Alexio's deeply cynical suspicions four months ago, and he slammed the phone down before he could say or do something he might regret. Like fire him. Alexio had no one to blame but himself.

He looked at the phone belligerently. The fact was that he had no desire for work. He had desire only for one thing and he was very much afraid that he had just let that one thing slip out of his grasp.

He picked up the phone again and dialled. After a few seconds a recording of Sidonie's voice sounded in his ear: *'I'm sorry I can't take your call. Leave me a message and I'll get back to you.*

Short, economical. Up-front. Alexio felt sick, and the back of his neck prickled. He didn't leave a message. He made another call and asked Tante Josephine if Sidonie had left her yet.

Tante Josephine answered him and the panic rose high enough in his throat to strangle him.

He forced himself to sound calm. 'When did she leave?'

She told him and Alexio did rapid calculations in his head. Somehow he managed to get out something vaguely coherent and then he put down the phone and stood up. And then he sat down again abruptly. Alexio didn't know what to do, and he was filled with a sense that for the first time in his largely charmed life he couldn't predict the outcome with his usual arrogance.

An image of his brother Rafaele came into his mind's eye, and he recalled how turbulent his emotions had been at seeing his brother embrace love and a family. Alexio realised now that he'd been poisonously jealous of his brother. Jealous of what he'd reached out for when everything in his life should have told him it wasn't possible.

Something was swelling inside Alexio's chest now—something bigger than the past. And with it came the fear that had held him back that morning. But for the first time Alexio didn't fight it. And then he felt another very fledgling feeling take hold: *hope*. Did he dare to think that he too could reach out and take hold of something he'd once believed in? Even if there might be nothing on the other side?

With a grim sense of resolve, and knowing that he just didn't have a choice any more, Alexio made the first of a series of calls and then instructed his driver to have the car ready.

CHAPTER TEN

SIDONIE SAT IN her seat, legs tucked up beneath her, and looked out of the small oval window of the plane. A faint heat haze shimmered off the tarmac outside. She felt bad about leaving her aunt behind, even if she *had* assured Sidonie she was fine. She was going to Dublin to enquire about getting back onto the college programme for her final year.

But then she felt the flutters in her belly and panic gripped her. How could she be thinking of going back to college when she was due to have her baby before Christmas? Tears pricked her eyes. She cursed her impetuousness. She hadn't really thought this through at all. She'd just wanted to get far away from Paris and Alexio's ongoing mistrust before he reduced her to rubble.

She couldn't believe she'd left herself wide open to his cynicism again.

She heard the sound of the air hostess saying, 'Your seat, sir.'

Sidonie's heart stopped for a moment and she looked around. An incredible sense of disappointment lanced her when she saw a small, very rotund man, sweating profusely, taking off his jacket before he sat down. She looked away, cursing herself again. What had she been hoping for? For history to repeat itself and Alexio to turn up when she wasn't even on one of his planes?

Sidonie choked back the tears and told herself that she was the biggest idiot on earth for letting her defences down so spectacularly. She bundled up her sweatshirt and put it under her head against the window, hoping to block everything out—including the take-off and landing and disturbing images of a cynical expression that softened only in passion.

'I'm sorry, sir, I'm afraid we've made a mistake with your seat. I'll have to move you.'

Sidonie woke up and blinked, surprised to see that they were in the air and she'd missed the take-off. Then she recalled why she was so tired and scowled at the memory. The air hostess was helping the man beside her out of his seat and apologising profusely while he complained vociferously.

Sidonie didn't mind. His elbow had been digging into her, and if no one else sat down she could—

'Is this seat taken?'

Sidonie stopped dead in the act of laying out her sweatshirt on the seat beside her as a pillow. She went hot and then cold. She looked up.

Alexio. In a dark suit and shirt. Looking dishevelled and a little wild.

In a daze, half wondering if she might be hallucinating, she said, 'Well, I was hoping that it would stay empty.'

Alexio grimaced. 'I'm sorry, it would appear that all the seats are taken. This is the only one left.'

Sidonie lifted up her sweatshirt and held it to her like protection. She tried to ignore the jump in her pulse at the way Alexio slipped off his jacket and sat down, infusing the small space with his scent and magnetism. The sense of *déjà vu* was heady.

Her eyes narrowed on him. She was wide awake now.

'How did you know where I was?' And then she answered herself. 'Tante Josephine.'

Alexio's mouth quirked but the smile didn't reach his eyes and for the first time Sidonie saw something in their depths she'd never seen before: nervousness. It made her pulse leap even more.

'Yes.'

Sidonie shook her head and tried to stave off the emotional pain of seeing him again—especially here. 'What do you want, Alexio?'

He shrugged minutely and looked tortured, and then he said, 'You...and our daughter.'

Sidonie fought back the tears and bit her lip before saying, 'I know you do. You feel a duty, a sense of responsibility...but it's not enough. I won't be that woman who takes from you just because you're the father of my child. And you don't trust me...'

Alexio's eyes burned fiercely now. He angled his body towards Sidonie, cocooning her from the rest of the plane. He took her hand and she could feel his trembling slightly. It stopped her from pulling back.

'I do trust you, Sid...*Sidonie*...'

Sidonie's heart clenched at the way he'd corrected himself.

His grip on her hand tightened. 'I *do*. I should never have said what I said earlier. It was stupid and I'm an ass. I didn't mean it for a second. It was a reflex. I was still clinging on to the last tiny piece of my cynical soul because I was too scared to let my past go... I was nine when my mother told me not to believe in love, that it was a fairytale. I watched her and my father annihilate each other all my life... I thought that was normal. I always chose women who were emotionally aloof...who demanded nothing. Because I had nothing to give. And then I met you, and for the first time I wanted more.'

His mouth twisted with self-recrimination.

'And yet at the first opportunity I chose to mistrust you, and then I turned my back on you...telling myself that I'd been a fool to expect anything more.'

Feeling shaky and light-headed, Sidonie said, 'That phone call was very bad luck...'

Alexio's mouth was still tight. 'But I gave you no chance to defend yourself—and why would you want to after I'd had you investigated like a common criminal?'

Sidonie wanted to touch his jaw but she held back. This moment felt very fragile. 'I can't escape the fact that my mother *was* a criminal. That's pretty damning, even if you hadn't overheard me talking to Tante Josephine. That's partly why I agreed with you when you asked if I'd set out to seduce you once I knew who you were... I felt it was hopeless...'

'The last four months have felt pretty hopeless.' Alexio's voice was bleak.

Sidonie said quietly, 'You were the first person I'd trusted in a really long time—if ever—and you hurt me...'

Contrition made Alexio's face look old all of a sudden. He went grey. 'I know. And I don't expect you to forgive me... But I wanted to tell you something.'

Sidonie looked at him and her belly hollowed out. 'What?'

His hand tightened on hers. His voice was so rough and his accent so strong that she almost couldn't make out what he was saying.

'I've fallen in love with you.'

His words dropped between them. Sidonie struggled to believe she hadn't dreamt them up.

He smiled, and it was almost sad. 'I think I fell for you on that plane...' His smile faded. 'If you give me a chance I'll spend the rest of my life making it up to you...'

Sidonie shrank back, pulling her hand free. She shook

her head, everything within her trying to dampen down the incredibly sweet swelling of joy. The fall would be too great if—

'You can't mean it…you're just saying that.'

Alexio looked fierce and affronted. 'I've never, ever said that to another woman and I never intend to.'

Sidonie felt a mix of tears and laughter vying for supremacy. But still she couldn't afford to believe. Visions of her stepfather's sad face came back to haunt her. Sad because he'd loved his wife his whole life when she hadn't loved him. Even though he'd sacrificed so much to be there for her. Alexio was saying this…but he couldn't love her as much as she loved him.

'You don't…don't mean it,' she got out, too scared to hope for even a second.

Alexio reached for her and put his hands on the bottom of her top, pulling it up to reveal her belly. Sidonie squeaked with shock, but before she could stop him Alexio was putting his big hands on her, spanning the small compact swell, and he was bending down, his mouth close to her bump, saying with a none too steady voice, 'Belle…I'm doing my best, here, to convince your mother that I love her and trust her and want to spend the rest of my life with her…and you…but it's not going so well. I don't think she believes me.'

Sidonie felt a very definite kick then—the first proper kick apart from the flutters. In shock, her eyes wide, she watched as Alexio came back up, his hands still on her belly.

There was a look of wonder on his face. 'I felt that…'

And then the look cleared, to be replaced with one of determination.

'Belle is clearly on my side. It's two against one.'

Sidonie couldn't prevent the tears from clogging her throat and flooding her eyes. She was overwhelmed by

Alexio's hands on her belly, the baby kicking for the first time…him saying he loved her.

But she ignored all that for a moment and choked out, 'I thought you said we couldn't call her Belle…'

Alexio smiled, and this time it looked slightly less nervous. 'It's growing on me—and Tante Josephine will never forgive me if we call her something else. But next time it's my choice.'

'Next time?' Sidonie choked out through even more tears.

Alexio was just a blur now, and his hands left her belly to come up and cup her face, thumbs wiping at her tears.

'Next time…if you'll have me,' he said gently, 'And the next time and the next time…'

And then his mouth was on hers and Sidonie was shaking too much to do anything but submit and allow herself the first sliver of belief that this was real and that Alexio meant what he was saying.

When he pulled back Sidonie's mouth tingled. His hands were still on her jaw, cupping her face. She looked into his eyes, searching, and all she could see there was pure… *emotion*. For the first time. No shadows. No cynicism.

She took a deep shaky breath. 'Alexio…'

'Yes…?'

'I love you too…even though you really hurt me. I fell for you when we first met and I never stopped. I'm still falling. Every time I look at you. I told myself I hated you…but I couldn't.'

Alexio's hands tightened around her and his gaze grew suspiciously bright. 'You love me?'

Sidonie wanted to take a snapshot of this moment. Alexio Christakos, multi-billionaire and playboy. Arrogance and confidence personified. Eyes shining with tears, doubting her word.

She reached up to touch his face, feeling the spiky

prickle of his stubble. He was a different man from the one who had so coolly laid out his plan that morning. He'd been hiding all this emotion. Suppressing it.

'Of course I love you. I love you so much that I'm terrified I love you more than you love me.'

Alexio just looked at her for a long moment and shook his head, smiling a little ruefully. 'Not possible, I'm afraid. You're getting the full force of years and years of repressed loving and then some more...'

He reached into his pocket for something, and pulled out a small black box. Sidonie looked down at it and back up.

Alexio looked nervous again. 'Sid... *Sidonie*...'

'No...' she said urgently, and then, more shyly, 'I like it when you call me that... I just... I was angry...'

She could see the pain in his eyes at that and she touched his jaw. Alexio dragged his gaze away and opened the box. Sidonie looked down and gasped when she saw a stunning heart-shaped diamond ring glittering up at her. Alexio took the ring out of the box. He took her left hand in his and looked at her so deeply that he took her breath away and made fresh tears well.

Looking endearingly unlike himself, palpably nervous, he asked, 'Will you marry me, Sidonie Fitzgerald?'

The tears overflowed and fell. Sidonie couldn't speak. She was too overcome.

Suddenly Alexio disappeared again, down towards her bump, and she heard him say, 'Belle, I've just asked—'

Alexio yelped when Sidonie grabbed his hair and pulled him back up.

'Yes!' She looked at him. 'Yes...' she said again, framing his face with her hands. 'I'll marry you, Alexio.'

Alexio kissed the palm of her hand and then took it in his again, to slide the ring onto her finger. 'I had a jeweller meet me at the plane and I picked that one out because it reminded me of your pure heart...but I can change it...'

Sidonie shook her head, looking at the ring glinting at her. 'No..' She felt more tears coming after what he'd just said. 'I love it…and it's really glittery.'

Alexio pulled her in close. 'I'll give you glittery things for the rest of our lives…'

Sidonie stiffened and pulled back, making Alexio frown.

'No… I don't want anything from you, Alexio… I mean it. I know you say you trust me, but I don't want you to ever doubt that I want nothing from you except you. I won't marry you until I can sign something that says I'm not after you for your money.'

Alexio sighed. 'Sid, don't be ridiculous.'

Sidonie pulled away and dragged her top down over her bump. She shook her head again and crossed her arms. 'No marriage unless you agree.'

Sidonie saw Alexio's eyes slide down to her bump and she put a hand over it.

'And no more cutesy manipulation of our daughter before she's even born.'

Alexio rolled his eyes heavenward and then threw up his hands. 'Okay—fine.'

His eyes glinted with determination then and he reached for her, pulling her into him so tightly that she didn't know where she ended and he began. Sidonie slid her arms around his waist and snuggled against him. They rested like that for a long moment, the calm after the storm.

'Sid?'

'Hmm?'

'Are you going to sleep?'

Sidonie nodded her head against Alexio's chest and said sleepily, happily, 'It's those hormones again. I have a feeling you're going to be keeping me up late, so I should really nap now. And also pregnant women shouldn't be subjected to too much excitement—it takes it out of us.'

She felt Alexio tense slightly and heard his affronted,

'What happened last night was more than hormones and you know it. Luckily we have the rest of our lives for me to prove it to you...'

The rest of our lives...

Sidonie smiled and moved closer to Alexio, deeper into his embrace, and he moved slightly so that he could put a possessive hand over her belly, setting off a chain reaction of desire.

'Okay,' she admitted sheepishly, lifting her head to look at him. 'Maybe it wasn't just pregnancy hormones...'

Alexio cupped her jaw with his hand and looked down at her. 'Excuse my French in front of Belle,' he said with a wicked smile, 'but damn right it wasn't.'

Two days later, Dublin

'Now I just want to make absolutely sure I haven't missed any loopholes or sneaky amendments. This was all drawn up very quickly because my fiancé has arranged our marriage for two weeks' time in Paris.'

Sidonie ignored the snort of insult from the man pacing the solicitor's office. She smiled sweetly at Mr Keane, who looked as if he was having trouble holding back nervous hysterics. No doubt he hadn't expected to see one of the world's foremost self-made billionaires in his office, never mind in this position.

Sidonie went on. 'Is it absolutely clear that if we divorce—'

'There will never be a divorce,' came the fierce pronouncement.

Sidonie rolled her eyes at the solicitor and then looked at her fiancé.

'Well, of course *now* we don't think there'll be a divorce, but you never know what will happen in life and I want to make sure that if and when such a time comes I walk away with not a cent of your fortune.'

Sidonie felt absolutely sure that there would be no divorce either, but it wasn't a bad thing to keep an alpha male like Alexio on his toes.

Alexio was bristling. He stalked over and put his hands down on the desk to glare at Sidonie. The intensity of that glare was diminished somewhat by the way he looked at her mouth so hungrily.

'There will not be a divorce while there is breath in my body.'

Sidonie stretched up and pressed a kiss to Alexio's cheek, causing his expression to turn positively nuclear. 'Well, we have to get married first, of course. Don't get all excited.'

She turned and smiled again at the very flushed-looking solicitor. 'So, in the event of a divorce any children will be provided for, and custody arrangements have been outlined, but I will get nothing—is that right?'

The solicitor ran a pudgy finger underneath his collar, his gaze flicking uneasily to the man who all but towered over his pregnant fiancée. Having had a lot of experience with pregnant women, thanks to his own healthy brood of seven children, he figured the lesser of two evils right now was Alexio Christakos, even if he *was* paying his bill and practically had steam coming out of his ears.

'Yes, that's exactly it, Miss Fitzgerald.'

'And ninety per cent of the money that Mr Christakos is insisting on giving me as an allowance has been designated to the various charities I mentioned?'

The solicitor quickly scanned the pages again and said, 'Yes, I believe so.'

'Great!'

Sidonie reached over and took the pen and signed her name with a flourish. Then she smiled sweetly at Alexio and handed the pen to him. He signed on the line with much unintelligible muttering under his breath.

Two weeks later a radiant and glowing Sidonie walked down the aisle of the biggest *mairie* in Paris on the arm of her matron of honour—her aunt, who grinned from ear to ear and was resplendent in a lavender suit. It had been bought by Alexio, who had grumbled that at least he could lavish gifts on *someone*.

Alexio hadn't had to turn and see Sidonie arrive. He'd already been waiting impatiently for her to appear.

He was still unprepared, though, when she did. His breath caught and he couldn't stop the tears clogging his throat and making his eyes shine. He'd been holding his emotions back all his life and now they overflowed. And he loved it. He'd even been oblivious to his brother Rafaele's smug *welcome to the club* look.

Sidonie's hair was half up, half down, held in place with a plain diamond art deco clip. She wore no other jewellery apart from her engagement ring. Her dress was strapless and had an empire line under her bust to accommodate her growing bump. The off-white material fell in loose, unstructured folds to the floor. Her skin glowed, and as she came closer, her eyes fixed on his, his heart almost stopped at the sheer strength of his love all over again.

He held out his hand to her and she put hers in his and smiled at him. At that moment Alexio felt all the pieces of his life slide into place, and he drew the love of his life forward by his side and hoped that they could get to the kiss as fast as possible.

Outside the office of the *mairie* afterwards, Cesar da Silva thrust his hands into his pockets. It had been a mistake to come. He didn't know what had got into him, but that morning he'd seen the invitation to Alexio's wedding on his desk and something had compelled him to make the journey to Paris from Spain.

He'd arrived late and stood at the back of the civil office. Alexio and his wife had had their backs to him as the ceremony was conducted, but he'd seen his other half-brother, Rafaele, near the front, holding a small boy high in his arms, with a dark-haired woman beside him, her arm around his waist. His wife.

He'd been invited to their wedding too, just months before, but the rage within him had still been too fierce for him even to contemplate it. The rage he'd felt at finally coming face to face with his half-brothers at his mother's funeral. The rage he'd felt at the evidence that she'd loved them above him. That she hadn't abandoned *them*.

But he knew it wasn't their fault. Whatever the stain had been on Cesar's personality that had led their mother to leave him behind had nothing to do with them. Maybe, he surmised cynically, they were just more lovable.

God knew, he'd felt dark for so long he was constantly surprised that people didn't run in terror when they looked into his eyes and saw nothing light. But they didn't run. And especially not women. It seemed the darker he felt, the stronger the draw to his lovers. More than one had been under the erroneous impression that they could *heal* Cesar of the darkness in his soul.

He wasn't surprised at women's eagerness to put up with his less than sunny nature; after all he was one of the richest men in the world. His mother had taught him that lesson very early on. After cutting Cesar from her life like a useless appendage she'd gone on to feather her nest in fine style—first with an Italian count and then, after he'd lost everything, a Greek tycoon.

He could see Rafaele putting his son down now—an adorable-looking little boy. *His nephew.* Cesar felt it like a punch to his gut. He'd been about the same age when his mother had left him with his grandparents and everything had gone dark and cold. To see that small boy now, swinging between his parents' hands, was almost too much to bear.

And then his youngest half-brother Alexio emerged from the *mairie*'s office with his new wife. His *pregnant* wife. More new life unfolding.

The pain in Cesar's chest increased. They were beaming. Eyes only on each other. Besotted. Cesar could feel his blackness spreading out…infecting the people around him like a virus. He caught one or two double-takes. People were wary around him. Women were fascinated, lustful. Covetous.

It gave him no measure of satisfaction to be as blessed as his brothers in his physical appearance. It compounded his cynicism. His looks merely sweetened the prospect for avaricious lovers, and they had proved to him from an early age that women were shallow. If he had nothing they'd still want him, but they wouldn't have to put on the elaborate pretence of not being interested in his fortune. Sometimes he almost felt sorry for them, watching them contort themselves into what they thought he wanted them to be.

Alexio was lifting his new wife into his arms now. Hearing her squeal of happiness, and seeing her throw her bouquet high in the air behind her so the women could catch it, made something break apart inside Cesar. He had to get away. He shouldn't have come. He would taint this happiness with his presence.

But just as he turned someone caught his arm, and he looked back to see Rafaele, with his son in his arms. The small boy was looking at Cesar curiously and he could see that he'd inherited his grandmother's eyes. *His* eyes. He felt weak.

As if Rafaele could see and understand the wild need to escape in Cesar's chest, he said, 'Whatever you might think our lives were like with our mother...they *weren't*. I'll tell Alexio you came. Maybe we'll see you again...?'

Cesar was slightly stunned at Rafaele's words. And at the way he'd seen his need to get out of there. That he wasn't pushing for more.

His chest feeling tight, Cesar nodded and bit out, 'Give him my best wishes.'

And then he turned and walked away quickly from that happy scene, before his wondering about what Rafaele had meant about their mother could tear him open completely and expose the dried husk of his soul to the light.

* * * * *

WHEN DA SILVA BREAKS THE RULES

PROLOGUE

CESAR DA SILVA hated to admit that coming here had had any effect on him, but his gut was heavy and tight as he stood on the path near the grave. He asked himself again why he'd even come and reflexively his fingers closed around the small velvet pouch with its heavy weight in his hand. He'd almost forgotten about it.

He smiled cynically. Who would have thought that at the age of thirty-seven he'd be obeying urges and compulsions? Usually he was the king of logic and reason.

People drifted away from the open grave a short distance across the hilly green space. Ornate mini-mausoleum-style headstones dotted the cemetery in the hills of Athens, its grass no doubt kept generously watered in the Greek heat.

Finally there were only two men left by the grave. Both tall, of similar height, with dark hair. One had slightly darker and shorter hair than the other. They were broad, as Cesar was, with powerful builds.

It was no wonder they were all similar. He was their half-brother. And they had no idea he even existed. He saw one put his hand on the shoulder of the other. They were Rafaele Falcone and Alexio Christakos. They all shared the same mother, but had different fathers.

Cesar waited for icy rage to surge upwards upon seeing this evidence of the family he'd always been denied, but instead he felt a kind of aching emptiness. They came towards him then, talking in quiet voices. Cesar caught his youngest half-brother's words on the slight breeze— something like, *'Couldn't even clean up for the funeral...?'*

Falcone replied indistinctly, with a quirk to his mouth, and Christakos riposted, smiling too.

The emptiness receded and anger rose up within Cesar. But it was a different kind of anger. These men were joking, joshing, just feet away from their mother's grave. And since when did Cesar feel protective of the woman who had taught him from the age of three that he could depend on no one?

Galvanised by that very unwelcome revelation, Cesar moved forward and Falcone looked up, words dying on his lips, smile fading. Falcone's gaze was enquiring at first and then, as Cesar drilled holes into him with his stare, it became something else. Cold.

With a quick flick of a glance to the younger man by his half-brother's side, Cesar noted that they'd also all inherited varying shades of their beautiful but treacherous mother's green eyes.

'May we help you?' Falcone asked coolly.

Cesar glanced over them both again and then at the open grave in the distance. He asked, with a derisive curl to his lip, 'Are there any more of us?'

Falcone looked at Christakos, who was frowning, and said, *'Us?* What are you talking about?'

Cesar pushed down the spreading blackness within him and said with ominous quiet, 'You don't remember, do you?'

But he could see from the dawning shock that his half-brother did, and Cesar didn't like the way something inside him tightened at that recognition. Those light green eyes widened imperceptibly. He paled.

Cesar's voice was rough in the still, quiet air. 'She brought you to my home—you must have been nearly three, and I was almost seven. She wanted to take me with her then, but I wouldn't leave. Not after she'd abandoned me.'

In a slightly hoarse voice Falcone asked, 'Who *are* you?'

Cesar smiled, but it didn't meet his eyes. 'I'm your older brother—*half-brother*. My name is Cesar Da Silva. I came today to pay my respects to the woman who gave me life…not that she deserved it. I was curious to see if any more would crawl out of the woodwork, but it looks like it's just us.'

Christakos erupted. 'What the *hell*—?'

Cesar cast him a cold glance. Somewhere deep down he felt a twinge of conscience for imparting the news like this, on this day. But then he recalled the long, aching years of dark loneliness, knowing that these two men had *not* been abandoned, and crushed it ruthlessly.

Falcone still looked slightly shell-shocked. He gestured to his half-brother. 'This is Alexio Christakos…our younger brother.'

Cesar knew exactly who he was—who they both were. He'd always known. Because his grandparents had made sure he'd known every single little thing about them. He bit out, 'Three brothers by three fathers…and yet she didn't abandon either of *you* to the wolves.'

He stepped forward then, and Alexio stepped forward too. The two men stood almost nose to nose, Cesar topping his youngest brother in height only by an inch.

He gritted out, 'I didn't come here to fight you, brother. I have no issue with either of you.' *Liar*, a small voice chided.

Alexio's mouth thinned, 'Only with our dead mother, *if* what you say is true.'

Cesar smiled, but it was bitter. 'Oh, it's true all right—more's the pity.' He stepped around Alexio then, before either man could see the rise of an emotion he couldn't name, and walked to the open grave.

He took the velvet pouch out of his pocket and dropped it down into the dark space, where it fell onto the coffin with a hollow thud. In the pouch was a very old silver medallion featuring the patron saint of bullfighters: San Pedro Regalado.

Even now the bitter memory was vivid. His mother was in a black suit, hair drawn back, Her features as exquisitely beautiful as any he'd ever seen. Eyes raw from crying. She'd taken the medallion from where it hung around her neck on a piece of worn rope and had put it around his neck. She had tucked it under his shirt and said, *'He will protect you, Cesar. Because I can't at the moment. Don't ever take it off. And I promise I will come back for you soon.'*

But she hadn't come back. Not for a long time. And when she finally had it had been too late. Something had withered and died inside him. *Hope.*

Cesar had taken off the medallion the night he'd let that hope die. He'd been six years old. He'd known then that nothing could protect him except himself. She deserved to have the medallion back now—he'd had no need of it for a long time.

Eventually Cesar turned and walked back to where his half-brothers were still standing, faces inscrutable. He might have smiled, if he'd been able, to recognise this familiar trait. An ache gripped him in the region of his chest where he knew his heart should be. But as he knew well, and as he'd been told numerous times by angry lovers, he had no heart.

After a taut silence Cesar knew he had nothing to say to these men. These strangers. He didn't even feel envy any more. He felt empty.

He turned and got into the back of his car and curtly instructed his driver to go. It was done. He'd said goodbye to his mother, which was more than she'd ever deserved, and if there was one tiny piece of his soul that hadn't shrivelled up by now then maybe it could be saved.

CHAPTER ONE

Castillo Da Silva, near Salamanca

CESAR WAS HOT, sweaty, grimy and thoroughly disgruntled. All he wanted was a cold shower and a stiff drink. A punishing ride around his vast estate on his favourite stallion had failed to put a dent in the dark cloud that had clung to him since his return that afternoon from his half-brother Alexio's wedding in Paris. Those scenes of chirpy happiness still grated on his soul.

It also irritated him intensely that he'd given in to the rogue compulsion to go.

As he neared the stables his black mood increased on seeing the evidence of a serious breach of his privacy. A film was due to start shooting on his estate after the weekend, for the next four weeks. If that wasn't bad enough, the stars, director and producers were all staying *in* the *castillo*.

He wasn't unaware of his complicated relationship to his home. It was both prison and sanctuary. But one thing was sure: Cesar hated his privacy being invaded like this.

Huge equipment trucks lined his driveway. People were wandering about holding clipboards, speaking into walkie talkies. A massive marquee had been set up, where locals from the nearby town were being decked out as extras in nineteenth-century garb.

All that was missing was a circus tent with flags flying and a clown outside saying, *Roll up! Roll up!*

One of his biggest stable yards had been cleared out so that they could use it as the unit base. The unit base, as a film assistant had explained earnestly to Cesar, was where the actors got ready every day and where the crew would eat. As if he cared!

But he'd feigned interest for the benefit of his friend Juan Cortez, who was the Lord Mayor of Villaporto, the local town, and the reason why Cesar had given this idea even half a second's consideration. They'd been friends since the age of ten, when they'd both had to admit defeat during a fist fight or remain fighting till dawn and lose all their teeth. And they would have—both were stubborn enough.

As his friend had pointed out, 'Nearly everyone has been employed in some capacity—accommodation, catering, locations, the art department. Even my mother is involved in making clothes for the extras and putting up some of the crew. I haven't seen her so excited in years.'

Cesar couldn't fail to acknowledge the morale and economic boost the film had already brought to the locale. He was known in the press for his ruthless dealings with people and businesses—one journalist had likened his methods to those of the cold, dead-eyed shark before it ate you whole. But Cesar wasn't completely heartless—especially if it involved his own local community.

More than one person caught a glimpse of his glowering features and looked away hurriedly, but Cesar was oblivious, already figuring out how he could rearrange his schedule to make sure he was away for as much of the next four weeks as possible.

To his relief, his own private stable yard, which was strictly off-limits to the crew, was empty when he returned. He wasn't in the mood to deal with anyone—not even a groom. After unsaddling his horse and hosing him down, Cesar led him back to his stall and made sure he was secure, patting his still quivering flesh after their exertion.

It was only when he was turning to leave again that Cesar spotted a movement out of the corner of his eye and turned to look.

And stopped breathing, and thinking.

In the other corner of the quiet stable stood a woman. Cesar felt slightly dizzy for a moment and wondered if he was seeing an apparition.

She was wearing a white corset that cinched in her waist to almost impossible proportions while provocatively pushing up the abundant swells of her breasts. Long wavy golden hair was pulled back from an ethereally beautiful face and left to tumble down her back. Very feminine hips curved out from that tiny waist and a long, voluminous skirt almost touched the ground.

She was stunning…exquisite. She was Venus incarnate. She couldn't be real. Nothing so perfect existed in reality.

Almost without realising that he was moving, Cesar closed the distance between them. She didn't move. Just stared at him, looking as transfixed as he felt. Imbuing the moment with an even headier other-worldly feeling.

Her eyes were huge and blue…piercing. She was tiny, and it seemed to call to some deep, primal part of him. Evoking an alien urge to protect.

Her face was small and heart-shaped, but with an inherent strength that elevated it out of the merely beautiful to the extraordinary. High cheekbones. Elegant straight nose. A full, lush mouth made for sin and sinners. Skin like alabaster.

There was a beauty spot close to the edge of her upper lip. She exuded an earthy and very feminine sexual allure. She couldn't be real. Yet every single ounce of his masculinity was humming and throbbing in reaction to her luminosity.

As if to check that he wasn't losing it completely, Cesar reached out a hand, noting with almost dispassionate surprise that it trembled slightly. He cupped his hand near her cheek and jaw, without actually touching her, almost afraid that she might disappear if he did...

And then he touched her...and she didn't disappear. She was *real*. Warm. Skin as soft as silk.

A movement made his eyes drop and he saw her chest moving up and down rapidly with her breaths.

'Dios,' he said faintly, almost to himself, 'you are real.'

Her mouth opened. Cesar saw small, even white teeth. Her tongue-tip pink. She said, 'I...' and then stopped.

Just that one tiny word had been uttered in a husky voice, making Cesar's whole body tighten with a need that was unprecedented.

Sliding his fingers further around her jaw to the back of her neck, silky hair tickling his hand, Cesar tugged her into him and after a minute hesitation she came, stumbling ever so slightly. All he knew, once he felt the barest whisper of a touch of her body to his, was that he couldn't hold back now even if a thousand men tried to stop him.

He lowered his head and his mouth touched hers, and all that sweet, soft voluptuousness pierced him right to the centre of his being, and threw him into the pit of a fire of lust so strong it obliterated everything he knew, or thought he knew.

Cesar felt her hands clutching at him, grabbing his shirt. Any resistance vanished when her mouth opened under his, and his arms tightened around her as his hungry tongue thrust into that hot, moist cavern.

However sweet that first initial taste had been, it turned to pure sin. Decadent and rich. Her tongue was sharp and smooth, teasing. Stoking his levels of arousal so that every bit of blood seemed to be rushing to the centre of his body, making that shaft of flesh lengthen and stiffen painfully.

Moving his hands to her waist, encircling it, Cesar almost groaned aloud when he felt his fingers meet. That evidence of her intense femininity pushed his body over the edge, made it betray him as if he were an over-sexed teenager.

He could feel her chest, struggling with constricted breath, moving up and down rapidly. Blood surging anew, Cesar lifted a hand and dragged it up between their bodies, itching to touch that smooth pale skin.

When he came into contact with the swell of one breast his body pulsed with a need that shocked him. He broke the contact of their mouths for a moment, resting his forehead against hers, overwhelmed at the strength of his desire.

'Please…'

Her voice sounded even huskier…needy. The way he felt. He needed this woman *now*. Needed to free himself and lift up her skirts and plunge right into the centre of that taut, smooth body. To feel her legs wrap around him.

On some very dim and distant level Cesar was aware that he had become animalistic. Reduced to the cravings and needs of a base animal in an effort to achieve a kind of satisfaction he'd never anticipated before.

But that still couldn't stop him. Not after that husky *please* had filled the space between them.

Branding her mouth with his again, the kiss was open-mouthed and carnal. Electrifying.

In the act of lifting up her skirts, almost desperate now, Cesar jerked and flinched when a flash of light seemed to illuminate the world for a second. Like the crack of a whip. Shattering the heady moment.

Lifting his head from where their mouths were welded together, Cesar could only see two huge pools of blue, ringed by long black lashes. That plump mouth was pink. He could feel her chest moving against his.

Then there was another flash, and a rapid jarring, clicking sound. He flinched again. Some vague notion of reality and sanity returned from a long distance. He turned his head, but it was the hardest thing to do—to look away from that face. Those eyes.

He saw a man standing at the entrance of the stables holding a camera up to his face. It was the equivalent of having a bucket of cold water thrown over him. Suddenly reality was back.

Cesar straightened up. Instinctively he pushed the woman behind him as he snarled at the man who was backing away, still shooting, 'Get out of here. *Now.*' One of Cesar's grooms appeared near the door and he rapped out at him, 'Get Security now—and get that man's camera.'

But the photographer had disappeared, and even though Cesar's groom darted away after him Cesar had the sinking feeling it would be too late. He'd reacted too late himself.

Becoming aware of rapid harsh breathing behind him, Cesar turned around.

And almost fell into the pit again when he saw those huge blue eyes staring up at him and that body which made him ache.

But reality had intruded. This woman was no apparition or ghost. She was flesh and blood, and he had just lost his legendary control spectacularly. *Dios*, had he gone mad?

Accusingly, Cesar asked, 'Who the hell *are* you?'

Lexie Anderson was barely aware of the sharp accusation in the deep, deliciously accented voice. She couldn't seem to get enough breath into her challenged lungs to speak. All she could ask herself was: *what the hell had just happened?*

She remembered wandering away from the camera tests

while they set up the lights and finding these quiet stables. She loved horses, so she had come in to investigate.

Then the peace had been shattered when this man had appeared in the courtyard on a huge black stallion. He'd swung down off the horse's back and from that moment on everything had got a little hazy.

Lexie had been mesmerised by his powerful physique and the play of muscles under his close-fitting polo top and jodhpurs as he'd tended to the horse. And that had been before she'd seen his face properly. When he'd heard her and turned around.

He was stunning. Beautiful. But with a masculine edge that made 'beautiful' sound too…pretty. He was hard. Edgy. Dark. Messy dark blond hair. A sensually sculpted mouth surrounded by stubble shadowing a very masculine jaw.

But it was his eyes that rendered Lexie a bit stupid and mute even now, as he waited for her reply. They were green—unusual and stark against dark olive skin. Not hazel, or golden, or light green. Something between all three. Unnerving. Mesmerising.

And he smelled of *man*. Sweat and musk and heat. Along with something tangy. Woodsy.

Lexie shook her head, as if that might make all this disappear. Maybe she was having some bizarre dream. Because she knew that what had just happened was unprecedented. She did not react to complete strangers by letting them kiss her, or by feeling as if she'd die if they didn't *keep* kissing her.

She remembered his big hands around her waist, then reaching under her skirts to pull them up, and how she'd burned between her legs for him to touch her there.

Now was most definitely *not* the time to be assimilating that cataclysmic information.

'I'm…' She stopped, her tongue feeling heavy in her

mouth. She tried again. 'I'm Lexie Anderson. I'm with the film.'

Lexie's face burned when she realised exactly how she was dressed, and how this man's eyes had widened when he'd seen her. Belatedly self-conscious, she went to cross her arms but realised the corset only made things worse—especially when those green eyes dropped to her heaving flesh again.

Feeling trapped now—literally backed into a corner—and not liking it, Lexie forced her legs to move, wobbly as they were, and stepped cautiously around him.

He turned to face her. Eyes cool, unreadable. Hands clenched into fists by his sides. 'You're Lexie Anderson... the lead actress?'

She nodded.

He looked at her, his eyes no longer unreadable now. Angry. 'And how did you get in here?'

She blinked, not understanding for a moment. 'I didn't see any sign or a gate...I just saw the horses—'

'It's off-limits here. You should leave—now.'

Anger gripped Lexie. She'd just behaved in a way that was completely out of character. The last thing she needed was to feel the lash of *his* censure. Stiffly, she replied, 'I didn't realise this was off-limits. If you can tell me how to get back to the unit base, I'll happily leave.'

His voice was harsh, curt. 'Turn left. It's at the end of the lane and to your right.'

Seething inwardly now, because she had been over-come by the first rush of physical desire she'd ever felt, and it had been for some anonymous person who worked at the castle and not even someone she *knew* or who was particularly charming, Lexie stalked off, tense as a board.

Then she heard the man curse and he commanded, 'Wait. Stop.'

Lexie stopped, breathing hard, and turned reluctantly again, rigid with tension.

He walked towards her, his movements powerfully agile, and she stepped back. His eyes flashed but she just tipped up her chin. What was wrong with her judgement? There wasn't anything remotely forgiving or alluring about this man. He was all hard edges and brooding energy.

He looked grim. 'That was a paparazzo. He got our picture.'

She'd forgotten. Her brain was refusing to work properly. Lexie could feel her blood draining south. The man must have feared she was about to faint or something, because he took her arm and none too gently drew her over to a haystack by the entrance, where he all but pushed her down onto it.

She ripped her arm free and glared up at him, hating the betraying quiver in her belly at his touch. 'There's no need to manhandle me. I'm perfectly fine.'

As if to confirm her worst suspicions, the young groom came running back, his face red.

'Well?' barked the man.

Lexie felt like standing up and telling him to go and take out his aggression on someone his own size, but she was disgusted to feel that her legs might not hold her up.

'Señor Da Silva…'

The groom spoke quickly after that, in incomprehensible Spanish, but Lexie was now gaping at the tall, angry man who was answering equally gutturally and quickly, making the groom turn puce and rush off again.

Lexie was too shocked to care for the groom's welfare any more. He turned back to her and she said faintly, 'You're Cesar Da Silva…?'

'Yes.'

He didn't seem to be too thrilled she'd made the connection. She'd thought he was a worker! Lexie hadn't recognised him as the owner of this entire estate because he was famously reclusive. Also, she'd never expected *the* Cesar Da Silva to be so young and gorgeous.

She had to will down her mortification when she thought of how she'd been all but crawling all over him like a hungry little kitten only minutes before. Begging. *'Please.'*

Oh, God.

She stood up. She had to get out of here. This was not her. She'd been invaded by some kind of body-snatcher.

'Where do you think you're going?'

Lexie looked at him. Anger flashed up again—at him and herself. She put her hands on her hips. 'You just told me to leave, didn't you? So I'm leaving.'

She moved around him again, towards the entrance, relieved that her legs were working.

'Wait.'

Lexie stopped and sighed heavily, turned around. She arched a brow, hiding how damn intimidating she thought he was. 'What now?'

He couldn't have looked more stern. 'That photographer got away. My groom saw him get into a car before any of the security guards could be alerted. I would imagine that right about now he's emailing pictures of us to any number of agencies around the world.'

Lexie felt sick. She felt even sicker to think that she was potentially going to be splashed across the tabloids *again*. And with Cesar Da Silva, one of the most reclusive billionaires in the world. It would be a sensation and it was the last thing she needed—*more* intense media interest.

She bit her lip. 'This isn't good.'

'No,' Da Silva agreed, 'it's not. I have no desire to become the centre of some grubby little tabloid sensation.'

Lexie glared at him, incensed. 'Well, neither do I.' She pointed a finger at him. 'And *you* kissed *me*.'

'You didn't stop me,' he shot back. 'And what were you doing in here anyway?'

Lexie burned. No, she hadn't stopped him. Anything but. She'd been caught up in a dreamlike state of…hot insanity.

'I told you.' Her voice was stiff, with the full ramifications of what had happened sinking in. 'I saw the stables, I wanted to see the horses… We're doing camera tests with Make-up and Wardrobe, and while they were setting up the lighting…'

She tensed as realisation hit.

'The camera tests! I have to go back—they'll be looking for me.'

Lexie went to rush off, but her arm was caught by a big hand. She turned and gritted her jaw. Those green eyes were like burning gems in his spectacular face. His hand on her arm was hot.

'This isn't over—'

Just then a PA rushed into the yard, breathless. 'Lexie, *there* you are. We've been looking all over for you. They're ready to shoot again.'

Lexie pulled free of Cesar Da Silva's grip. She could see his irritation at the interruption but she was glad, needing to get away from his disturbing presence and so she could try to assimilate what had just happened.

Lexie tore her gaze from his and hurried after the officious PA, who was speaking into the walkie-talkie microphone that came out of her sleeve near her wrist. Lexie heard her saying, 'Found her…coming now…one minute…'

Her head was reeling. She felt as if in the space of just that last…fifteen minutes?…her entire world had been altered in some very fundamental way.

She'd let that man…who had been a complete stranger… walk up to her and kiss her. Without a second's hesitation. And not just kiss her…*devour* her. And she'd kissed him back.

She could still feel that dizzying, rushing sweep of desire like a wave through her body. Impossible to ignore or deny. Immediate. All-consuming.

It was crazy, but she'd felt protected by his much larger bulk when he'd put her behind him as soon as he'd seen the paparazzo. Lexie wasn't used to feeling tiny, or in need of protection, even though she *was* physically small at five foot two. She'd been standing up for herself for so long now that she wasn't usually taken unawares in a situation like that. It sent a shiver of unease through her.

The photographer.

She felt sick again. Memories of lurid headlines and pictures rose up. Before she could dwell on it though, they'd entered the yard where the camera tests were taking place and everyone snapped to attention as soon as she appeared.

The cameraman beckoned her over. 'Right, Lexie, we need you over here on your mark, please.'

Cesar paced back and forth in his office, behind his desk. If it were at all possible his black mood had just become even blacker. Like a living, seething thing crackling around him. He had a file open on his desk and there were clippings and pictures strewn across it.

It was a file on Lexie Anderson. And it was not pretty.

One of the film assistants had furnished Cesar's office with files on everyone involved in the film. As much for security purposes as for a little general knowledge about the cast and crew. He hadn't even looked at them before now, because he hadn't been interested.

The files generally just held people's CVs. Except for Lexie's file. Her file was fat, not only with her CV, covering work which consisted mainly of TV and some indie movies before she'd shot to stardom via some vacuous-looking action movies, but also with numerous clippings from papers and magazines.

There were pictures of her, scantily clad, for a lads' magazine some years previously. One image showed her posing as some sort of half-dressed cheerleader, in nothing but thigh-high socks, knickers and a cardigan, teasingly open just enough to show off the voluptuous swells of her breasts and the sensual curve of her tiny waist. Her hair was down and tumbling sexily over her shoulders.

It was exactly the kind of image that Cesar found a complete turn-off, but right now he was having to battle with his own body to stop it responding as helplessly as if he were an over-sexed teenager all over again.

Cesar cursed and picked up the picture, throwing it aside. It fluttered to the floor. She was an actress. That was what she did.

But much worse than that were the more recent pictures and headlines: *Luscious Lexie—Homewrecker!* The tabloids had indulged in a feeding frenzy because she had been involved with a married actor who had subsequently left his heartbroken wife and children. He and Lexie weren't together now, though. According to the salacious copy, once he'd left his wife, heartless Lexie hadn't been interested any more.

Cesar knew that he couldn't have cared less what any lead actress got up to in her spare time, or with whom. But he'd kissed this woman in a moment of extreme madness only a short time before.

The imprint of that petite lush body against his was still branded into his memory. No woman had *ever* got him so hot that he'd lost control like that. He'd been moments away from backing her into a wall and thrusting up into her slick body if they hadn't been interrupted by the paparazzo when they had.

Cesar cursed. And then his phone rang. He answered it abruptly.

His solicitor's voice came down the line, 'Cesar, I've got some news you're not going to like.'

If his solicitor could have seen Cesar's expression right then he probably would have put the phone down and run. But he couldn't, so he went on, oblivious.

'You were photographed at Alexio Christakos's wedding this morning in Paris.'

'So?' Cesar offered curtly, his mind still full of lurid images of Lexie Anderson and her effect on his body.

His solicitor in Madrid sighed heavily. 'Well, it would appear that some very industrious reporter decided to do a quick search, to see if there was any connection between you and Christakos. They came up with the fact that the recently deceased Esperanza Christakos was briefly married to one Joaquin Da Silva, years before she became a renowned model.'

For a second Cesar saw only blackness. He sat down. 'How did they find this?'

'It's not a secret who your mother was, Cesar,' his solicitor pointed out carefully. 'It's just never been discovered before...the connection...'

Cesar knew this. His mother had left so long ago that no one had ever seemed to have the inclination to go digging. He came from the Da Silva dynasty and that was all people cared out.

Until now.

Cesar managed to give an instruction to his solicitor to monitor the media attention closely and put his phone down.

The press would have a field day. He was the estranged half-brother of two of the most renowned entrepreneurs in the world. It would be open season on prying into their lives. For speculating on why nobody had ever spotted the connection before now. And so on, and so on.

He was well aware that this was hardly big news—people discovered half-siblings all the time. What he wasn't prepared for was the prospect of ignominious media intrusion into an area of his life that had always been shut away. Not acknowledged.

The only time the reality of his brothers had been acknowledged, it had been used to taunt him. To drive home the fact that he was not the chosen one. That he could trust no one. Ever. As much as he hated to admit it, the scar was still deep. He only had to think back to earlier that day to remember how it had felt to be so black and bitter next to their happiness and ease with the world. A world that had taught them they could trust. That mothers didn't leave you behind.

Cesar cursed the maudlin direction of his thinking. Cursed himself again for having gone to Christakos's wedding.

With this film on his estate his privacy was already being well and truly eroded. Now this.

And then another picture of Lexie caught Cesar's eye and a headache started to throb behind his right temple. He feared that the reclusive life he'd lived for so long was about to slip out of his grasp unless he could do some serious damage limitation.

CHAPTER TWO

'Miss Anderson? Mr Da Silva would like to see you in his office, if you could spare a few minutes?'

Lexie knew it wasn't really a question. It was an order, and she chafed at the autocracy, already imagining his dark, forbidding expression. He'd been a complete stranger to her less than a couple of hours ago, known only by his reputation and name, yet now his saturnine image was branded like a searing tattoo on her brain. *His taste…*

Hiding her reaction, Lexie just shrugged her shoulders lightly and smiled. 'Sure.'

She followed the smartly dressed young woman down a long hallway. She'd just arrived back at the *castillo* from the camera tests and was dressed in her own clothes again. Worn jeans and sneakers. A dusky pink long-sleeved cashmere top, which suddenly felt way too clingy.

The make-up artist had scrubbed her face clean and she'd left her hair down, so now she had no armour at all. She hated the impulse she had to check her reflection.

Lexie hadn't had much time yet to look around the *castillo* as she'd been busy since they'd arrived, doing rehearsals and fittings. It was massive, and very gothic. The overall impression was dark and forbidding. Oppressive. Not unlike its owner. Lexie smiled to herself but it was tight.

A stern housekeeper had shown her to her room when

she'd arrived: dressed in black, hair pulled back in a tight, unforgiving bun. She might have stepped straight out of an oil masterpiece depicting the Spanish Inquisition era.

Lexie's bedroom was part of an opulent suite of rooms complete with an elaborate four-poster bed. Reds and golds. Antique furniture. A chaise longue. While it wasn't her style, she had to admit that it was helping her get into character for the film. She was playing a courtesan from the nineteenth century, who was torn between leaving her profession for her illegitimate son and a villainous lover who didn't want to let her go.

It was a dark, tragic tale, and the director was acclaimed. This film was very important to her—and not just for professional and economic reasons. One scene in particular had compelled Lexie to say yes, as she had known it would be her own personal catharsis to act it out. But she didn't want to think of that now.

After a series of soulless but financially beneficial action movies, this was Lexie's first chance to remind people that she could actually act. And hopefully move away from that hideous *Luscious Lexie* image the tabloids had branded her with. Not entirely unjustly, she hated to admit.

The young woman stopped outside a massive door and knocked. Lexie's mind emptied. Her heart went *thump* and her throat felt dry.

She heard the deep and curt *'Sí?'* And then the woman was opening the door. Lexie felt as if she was nine again, being hauled up in front of the head nun at her school for some transgression.

But then Cesar Da Silva was standing in the doorway, filling it. The woman melted away. He'd changed. Washed. Lexie could smell his scent—that distinctive woodsy smell. But without the earthy musk of earlier. It was no less heady, though.

Wearing a white shirt and dark trousers should have

made him appear more urbane. It didn't. The material of his shirt was fine enough to see the darkness of his skin underneath. He stood back and held out an arm, stretching his shirt across his chest. Lexie saw defined hard muscles. Heat flooded between her legs.

'Come in.'

Lexie straightened her spine and walked past him into a massive office.

She was momentarily distracted by its sheer grandeur as he closed the door behind them. It was shaped like an oval, with a parquet floor, and it had an ante-room that looked like a library, with floor-to-ceiling shelves of books upon books.

Something very private and poignant gripped her inside.

'Please, take a seat.'

Da Silva had moved behind his desk, hands resting lightly on top, but not disguising his obvious tension. The desk was huge, awe-inspiring. A very serious affair, holding all sorts of computers and machines and phones.

And yet less than two hours ago she and this man had mutually combusted and she had been oblivious to who he was.

Feeling uncharacteristically awkward, she started, 'Look, Mr Da Silva—'

'I think we've gone beyond that, don't you?' His face was mirthless and hard.

Lexie wondered for a crazy moment what he would look like if he smiled. Genuinely smiled.

She burned inwardly at that rogue little thought, and in rejection of his autocratic tone. 'I...well, yes.'

Her big slouchy handbag was slung over her shoulder. She let it slip down now, and held it in front of her like a shield. Something was telling her this wouldn't be a quick meeting.

A bright colour caught her eye then, and she glanced

down to see a photo of herself on the ground. Frowning, she bent to pick it up. When she registered the image, her insides roiled. She'd been twenty-one. Completely naive. Cringing inside with embarrassment. Not that you'd know it from the picture. She'd been hiding behind a well-developed wall of confidence and nonchalance that hadn't come easily.

She held the picture between thumb and forefinger and looked at Cesar across the desk. He was totally unrepentant. Something hard settled into her gut. The awareness she had of his sheer masculine physicality made her feel like a fool. And very vulnerable—which she did not welcome. It had been a long time since she'd allowed anyone to make her feel that way.

Then she saw the open file and all the other cuttings and clippings and pictures. She didn't have to read the lurid headlines to know what the characters said even from here, upside down. *Luscious Lexie.*

She went icy. Her bag slipped to the floor unnoticed.

'What is this?'

'This,' Cesar da Silva offered tautly, 'is your life, I believe.'

Lexie looked at Cesar and right at that moment despised him. She'd barely exchanged more than twenty sentences with the man, and he'd displayed not an ounce of charm, yet she'd blithely allowed him to be more intimate with her than any other man had ever been.

Her conscience mocked her. That wasn't technically true, of course. But the other experience in her life hadn't been consensually intimate. It had been a horrifically brutal parody of intimacy.

Lexie forced her mind away from that and raged inwardly at the injustice of his evident blind belief in the lies spread before him. She hated that a part of her wanted to curl up and cringe at how all this *evidence* was laid out so starkly across his desk. Ugly.

She forced her voice to be light, to hide the raging tumult. 'And do you believe everything you read in the papers, Mr Da Silva?'

He gritted out, 'Call me Cesar.'

Lexie smiled prettily, hiding her ire, 'Well, when you ask so nicely...*Cesar.*'

'I don't care enough to give the time to believe or disbelieve. I couldn't really care less about your tawdry sex life with married men.'

Lexie saw red. She literally saw a flash of red. She forced air into her lungs. Clenching her jaw so tight it hurt, she bit out, 'Well, then, perhaps you'd be so kind as to let me know what you want to discuss so that I can get on with my *tawdry* life.'

Cesar had to force back the urge to smile for a second. She'd surprised him. Standing up to him so fiercely. Like a tiny virago. Or a pocket Venus.

It took an immense physical effort not to let his gaze drop and linger on the swell of her breasts under the clinging soft material of her top. Or to investigate just how snugly those worn jeans fitted her bottom.

When she'd walked in he'd taken in the slim, shapely legs. The very feminine swell of her hips. She was the perfect hourglass, all wrapped up in a petite, intoxicating package. Her hair was loose and wavy over her shoulders. Bright against the dark wood of his office. *Against the darkness of the castillo.* Something lanced him in a place that was buried, deep and secret. He didn't welcome it.

He didn't like that he'd also noticed her beauty spot was gone. The artifice of make-up. It mocked him for believing himself to have been in some sort of a dream earlier.

For thinking she was some sort of goddess siren straight out of a Greek myth.

But she was no less alluring now in modern clothes than she had been in a corset and petticoats. In fact, now that Cesar knew the flesh her clothes concealed, it was almost worse.

And he'd just been ruder to this woman than he'd ever been to another in his life.

He could actually be urbane. Charming. But as soon as he'd laid eyes on her again he'd felt animalistic. Feral. Even now his blood thundered, roared. For her. And she wasn't even remotely his type.

He ran a hand through his hair impatiently. His conscience demanded of him that he say, 'Look, maybe we can start again. Take a seat.'

Lexie oozed tension and quivering insult. And he couldn't blame her. Even if her less than pristine life *was* spread all over his desk.

'I'm fine standing, thank you. And where, might I ask, did you get your hands on what appears to be a veritable scrapbook of my finest moments?'

Her voice could have cut through steel it was so icy. Cesar almost winced.

'Someone working on the film compiled information on the cast and crew.' His eye caught another lurid shot of Lexie pouting over the bonnet of a car. His body tightened. He willed himself to cling on to some control. 'It would appear that person was a little over-zealous with the back catalogue of your work.'

Lexie flushed, her cheeks filling with dark colour, and Cesar felt his conscience twinge again. As if *he* was in the wrong. When this woman was standing there with her chin tilted up, defiant in the face of her less than stellar reputation.

She came forward and Cesar's gaze couldn't help but

drop to where her breasts swayed gently under her top. She stopped at the other side of the desk and put her hands on it and glared at him, her huge blue eyes sending out daggers of ice.

She plucked out the image of her on the car and held it up accusingly. '*This* is not a back catalogue of work. *This* is a naive young girl, trying to get on in a ruthless cutthroat business—a girl who didn't have the confidence or economic security to say no to bullying agents and photographers.'

She spat out the words.

'You might consider that the next time you find it so easy to judge someone you were only too happy to kiss without even knowing who she was.'

Before Cesar could respond to her spiky defence, not liking the rush of a very alien emotion within him, she'd gathered up all the cuttings and pictures, her CV and headshots, and marched over to a nearby bin, dumping the lot.

She turned around, her hair shimmering as it moved over her shoulder. She crossed her arms. 'Now, what was it you wanted to discuss?'

Lexie hated that her body was humming with awareness for this man. Who was blissfully immune to the angry emotions he was arousing.

What a judgmental, supercilious, arrogant, smallminded—

'I owe you an apology,' he said tightly.

Lexie blinked. The anger inside her suffered a bodyblow. 'Yes, you do.'

His mouth was a grim line. 'I had no right to judge you on the basis of those pictures.'

'No, you didn't,' Lexie snapped, but then she flushed again when she thought of another similar shoot she'd done relatively recently—albeit for a much more up-market publication and with a world-famous photographer. But still, she couldn't exactly claim the moral high ground either…

'It's fine,' she dismissed airily, 'let's forget about it.'

He sighed heavily then, and opened up the laptop that was on the desk in front of him. 'You should see this.'

Trepidation skittered over her skin. Warily Lexie walked around the desk until she could see the laptop, acutely conscious of her proximity to him. When she saw the images, though, her belly swooped alarmingly.

It was her, and him, locked in a clinch that looked positively X-rated. Both his hands were under her skirt, pulling it up, baring her legs. Her breasts seemed about to explode from her corset, crushed against his chest. Their mouths were locked together in a passionate kiss, their eyes closed. Lexie's hands gripped his shirt so tightly that her knuckles were white. And just like that it all came back in a rush: the desperation, the craving, the *aching*. The need.

Lexie could feel heat from behind her. She swallowed. There could be no mistaking that whatever had happened between them had consumed them both. It was not a comfort.

'Where is this?' she asked hoarsely, unable to stop looking away from the image with some kind of sick fascination.

'It's on a well-known internet gossip website. It's only a matter of time before it hits the papers.'

Lexie backed away from the laptop as if it might explode…retreating around the desk, feeling marginally safer once something solid was between them.

Cesar's eyes were glittering. His disdain was palpable. He might have just apologised, and surprised her by doing so, but there was no mistaking his disapproval of the entire situation.

Stung, Lexie said defensively, 'There were two of us there.'

He was grim. 'I'm aware of that, believe me.'

'So…' She swallowed painfully, thinking of the inevitable re-igniting of press interest and the weariness and fear of exposure that would provoke. 'What now?'

Cesar looked at her for a long moment and crossed his arms. 'We contain it.'

Lexie frowned. 'What do you mean…contain it?'

'We don't give it air to breathe. You're here in the *castillo* for the next four weeks. There should be no reason why it won't die a death if they have nothing to work with.'

Something icy touched Lexie's spine. 'What are you talking about exactly?'

A muscle pulsed in Cesar's jaw. 'What I'm talking about is that you don't leave this estate.'

Fire doused the ice. Lexie pointed at herself. '*I* don't leave the estate? What about you?'

Cesar shrugged minutely, arrogant. 'Well, of course I will have to leave. I have business to attend to.'

Lexie emitted a laugh that sounded far too close to panic for her liking. 'After a passionate embrace is plastered all over the world's press, you appear in public with me nowhere to be seen…do you know how that'll look?' She answered herself before he could. 'It'll look as if you're rejecting me and the press will be all over it like a rash.'

Cesar's jaw pulsed again. Clearly he was not used to having anyone question his motives. 'You will be protected in here from the press.'

'Oh, really?' asked Lexie. 'That paparazzo managed to get in, and I assume even a reclusive fossil like you has heard of camera phones?'

She was so angry right then at Cesar's preposterous plan that she barely noticed that he'd moved around the desk, or that his eyes flashed dangerously at her childish insult.

'What's to stop some enterprising crew member from snapping pictures of *poor jilted Lexie* on the set of her new film…?' Lexie was on a roll now, pacing back and forth. 'The press will love documenting *your* exploits while I'm the rejected fool, locked in the castle.'

Lexie stopped and rounded on Cesar, who was at the other side of the desk now and far too close and tall and dark. She took a step back.

She shook her head. 'No way. I'm not going to be incarcerated in this grim fortress just to make life easier for *you*. I'd planned to visit Lisbon, Salamanca…*Madrid!*' That last came out with more than a little desperation.

Lexie had dark memories of being all but locked up once before, and it wasn't going to happen again in her lifetime—not even on an estate as palatial as this one.

Cesar looked at Lexie and was momentarily distracted by her sheer vibrancy and beauty. Her cheeks were pink with indignation, her eyes huge and glittering. Her chest was heaving. As she'd paced back and forth energy had crackled around her like electricity.

Her words hit him then: *I'm not going to be incarcerated in this grim fortress…* He felt like cracking a bleak smile. He knew only too well what that was like. And he could sympathise with her rejection of the idea.

He rested back against his desk and crossed his arms, because right now they itched to reach out and grab her and pull her into him. So close to her like this he could smell her scent, all but feel those provocative curves pressed against him.

His body tightened, blood rushed south. He cursed silently.

'So…what would be *your* suggestion, then?'

Lexie blinked. Cesar marvelled that her every thought was mirrored on that expressive face and in those huge eyes. He'd never seen anything like it. He was used to women putting on a front, trying hard to be mysterious.

She bit her lip and that was even worse. *He* wanted to bite that lip.

She looked at him. 'We go public.'

Cesar's eyes snapped up from her mouth to her eyes. His crossed arms dropped. 'We go *what*?'

'We go public,' she repeated.

'As in…?'

Her eyes flashed brilliant blue, like fire. 'As in we are seen together. As in we go out in public. As in we let people think that we are having an affair.'

Cesar tensed for the inevitable rush of rejection at that proposition. He didn't *do* high publicity—especially not with women like Lexie, whose second home was among the tabloids. Whose life was laid out in a series of lurid pictures amid salacious headlines.

But it didn't come. The rejection. What did come was an intense spiking of anticipation in his already hot blood. His brain clicked and whirred at the thought of this audacious plan. The news of his half-brothers would be hitting the newsstands possibly as soon as tomorrow…

'Well?'

Lexie's voice cut through the snarl of thoughts in Cesar's head. Somehow, without analysing it fully right now, he knew that a news story featuring *them* would inevitably be more colourful and interesting than one about his family connections. That would be diminished in favour of a far more scandalous story: *Reclusive billionaire beds homewrecking Luscious Lexie.*

'I think,' Cesar said slowly, letting his eyes fill with Lexie again, 'that your idea has some merit.'

Some of the tension left her shoulders even as she crossed her arms, which pushed the swells of her breasts up. *Dios*, Cesar cursed again silently. Suddenly all rational thoughts of distracting the press via a story about him and Lexie fled, to be replaced with the very *real* urge to touch the woman in front of him.

'Good,' she said now. 'Because I really do think that's the best solution. And the fairest.' Her mouth firmed. 'I know the press, and sometimes you have to play them at their own game rather than fight them.'

She lifted her chin then, and something about the move was so endearingly spiky that Cesar had to stop himself from reaching out to trail his fingers across her jaw. Out of nowhere came a surge of something that felt almost like *protectiveness*.

His hands curled around the edge of his desk beside his hips. He forced his mind back to the conversation. 'I have a charity auction to attend in Salamanca next weekend. We can go to that.' The devil inside him compelled him to continue. 'And we'll have to be convincing, Lexie.'

Those big blue eyes narrowed. 'Convincing?'

Cesar smiled, the anticipation inside him tightening now. 'Convincing…as lovers.'

Lexie's arms tightened, pushing those firm swells up even more. 'Oh…well, yes. I mean, that's obvious…but that'll be easy enough… I mean…I'm an actress after all.'

Suddenly the confident woman of only a few moments ago was not at all sure of herself. Cesar was more intrigued than he liked to admit. He shifted on the desk, crossing one ankle over the other, and noted how Lexie's eyes dropped to his mid-section for a second before skittering away again.

But then the suggestion that she'd have to *act* with Cesar hit home and made something hot and dark pierce him inside. He tensed. 'So what happened earlier, Lexie? Were you just practising your *acting* skills on the nearest stable hand you could find?'

She looked at him. 'No. It wasn't like that.'

Cesar felt more exposed than he liked to. 'So what *was* it like?'

For a second he fancied that the turmoil he could see in those blue depths mirrored the part of him that still couldn't make sense of what had happened. But the very suggestion that it had been in any way within *her* control and not his made something snap inside him.

He straightened up and did what his hands had been itching to do ever since she'd walked into his study. He reached for her and pulled her into him, and something treacherous in his mind quietened as soon as those soft curves fell against him.

Her hands were pressed against his chest and a soft *oof* escaped her mouth: a sigh of shock. She looked up. 'What are you doing?'

Cesar's body was already hardening against hers. An automatic and helpless reaction to her proximity and touch. He hated this feeling of being out of control—it had been a long day of that very unwelcome sensation. He gritted out, 'I'm seeing how good you are at improvisation.'

And then he bent his head to hers, and her mouth was as firm and yet as soft as he remembered, and those lush contours sent his brain into a tailspin all over again.

Lexie was drowning. Her hands looked for purchase anywhere she could find it to try and cling on. Cesar's mouth was searing and hot. Hard. His arms were welded tight around her. She was off-balance and plastered against him, breasts crushed against rock-hard contours. One of his hands moved up to her head, angling it. Their mouths were open, tongues touching and tasting. Stroking, sucking.

Lexie wanted to wrap her arms around his neck and rub herself up and down his hard length, seeking to assuage the stinging in her nipples and the ache growing inside her.

She could feel a hard ridge against her belly and it caused a spasm of damp desire between her legs.

And then the haze lifted ever so slightly, when he took his mouth away for a moment and she remembered his grim look and what he'd said, *'I'm seeing how good you are at improvisation.'*

As if a cold bucket of water had been thrown over her Lexie jerked backwards, almost stumbling in an effort to right herself. She was shaky all over, breathing heavily. Cesar was resting on the edge of the desk, barely a hair out of place, even if his cheeks were flushed and eyes were glittering brightly.

Lexie wasn't ready for this onslaught of physical sensations and feelings. Barely able to get her head around articulating much, she asked, a little redundantly, 'What was that in aid of?'

'Proving that it will be no hardship to *act* out being lovers. In fact it's almost inevitable that we will *become* lovers.'

Lexie rebelled at that arrogant tone even as her body betrayed her spectacularly. 'Don't flatter yourself, Mr Da Silva.'

He smiled. 'It's Cesar, please.'

Lexie felt dizzy at how quickly this man was dismantling the bricks and mortar that had protected her for years. She couldn't analyse it now, but she knew that he must have connected with her on some very deep level for her to have allowed him to kiss her—not once, but twice. Without even putting up a fight.

Panic galvanised her and she reached down and picked up her bag, slung it over her shoulder. She forced herself to look at Cesar but it was hard. The air between them was saturated with electricity and tension and something else far more disturbing and new to Lexie: *Desire.*

She hated to admit that she was also stung to think

that he believed she was the kind of person who would just widen her eyes and say yes to such an autocratic announcement.

She bit out, 'I am *not* an easy lay, Cesar. Evidently you believe what you read in the papers, but I can assure you that I am perfectly capable of controlling myself. I am interested in putting forward a united front in order to get the press off our backs...that is all.'

Cesar stared at her for a long moment and then shrugged. He folded his arms across that wide chest, making the muscles of his arms bunch against the silk of his shirt.

'We'll see,' he said carelessly. As if he truly didn't care if she tumbled into his bed one way or the other. As if he knew that she would be helpless to resist him when the time came.

Curbing the urge to take her bag and swing it at his head, Lexie backed away to the door, her blood boiling—and not just from his words and that arrogance. She turned around and was reaching for the doorknob, relishing the prospect of removing herself from his orbit, when he called her name softly.

With the utmost reluctance Lexie gritted her jaw and turned around, keeping her hand on the door. He was still sitting there, eyes hooded, watching her.

'Don't forget...next weekend...Salamanca. That's if you still want us to proceed with *your* suggestion.'

For a second Lexie contemplated the alternative and saw herself pacing up and down the dark *castillo* corridors or in the grounds. Trapped. With the press digging her life up again. Speculating. She went cold at that prospect. There was no choice.

She managed to say icily, 'I won't forget.' And then she pulled the door open and left, with her dignity feeling badly battered.

CHAPTER THREE

WHEN LEXIE GOT to her room she paced. Full of pent-up energy. Hot and then cold at the same time when she reconsidered the equally disturbing prospects of appearing in public *with* Cesar and *not*. And the ramifications of the press's interest in her if that was the case.

There was no doubt about it: appearing with Cesar would be the better scenario. It was only in the last few weeks that the tabloids' interest in *'Luscious Lexie the homewrecker'* had let up. If she was going to become press fodder again so soon, then she would *not* be the victim.

Cesar was unmarried. A bachelor. An affair with him would be old news very fast. And, she realised with some cynicism, it couldn't hurt the film to be linked to this kind of publicity.

What she hadn't counted on was the attraction she felt for Cesar. She'd just kissed him back again, as passionately as she had earlier, with no qualms. No hesitation! It was as if as soon as he touched her some ever-vigilant switch in her brain turned to *off* and she became mute. Acquiescent.

She held out her hands and noted that even now they were trembling slightly. Disgusted, she shoved them under her arms and then spied her electronic tablet. She marched over and opened it up.

She hated herself for it, but she found herself searching for Cesar Da Silva Girlfriend. Predictably not much came up except a few photos of him at events with beautiful women. They were all tall, brunette. Sleek. Classy. One was a UN diplomat. The next an attaché to a world leader. Another was a human rights lawyer.

There were also pictures of Cesar with world leaders at economic summits.

Lexie put a hand to her mouth to stem a slight surge of hysteria. She was seriously out of her depth with this man, and she didn't like her feeling of insecurity when she was faced with the evidence of his previous lovers' undoubted intellectual accomplishments. The plan for them to appear as lovers mocked her now. Who would ever believe he'd choose *her*?

Feeling like a stalker, she looked up his background. To her surprise, a new news article popped up. And a picture of him from earlier that very day, taken at a wedding in Paris. Lexie frowned for a second, wondering how he could have come from Paris back to the *castillo* in such a short space of time—and then she recalled hearing a helicopter earlier. Of course—to a man like Cesar Da Silva travel between European bases was far removed from most people's more tedious, lengthy experiences.

She focused on the short piece again. It had been the wedding of Alexio Christakos and his very pretty bride—someone called Sidonie. The article seemed to be implying that a familial relationship existed between Alexio Christakos and Cesar Da Silva. And also another man: Rafaele Falcone.

Lexie frowned. She knew Christakos and Falcone were half-brothers. They'd been notoriously eligible bachelors before settling down. So...what? Cesar was related to these men? Lexie kept searching and found a very brief reference to his father. Joaquin Da Silva had been famously disinherited from his family after leaving to train as a bullfighter.

He'd achieved some fame early on, before dying tragically in a goring by a bull.

There wasn't much else apart from Cesar's current accomplishments, of which there seemed to be many. He was listed as one of the world's leading philanthropists.

The picture of Cesar at the wedding caught her eye again. She looked more closely. There was a definite resemblance between the two men. And Rafaele Falcone. She couldn't be sure, but it looked as if they all shared varying shades of green eyes. Unusual. *Too* unusual.

A suspicion slid into place inside Lexie. He'd agreed so quickly to appearing in public with her, when all the evidence pointed to a man who would find that kind of exposure anathema. *He wants me.* Lexie shivered at the thought. Was he prepared to court the press's attention just to get her into bed? That idea was both intoxicating and terrifying.

But perhaps Cesar had his own reasons for wanting to divert the press? If something was about to break about his family? She didn't like it, but a feeling of empathy gripped her. And curiosity...

Just then a knock sounded on her door. Lexie's heart jumped. She put the cover over her tablet's screen and went to the door, steeling herself. But when she opened it, it was Tom—the producer. An acute dart of disappointment made her want to scowl.

She forced a smile. 'Tom?'

He held up his own tablet to reveal the same picture of the kiss that Cesar had shown her just a short while before. Her insides tightened again at seeing herself in such an alien and lurid pose.

'Ah...' she said.

'Ah...' the older man echoed. 'I didn't realise you had history with Da Silva. You never mentioned anything...'

'I don't really want to discuss it, Tom, if that's all right.'

'Look,' he said quickly, mollifying her, 'I'm not complaining, Lexie—far from it. This is PR gold dust for the film. *If* you two are…together.'

Tom was obviously concerned that an affair between her and Cesar Da Silva might jeopardise filming if it wasn't all that it seemed. He could throw them off his estate at any moment if he so wished.

Lexie's jaw was tight. She imagined the press furore after they appeared in public next week. 'Yes…' she said reluctantly, as if not even wanting to give the words oxygen. 'We are…together.'

The relief that crossed the producer's face was almost comical. 'Okay, that's good. I mean, like I said, it's gold dust for the film. We could never have generated this much press just by—'

'Tom?' Lexie cut him off, forcing another smile. 'I'd appreciate an early night. I've a lot of prep to do this weekend before we start shooting on Monday.'

He backed away, putting a hand up. 'Of course. I'll leave you to it. Night, Lexie.'

When he was gone she sagged back against the door with relief. Out of the past, the words of her counsellor came back to her: *'Lexie, one day you'll meet someone and you'll feel desire. And you'll feel safe enough to explore it…and heal.'*

Lexie stifled a semi-hysterical giggle. She'd felt it today, all right, but she didn't feel safe right now. She felt in mortal danger. Especially when she thought of those distinctive green eyes and that hard-boned face…and that powerful body. That dark, brooding energy…

She felt anything but safe.

She thought again of Cesar's nonchalant assertion that they would become lovers. A dart of anger gripped her insides. He was obviously used to women falling at his feet if he could make such a declaration. He had no idea of the scars that scored her insides like tattoos. Not visible to the naked eye, but she felt them every day. Scars she'd fought hard to overcome so she could function and live and work.

She resented Cesar Da Silva right then for inserting himself so solidly and irrevocably into her life. And yet she had no one to blame but herself.

Sighing volubly, Lexie pushed off the door and vowed to do whatever it took to focus on the most important thing in her life right now: the job she had to fulfil for the next four weeks. Her *real* acting job, as opposed to the acting she'd be doing in a week's time. Although that filled her with a lot more trepidation because she was afraid that she wouldn't have to act at all.

Midway through the following week Lexie was pacing back and forth on the set while they set up the cameras for a new shot. She was listening to the script on her mp3 player and repeating her lines to herself.

They were shooting not far from the *castillo*, in a walled garden. Inevitably, though, her thoughts deviated yet again to the person who had dominated almost every waking and sleeping moment since she'd met him, in spite of her best efforts.

He'd appeared to watch the filming at various intervals, effortlessly unsettling Lexie in the process. If he was around she became acutely self-conscious. And being dressed in cleavage-revealing nineteenth-century garb didn't help.

Right then, just as she was sighing with relief that he *hadn't* appeared today, he did appear—as if conjured up from her overheated imagination—striding towards her on the narrow path. She had nowhere to go. Trapped. All of the crew were busy working, oblivious to the seismic physical reaction inside Lexie as Cesar bore down on her in a secluded part of the garden.

Her heart sped up. She went hot all over. Pinpricks of sensation moved across her skin. Nipples tightened against her bodice. The corset became even more constrictive. She pulled the long coat she wore to keep warm more closely around her, to try and hide some of her far too buxom cleavage. She took the earphones out of her ears and fought the urge to take several steps back.

Cesar came to a stop in front of her. It didn't help that he was dressed in much the same way as when she'd seen him for the first time, in a close-fitting polo shirt and jodhpurs. Hair mussed. Jaw stubbled. He'd obviously just been riding.

For a bizarre second Lexie actually couldn't speak. His eyes were hypnotic. When *he* spoke, it jarred her out of the daze she was in.

'I've arranged for my assistant to have some clothes delivered to you from a boutique in Salamanca.'

Lexie looked at him blankly. 'Clothes?'

'For the weekend…for future events.'

Suddenly Lexie realised what he meant, and immediately chafed at the implication that he had to buy clothes for her because she wasn't as classy or elegant as his other lovers. And she hated that she'd thought that.

Stiffly she said, 'You really don't need to do that.' Lexie knew she was out of his league; she didn't need a reminder.

Cesar was obdurate. 'Well, it's too late. They've been delivered to your suite.'

Lexie opened her mouth again, but Cesar put up a hand.

'If you don't want to use them, that's fine. See what's there and decide. It's no big deal.'

No, thought Lexie churlishly, because all it had taken was a mere snap of his fingers. She looked at him suspiciously. 'How did you know what size I was?' She immediately regretted asking the question when his gaze swept up and down her body. What he could see of it...

'I asked the costume designer, just to be safe, but my own estimation wasn't far off.'

Lexie burned with indignation and something much hotter to imagine Cesar guessing her vital statistics.

Just then a PA came close and hovered. When Lexie looked at her she made a signal that she was required. Lexie looked back at Cesar and said, with evident relief, 'I have to go. They're ready to shoot again.'

But he didn't get out of the way. And Lexie knew she wasn't supposed to step onto the manicured lawn.

She was about to open her mouth when he moved closer and put a hand around the back of her bare neck, exposed because her hair was up in a complicated chignon. He bent down and pressed a fleeting but hot kiss to her mouth, and then pulled back, letting her go.

Lexie tingled all over. Her head felt fuzzy. 'What was that for?'

Cesar smiled, but it didn't reach his eyes, and Lexie felt something tug inside her, wondering again what he'd look like if he *really* smiled.

'As you so memorably pointed out, there are camera phones around. I'm just being vigilant.'

Lexie flushed to recall what she'd said to him. There was nothing remotely fossil-like about this man. He was all bristling, virile energy.

Faintly she said, 'Celeste will have to retouch my lipstick.'

He smirked. 'Well, you'd better run along and let Celeste do that.'

For a second Lexie blinked at him. There was a tantalising glimmer of something lighter between them. But then he was turning and striding back the way he'd come, and as Lexie walked over to the main hub of the set she couldn't be unaware of several appreciative female *and* male glances that lingered in his direction and then on her with undisguised envy.

Cesar was waiting for Lexie in the main *castillo* drawing room three days later. Looking back on the last tumultuous week, he did not relish the twisting and turning of events since he'd taken one look at that woman and his brains had migrated to his pants.

Cesar was renowned for lots of things: his inestimable wealth; philanthropy; scarily incisive business acumen; a zealous desire for privacy; success. And control. Above all control over his emotions. He'd become a master of controlling them from a young age. Too young.

His usual choice of woman was tall and brunette. Elegant. Classic. Not blonde, petite and curvy, with blue eyes big enough to drown in. And with a dubious reputation splashed across the tabloids.

On some level he'd always sought to stay away from prying eyes, as if somehow they might see something in him that he couldn't articulate himself. A darkness that had clung to him for a long time. The stench of abandonment. The cruelty of neglect and a lack of care. It had been like an invisible stain on his skin.

Yet for someone who had spent his life largely on the periphery of the media glare, largely due to his very *non*-scandalous social life, the prospect of suddenly being thrust front and centre was not having the effect he might have expected.

Of course he didn't relish the idea. But at the same time it didn't fill him with repugnance.

Cesar poured himself a drink and smiled grimly. Right now though, all those concerns were receding and being replaced by something else. Some*one* else. Lexie Anderson. Cesar had been due to go to North Africa that week, to attend a meeting about aid, but had cancelled it on the flimsy pretext of wanting to make sure that the first week of filming went smoothly.

Cesar would be the first to admit that he had dismissed the film industry as flaky and narcissistic, but just one week had proved him wrong. The crew were tireless and worked twelve- and thirteen-hour days—if not longer. He was also surprised by how quickly and well they worked as a cohesive unit.

The producer had explained that most of them had worked together before, but there were lots of inexperienced locals in the mix and Cesar had witnessed more than one incident of a more experienced crew member patiently showing someone the ropes.

Lexie was one of the most tireless. Standing for long minutes on a mark while the lighting crew and cameraman worked around her. Her co-star would invariably go back to his trailer. Cesar had found out that she could have insisted they use a stand-in but had wanted to be there herself. He had to admit that he hadn't really expected her work ethic to be that strong.

She was popular. Especially with the male members of the crew. Cesar was more aware of that than he liked to admit. He'd never been jealous because of a woman before and he didn't welcome jealousy's appearance.

He heard a sound then, and with something whispering over his skin like a warning Cesar took a breath and turned around.

Bombshell. That was the only word that seemed to compute in his head when he saw the woman standing in the doorway. Her effect on him was like a bomb too—exploding out to every extremity and making his flesh surge as blood pumped south.

He took in details, as if he couldn't handle the full reality. Glossy blonde hair, trailing over one shoulder in classic screen siren waves. Pale skin. Slim bare arms. A sleeveless gold lamé dress that fell to the floor in a swirl of glamorous luxury.

She was poured into it, and the material highlighted her curves to almost indecent proportions. The deep, plunging vee of the neckline drew his eye to that abundant cleavage.

She was every inch the glittering movie star. And the most provocatively beautiful woman Cesar had ever seen in his life. He knew that if they hadn't already kissed, if he hadn't already seen her up close, he might have seen her like this and dismissed her as too garish. But right now he could no more dismiss her than recall his own name.

His hands clenched so tightly that he heard a crack, and he looked down stupidly to see his heavy Waterford crystal glass about to break in his hand.

He put it down on the sideboard with a clatter that jarred his ragged and sensitised nerve-endings.

She moved into the room, and the sinuous sway of her hips nearly undid him. Normally he had finesse. He could utter platitudes to women like *You look beautiful*. But right now all he could do was say gruffly, 'My driver is waiting outside—we should go.'

Lexie fought down a betraying quiver of insecurity as she preceded Cesar out of the room, and cursed herself for wanting his reassurance that she looked okay and not too over the top. Her dresses were normally fine—fairly standard designer fare, given to her after photo shoots or premieres—but when she'd compared them to the finery he'd ordered there had been no competition. She'd had to choose one of his.

She had not been prepared for his impact on her in a classic black tuxedo. It was obviously a bespoke suit, moulded to his powerful body in a way that most men's weren't. It should have made him appear civilised. Just like trousers and a shirt should make him look civilised. But the structured clothes only made him seem more raw. Untamed.

His hair was always on the slightly messy side, and Lexie didn't like the way that small detail already felt familiar. But his jaw was clean-shaven, and somehow it gave him a more youthful air.

He took her arm with one big hand and Lexie had to curb her response not to jump. She could feel slightly rough calluses. It made her think of how he'd looked swinging lithely from that huge horse the first time she'd seen him... muscles bunching and quivering. He was no mere soft-palmed money man. The very heart of her feminine core grew hot and damp.

She tried to pull her arm free but his hand was firm. She sent him a sharp glance, irritated at his effect on her, which quickly turned to something else when she saw him gazing at her intently. His hand slid down her arm and took her hand. It was a relatively chaste gesture, and yet it had an almost embarrassing effect on Lexie.

She let herself be led to the exclusive black car and Cesar let her go so she could slide into the back, with the driver holding the door open solicitously.

When he got in on the other side he sent her a look that made Lexie feel utterly exposed. As if he'd been toying with her, taking her hand like that.

Feeling unbearably prickly, Lexie stared out of the window. Anything to escape that dark green mocking gaze.

His voice was cool. 'This was your suggestion, you know. You don't have to look as if you're about to go to the gallows.'

Lexie tensed and felt angry. She turned back to Cesar. 'I don't regret my suggestion for a second. It's still the best option.'

The tinted windows gave the back of the car a disturbingly cocoon-like atmosphere. And since when had the privacy window gone up? Lexie's skin prickled. She could have sworn it had been down when they'd got in. And was it her or had the temperature in the back of the car just shot up by about a thousand degrees?

Cesar was lounging on the other side of the car like a pasha surveying his concubine. She almost wished he was glowering at her, as he had done that first day. She could handle that. She couldn't handle this far more ambiguous energy swirling between them.

Feeling a kind of desperation rising up, she said, 'What happened before…the kissing…it won't happen again.' *So why can't you stop thinking about what it would be like to be kissed again…and more?*

Something in Cesar's eyes flashed, but he said easily, 'We can't stand ten feet apart, Lexie. We'll have to… touch…display moments of affection. Surely it shouldn't be so hard for you to feign besotted devotion?'

That prickliness was lodging in Lexie's gut, and it made her say waspishly, 'Yes, well, I'm not the only one who has to be convincing.'

Before she could react, Cesar had reached for her hand and taken it in a firm grip. Lexie gasped as he brought it to his mouth and kissed her sensitive inner palm. It felt shockingly intimate, and a shard of pure sensation pulled at her belly and groin.

He took his mouth away, eyes glittering fiercely. 'Is that convincing enough for you?'

Lexie knew her eyes were wide, her breathing choppy. He'd just kissed her hand and she was a puddle. *Her hand!* She yanked it away before he could make a complete fool of her.

Cesar saw how Lexie shrank back and everything in him rejected that even as he saw the signs of mutual attraction: the hectic pulse at the base of her neck, flushed cheeks.

Almost accusingly she said, 'You don't look like the type of guy who relishes PDA.'

Cesar bit back the urge to clamp his hands around that tiny waist and haul her into him to show her *exactly* what he thought of PDA. Every time she moved her breasts moved with her, deepening that enticing line of cleavage. But a warning bell went off in his head. She was right, and it irked him that she'd read him so easily.

He *didn't* like public displays of affection *at all*. In fact he really wasn't a tactile person. He usually discouraged his lovers from touching him, preferring to keep their contact confined to the bedroom.

Human touch had been non-existent when he was growing up in the *castillo*. When it had come it had been rough, perfunctory. *Unloving*. A minute shove. A clip around the ear for some transgression. Worse after he'd been caught rolling around in the dirt with Juan Cortez, swinging punches at each other.

If a lover slipped her hand into his, or wound her arm through his, his first instinct was to flinch away. Except right now all he could do was see the wide chasm of distance between him and Lexie in the back of the car and resent it.

Salamanca wasn't far. And it was for *that* reason, Cesar told himself, that he said softly, 'Come closer.'

'*You* come closer,' Lexie responded spikily.

Unbidden, Cesar felt a burgeoning…lightness within him. He even felt a rare smile tip the corners of his mouth.

'I asked first.'

Lexie's expression turned mutinous and had a direct effect on Cesar's already raging blood. Arrowing directly to his groin.

'Lexie,' he growled, 'if you can't bring yourself to move

closer in the back of a car, with no one watching, how do you expect us to convince a wall of paparazzi?'

With palpable reluctance Lexie huffed a sigh and moved across the seat, still keeping a healthy few inches of space between them. Cesar was intrigued. She was spiky, confident. And yet she showed these tantalising glimpses of another side altogether...one less sure of herself.

Her faintly floral scent tickled his nostrils. He fought not to just grab her and haul her onto his lap.

'So, tell me something about yourself...'

'Like what?' Lexie's voice was almost sharp.

Even more intriguing. She was seriously unsettled.

'How did you get started as an actress?'

Lexie glanced at Cesar. The sensation that he was seeing a part of her that no one else cared to observe was acute and uncomfortable. Once again all of her deepest secrets and vulnerabilities felt very close to the surface, as if he might just peel a section of her skin back and see them all laid bare.

Right now, facing a barrage of photographers and pretending to be this man's lover would be infinitely preferable to this intimate cocoon in the back of the car. Then she remembered the awful, excoriating feeling of seeing her life spread across his desk in a series of lurid pictures and she said with faux sweetness, 'You mean you skipped the part about the casting couch in that extensive research file?'

That earned her a twitching muscle in his jaw that distracted Lexie momentarily. His jaw was so hard, so resolute. As if hewn from a lifetime of clenching it.

His voice was equally hard. Clearly he did not welcome her sarcasm. 'I'd like to know how you really got started.'

Lexie's belly dipped ominously and she looked at him suspiciously. He seemed to be genuinely interested. But that reminded her uncomfortably of how she'd once believed someone else had been *genuinely interested*. That experience had left her splashed all over the tabloids, with her reputation ground into the muck. Mocking her for how quickly she'd trusted the first person who had appeared to want to know the real her. After she'd lived a lifetime protecting herself.

The reminder was not welcome now.

In a desperate bid to avoid this, Lexie racked her brain for a pithy and superficial answer. But his gaze was too direct. Too...unforgiving.

'Well,' she started reluctantly, 'I was in a shop one day... I'd just moved to London from Ireland. I was sixteen.'

He frowned. 'You're Irish?'

She nodded, hiding the dart of pain. 'Originally, yes.' When he said nothing more, she continued. 'I was in this shop...and a young kid was in front of me. Suddenly, out of nowhere, the owner accused him of shoplifting—which he hadn't done. So I stepped in and defended him.'

Lexie shuddered slightly when she recalled the oily owner's eyes devouring her overly buxom curves. She'd developed early—another unwelcome reminder right now.

'The next thing I knew,' Lexie went on, eager not to think of that time, 'I was shouting at him. I told the kid to run...and then a woman arrived.' Lexie looked at Cesar, but he was just watching her. She felt silly. 'Look, this is a really boring story...'

'I want to hear it. Go on.'

Lexie glanced away and then looked back after a moment. His gaze was intent. She took a breath. 'The woman had heard me shouting and came to investigate. She stepped in and defused the situation. Afterwards she took me for a coffee. She told me she was a casting director and asked if I'd like to audition for a part in a short film.'

Lexie recalled how bleak those days in London had

been. How alone she'd felt. How impoverished. Vulnerable, but trying to be strong...optimistic...

'So I said yes...and I got a leading role in the film. It was shown in the fringe category at the Cannes Film Festival the following year, and it won an award.' She shrugged one slim shoulder, self-conscious all of a sudden, but determined not to let him see how easily he seemed to be able to unsettle her. 'That's it. That's how I got started. But it was a rocky road... I had an unscrupulous agent for a while... It takes time to realise who has your best interests at heart.'

For a long moment Cesar was silent, and then he said, 'I'd imagine if anyone had tried to lure you onto a casting couch you would have subjected them to the same treatment as that shop owner.'

A dart of unexpected warmth pierced Lexie—and then she thought of the lurid photo shoots she'd done and the warmth fizzled out. 'Unfortunately I wasn't always so sure of what to say no to...'

Something in the air shifted between them. Lexie couldn't look away from Cesar's gaze. It was hypnotic. He seemed a lot closer. For an awful churning moment she wondered if she had moved closer to him without even realising?

'You didn't say no when I kissed you in the stable.' His voice was deep, rough.

Breath was suddenly in very short supply to Lexie's lungs. 'Proof that my track record doesn't appear to be improving with age.'

Her brain was short-circuiting. Was it only a week since she'd first kissed this man? It felt as if aeons had passed. Cesar slid an arm around her waist, pulling her into him. She gasped, filled with a fatal but delicious hot lethargy that urged her not to think. Just to feel. He was going to kiss her, and all Lexie felt was intense anticipation. Her blood was sizzling.

His mouth touched hers. Soft, coaxing. Taking Lexie by surprise. Dismantling any feeble defences she had. His other arm pulled her in even closer and lust exploded deep in her solar plexus.

His mouth was firmer now—insisting, demanding that she respond. As the last shred of trepidation melted away Lexie's mouth opened, and Cesar's attack was brutally sensual and complete. His tongue was stroking hers, sucking it, forcing her to respond.

Without even being aware of it, Lexie touched his jaw, her fingers spreading, threading through his hair, gripping it. Learning the shape of his skull.

One of his hands cupped the weight of her breast and it sent no flares of danger into her brain. Only a desire for *more*. She arched into that hand and heard a low, feral growl of approval.

When his hand left her breast and his mouth left hers she let out a husky breath of disappointment. She opened heavy eyes to see two dark glittering pools of green and black, swirling with depths that reached inside her and tugged hard.

Cesar's fingers slid under the strap of her dress, dislodging it. Her heart-rate accelerated. The first tendrils of panic pierced the haze of heat.

'Cesar... I...'

'Shh...' he said, and that hand was busy peeling down the strap of her dress.

As if knowing just how to subdue those faint tendrils of panic, he kissed her again, pulling her under even more. Making her hot, making her *need*. Making something tight coil inside her until she had to move to try and alleviate it.

When air whistled over the bare slope of her breast Lexie tore her mouth away, breathing hard. Cesar was breathing harshly too. He was looking down, and she followed his gaze to see her breast, its nipple pink and tight and pouting. His hand seemed huge and dark against her pale skin.

'*Dios*...you are truly exquisite.'

His thumb moved back and forth over her nipple, making it pucker, grow harder. She bit her lip to stop from crying out at the exquisite feeling. The tightening sensation deep in her belly was sharper. She could feel wetness between her legs, against her panties.

She couldn't think...couldn't rationalise. She wanted to know how his mouth would feel on her. Tasting her... His tongue... But something was trying to break through. Sense, sanity...self-preservation?

Cesar pulled away from her abruptly, adjusting her dress at the same time, covering her up, and then Lexie heard it: the insistent knocking on the privacy window. A cold wind whistled over her skin.

She felt completely dazed, and could only watch as Cesar, who looked as if nothing had happened, pressed a button and said a few words in Spanish. He turned back to her, but already shame and embarrassment were clawing up inside Lexie.

An insidious image of his usual lovers inserted itself into her brain. She would bet that he didn't subject *those* cool beauties to such sensual attacks in the back of his car.

She pulled the strap of her dress up fully, covering her sensitised breast. Through the window behind Cesar's head she could see people milling, see the flashing pops of cameras. See security people waiting for them to emerge.

Realisation sank into her belly like a cold stone. Of *course* he didn't normally do this. He'd engineered that kiss purely because he'd known exactly how close to Salamanca they were. He'd known they were about to emerge from the car and had wanted to make things look as *authentic* as possible.

She couldn't meet his gaze, and tried to pull away

when his fingers caught her chin. 'What?' she spat out, livid with herself for the dart of hurt that she shouldn't be feeling. 'Do I not appear sufficiently dishevelled to make the paparazzi believe we've been making out like teenagers?'

He flushed angrily. His accent was stronger. 'That was not premeditated, Lexie. But now that you mention it...'

Eyes sparking, Cesar covered her lips with his mouth again and Lexie fought him, closing her mouth. But with expert precision and ruthless intent Cesar proceeded to show her just how pathetic her little outburst had been. Within seconds her mouth was open under his and he was bending her head back with the force of his kiss. And she was matching him, her anger heightening the tension between them.

Cesar was losing it. He knew he was losing it. But he couldn't take his mouth off Lexie's. He'd never tasted anything so sweet. Or so wicked. The way her lush mouth softened under his...the feel of that body under his hands. Her breast...that hard peak under his thumb... He'd wanted to taste it.

Dios.

Cesar finally pulled back, heart hammering. He did *not* ravish women in the back of his car. He was cool, calm, controlled.

Right now he felt anything but. He could hardly see straight. His body was on fire.

Lexie was looking at him with huge bruised eyes. She thought he'd done that on purpose. And he had—but not for the reasons she obviously suspected. He'd wanted to make sure there was no ambiguity about how he felt about her.

He cupped that delicate jaw, a little aghast that his hand shook minutely. Her mouth was pink, swollen. He couldn't help running his thumb across that pouting lower lip, feeling its fleshy softness.

'Make no mistake, Lexie, I want you…and not just to distract the crowds. You know the truth of what I said earlier. We will be lovers for real.'

CHAPTER FOUR

WE WILL BE lovers for real.

Lexie's hand was held tight in Cesar's. She hadn't had time to respond because the driver had opened the car door. And, as much as she wanted to pull free, right now she needed the support. They'd just run the gauntlet of the press outside. Lexie had felt so raw after those kisses that she'd probably looked as green as an *ingenue* at her first premiere.

Cesar had seemed as cool as a cucumber. He'd even rustled up a smile. It was galling. Shouldn't he be the one flinching and snarling?

Lexie finally managed to pull her hand free, once they were in the marble lobby of the very exclusive hotel that was hosting the event.

Cesar frowned. 'Are you all right?'

Lexie wanted to scream. She felt wild, dishevelled. Not herself. 'Not really,' she ground out. 'I need to freshen up before we go in.'

She spotted the powder room and made a beeline for it. Once inside she found it was mercifully empty and she let out a great shuddering sigh of relief. When she looked in the mirror she nearly lost the ability to breathe again.

Her hair was mussed. Cheeks bright pink, mouth swollen. Eyes huge and glittering far too brightly. Lexie pulled tissues out of the box and started to repair the damage.

Damn him. She cursed him roundly. Once again she was floored by how instantaneous his effect on her was and how her body betrayed her every time, jumping gleefully into the fire without any hesitation.

When Lexie was done she surveyed herself again and caught her own eyes in the reflection. There were shadows and secrets in their depths that only she could see. Someone like Cesar could never guess at them. She might be stronger now, but once she'd been utterly broken and had never thought she'd be whole again.

But when Cesar touched her it made her feel whole. It made her forget everything. Forget what had happened to her. There was none of the reflexive instinctive fear that had come when other men had kissed her—even if that had been in the safe environment of a film set.

We will be lovers.

Lexie couldn't seem to stem the tiny flicker of hope inside her. As inconceivable as it seemed...as unsuitable as Cesar Da Silva was...perhaps he was the one who could repair something in her that she had believed destroyed a long time ago? Just allowing that thought to enter her head made Lexie sway on her feet as a giddy mix of excitement and terror rushed up inside her.

There was a knock at the door, and then, 'Lexie, are you okay?'

Lexie's breath jammed in her throat. Her recent thoughts were too nebulous, too scary. She called out threadily, 'I'm fine. I'll be out in a second.'

When she did emerge she didn't like the spurt of emotion at seeing him leaning nonchalantly against a pillar, nor the way his gaze raked her face. He straightened up and just like that her mind started becoming fuzzy again.

She reined herself in with an effort. More people were milling around now, but to Lexie's relief he didn't take her hand again. He put it to her lower back instead, to guide her into the main ballroom where the dinner was being held. His touch burned like a brand through the back of her dress.

Lexie didn't like how aware she was of other women staring at Cesar, of the flurry of whispers that would stop as they grew close only to start up again after they'd passed. It reminded her uncomfortably of what it had been like to walk into a crowded room after the story had broken about her and Jonathan Saunders.

Cesar guided her to a seat and once she was sitting took his own, beside her. He stretched his arm out behind her, and his thumb was rubbing back and forth across the top of her bare back. Lexie almost closed her eyes as her body responded violently: nipples peaking, belly softening, warmth pooling and spreading.

His voice came close to her ear. Too close. 'Relax. You look as if you're about to shatter into pieces.'

Lexie opened her eyes and turned her head, and Cesar's face was so close she could see the darker flecks of green in his eyes. Green on green—an ocean. She had the bizarre urge to reach up and touch his face, and had to curl her hand into a fist to stop herself.

The line of his cheek was a blade, giving his features that edgy saturnine impression. Something came over her—perhaps the knowledge that she could touch him in public as it would be expected. She lifted her hand and touched his jaw. She felt it clench under her hand and looked at him. His eyes had darkened and something hard shone through their depths. Cynicism.

It made her snatch her hand back. But not before he caught it with lightning swiftness and captured it, pressing an open-mouthed kiss to the skin just as he had in the car. It was no less devastating this time.

'You are quite the actress...'

Before Lexie could respond with some acid retort that

might deflect from the fact that a scary poignancy had gripped her on seeing that cynicism, a menu was being handed to her by a waiter and she had to accept it. There was no room for poignancy; she didn't care if Cesar was cynical.

Lexie stared at the menu blankly for a moment as she regained her composure. Damn the man. *Again.*

But of course the menu still remained largely incomprehensible to her. Another kind of dismay filled her—especially when she was so keyed up. She didn't need this particular vulnerability right now.

'It helps if you turn the menu the right way up.'

His voice was low and gently mocking. Lexie's hands tightened on the thick vellum as embarrassment washed through her in waves, making her hot. She sent a glare to Cesar, who had that tantalising smile playing around his mouth again.

She turned the menu around but of course that made no difference. She could see the waiters taking orders now and started to panic. With the utmost reluctance she said to Cesar, in a low voice, 'What would you recommend?'

He glanced at her for a moment and then perused his own menu and said, 'Personally I'd recommend the quail starter—'

'Quail?' Lexie asked, feeling ill at the thought.

Cesar looked at her. 'Well, there's a brie starter too.'

'I'll have that,' Lexie said with relief.

Cesar glanced back at the menu. 'Then there's a choice of salmon risotto, beef carpaccio...'

'The beef,' Lexie said, too ashamed to look at Cesar. Especially when she thought of his multi-lingual lovers who would be well used to these situations.

He said from beside her, 'Not everyone is used to menus in French—it's nothing to be embarrassed about.'

Lexie's own mortification made her lash out. 'Don't patronise me, Cesar. I'm not stupid, I'm just—'

But before she could finish a waiter had arrived and Cesar was ordering for both of them. Lexie clamped her mouth shut. Did she *have* to let every tiny detail of her life out whenever she opened her mouth?

When the waiter moved on Cesar's attention was taken by someone sitting to his left, and Lexie was facing a table full of people looking at her with varying degrees of curiosity.

To her immediate right was an older woman who leaned into Lexie and said in an American accent, 'My dear, you've quite set the cat among the pigeons, arriving with one of the most eligible bachelors in the world.'

Lexie smiled weakly. To her relief, she discovered that the woman was as charming as she was obviously eccentric and rich, and she regaled Lexie with stories of her expat life in Spain.

Relieved to have an excuse to avoid that green-eyed scrutiny, Lexie conversed enthusiastically with the woman.

Cesar willed himself to relax for the umpteenth time. The food had been served and eaten. Lexie had managed to spend most if not all that time ignoring him. It was unprecedented. He'd never had this experience with a woman before. And certainly not with one he'd kissed.

When he'd noticed her struggling with the menu, and that she'd had it upside down, a lurch of emotion had tightened his gut. He remembered her story about how she'd got started in the industry, leaving home so young, and presumably leaving school. She hadn't gone to university. She obviously wasn't as sophisticated as the women he was used to. And yet there was something refreshing about that.

Just before they'd been interrupted she'd said angrily, *'I'm not stupid.'* But that was one thing that had never come into his mind. Lexie Anderson had more intelligence sparking out of those blue eyes than he'd ever seen in his life.

With some of his previous lovers Cesar had found himself calling things off purely because of mental exhaustion. It was as if they felt they had to prove to him what worthy candidates they were by conversing in three languages at once, about complicated political systems that he had no interest in. And in the bedroom more than one had been keen to initiate kinky scenarios that had felt anything but sexy.

But with Lexie…every time he looked at her he felt kinky. He wanted to tie her down to some flat soft surface and ravish her.

Perhaps it was due to the fact that when they'd stepped out of the car earlier, to face the press, his body had still been humming with an overload of sexual frustration, but the experience hadn't been half as painful as he'd imagined. Having Lexie by his side had seemed to mitigate his usual excoriating feeling that the lenses of the paparazzi had some kind of X-ray vision.

When he saw her dining companion get up to leave the table he felt a rush of satisfaction. Now she would have to turn back to *him*. Cesar wasn't unaware of the looks she'd been drawing all evening in that provocative dress. She outshone every other woman. Literally. Cesar couldn't even recall seeing another woman. It was as if she'd blinded him. *With lust.*

He didn't like the hot spokes of anger that lanced him every time he caught some man's gaze sliding to her abundant curves.

Lexie could sense Cesar beside her. Waiting… Mrs Carmichael had gone to the bathroom and she was ready for his gaze to be censorious for having avoided him so obviously.

Taking a breath, she turned back—and just like that a jolt of pure electricity shot through her belly. Cesar had his hand on the back of her chair again, far too close for comfort. He'd taken off his jacket and his shirt was pulled taut across his chest, doing little to hide that stunning musculature.

He spoke. 'What I said earlier…before you turned your back on me so comprehensively…'

Lexie flushed and was about to remonstrate, but she knew she couldn't. She felt like a child.

'Mrs Carmichael was interesting,' she supplied a touch defensively.

'I know Mrs Carmichael very well and she *is* interesting.' His lip curled slightly. 'About the most interesting person here.'

Lexie glanced around at the very important-looking men and women. 'But aren't these your friends?'

Cesar all but snorted, surprising Lexie.

'They pretend to be my friends because I come and bid an obscene amount of money at their auction and then go. The only reason I do it is because I believe in this particular charity and because the money goes directly to the source, rather than via a dozen government agencies.'

'Oh,' Lexie answered, a little taken aback at Cesar's words.

She'd have put him in the same category as many rich people who contributed to charity for far too cynical reasons. But this *was* a worthy charity; it was aimed at combatting sex trafficking—a cause close to Lexie's own heart. She knew it was not one that was especially 'trendy' in the media, so the fact that Cesar was endorsing it had to help.

'Mrs Carmichael told me about it.'

Cesar picked up a card with his free hand and held it out to her. 'Here's a list of items to be auctioned—see if anything takes your fancy.'

His insouciance and his air of almost bored expectation that she would expect to be indulged made Lexie feel bizarrely disappointed. Then the fact that she couldn't *read* the card sent a spurt of anger up her spine. Something bitter gripped her.

She whispered angrily, 'I might not be as intellectual as your usual lovers, Cesar, but you really don't have to treat me like some kind of bimbo just because I'm blonde and—'

'That's enough.' Cesar straightened up, his hand tensing across the back of her chair, his fingers touching her neck in a very light but subtle admonishment.

She tensed against her inevitable reaction and could have laughed. To all the world they must look besotted. Close together, staring at each other, intent...

She could see in his face that he was surprised at her response. She moved, dislodging his hand slightly. 'I'm sorry. I overreacted.'

Cesar grimaced faintly. 'I didn't mean for it to sound so dismissive or flippant.'

Lexie was once again taken aback by his ability to apologise. Slightly mollified, she said, 'Maybe I'll want to bid on something myself?'

To give Cesar his due, he didn't laugh before he said, 'Do you know how much the cheapest item is marked at?'

Lexie shook her head. He glanced down and then looked back up, naming a price. She paled and said faintly, 'I guess I won't be bidding, then.'

Cesar handed her the card and Lexie took it. She should really tell him—especially if he was going to have her so on edge—that even reading a menu would be a challenge for her.

'About the menu earlier...I should explain—'

'No.' He shook his head. 'I didn't mean to imply for a second that you're stupid.'

Now Lexie shook her head, regretting her defensive response. 'The reason I wasn't reading the menu very well was because I'm severely dyslexic.'

Lexie could feel her insides contracting, as if she were waiting for a look of disdain in Cesar's eyes. She'd seen it before.

But that didn't happen. He just said, 'And…?'

Lexie blanched. 'And…I can read perfectly well, but if I'm stressed…or under pressure…it becomes nearly impossible. I just need time.'

Cesar moved closer, his fingers whispering over her skin, under her hair. Lexie repressed a shiver of sensation.

'And are you?' he asked. 'Stressed? Under pressure?'

She wondered how it would be if she told him about the severe pressure and stress she felt under right now, with her body sparking and firing on levels she'd never even been aware of before.

Instead she said dryly, 'A little.'

He moved back slightly. 'You should have told me. A good friend of mine is dyslexic and he uses special software to help him. I'm sure I don't need to tell you of the renowned geniuses who had dyslexia but didn't let it hold them back.'

'Of course you don't,' Lexie said, almost feeling cross that Cesar was the one defending dyslexia and not her! 'I go to some of my local schools in London and talk to the kids about it—help them see that it won't limit them.'

He frowned, 'How do you manage with the scripts for your films?'

Lexie fiddled with her napkin self-consciously. 'I usually get an actor friend of mine to read them out. I record them, then I transfer them to my mp3 player…'

Someone sounded a gavel just then, and Lexie looked away with an effort. She was so engrossed in *him*. But people were sitting down again and she was glad of the interruption.

Not that long ago another man had duped her into thinking he was interested in her and she'd almost fallen for it. Now Cesar was coming perilously close to making her believe that *he* was interested but she knew that it was just lust. The spike of excitement in her gut was shameful, but she couldn't ignore it.

Cesar's attention had turned to the front. And then Lexie found herself distracted as with admirable nonchalance he made bids on the most expensive lots, only to get an assurance from the auctioneer that the lots he'd bought would be raffled for free at the charity for its workers.

When it was over, and Cesar had spent more money than Lexie had ever heard of, he turned to her and said brusquely, 'Are you ready to go?'

She nodded, too intimidated by what she'd seen to say a word. Lexie could see all the sycophants vying for his attention as they left, but he didn't stop for anyone, his hand on her back again.

His car and driver were waiting outside, as if psychically informed of his departure, but Lexie knew it must have been a series of frantic Chinese whispers from the staff, who had been watching his every move like a hawk.

Once they were in the back of the car, the darkness closed around them like a blanket, cutting out sounds, cutting out reality. It made Lexie exceedingly nervous and she scooted right over to her side of the car. The thought of Cesar kissing her again in this seductive gloom was far too scary to contemplate, even if the thought of his words *we will be lovers* tantalised her more than she cared to admit.

Through the tinted windows Lexie could see the lights of Salamanca glittering. It distracted her. She said on an awed breath, 'It's so beautiful…'

After a moment Lexie head Cesar say something to his driver in the front and then the car was turning around.

She looked at Cesar. 'Wait…what are you doing?'

A little gruffly he said, 'You should see the Plaza Mayor at night when it's lit up.'

After watching how generous he'd been to the charity, Lexie was mortified to think that he might feel the need to act as tour guide. 'It's fine,' she protested. 'I can come back again some evening.'

He ignored that and asked, 'Are you hungry for something sweet?'

Lexie blinked in the gloom. She hadn't had dessert. How did the man know she had a sweet tooth?

'A little…maybe…but really we don't—'

He cut her off. 'I know a place. We'll go there.'

The car parked on a street where couples strolled arm in arm. Cesar got out, and by the time Lexie had her door open he was standing waiting, holding out a hand for her to take. Muttering her thanks, she let him help her.

The early autumn air had a slight nip, and before Lexie could say anything she felt Cesar's dinner jacket being settled around her shoulders. His warmth and scent surrounded her like an intoxicating cloak.

When he took her hand Lexie had to battle the urge to pull it free again. The truth was she liked the way it felt to have her hand in his. She glanced up at Cesar and saw that his bow-tie was gone and the top button of his shirt was open. It made him appear rakish.

Lexie was attracting attention in her long gold dress. 'Do you think the photographers will be around here?'

Cesar looked down at her. 'They could be—they saw us leave.'

They rounded a corner then, and Lexie's mind blanked at the beauty before them. Salamanca's famous Plaza Mayor was lit up in golden lights. They spilled from everywhere and illuminated the huge ancient buildings. It was like the inside of a magical golden ornament. Lexie had known the old part of the city was a UNESCO heritage protected site and now she knew why. The square was huge...awe-inspiring.

Cesar led her across the airy space and she felt tiny in the midst of the baroque grandeur. When she was able to stop looking up and gaping at the beautifully ornate buildings, she saw that they'd stopped outside one of the cafés which was still open.

A small old man came rushing out, welcoming Cesar effusively and offering them a table under one of the massive arches that lined the square. They sat down. Lexie was relieved and disappointed in equal measure to get her hand back.

Cesar asked, 'What kind of dessert do you like?'

Feeling very bemused at being here with him, Lexie said, 'Anything...cakes...pastries.'

He arched a brow. 'Coffee?'

She nodded. 'Yes, please.'

Cesar said a few words to the proprietor, who looked as if he was about to burst with pride at having such an esteemed guest—clearly he knew who Cesar was.

A few people lingered over coffee, glasses of wine. Cesar's jacket swam on Lexie, but his warmth still tantalised her skin. It was incredibly seductive.

The owner bustled back out, with another young man following him. They set down coffee and a tray of different desserts. Lexie's mouth watered. When they'd left, Cesar explained what they were. There was an almond sponge cake, candied almonds, small fritters filled with cream, sweet puff pastry, small chocolate cakes...

Lexie groaned after she'd tasted some of the delicious pastry. 'If only I didn't have to worry about getting back into that corset in a couple of days.'

Cesar paused in the act of drinking his coffee and looked at her. Lexie looked back. The air between them sizzled. That moment in the back of the car earlier invaded her head like a lurid B movie.

He put his cup down. 'When I saw you for the first time I thought you were some kind of an apparition. That you weren't real.'

Lexie swallowed her dessert with difficulty. She remembered the transfixed expression on his face that day. She'd never forget it. While she hadn't thought he was an apparition, she'd felt something similar.

'I knew you were real...' she admitted. 'But I know what you mean. I wasn't meant to be there.'

Cesar grimaced. 'I was harsh on you.'

Lexie glanced down at her coffee and shrugged. 'Your privacy had been comprehensively invaded by hundreds of strangers...'

'I'd also just returned from my half-brother's wedding in Paris.'

He sounded so grim that Lexie looked up again. She recalled seeing the pictures on the internet of that wedding, the speculation.

Her curiosity piqued, she asked, 'So you *are* related, then?'

He frowned. 'Why do you ask?'

Lexie flushed, feeling like a stalker. 'I saw something on the internet when I went looking to see if there were any more pictures...of us.' It wasn't entirely untrue, she reassured herself.

Cesar's face was hard. 'Yes, it's true. He and Rafaele Falcone are my half-brothers.'

Lexie had the sense she was entering into a minefield. 'But this wasn't common knowledge?'

Cesar took a swift sip of his coffee and shook his head, putting the cup back down with a clatter. He was so tense all of a sudden that Lexie half expected him to jump up and stride away. But he didn't. Although for the first time his gaze was avoiding hers.

'We had the same mother but different fathers.'

'You didn't know them growing up?'

He shook his head and then speared her with a look that she couldn't read.

'No. I just knew of them. My mother was more interested in a life of opulence and luxury to think about cosy reunions, or to worry about the fact that she'd abandoned her eldest son.'

A multitude of questions hit Lexie. Why had his mother left him? But then that very first niggle of suspicion she'd had came back. 'Does that have anything to do with... *this*?' she asked carefully.

Cesar frowned. 'What do you mean?'

Lexie wasn't even sure herself. She only knew that she was feeling increasingly exposed on a level she didn't welcome.

'I mean, does the fact that it's come out about your brothers have anything to do with the fact that you were happy to agree for us to be seen together in public?'

His mouth tightened. 'I will admit that I saw an advantage in allowing another story to take precedence.'

Lexie had suspected that this might be a possibility. So why was a feeling of hurt blooming deep inside? A snide voice answered her—because she'd been seduced by his touch and his words into thinking his desire for her was his only motivation.

Of course someone like Cesar Da Silva would normally prefer to keep her tucked away out of sight, so that he could make it look as if that first kiss had been some crazy brief aberration. It had been his initial reaction.

Why hadn't she even questioned it properly at the time? His ready compliance? Because he'd turned her brain to mush exactly at the same time as he'd turned her insides molten.

She thought of the bathroom earlier—when she'd entertained the notion of their becoming lovers for a moment. The dizzying rush of exhilaration that had gripped her. *God*, she'd been so easily caught.

Lexie looked away from him and blindly picked up her cup again, not even noticing when some coffee sloshed over the rim to fall on her dress. Suddenly she couldn't stand it—being under his cool assessing scrutiny.

Almost knocking the small table over with her jerkiness, she stood up, any inherent ability to act deserting her. 'Would you mind if we left now? I'm quite tired…it's been a long week.'

She whirled away from the table and started to walk. Agitation was rising up from her gullet and also a kind of panic. Panic that she'd not thought more clearly that *obviously* he'd have an ulterior motive for wanting to be seen in public with her. He'd just been toying with her, while she'd been perilously close to proving how easily duped she could be—*again.*

She vaguely heard a muttered curse and some change being thrown on the table and just when she'd reached the middle of the golden square which by now was almost empty, her arm was caught in a big hand. She was spun around to face a familiar glowering expression. She welcomed it.

'What the hell was that about, Lexie?'

She wrenched her arm out of Cesar's grip, dislodging his coat from her shoulders. It fell to the ground, unnoticed by either of them. Words trembled on her lips, but if she uttered them she only risked exposing herself even more.

His lip curled. 'You find the fact that I have my own reasons to avoid the press digging into my life unpalatable?

That I was left behind like some unwanted luggage, with half-siblings who never even knew I existed?'

'What?' Lexie said, his words shocking her out of her own turmoil for a moment. 'No! Of course not... I didn't even know anything about your family.'

Cesar's mouth was tight. 'My mother hoped to get a good deal by bringing me back to the family home, but she hadn't banked on my grandparents giving her an ultimatum: just me or neither of us. So she left me behind.'

Lexie's agitation drained away. She put out a hand, 'Cesar...I had no idea.'

He stepped back. The huge magnificent square seemed to frame him in a leonine glow, making his masculinity even more impressive.

'That's what is about to hit the papers any day now. The full lurid story of Esperanza Christakos—née Falcone, née Da Silva—her rise from poverty to incalculable wealth and fame. And the gory details of the son she abandoned.'

Even as his words touched a painful nerve within Lexie she let out a tiny gasp of recognition at the name. She'd never put two and two together and realised that the world-famous beauty had been related to his brothers—*or him*.

She shook her head. 'I didn't know anything about her.'

Cesar, clearly angry at himself for letting all that spill out, said curtly, 'Well, *what*, then? If not that?'

Lexie's equilibrium was all over the place again. How could she articulate the fact that she was hurt because he evidently hadn't been motivated to appear with her in public simply out of sheer desire? When all along she'd protested vehemently at his arrogant assertion that they'd become lovers even as she'd pathetically melted whenever he touched her. And yet now that he clearly had another motivation it only highlighted her inner confusion and the tumultuous desires he evoked within her.

She searched his face for any hint of softness. But found

none. She realised then just how truly hard he was, and couldn't stop the tug of emotion at imagining a small child being left in that huge grim *castillo* without his mother.

Racking her brain for a way not to betray herself, she avoided his question and said weakly, 'We don't have to do this…if you don't want to.'

Right now even the prospect of staying in the *castillo* to avoid the press was more appealing than the thought of exposing herself like this again.

Cesar moved closer. His face wasn't so hard now. There was an explicit gleam in his eye that had a direct effect on Lexie's blood.

She spoke quickly, to hide her frayed nerves. 'Maybe this isn't such a good idea. If we stop now we can make it look like it was just a brief…fling.'

Cesar shook his head and said in that deep voice, 'We've gone too far to turn back now.'

Lexie's heart thumped hard. Her mouth dried. Treacherously, she didn't feel inclined to argue.

He said then, 'We both have our reasons for doing this, Lexie…and we're adults. This happened in the first place because we took one look at each other and couldn't keep our hands off each other.'

She thought of what he'd told her about his half-brothers. About his desire to avoid press intrusion around what was obviously a tender subject. Even though she didn't know the full story it resonated within her. She too had secrets to keep—dark ones. She found herself feeling a dangerous kinship with him. They were in this together.

He was sliding his hands and arms around her waist now, tugging her unresisting her body into his. All Lexie could feel was steel. Warmth and steel.

She put her hands on his chest. The moment felt slightly unreal. They were surrounded by the golden shimmering lights of the square.

Lexie's recent feelings of exposure and vulnerability were nowhere to be felt when Cesar's mouth touched hers. And they were certainly nowhere to be found in the almost shameless way she responded so quickly—opening her mouth, inviting him in, arching closer, demanding more.

There was a flash from nearby and it made her jerk in Cesar's arms. He pulled back, cursing. A photographer was feet away, snapping them. She felt Cesar tense but he made no move to stop the photographer, who was already walking away, checking his digital images.

Cesar turned back to Lexie and there was a distinctly satisfied gleam in his eyes. 'There goes any chance to protest that this was just a brief fling.' The satisfied gleam became something else—*hotter*. 'Whatever our reasons were, it's about *us* now. I want you. And you want me. It's that simple.'

CHAPTER FIVE

ABOUT AN HOUR later Lexie lay in bed with his words reverberating in her head. After that moment in the middle of that beautiful square Cesar had said nothing else. He'd just taken her by the hand and led her back to the car.

They'd remained in silence for the journey, as if both contemplating what lay ahead. Lexie's mind had been slightly numb, though. Too full to be able to tease out the different strands.

When they'd returned to the *castillo* the dour housekeeper had met them and told Cesar that he had some phone calls he must return. Lexie had welcomed the chance to escape, pleading tiredness, but she hadn't missed the intensity of Cesar's expression as he'd bade her goodnight. It had set a fire alight deep in her belly.

She could feel it now. As if she'd been awoken on some deep level. This hadn't happened with Jonathan Saunders, her *alleged* married lover... He'd appealed to an altogether less visceral side of her. Perhaps he'd appealed to the part of her that had finally been ready to trust again and she'd just chosen unwisely.

Suddenly that revelation made her heart beat fast. Perhaps she hadn't lost it completely. Perhaps she was still in control. This was totally different from what had happened before. There was no hint of scandal.

Cesar had not touched her innermost feelings and secrets. *He hadn't,* she told herself fiercely in the dark. He'd kissed her and she'd come alive. That was all. It was *physical*. And if anyone was long overdue their awakening it was her. She'd just got a little confused for a moment. Confused lust with feelings. Cesar was offering her a chance to explore this sexual attraction. And she realised with an almost desperate feeling that she wanted to. With *this* man.

What he'd revealed about his brothers and mother struck her again. That feeling of empathy. She knew exactly what it was like to want to avoid scrutiny of your most private self.

Cesar was a cynical being. It oozed from every part of him. Cynical and dark... She could appreciate why now. Lexie was cynical too—it had been branded onto her at an early age when she'd come face to face with the harshest side of life.

She'd prided herself on cultivating a sense of optimism over the years, but she knew that cynical shell hadn't really worn away completely. She could be as cynical as him now. More so. She had infinitely more to gain from this than he could ever realise.

And when the time came to walk away Cesar could go back to his classically coiffed intellectual lovers and Lexie would have achieved a personal emancipation she'd only ever dreamed about.

It was that simple.

'Thanks for a great day, everyone, that's a wrap.'

Lexie let out a sigh of relief. They'd finished shooting their scenes in the walled garden and would be moving further into the *castillo* estate for the rest of the week.

Cesar had been absent from the set all day, and Lexie had been glad of the space to try and get her bearings and remember that she was here to work. But her assertion to herself that she'd been glad of the space mocked her.

She hadn't seen Cesar since Saturday night, when he'd left her hot and bothered with that look. She'd felt so antsy on Sunday that she'd gone out for a long walk around the estate—and still no sign of Cesar.

After coming to the momentous personal decision that she would embark on an affair with him, she felt suddenly deflated now he'd disappeared into thin air. Without his unerring ability to distract her, and hypnotise her with his charisma and intensity, Lexie felt vulnerable.

She cursed herself for those weak feelings as she scrubbed her face clean in the empty make-up truck. It took her so long to get out of her costume that the base was usually quiet when she left. Only the wardrobe crew were still there, and the facility men who looked after the trailers. And the second assistant director, whose job it was to make sure Lexie was everywhere she needed to be and on time.

Lexie called goodnight and made her way back to the *castillo*. She didn't like the frisson of loneliness that assailed her and scowled at herself.

She was still scowling when she entered the *castillo* and ran straight into a wall. Except this wall was warm and it had hands that came around her arms, steadying her.

The singing rush of warmth and excitement made her scowl even more as she looked up into the elusive Cesar Da Silva's face. Damn him.

'I was just coming to find you.'

'Well, as you can see I'm here,' Lexie said testily, irritated at being irritated.

Cesar whistled softly. 'Bad day at the office, dear?'

His unexpected dry humour sparked something inside Lexie, but she pulled free of his hands before he could see it. She didn't want him to be flirty or endearing.

'I'm sorry,' she blurted out, avoiding his eye. 'It has been a long day.' *Liar,* her conscience mocked her.

She felt self-conscious in comfy leggings and a loose shirt. Face clean, hair pulled back into a messy knot. For all she knew he might have been wining and dining some dark beauty last night...

Cesar cut through her feverish thoughts.

'Those phone calls the other night...one of them resulted in me having to attend an urgent meeting in Paris early this morning, so I left yesterday.'

Lexie fought to repress the crazy lurch of relief. She shrugged a shoulder minutely and said airily, 'Really? I didn't notice.'

Cesar came close and tipped Lexie's jaw up so she had to look at him. She hated being small right now. If she'd been taller she could have eyeballed Cesar.

'Liar,' he said softly. 'Because I was aware of every minute I was away from this place.'

His words made air whoosh out of Lexie's lungs. An instantaneous bubble of lightness infused her blood. She couldn't help a rueful smile. 'Well, your meeting can't have been very exciting.'

Cesar shook his head. 'It was deadly dull.'

The air sizzled between them. And just like that all of Lexie's doubts and fears melted away again. His effect on her was ridiculous. But she couldn't resist.

He took his hand away. 'We hit the papers today...I thought you'd want to see.'

Lexie fought not to let him see how much he affected her. 'Of course.'

He stepped back. 'We can go to my apartment—it's more private.'

Lexie looked at him as he started to walk away. 'Your apartment?'

She walked quickly to keep up with him. He glanced at her and then took her hand, setting off a million butterflies.

'I have my own apartment here within the *castillo*.'

Curious as to what it might be like, in such a mausoleum of a castle, Lexie followed him down a warren of corridors, passing the study where she'd had that first cataclysmic conversation with him.

He stopped outside a door that had a keypad lock and entered a code. The door swung open. As he walked in and Lexie followed, her hand still in his, her jaw dropped. It was like stepping into another world.

The apartment was huge, cavernous. Like stepping into Narnia from behind the coats in the wardrobe. One side was dominated by a massive wall of windows. On the other side was a modern state-of-the-art kitchen. Steel and chrome with industrial lights.

The floor was wooden—parquet, like his office—and strewn with huge oriental rugs, softening it. One corner of the room was filled with three old battered leather couches and a low coffee table. A TV and music system. Along that wall was nothing but shelves and books—rows and rows of books.

Lexie felt that pang again. She loved books and reading, but for her it was a torturous process. Remembering how Cesar had responded to her dyslexia made her melt a little more.

'I have an office through here.'

As Lexie followed Cesar she saw another door, and glanced in as they passed to see a huge bedroom with a massive bed, sheets tangled on top. The image was incendiary and unbelievably intimate. She felt herself blushing. Would she be in that bed with him soon? Limbs entwined?

Her face was burning when he let her hand go inside the office. She was glad the lighting was dim and looked around. This was obviously a private study. Not as imposing as his other one, but somewhere he obviously spent a lot of time. Books were strewn around…papers. It was lived in. Comfortable. Messier than she would have imagined for someone who seemed so controlled.

He had some newspapers on the desk and turned one around to face her. Carefully keeping her expression neutral, she read the headline.

Hot! Hot! Hot! Luscious Lexie bags the world's most reclusive bachelor and richest man!

It was more or less what she had expected, but still a blow to her gut. She couldn't take her eyes off the pictures. One was of them arriving at the function the other night, her hand in his. She was practically welded to his body. She hadn't even realised that she'd been stuck to him like that. Her eyes were huge. Like a deer in headlights. Pathetic.

Another showed his head bending to hers. She couldn't remember what he'd said—something about going inside after another minute. But it looked as if he was whispering a sweet nothing. Her face was turned to his.

And one last one was a shot from inside the hotel; it must have been taken by a guest or a waiter on a camera phone. They were at the table, his arm around the back of her chair, heads close together.

Lexie felt horribly exposed, even though she was used to seeing her picture in the papers by now. But not like this. These showed just how enticing and fascinating she found this dark and difficult man. She was relieved that there didn't seem to be any pictures from the square. Even now those moments felt raw.

Cesar was perched on the edge of his desk, one powerful thigh in her eyeline, distracting her.

His voice sounding far too smug, he said, 'They look convincing…although you'd be more used to this sort of thing than me.'

Feeling prickly at his tone—obviously the experience

had been far more cataclysmic for her—and hating that he evidently believed in her guilt, Lexie stepped back and blurted out, 'I had nothing to do with ending up in the tabloids with that man.'

Cesar frowned. 'What do you mean?'

Lexie started to pace, agitated. Dammit, she didn't have to explain herself to this man. But…treacherously…she wanted to. Even if Cesar wasn't really interested.

She stopped pacing and faced him, crossing her arms in a classic defence pose. 'I didn't have an affair with that man.'

His eyes narrowed on her. 'So how did it come about?'

'Jonathan Saunders…' Lexie stopped for a moment. Even saying his name made her angry. 'We'd just done a small West End play together for a few weeks. I'd worked with him years before on my very first short film. He'd been nice to me at the time—kind of like a mentor. I considered us friends… During the play he made a point of hanging out with me. Making sure I got home okay. Stuff like that.'

Lexie felt queasy to think that his easy affection and hands-off attention had sneaked under her skin so that she'd believed she could trust him. And even though she hadn't really felt anything for him physically, she'd believed him to be a genuine friend. She'd been susceptible enough to consider that if he made a physical move she'd give him a chance. The thought made her skin crawl now.

'After we'd finished the play he called around one day and he was in a state, saying he needed somewhere to stay. He had some story about being chucked out of his house because he couldn't afford to pay the rent. I knew he wasn't that successful as an actor—it seemed believable. I had a spare room so I offered it to him and he moved in for about a week.'

'Did you sleep with him?'

Cesar's voice was sharp and Lexie glared at him, annoyed with herself for even bringing it up. It was only exposing her even more.

'I told you I didn't have an affair with him.'

'So what happened?'

'He left early one morning, and I only found out because there was banging on the door. I'd been asleep. I figured it was him—that he'd left something behind—he'd started rehearsals for a new play. I was half asleep, and when I opened the door the street was full of photographers.'

Lexie's face burned.

'I was dressed in night clothes...barely awake... I discovered later that Jonathan was actually married and had had a huge row with his wife because she'd found out he was having an affair and that his girlfriend was pregnant.'

Her mouth went tight.

'He'd known it was coming, because he'd been tipped off by his lover that the press suspected something, so he cultivated me. Made friends. Got me to trust him so that he could use me to be the fall guy when he wanted to protect his *real* girlfriend. He was terrified they'd track her down.'

Lexie sighed.

'His lover was the wife of a prominent Conservative cabinet minister; she wanted to avoid scandal at all costs. He figured *I* was a better prospect to throw to the ravenous press and he set me up well—living with me for a week, letting them believe we'd moved in together.'

Lexie looked at Cesar.

'I hadn't even known he was married. He'd said nothing at all about his wife. Or kids.'

'Why didn't you defend yourself once you knew the truth?'

Because she hadn't wanted to give the press any excuse to look into her background in case of what they might find.

A feeling of *déja vu* struck her. Here she was again, feeling the urge to *trust*, to believe. But if the last few minutes of rehashing the events of that unfortunate period told her anything it was that she couldn't trust. Not really. So she shrugged minutely. 'I didn't want to add fuel to the fire…attract even more attention. And I felt sorry for his wife and kids.'

She avoided his gaze. At least that was part of the truth.

There was something achingly vulnerable about Lexie as she stood in front of Cesar with her arms crossed so tight. He might have told himself before that he couldn't care less what she'd done, but right now he did care. And the fact that she hadn't slept with that guy made a tightness ease in him. Even as he wanted to find him and punch him. And that surprised him. Women didn't arouse feelings of protectiveness within him, a desire to avenge them. He shouldn't care.

A second too late Cesar saw that her eye had caught one of the other newspapers that had been delivered. A different headline: *Cesar Da Silva's long-lost family!*

Before he could stop her she'd reached out to pull the paper free. On the cover were recent photographs of all three men: Cesar, Rafaele and Alexio. And another of their beautiful mother. Shining out from all four photos was the undeniable genetic link of their green eyes.

Cesar stood up. Tense.

Lexie said slowly, 'That's where your green eyes come from. She was very beautiful, your mother.'

'Yes, she was,' Cesar said tightly, his skin prickling at having Lexie looking at the blatant evidence of his mother's lack of love for him. It made him feel raw again when he thought of the other night—how Lexie had all but run from the table in the square. When his irrational feeling had been that she'd seen the darkness in his soul and was repulsed by it.

Lexie gazed at him now and all he could see were those blue eyes. Something in him tightened when he saw the compassion in their depths, but it didn't make him want to run.

'Well,' she said a little awkwardly, dropping the paper down, 'I should go. I have an early start again tomorrow.'

When she turned to leave Cesar rejected it with every fibre of his being. 'Wait.'

He reached out and put his hands on her elbows, pulled her into him until their bodies were flush. The palms of her hands landed on his chest and his entire body thrummed with need.

His eyes roved over her face, as if learning every tiny detail.

'*Dios,*' he muttered. 'You are so beautiful.'

Lexie tried to duck her face. 'I'm not.'

'You are...' Cesar's ferocity made her look up. '...stunning. And I want you more than I've ever wanted anyone.'

Lexie felt the excitement in her blood obliterating the scary empathy that had come as soon as she'd seen the picture of Cesar and his half-brothers and mother. She'd *felt* the tension in his body.

Cesar's head dipped and his mouth found hers unerringly. She fell headlong into the flaming pit of the kiss. It burnt her up from the inside out, from the depths of her being.

This was *right*. She felt it in her bones. She trusted this, whether she liked to admit it or not. Her hands gripped his biceps in order to stay standing, and she came up on tiptoe, straining even closer.

Cesar undid her hair and she could feel it fall loose behind her shoulders. He was backing her towards something, and when she felt something solid behind her she realised dimly it must be his desk.

Still their mouths were clinging to one another, their

tongues tangling in a heady dance. Cesar lifted Lexie effortlessly until she was sitting on the desk. Instinctively she hooked a leg around one of his and heard his growl of approval as it brought his body into contact with hers.

The hard press of his arousal against her belly only set off another spasm of lust deep in her body. And between her legs. This was infinitely preferable to trying to rationalise her thoughts and feelings.

His hand was between them, unbuttoning her shirt. Lexie felt hot. Yearned for air, a breeze. His touch. When it fell open he pushed it off one shoulder, taking her bra strap with it, tugging it down her arm.

She wanted only one thing: *more*. When Cesar took his mouth from hers they were both breathing harshly. Somewhere she heard the ring of a phone—a mobile. She tensed.

He said gutturally, 'It doesn't matter.'

Lexie felt dazed, despite the intrusion of the phone. 'I want to see you.'

Standing up straight for a moment, Cesar undid his buttons and opened his shirt. Lexie closed her eyes when the intoxicating scent of man and musk hit her nostrils. Like when she'd first seen him.

When she opened them again they widened. He was magnificent. Broad and hard muscled. Dark blond hair dusted his chest, drawing her eye down to where it bisected the ridges of his abdomen muscles in a line and then disappeared into his pants.

And just like that Lexie became aware of being out of her depth. Overwhelmed. She knew that if they didn't stop now this would end in bed, and as much as she thought she wanted that she wasn't sure if she was really ready. And she realised a small part of her needed to know that he would stop.

She put a hand on his chest and felt him tense. It almost made her forget her intention.

'Wait…' Her voice felt rough, breathy. 'This is moving so fast…'

She looked up at him, wishing she could read what was in those green depths. Decipher that inscrutable expression.

Cesar stepped back and Lexie let her hand drop. It felt as if a chasm had opened between them. With a shaky hand she pulled her shirt and bra strap back up. She couldn't really think straight when Cesar was half clothed in front of her, and cringed as she realised it was only seconds ago that she'd been begging to *see* him.

Humiliation scored her insides. She was damaged. She couldn't just throw caution to the wind and do this. That was the problem.

She slid off the table, her legs unsteady. Between them she throbbed lightly. Mockingly.

Expecting Cesar to be irritated, put out, she caught her breath when she looked up at him and he smiled. Lexie nearly had to put her hands behind her to catch the desk. *Lord.* When he smiled something inside her ached because she hadn't really seen him smile before now.

He moved close again and rubbed his thumb across her bottom lip. His smile faded. 'We want each other.'

Lexie's heart thumped. Hard. 'Yes…' How could she deny it? God. She felt as gauche as a sixteen-year-old contemplating her first make-out session. But then she'd never had that experience.

'Next weekend there's a function in Madrid. You said you wanted to see the city?'

Her head felt fuzzy. Had she?

But Cesar didn't even bother to wait for her agreement, he just said, 'We'll go together. I have an apartment there so we can stay overnight.'

Lexie's heart nearly pounded out of her chest at the

thought but she managed to nod. 'It'll be good for us to be seen together. It'll be good for the press.'

'Yes,' Cesar agreed equably. 'But it's not just about that, Lexie. It's for *us*.'

When Lexie had left Cesar had to wait another few minutes for his body to cool down. He'd been ready to lift her up and carry her into his bedroom. His conscience mocked him—as if he could have held back from taking her right there on his desk.

When she'd pulled back, put her hand on his chest, everything within him had screamed with rejection. And then he'd come to his senses and realised just how close to the edge he was. So he'd welcomed a little space…sanity.

He was a civilised man, even though the last time he could remember feeling remotely civilised was over a week ago—just before he'd laid eyes on Lexie Anderson for the first time.

Cesar went to the window that looked out over a private section of the *castillo* gardens, tucking one arm under the other across his chest.

Something skated over his skin…a very old memory. A feeling. Vulnerability. He didn't like it. It harked back to a time before he'd made sure he was immune to such weaknesses.

He wanted Lexie, but she was dangerous. Because when he was near her he seemed to forget himself. His mouth tightened.

Everything in him had always urged him to trust nothing—and especially not women. After all, his mother and grandmother had taught him that lesson very well.

A memory came back, blindsiding him: his grandmother, dragging him painfully up to a first-floor window. Forcing him to sit down on the window seat. Every day, for hours on end. Before and after his lessons. Because she'd found him there one day. Watching...waiting.

'If you like it here so much then you'll do it every day. Watch, Cesar. *Watch*. See how she does not return for you. And when you tell me that you believe me we can stop playing this game.'

Cesar could remember glaring at his grandmother's thin, bitter face mulishly before she'd taken his ear painfully and pulled his face back to the window. Tears of pain had sprung into his eyes but he'd blinked them back. Loath to show her any emotion. Because even at that tender age of five he'd already known better.

And so he'd looked out of the window—fiercely—for hours on end, willing the figure of his mother to appear. Sometimes he'd thought he'd seen something, but it had only been a mirage. It had taken another full year before he'd finally told his grandmother what she wanted to hear.

His grandmother had made sure that he would see pictures of his mother enjoying her life in Paris. Becoming successful. Famous. A model. Having another son. His half-brother. Forgetting about *him*.

His mother *had* come back, with his younger brother, another year after that. The shattering pain of seeing his brother's hand in hers had been unbearable. He'd hated her—hated them both so much that he'd rejected her right back.

He'd lost his father before he'd even really known him. Then his mother had left him behind like a piece of unwanted luggage. Cesar's grandmother and grandfather had shown nothing but disdain and faint tolerance for their grandson. Their only motivation in making him heir had been their own greed and fanatical obsession with the family name.

The past finally receded from Cesar's head. He castigated himself for letting a woman, no matter how alluring, have this effect on him, for making him think about those things again. He *wanted* Lexie—pure and simple.

He was impervious to anything above and beyond sating himself with her. He would never want anything more with a woman than momentary satisfaction. And Lexie was no different.

CHAPTER SIX

Towards the end of that second week Lexie's nerves were jagged and fraying. It was almost certainly because of the constant presence of Cesar on the set. She felt his gaze on her like a physical touch sometimes.

She wasn't used to this. This excruciating build-up of sexual awareness and frustration. She hated Cesar for having done this to her, having this hold over her, while in the same breath she wished he would just stride across the set and take her in his arms and kiss her to make her head stop spinning.

But it wasn't just the physical sensations. He seemed to have snuck deeper. And she couldn't believe she was in danger of being gullible all over again even though this was infinitely different from what had happened with Jonathan Saunders.

Madrid and the weekend loomed large. The irony was not lost on Lexie—she was playing the part of a jaded sexual libertine and yet she had no idea of the reality of what that should feel like. She felt like a fraud, and gave thanks that no one seemed to have called her on it yet.

But after this weekend, a sly voice pointed out, *you'll know exactly what it feels like.*

When they finally called a wrap that day, and Lexie saw that it was Cesar waiting for her with a golf buggy to get her back to the unit base instead of one of the PAs, she snapped and said caustically, 'Don't you have a world leader to meet or something equally important to do?'

Cesar just looked incredibly sanguine and stepped out of the buggy to help her in, saying *sotto voce*, 'I'm your besotted lover, remember?'

Lexie stifled a snort and pulled the coat she wore to keep warm around her, hiding her voluptuous curves in the elaborate dress.

And then she felt churlish. She glanced at Cesar's patrician profile. He was even more gorgeous dressed down in faded jeans and a long-sleeved top. Workmanlike boots. He looked younger like this, less intimidating. Less a titan of industry.

As much as his presence on the set unnerved her, she'd come to expect it now. Two days ago she'd been waiting for the camera to be set up and had wandered behind one of the equipment trucks to find Cesar deep in conversation with one of the oldest members of the crew. A veteran who had worked on some of the biggest films ever made.

Cesar had been listening intently and asking him about his career. The effect this had had on Lexie was nothing short of pathetic. It had been akin to seeing Cesar cradle a small puppy. Inducing warmth, tenderness. *Danger.*

When they reached the base Cesar helped her from the buggy and opened the door of her trailer for her. Before she could go in, though, he caught her hand.

She looked at him warily.

'I have to go to London tomorrow morning for twenty-four hours. But I'll be back to take you to Madrid on Saturday. We'll leave after lunch.'

He let her hand go to cup the back of her neck, drawing her to him. Even though Lexie had a split second of realisation that he was going to kiss her the touch of his mouth to hers was still like an electric shock, infusing her blood with energy and heat. It was a chaste kiss, and he drew back almost as soon as it had started. But Lexie wanted more.

'Till then.' He let her go, stepped back.

Lexie's heart was beating fast. This was the moment. She could say something now—back out, not go through with it. *Stay safe.*

She opened her mouth. Cesar's green gaze was almost black. And, treacherously, she shut her mouth without saying anything. A recklessness within her was urging her to seize the moment.

Lexie saw other crew members arriving back from the set. Her dresser hurrying to help her out of her costume.

She took a breath. 'Fine, I'll be ready.'

Cesar smiled and it was distinctly predatory. 'I look forward to it. Don't miss me too much, will you?'

Lexie wanted to make a face but he was already turning to go. She really didn't like the impulse she felt to run after him and beg him to take her with him.

On Saturday Lexie was dressed casually, in a stripy long-sleeved top, a long, loose, gypsy-style skirt and soft boots. She had a weekend bag and was waiting for Cesar in the imposing reception hall of the *castillo*, trying not to think about the butterflies fluttering around in her belly at the prospect of seeing him again, or to think too much about what the weekend would bring.

So she thought of the difference between his private apartment and its soaring modern space and the rest of the *castillo*. So different. It made her wonder what it must have been like to grow up here…and why his mother had left him behind.

Something caught Lexie's eye through a doorway and she put down her bags for a moment to walk into a long formal room. It was filled with portraits and she shivered a little as she looked at them. They were all so stern and forbidding—much like the dour *castillo* housekeeper.

She walked around them and came to the most recent ones. Lexie figured they had to be of Cesar's grandparents. They appeared sterner than all the rest put together and she shivered again.

'Cold?'

Lexie jumped and put a hand to her heart, looking around to see Cesar lounging against the door frame, watching her. She took him in. He was wearing dark trousers and an open-necked shirt. He looked smart, yet casual. Gorgeous.

'You startled me.'

He straightened up and came in, hands in his pockets, which made her feel minutely safer. Her skin was hot. And an ache she'd not even been aware of noticing eased. *She'd missed him.* For one day.

Dragging her eyes away from him, she regarded the portraits again. 'Are these your grandparents?'

He stood beside her and a frisson of electricity shot straight to her groin.

He sounded grim. 'Yes, that's them.'

Lexie was curious. 'What were they like?'

He was clipped. 'Cold, cruel, snobbish. Obsessed with the family legacy.'

She looked at him and almost gasped at how hard his face had become. Stark. Pained.

'What did they do to you?'

He smiled, but it was hard. 'What *didn't* they do? My grandmother's particular favourite hobby was getting me to compile scrapbooks of newspaper cuttings featuring my mother and half-brothers, further driving home the message that they wanted nothing to do with me.'

Lexie stared at Cesar, too shocked to say anything for a moment. No wonder there was such tension in him when he mentioned his family. And yet he'd gone to that wedding... He glanced at her and she could see it in his eyes: *Not up for further discussion.* What surprised Lexie was the wave of rage she felt welling inside her at the horrific cruelty he'd endured.

'What happened to your father? Is it true that he was a bullfighter?'

Cesar looked away again and Lexie thought he would ignore her, but then he said, 'He rebelled. He wanted out and wanted nothing to do with his inheritance. So he did what he could to ensure that his family would disown him: he became a bullfighter. It was the worst insult to his parents he could think of. And they duly disinherited him.'

'Your mother...?'

Cesar kept his eyes on the portraits.

'My mother was from a small town down south, where my father went to train as a bullfighter. She was poor. He fell in love and they got married, had me.'

'Did she know who he was? Where he'd come from?'

Now Cesar looked at Lexie, and she almost took a step back at the cynicism etched on his face. He seemed older in that moment.

'Of course she did. That's why she targeted him. If he hadn't died she probably would have persuaded him to return home—especially once they'd had me.'

Lexie tried to hide her dismay at seeing this side of him. He seemed utterly unapproachable at that moment.

'You don't know that for sure, though...' she said, almost hopefully.

'Of course I know,' he dismissed coldly. 'As soon as my father died she brought me here, but my grandparents wanted nothing to do with her. Only me. They realised that their legacy would be secure with an heir. Once she knew there was nothing she could gain, she left.'

Lexie put a hand to her belly in a reflexive action as

the old pain flared inside her hearing his words. To think of the awful wrench it must have been for his mother to give him up. No matter what he said, she couldn't have been that cruel.

'But she came back…? You said that she came back some years later.'

A bleak look flashed across Cesar's face, but it was so fleeting that Lexie wasn't even sure she'd seen it.

'Yes, she did. Maybe she thought she could benefit then. But it was too late.'

'How old were you?'

'Almost seven.'

Lexie gasped. 'But that's so young…you were still so young. Why didn't you go with her?'

Even as she realised that Cesar wasn't going to answer her she had a moment of intuition. He'd been left here when he was so tiny, yet he had been old enough to remember. Remember his mother walking away. Lexie couldn't even begin to imagine what had broken inside him in those years after his mother had left him. Broken so badly that he'd let her walk away from him again.

Cesar stepped back and said, 'We should go. The plane is ready.'

After a short trip in a sleek Land Rover to a local airstrip, Lexie knew she shouldn't have been surprised to see a small private plane waiting for them—reminding her, as if she needed it, just who she was dealing with.

Except the man she was dealing with had just shown her a side of himself that was raw and bleak, and she couldn't stop her chest from aching. Even though she knew that he wouldn't thank her for it. He hadn't had to say a word for her to know that he would scorn the slightest hint of pity.

Cesar parked the car and swung out of the driver's seat

with lithe grace. He'd come around to help Lexie out before she could object, taking her hand in his firm grip.

An assistant took their bags to the plane. The pilot was waiting to greet them, and then they were stepping into the plush, luxurious world of the super-rich. Although Lexie was still a bit too shaken up by what Cesar had revealed to truly enjoy this novel experience.

A steward showed her to her seat solicitously, and Cesar took the seat opposite. There was no waiting for other people to arrive, to sit down. Once they were in they buckled up and the plane was moving.

In a bid to try and shake some of the residual melancholy she felt at hearing about Cesar's less than happy-sounding childhood, Lexie asked, 'So what's the function this evening?'

Cesar stretched out his long legs across the aisle. 'It's a dinner and Spanish music event at the Italian Ambassador's residence.'

Lexie felt her stomach plummet. 'Seriously? But I've never met an ambassador in my life…I won't know what to say—'

He leaned across and took one of her hands out of her lap and held it to his mouth, kissing it. Effectively shutting her up. The air in the cabin seemed to get hot and sultry.

'You don't have to worry about saying anything. They're not going to present you with an IQ questionnaire before dinner to see if you qualify.'

Lexie hated this insecurity that stemmed not only from her dyslexia but from having left school early. 'But they'll be talking about politics and the EU and economics…'

'And,' Cesar replied without hesitation, 'if they do I can't imagine that you wouldn't know just as much if not more than them. These are *people*, Lexie, they're not intellectual giants.'

'Well, you are…' She was being distracted by the hypnotic stroke of Cesar's thumb on the underside of her wrist. His thumb stopped and he frowned at her.

'Where on earth do you get that from?'

Lexie shrugged, feeling exposed again for having researched him in the beginning.

'You're one of the most successful men in the world... you go to economic forums...all those books in your study and apartment...'

Cesar's mouth twisted. 'All those books in my study belong to my family. The only reason I haven't ever got rid of them is in case I need them for reference and for reasons of pure vanity—because they look good.' Then he said, 'Me, though? The books I like reading are popular crime thrillers—nothing more intellectual than that, I assure you.'

Something shifted inside Lexie. An ominous feeling of tenderness welled up.

'And as for school...I was not a natural A student—far from it. I had to work for every one of my grades. Once my grandparents realised this they recruited the local swot— Juan Cortez, who is now the Mayor of Villaporto, the local town—to come and help me.'

The tenderness swelled. 'Are you still friends?'

Cesar smiled. Another rare, proper smile. Lexie had to stop herself from gripping his hand tighter.

'Yes, but only because we nearly killed each other when we were ten.'

Lexie asked impulsively, 'What happened?'

He looked rueful. 'I had issues with someone being smarter than me.' And then he said, 'I'm a hustler, Lexie. I go to these forums and meetings because I have inherited and manage a vast legacy. For a long time I thought I wanted to do what my father had done and turn my back on it, but then I realised that if I did and the fortune got carved up I'd be cutting off my nose to spite my face. I realised that I enjoyed being an entrepreneur—I was good at it. And once my grandparents died I could finally put the family's vast wealth to some good use.'

'How old were you when they died?'

Cesar's easiness vanished. 'Fifteen when my grandfather died and then eighteen when my grandmother died.'

Lexie squeezed his hand but said nothing. She could see the lack of grief for them in his eyes—it was almost defiant. Her own silly heart ached to think of him taking on all that responsibility at such a young age. And as a boy growing up with no love. The thing was, she knew what that felt like—albeit on a different level.

The lack of affection in her own family had come after shattering events and had never been repaired.

The steward appeared then, to offer them some refreshments, and Cesar let her hand go. To Lexie's relief the conversation turned to more neutral topics after that.

It felt like no time at all before they were descending into Madrid, and Lexie looked out of the window eagerly to catch her first glimpse of the capital city.

When they emerged from the plane after landing it was pleasantly warm with a hint of autumnal freshness. A car was waiting for them.

Cesar said in the back of the car, 'We'll go to the apartment and then I'm taking you out on a tour.'

'Okay,' Lexie answered. An incredibly light feeling was bubbling up inside her, and she was determined not to analyse it too carefully.

When Cesar put out his hand for her to come closer she didn't hesitate, sliding along the back seat until she was right beside him. His arm went around her, his fingers splaying provocatively just under Lexie's breast, making her toes curl in her shoes.

His apartment building was on a very grand, wide, tree-lined street. It was an old building, and his apartment was at the top. When he opened the door to let her in Lexie wasn't surprised to see that the same kind of modern design as was in his *castillo* apartment ran through this space too. The old building was the shell, but classic furniture and abstract paintings gave it a very contemporary and slightly eclectic Art Deco aesthetic. It oozed class and luxury. Good taste.

Lexie asked, as he led her down a corridor, 'Did you design this and your other apartment at the *castillo*?'

'Yes. A friend who is an architect helped me. Luc Sanchis. He oversaw the structural work and his team did the interiors.'

'Wow,' Lexie said, awed. Even she'd heard of the famous constructive architect.

Cesar stopped at a door. 'We've also come up with a plan to completely remodel the interior of the *castillo* but it's undergoing a lengthy planning permission process. As you can imagine it's protected because it's so old, and we have to incorporate that integrity with the new design.'

Lexie wrinkled her nose. 'I think it would be great... It's an amazing building, but...'

'Completely stuck in the Middle Ages and not in a good way?'

She smiled. 'If you say so. I couldn't possibly be so rude.'

He reached out and rubbed his thumb along her lower lip. Lexie's blood sizzled. And then, as if he had to make a physical effort to stop touching her, he gritted his jaw and let his hand drop.

He pushed open the door and let her precede him. It was a bedroom, with a massive en-suite bathroom and dressing room. The same Art Deco stamp on the furnishings. She loved it.

'This is your bedroom.'

She turned around, her heart speeding up. He was putting her bags at the bottom of the bed and turning around.

'I'm not even going to say it, Lexie... You know I want you. But this is your space.'

Beyond touched, and reassured in a very deep place that *needed* reassurance, Lexie got out a husky 'Thank you...'

A few hours later Cesar stood at the window in the reception room. He was waiting for Lexie, his hands stuck deep in the pockets of his black trousers. His hands had never itched so much in his life. The previous few hours had been both heaven and hell. Torture.

When he'd asked her how she'd like to see the city and she'd professed an interest in an open-top bus tour that was what they'd done.

He'd never done one of these tours in his life—it was completely alien to anything he'd normally do—but he had noticed them in various cities and always envied the kind of people who went on them.

Lexie had been like a child, her face lighting up to see the beautiful city. And Cesar had ended up inadvertently doing a better job of being tour guide than the actual tour guide. A small crowd had gathered around them on the top of the bus so they could hear his take on the various sites. It had helped that he spoke multiple languages.

Lexie had been laughing when they disembarked, because some of the American tourists had insisted on tipping him—one of the wealthiest men in the world!

In that moment, when Lexie had been laughing, Cesar had felt a dizzying rush of something that was also completely alien to him...it was only now that he could recognise it with a sort of incredulity. *Happiness.*

For a moment he'd felt pure, unadulterated ease. Joy. The blackness that seemed to be his constant companion had dissipated. And it had lasted even as Lexie had asked if they could walk back to the apartment because it wasn't far.

They'd stopped and had coffee and cakes on the way.

Cesar had never, ever spent such an enjoyable couple of hours with anyone.

The threads of that happiness lingered now, like a seductive caress. But Cesar was aware of something very strong inside him that refused to believe it. It was urging him to be vigilant, not to trust in this ephemeral feeling.

Anything that had felt vaguely like this had been ripped away from him at such an early age that now it seemed too...*easy.*

He heard a sound then, and turned around, and when he saw Lexie it was like a punch to his gut—it was that physical.

He couldn't have analysed what she was wearing in any kind of detail. All he knew was that it was black and seemed to cling to every curve she had with a precariousness that made Cesar's body stiffen in wanton reaction. Her shoulders were bare. Her hair was pulled back, revealing her long delicate neck.

She was a goddess.

Cesar walked over to her before he could melt into a pool of unrestrained lust and lock them both in this apartment until she finally gave in to him. He was actually afraid to touch her—afraid that if he did he'd turn into some feral being.

'My car is waiting outside.'

Lexie smiled, but Cesar could see a slight nervousness in her eyes. The thought of dinner? Was she feeling insecure? It made unwelcome protectiveness rise up, but lust was also rising, too high and fast for him to be able to focus on it or let it bother him.

He let her precede him, her scent light and fresh. Floral. Her long dress swung around her hips and legs, and Cesar all but closed his eyes and sent a prayer up to the God he hadn't consulted in a long time for the ability to show some restraint.

* * *

Lexie was finally relaxing. Although she knew it probably had as much to do with the second glass of wine she was on as the fact that the dinner was proving to be far less scary than she'd thought.

But the location was beyond intimidating in its grandeur. It was a very old palace in the centre of Madrid that had been turned into the Ambassador's residence. If everyone hadn't been in modern clothes it would have been hard to ascertain where the past ended and the present began under the soft, seductive lighting of hundreds of candles.

She'd imagined that people would be talking about complicated fiscal policies and the merits of a single currency, but they were actually far more interested in talking to her about the famous people she'd met and what they were really like.

She felt a large hand on her thigh and her lower body spasmed in pure need. She put her hand over his to remove it, but instead her fingers wound their way through his. Holding him there. Her body and her mind were in two different places...

She smiled brightly at the man beside her and took advantage of the lull in the conversation to turn and face Cesar on her other side.

He looked at her. 'Okay?'

She smiled wryly. 'I've been telling the esteemed Secretary to the Greek Ambassador exactly which celebrity tour he should take his kids on when they go to LA next month.'

Cesar smiled and leant forward to kiss her on the mouth. Lexie found herself wanting to cling to him, her fingers tightening on his on her thigh. *She was ready.* Her heart sped up at the thought even as old tendrils of fear made her trepidatious.

He drew back and his eyes were glowing dark green.

'There's a dance showpiece after dinner. We don't have to stay if you don't want to.'

Lexie shook her head, giving in to that fear like a coward, delaying the moment of inevitability. 'No, it's fine. I'd like to see it.'

As the dinner ended and they moved into the room where the showpiece was taking place Lexie seemed to be existing in a haze of shimmering heat. She was acutely aware of Cesar's every move.

Their afternoon on the bus had been delicious torture. Cesar had been dressed down, in jeans and a casual top and jacket. He'd pressed so close against her that she had barely taken in a word he'd said about any of the stunning monuments and squares they'd seen, all too aware of him.

He'd been so gracious and patient when the other tourists had wanted to listen to his explanations and she'd seen another side of him completely. He wasn't as misanthropic as first impressions would have led Lexie to believe—far from it. But she wondered if he even realised that himself.

They had front row seats for the dance performance— by a flamenco dancer. When the lights went down a hush went around the crowd and then a lone guitar started playing the most hauntingly beautiful Spanish music.

Lexie glanced at Cesar to find him staring at her with an intensity that made her insides liquefy. Only with extreme effort could she look away.

A spotlight lit up the small stage and a beautiful dark-haired woman with the lithe body of a dancer walked into the middle. She wore a long red dress, very plain and simple, red shoes, and a red flower in her hair.

She made the most exquisite shapes with her hands and body—typical flamenco postures. Then the hard soles and heels of her shoes started hitting the boards of the stage as the rhythm of the guitar picked up pace. Tiny hairs stood up on the back of Lexie's neck.

It was mesmerising. There was something so elemental and beautiful about this woman and the power in her body. It made a ball of emotion lodge in Lexie's chest and throat. She was acutely aware of the man beside her, of his sheer overwhelming masculinity. Something seemed to be flowing between them through the beat of the music, even though their thighs and arms were barely touching. It was carnal and earthy. Sexual.

The beat and power of the dancer's feet seemed to resonate with Lexie's heartbeat. Cesar had unlocked something powerful within her—something that she was finally connecting with herself after such a long time.

The beat of her own sexuality.

It was something she'd feared lost for ever, stolen from her too long ago ever to claim it back. Lexie wanted to look at Cesar again, but she was afraid that if she did, and he was looking at her, he'd see how raw her desire for him was.

She could see the sheen of exertion on the dancer's skin. The music and the dance were building and building. Lexie fancied she must have a similar sheen to *her* skin…she felt so hot. The expression on the woman's beautiful face was intense as her feet beat out the relentless passionate rhythm. Lexie felt it rise up through her body too.

As the music and the dance reached a crescendo, and as if he could sense how affected she was, Cesar's hand closed around Lexie's, his fingers twining through hers with an unmistakably possessive touch.

Her nipples pricked painfully. She was breathing harshly, every part of her body tingling with desire for the man beside her, as the music exploded and the woman came to a dead stop with her arms high in a proud and beautiful pose, her chest heaving with exertion. People started to clap rapturously. But still Lexie was almost afraid to look at Cesar.

'Lexie?'

She finally turned her head towards him and her world coalesced down to this moment and this man. She wanted him with a fierce drumbeat of need.

Another performer was coming on and she said impulsively, 'Would you mind if we left now?'

Cesar shook his head, a frankly explicit look coming into his eyes as if he could read what was on her mind, feel her desire. 'No—let's go before the next act starts.'

By the time they were walking out Lexie had taken deep breaths and regained some control. But she still trembled all over. Never had anything impacted her in such a deeply physical and visceral way as it had sitting beside this man and wanting him so badly that their very surroundings seemed to echo with it.

They were at the front of the residence now and Cesar's car was pulling up. The driver opened the door for her and Cesar got in on the other side. He reached for her almost immediately and Lexie went willingly.

Their mouths met and their kiss was hungry and desperate. Lexie's blood thundered and roared. She was still borne aloft on the sheer exhilaration of the dance. She drowned in the kiss, in the rough stroke of Cesar's tongue against hers and the feel of his arms around her.

By the time they reached the apartment she was half sitting on his lap, arms around his neck, mouth swollen, breathing fast.

Gently he took her arms down and opened his door before stepping out. He reached in and Lexie had one crazy moment of thinking she could just shut the door, instruct the driver to drive all the way back to the *castillo* and shut out the clamours of her body.

But she didn't. She'd already proved to herself that she was strong enough to withstand the worst things that could happen to a woman. She was certainly strong enough to withstand reclaiming her body and her right to sensual pleasure.

Lexie put her hand in Cesar's and let him pull her out. Keeping a tight grip on her hand, as if he was aware that a rogue part of her still wanted to escape, he greeted the concierge and led her to the lift. Once inside they didn't speak. But the air hummed with awareness and expectation. It was heavy.

When they entered his apartment and the door closed behind them the silence swirled around them. Lexie's heart was beating so hard she thought it had to be audible.

Cesar shrugged off his jacket and threw it over a chair haphazardly. Looking at Lexie, he pulled at his bow tie, undoing it. She was clutching her bag tightly, her eyes glued to his mouth, wanting it on hers again.

He reached down and took her bag, threw it aside to join his jacket. Then he put his hands on her arms.

'You're sure?'

After a moment Lexie nodded and said, 'I've never been more sure of anything in my life. Make love to me, Cesar.'

CHAPTER SEVEN

FOR A MOMENT Cesar did nothing, and a wave of cold clammy horror gripped Lexie as she imagined being rejected. But then he dipped, and she let out a little squeal when he lifted her into his arms against his chest.

He strode down the corridor, past her bedroom to another door on the opposite side. Lexie took in no details of the room he walked into beyond the fact that it was dark, palatial and had a massive bed.

He walked right over to it and let Lexie down, before reaching for a light and switching it on to put out a pool of golden light.

Light, Lexie thought. *Light is good.* The enormity of what she was doing was sinking in.

Reverently Cesar put his hands on Lexie's shoulders. She tried to calm her thundering pulse. Then he turned her around and it went haywire again.

He pulled the pins from her hair until it fell down. Then he brushed it aside over one shoulder. Lexie shivered when she felt him come close behind her, wrapping an arm around her midriff and pressing a kiss to her bare shoulder.

His fingers were on her zip at the back of her dress. Slowly, so slowly, he started to pull it down. The dress loosened around her chest and she curled her hands into fists to stop herself from impeding its progress as it fell forward and down.

Now she was bare from the waist up except for a strapless lace bra.

Cesar's hand had drawn the zip all the way to the top of her buttocks, where it ended. Then with both hands he pushed it over her hips so that it fell to the floor. She was aware of a rough indrawn breath, and then his hand was cupping her bottom in her silk French knickers, smoothing over her hip.

Her legs were losing their ability to hold her upright.

When he put his hands on her shoulders again, to turn her around, Lexie looked down. She felt hot, excited and scared. All at once. Cesar's hands were on her waist, pulling her into him.

'Lexie…look at me.'

She bit her lip, but looked up. His face was flushed, eyes glittering like dark jewels. His gaze dropped to her mouth, and then lower. Her skin went on fire.

He lifted a hand and cupped one breast. Her nipples were hard and stinging. Pushing against the lace of her bra. He brushed his thumb across one nipple, making Lexie gasp. Making her want more. *His mouth.*

Cesar sank back onto the bed and pulled her into him. Lexie nearly stumbled in her shoes and she kicked them off jerkily, steadying herself on his shoulders.

His hands closed around her waist again, and with her breasts at easy reaching distance for his mouth he explored her through the lace, his tongue laving the lace-covered tips, first one and then the other.

Lexie's hands were like claws gripping his shoulders. It was torture. The stinging chafing of the lace against those throbbing moist peaks. She almost sobbed with relief when he reached around to undo her bra and then cupped one breast before he encircled that aching naked tip with his wicked, hot mouth. It was exquisite.

Her hands moved to Cesar's head, fingers threading through silky strands of hair. When he tried to draw back she had to release him. She looked down, dazed, drunk. Instinctively she reached for his shirt, undoing his buttons, her breasts swaying with her movement.

He took over, emitting a soft growl of impatience when a button got caught, ripping it apart and off. Then his chest was bare. And gorgeous. Lexie had to sink down onto one thigh, unable to stand any more.

Cesar caught her to him with a strong arm, his other hand finding her chin and angling it so that he could plunder her mouth in a scorching hot kiss. He let that hand trail down to cup and massage her breast again, fingers pinching her stiff nipple.

Lexie squirmed. Between her legs she was stinging. Moist. Sensing her need even before she acknowledged it, Cesar moved his hand down over her waist. He pushed her legs open, his mouth still on hers, distracting her, until she felt those fingers exploring the delicate skin of her inner thigh. She held her breath as they trailed over her sex, hidden under the silk of her panties.

Lexie broke the kiss. Cesar's eyes were half lidded, hot with need. She was clinging to him and his hand was *there*, right where she felt swollen and needy. He was pressing against her flesh, moving rhythmically.

In a fast-moving world that had been reduced to all things physical Lexie tried to cling onto reality and the feeling that she could trust Cesar.

She put her hand on his wrist, stopping his movements, and said threadily, 'I don't want you to hurt me.'

He could never know the wealth of history behind that plea.

He frowned and removed his hand, bringing it up to touch her jaw again.

'I would never hurt you. We'll take this slow, okay?'

Lexie nodded. Relief flooded her. In a smooth move, Cesar lifted her from his lap and onto the bed. She sank back and looked up, watching him undo his trousers and push them down.

Her eyes widened on the bulge in his boxers, and they widened even more when he'd dispensed with the rest of his clothes and put his hands to the edges of those boxers. He pushed them down and his erection was freed.

Lexie waited for rejection, revulsion, fear…but it didn't come. She only felt intense excitement. And need. Euphoria bubbled up inside her. Lightness. When Cesar bent down and put his hands to her panties she lifted her hips to let him pull them down.

His body was awe-inspiring. He was a very masculine man in his prime. Broad through the chest and shoulders, slimming to lean hips, and down to powerful buttocks and thighs.

He came down on the bed beside her, on one arm, and looked at her. His gaze left scorching hot trails where it rested on her curves. 'You're more beautiful than anything I've ever seen.' He ran his hand up and down her body, barely skimming, teasing her.

Lexie touched his jaw reverently, feeling the tough line under her fingers, following the line of his cheek down to his mouth, tracing that sensual shape.

Her belly contracted when he caught her hand and sucked one finger deep. Then he took her finger out of his mouth and, not taking his eyes off her, trailed his hand down over her breasts to the curls protecting her sex.

Gently, he encouraged her to open her legs. Lexie held her breath. Keeping the heel of his hand against her, he explored her with his finger, seeking the seam of her body and parting it, releasing her desire to smooth his passage.

She was breathing again, but it was laboured as Cesar moved his fingers over her and pressed his palm against her. Without her even knowing it Lexie's body was moving, hips twitching, circling, seeking more.

He bent his head and took her mouth, and she almost sobbed into it when she felt him thrust one finger inside her. Her hands had to hold onto something and she found his arms, fingers digging into hard muscles. Cesar shifted and she could feel his erection against her hip.

She was too shy to reach out and touch it, but she wanted to. Wanted to explore what all that power would feel like encased in silken skin.

But right now his finger was moving in and out of her body and causing sensations such as Lexie had never experienced before. There was a delicious tightening feeling, building and building. An urgency. A desire for more.

When one finger became two, and Cesar's tongue thrust deep into her mouth, her hands tightened on him.

He broke away. '*Dios*…you're so responsive…I don't know how slow I can go…you're killing me.'

Lexie blinked. Cesar looked like a dark golden lion in the dim light. She whispered throatily, 'Don't go slow.'

He gazed at her, his breath coming sharp and fast. He was on the edges of his control…she could sense it. Right then Lexie felt invincible. Strong. In control.

Cesar disappeared for a moment and Lexie heard a drawer open and shut, then the sound of foil ripping. He came back and she saw him smoothing protection onto his erection.

A spurt of jealousy that he was touching himself so intimately caught her unawares, making her want to giggle with the sheer joy of discovering her own body again. Of being here and feeling *safe*.

Cesar came over her, careful not to crush her, but the weight of his naked body over hers was something Lexie craved. She reached for his body, clasping him, urging him down.

He cursed. 'I don't want to hurt you.'

'You won't,' she said, and meant it, feeling emotional.

Lexie felt him push her legs apart further with his hips, stretching her. Poised above her, he nearly undid her when he pushed some hair back off her hot cheek and pressed a kiss to her mouth. As if somehow...he *knew*.

And then she felt him—hard, forceful, pushing into her, seeking her acceptance. Her body resisted and Lexie sucked in a breath. She willed herself not to let the darkness of her past reach out to poison this moment. She willed her body to relax, to *trust*.

After several heart-stopping moments, punctuated only by their harsh breathing, she felt a shift and Cesar's body slid in a little more. Filling her.

'You're so small...so tight.'

She moved her hips experimentally and earned herself a long, low growl from Cesar that sounded feral.

She could see the cost of his restraint showing on his face, in his tense shoulders. He reached down a hand and moved it under her thigh, encouraging her to lift her leg around his waist.

The movement brought him deeper into her body, and now Lexie groaned as excitement built, a restless, surging yearning for a deeper connection between their bodies.

She lifted her other leg and Cesar pulled out before sliding back in, his body huge and powerful. He angled his body so that he was thrusting as deep as possible. He put a hand between them and found the cluster of cells at the juncture of her thighs. Lexie gasped out loud as that building excitement shot right through her core.

Her whole body was alive with a deep mystical energy, coiling and binding her to this man with an invisible weave. Cesar's chest touched hers, hair a delicious friction against her breasts. Lexie arched her back to ask mindlessly for *more*.

Cesar's movements were becoming more urgent, stronger. Faster. Her heels were digging into his muscular buttocks, driving his body deeper into hers, holding him to her.

She could feel wave after wave of ecstasy washing through her until they gathered such force that she begged Cesar to release her from the torture and let her fly. But she wasn't coherent.

He bent his head and kissed her. 'It's okay, *querida*, I'll catch you.'

Those words unlocked the tension and Lexie soared on a blissful plateau of pleasure so intense that it was almost painful. And as she fell, feeling the powerful contractions of her body around Cesar's, she bit his shoulder to stop herself from screaming out loud. His own body tensed powerfully before he let out a guttural shout, and he fell just behind her.

Cesar's brain was in meltdown. Even now he could still feel the ripples of Lexie's orgasm keeping his body hard, not letting him come down completely from the most intense climax he'd ever experienced.

It was the most difficult thing in the world to break the connection between their bodies, but Cesar gritted his jaw and moved, releasing them both. Lexie winced minutely. Her eyes were wide, cheeks flushed, hair in disarray around her head.

He moved so that he didn't crush her and came onto his side, pulling her into him so that they were face to face. Normally when Cesar made love to a woman he felt the overwhelming need to get away. Right now it was the last thing on his mind. She fitted him. One leg was still looped over his thigh. The centre of her body was still flush with his, doing little to help his arousal subside.

He could only look at her. The expression on her face was as stunned as he felt. A lock of hair was across one hot cheek, damp with her sweat. He raised a hand, noted vaguely that it was trembling, and tucked her hair behind her ear.

As his normal faculties returned Cesar was aware of feeling more and more vulnerable. But still he couldn't seem to move, to be able to unweld his arms from around her.

Then he saw a brightness in her gaze in the dim light. Her mouth wobbling even as she bit into her lower lip to disguise it. Cesar's belly dropped as if from a great height as something very cold lanced him. He'd just assumed... been so focused on how intense it had been for him... Even though he'd believed it had been the same for her, but she was so small...

He could feel tremors in Lexie's body now—as if she was experiencing a delayed reaction. Cesar moved and came up on one arm, cold terror trickling through him. 'Did I hurt you?'

Rapidly she shook her head and Cesar saw her eyes fill in earnest now, felt the tremors in her body getting stronger. Her cheeks paled. Was she going into some kind of shock?

Her body, which had felt so warm and languorous seconds before, now felt cold. Galvanised by increasing panic, Cesar gathered Lexie into his arms and stood up from the bed, taking her with him. She curled up against his chest, making something like bile fill him at the thought that he'd hurt her. She said nothing.

He walked into the bathroom and straight into the shower, where he turned on the powerful spray of hot water and stood them both under it. He felt Lexie gasp, her body curl even tighter into him, and he also felt those tremors increase as she started crying in earnest.

Her face was buried in his chest and her slim back was heaving with the force of her sobs as her hands pressed against him.

Cesar felt as if his chest was being ripped apart by bare hands. 'Lexie...*Dios*...please tell me...did I hurt you?'

She shook her head against him. The slimmest sliver of relief went through him. Cesar rested his back against the wall and wasn't even sure how long he stayed like that, under the powerful spray, while Lexie sobbed in his arms. He could still feel the power of the emotion running through her slim body.

Eventually the storm passed and she became still. They were surrounded in hot steam. She started to move, and then he heard a husky, rough-sounding, 'You can put me down. I'm okay.'

Reluctantly, even though his arms were stiff, Cesar let her down until she stood. She wouldn't look at him and he had to tip her chin up. When he saw those huge bruised eyes and her swollen mouth he had to curb his almost instantaneous reaction. *Again.* Already...

'Lexie...what...?'

She shook her head, came close, put her hands on his chest. 'You didn't hurt me...' Her voice sounded raw. 'The opposite. I promise.'

Cesar frowned as water ran in rivulets down their bodies, plastering their hair to their skulls. 'But...why?'

Lexie ducked her head, resting her forehead against him for a moment and making something incredibly alien flood through Cesar. Then she looked up again, 'I just... It's never been like that. That's all.'

Cesar had the distinct feeling that that *wasn't* all, but

something held him back from forcing her to explain. He hadn't hurt her. The relief was almost overwhelming.

'Come on,' he said gruffly. 'Let's get out.'

He turned off the water and stepped out, reaching back for Lexie. She emerged from the steam, taking his hand, and he couldn't stop his gaze from devouring those naked curves greedily. She was looking at him too, and Cesar had to stop himself from pressing her up against the shower wall and taking her there and then.

Instead he wrapped a towel around her and her hair. She stood as mute as a child and let him dry her off, and after he'd dried himself roughly he took her back into the bedroom.

He dropped his towel and gently took hers off and led her back to the bed. Her hair was damp but she didn't look inclined to dry it. He could see her eyes heavy with the need to sleep. Heavy after the outpouring of emotion that had left tentacles of panic inside him at the thought that he'd hurt her.

She crawled into the bed and lay down, and Cesar looked at her before getting in beside her. This was anathema to him—sharing a bed after lovemaking. But it was something he wasn't in a position to question right now.

Lexie burrowed straight into his arms, wrapping her legs around him, resting her head on his chest. Those soft abundant curves melted into him. His heart thudding unevenly, it was only when he could feel her body relax into sleep and her hold on him loosen that he was able to relax himself.

When Lexie woke up she opened her eyes and blinked at the dawn light coming in through long grand windows. She felt completely disorientated. Her body felt...different. Heavy. Lethargic. *Sated*. Hers...

She became aware of something moving steadily under

her cheek. *Cesar's chest.* She lifted her head and looked up to see him asleep. Dark stubble lined his jaw. And then her eye caught something else and she let out a small gasp of dismay.

A neat row of small teeth marks scored the flesh of his shoulder. And suddenly Lexie was back in that moment of such extreme pleasure that she'd had to bite him to keep from screaming.

She ducked her head again quickly, face burning. It all came back…every scorching moment. Taking him into her body had been far more momentous and emotional than she would ever have imagined it might be.

She'd cried like a baby.

Lexie cringed to think of how she'd curled up into his chest and sobbed. How he'd asked if he'd hurt her. Far from it. She felt almost guilty—as if she'd misled him by not telling him about herself. As if she'd taken something she only had half a right to. This man would never know the precious gift he'd unwittingly given her.

A sense of liberation from the dark past rushed up in a giddying sweep of emotion so physically acute that Lexie had to move or risk waking him. And she wasn't ready for that assessing gaze to land on her just yet.

Moving stealthily, she managed to extricate herself and climb out of the bed without disturbing Cesar, who lay in a louche, sexy sprawl. She couldn't help stopping for a moment and looking at him covetously. He was so beautiful…his skin a deep olive, his chest broad and powerful, and lower… Her face burned even hotter at the thought of how he'd felt moving inside her. So gentle but so powerful.

Emotion tightened like a fist around her heart. On first acquaintance with this man, she never could have imagined he'd have so many hidden depths, or have the capacity to be so…*considerate.*

Lexie immediately dismissed the direction of her

thoughts when a kind of panic seized her guts. She had to lock off her emotions. This was purely physical. She'd gone into this with eyes wide open. It was an affair. And when the time came she would walk away with her head held high.

Lexie grabbed up her things and crept out of the room. Once she was in her own room she had a shower, before donning faded comfy jeans and a V-necked cashmere top. She pulled her hair back into a ponytail and went to find the kitchen.

Lexie had found a radio station playing classical Spanish music and was blissfully unaware of the tall man resting his shoulder against the door, arms crossed, as she made breakfast.

It was only when she turned around to find some salt and pepper that she saw him and nearly jumped out of her skin.

He straightened. 'Sorry, I didn't mean to startle you.'

Lexie flushed, still not ready to see him. Already a hum was starting in her blood. 'You didn't…' She flushed some more. 'I mean, you did—but it's okay.'

He was bare-chested and wearing jeans with the top button open. Lexie nearly melted. Her body was unaccustomed to this overload of sensations and desires.

He came into the kitchen, right up to her, and growled softly, 'I woke up alone.'

'I just…I woke up and you were asleep,' Lexie stammered. 'I didn't want to disturb you.'

A look she couldn't identify came into his eyes and he said, 'You didn't.'

He bent then, and pressed his mouth to hers. In an instant she was on fire, her mouth opening under his, seeking more. When he pulled back she was breathing fast.

She was out of her depth. This whole morning-after thing was totally alien to her.

In a bid to try and disguise her discomfiture Lexie turned back to where she was frying some eggs and bacon, glancing over her shoulder. 'I hope you don't mind... I found some food in the fridge. Are you hungry?'

She was babbling now.

Cesar just leant back against the island in the kitchen and said huskily, 'I'm starving.'

But the look he sent up and down Lexie's body told her he didn't mean for food. She bit her lip and tried to ignore her body's reaction. Was this even normal?

Somehow she managed to make something resembling breakfast and coffee, and to serve it up without it ending up all over the floor.

The state-of-the-art kitchen in Cesar's apartment led into a large open-plan dining/living space. She sat down at the table there and noticed that there were Sunday papers, and—thankfully—that Cesar had put a top on.

He saw her glance at the papers and explained, 'The concierge drops them in if I'm here.'

Lexie spotted something that piqued her interest and pulled one of the more tabloid-looking papers out of the pile—only to realise that the press had managed to catch her and Cesar on their open-top bus tour.

There were also pictures of them walking hand in hand back to the apartment.

Something about that sent acute disappointment to her gut. It had been a spontaneous moment. This tainted the memory. She said faintly, 'I never imagined they could have known that we'd be doing that.'

Cesar took a sip of coffee and said, almost absent-mindedly, 'I called my assistant—told her to tip them off anonymously.'

Something cold slithered into Lexie's gut. She put down

her fork and looked at Cesar and brought up a dim recollection of him on his phone briefly at one stage on the bus.

'But....' Lexie was about to ask him *why* when she stopped herself. Of *course* he'd wanted to tip them off. They were meant to be courting the press—for both their benefits. Why waste an opportunity to document it?

'But...?' he asked.

She hated to think it, even to acknowledge it, but she felt betrayed. And she shouldn't be feeling that. Because if she did then it meant that Cesar had attained a significance for her that she had no control over.

She forced a smile and shook her head. 'But nothing. Of course you should have tipped them off. It was a good opportunity to let them see us.'

Cesar watched Lexie continuing to eat her breakfast and something twisted inside him. She looked so young, so innocent.

When he'd woken up alone in the bed his immediate reaction had been irritation that she'd left. He'd been about to go and find her when he'd remembered her tears, that incredible outpouring of emotion, and like a coward he'd stopped. Not sure if he was ready to face that searing blue gaze in the morning light.

The look in her eyes just now, though, made him feel like a heel. His own conscience mocked him. Making that call to his assistant yesterday had come out of a gut reaction to how Lexie's lit-up face and smile had made him feel. A gut reaction to doing something so out of his comfort zone. Cesar didn't *do* quirky, fun sightseeing tours with lovers. He didn't engage with the public. But he had— and moreover he'd found himself enjoying it.

He was dark and brooding, and most people ran a mile when they saw him. But not when he was with Lexie.

And that, frankly, had terrified him. So he'd called Mercedes and once he'd instructed her to alert the press he'd felt that he *hadn't* lost his mind completely.

Now, absurdly, he felt guilty.

Lexie was taking a sip of coffee, wiping her mouth, avoiding his eyes. Cesar reached out and took her hand. He saw her tense and that guilt intensified. *Damn her.*

Warily she looked at him.

Carefully Cesar said, 'Our becoming lovers was inevitable. Diverting the media is a beneficial consequence for both of us.'

Lexie blinked. Cesar saw how her expression became inscrutable, hidden.

'Of course. I know that. Don't worry, Cesar, I'm not some soft-hearted teenager who is weaving fantasies around a happy-ever-after scenario. I know that doesn't exist. Believe me.'

Something about the harshness of her tone caught at Cesar's chest, making it ache even as everything within him urged him to agree with her, to feel relieved.

She stood up to take their plates and Cesar caught her wrist, said gruffly, 'Leave it. My housekeeper will attend to it later, when we're gone.'

He tugged her towards him until she put down the plates and fell, resisting, into his lap.

She huffed out, 'What are you doing?'

The feel of her soft, lithe body against his made a lie of every one of Cesar's last words. All he could think about was how much he wanted this woman. But Lexie was stiff in his arms and that made him feel slightly desperate.

His hand was on her waist and he could feel a sliver of silky skin under her top. He explored underneath, over the indent of her naked waist and higher. Already he could feel the effect, the softening and relaxing of her body into his.

'Lexie...'

Slowly she turned her head to his, and for a moment

there was something unguarded in the depths of her eyes. Something very raw and pained. But it didn't make Cesar want to run.

His exploring hand came into contact with the bare swell of her breast. *No bra.* And just like that lust surged between them, red-hot and powerful. Their mouths connected, their kiss deepened, Lexie groaned softly and Cesar cupped the full weight of that breast in his hand.

Weakly he drowned out the clamouring voices in his head that told him he was deluding himself if he believed that he was half as in control of this as he would have Lexie believe.

CHAPTER EIGHT

'*LET'S GO AGAIN,* folks.'

Lexie clenched her jaw. This was the thirteenth take, and if she fluffed her lines one more time more than one crew member would want to wring her neck. Including herself. The director called *action* and by some miracle Lexie managed to get through the dialogue with no mishaps.

There was an audible sigh of relief around the set. Everyone was tired. It was the end of the third week and fatigue was setting in. The prospect of another week here and then two weeks in London stretched like a never-ending horizon line.

As they called that scene complete and started to set up for the next one Lexie was whisked back to the unit base for a costume-change. She relished the time to try and gather her scattered and fragmented thoughts.

Since the previous cataclysmic weekend, and their return to the *castillo* from Madrid on Sunday, Lexie had been avoiding Cesar at every opportunity. It didn't help that he was almost constantly on set—hence her fluffed lines and general state of being flustered. But today he hadn't shown up, and that had nearly been worse.

Lexie was terrified that she'd gone and fallen for the first man who had come along and kissed her whole body awake—much like Sleeping Beauty in the fairy tale.

That was why she'd been avoiding Cesar all week. She

felt as if she wasn't in control of these new and overwhelming desires. It was like having a car and not really knowing how to drive it—being afraid that if she got behind the wheel it would careen off the road and cause mayhem and destruction.

She felt feverish, excited. Exactly like the soft-hearted teenager she'd mocked only days ago.

That weekend he'd only had to pull her onto his lap and kiss her before she'd been reduced to a puddle of lust, letting him take her back to bed and make love to her again and again. Showing her the heights her body could attain with just the barest sweep of his clever fingers against her body's core.

He had no idea who he was dealing with. The dark secrets Lexie harboured. But every time Cesar touched her she felt more and more exposed—as if sooner or later she wouldn't be able to stop it all tumbling out. Baring her soul to him.

So she'd been avoiding him. Like a coward. Even though all she could think about and dream about and yearn for was him.

It was affecting her work. And it didn't help that one scene in particular was due to be shot at the beginning of the following week and Lexie was dreading it, but unable to say anything to anyone about it.

After her dresser had left Lexie waited for the call to go back to set, pacing up and down her trailer, repeating her lines, trying to force all other thoughts out of her head.

When a knock came on her trailer door she said distractedly, 'I'll be out in a minute,' assuming that it was the call for set. But then the door opened and Lexie whirled around, copious amounts of silken layers rustling as she did so, only to see Cesar coming up the steps and entering.

Immediately the relatively big space was tiny. He closed the door behind him. He looked dark, gorgeous. Intent.

Lexie was breathless, and it only had a little to do with her costume. 'You shouldn't be here—they'll be calling for me in a minute.'

Cesar crossed his arms. '*Here* seems to be the only place I can find you without you avoiding me or hiding in your room.'

Lexie flushed, her whole body tingling just to be near him. She couldn't deny the sheer excitement that gripped her, the anticipation at the look in Cesar's eye. Especially when his gaze dropped to the swells of her breasts, made even more provocative than usual in the dress.

Lord, she wanted him right now. *Here*. Like some lurid parody of the stories she'd heard of actors and actresses behaving badly while shooting on location.

Cesar came towards her and Lexie had nowhere to escape to. He wrapped an arm around her waist and pulled her into him. Her body sang and, bizarrely, something inside her calmed. She felt more centred.

'Why have you been avoiding me all week?' he growled.

'Work…I need to concentrate on my work,' Lexie blurted out weakly.

His eyes flashed. 'Well, you're singularly to blame for *me* not being able to concentrate on a single thing.'

'Really?' Inordinate pleasure snaked through Lexie to hear that. To imagine this stern, unflappable man being distracted because of her. She felt like smiling.

'I don't play games, Lexie.'

She blanched. 'You think…you think I'm playing some *game*?'

His jaw was set, stern. Her belly swooped.

'Cesar…I'm not playing a game… I was avoiding you because last weekend… It's just been a long time for me.' *Try for ever,* said a small voice, but she blocked it out. 'I'm not used to this—I don't have *affairs*.'

Flustered, she ducked her head. Cesar put a finger to her chin to tip her face back up.

His gaze dropped to her cleavage and his voice was rough. '*Dios*…do you know what it does to me to see you in these dresses?' His eyes met hers again and his arm tightened around her. 'Come to my apartment this evening.'

Resistance was futile. Lexie felt herself dissolving, aching to say *yes*, let him take control so she didn't have to think or analyse. Just *be*.

'Okay.' She smiled, unable to keep it in.

Cesar was about to kiss her when a knock came on the door and a PA called out, 'Lexie, they're ready for you.'

Cesar stopped and Lexie almost groaned. 'Okay, thanks,' she called back.

Then he smiled, and it was wicked. 'I'll cook dinner. Come by when you've wrapped. Bring a weekend bag.'

Lexie almost rolled her eyes, 'My room is in the *castillo*. If I need anything surely I can just—?'

Cesar cut her off. 'Just…do it.'

'Okay,' Lexie said again, her smile turning wry at his autocratic tone.

She let Cesar lead her out to where her driver was waiting in the car to take her back to the set.

The following day Lexie grumbled good-naturedly, '*Why* can't you tell me where we're going?'

Cesar stopped abruptly and Lexie almost careened into him. He caught her hands and held them. The breeze had mussed up his hair. He looked vital, and so gorgeous that she sighed with pure appreciation. He looked darker too, all dressed in black.

He was mock stern. 'Just do as you're told.'

Lexie saw a staff member carrying their bags to a waiting helicopter. It was sitting on a landing pad at the back of the *castillo*.

Cesar had woken her early that morning and she'd stretched like a satisfied cat amongst his very tousled sheets before she'd even really realised the enormity of where she was.

In Cesar's bed, in his private apartment. After a night of lovemaking that had almost brought her to tears again. She'd only held them back with gritted teeth, determined not to let him see her get so emotional again.

But she couldn't help it. With every touch, every kiss, this man was rebuilding the very fabric of her soul. A fabric that had been torn apart brutally years before.

As instructed, she'd packed some things the previous evening and had gone to his apartment after work to find him waiting for her, busy in his kitchen making dinner. The sight had been so incongruous and so...*sexy* that Lexie had struggled to affect a nonchalance she hadn't felt.

Before she could say anything else Cesar took her by the hand and led her to the helicopter, bundling her inside. Lexie gave up trying to figure out where they were going and did as she was told, putting on earphones and buckling up.

Cesar leant over from his seat to help her just as the rotor blades started up outside, and adrenalin and excitement kicked in her belly.

He grinned at her. 'Don't worry—you'll like it, I promise.' And then he pressed a swift kiss to her mouth and sat back.

Lexie scowled at him, hating that his grin made her heart clench and that he could so easily affect her. But then her mind emptied as the chopper rose smoothly into the air and she saw the *castillo* drop away underneath them.

Cesar had obviously asked the pilot to take a tour of the estate, and he pointed out vineyards and more land than she had ever realised belonged to him. It was truly mind-boggling. And sobering to realise the extent of his responsibilities.

Then they were banking and heading away from where the sun had risen only a short while before. Lexie was transfixed by the changing landscape underneath them as they passed over low mountains and rivers.

Eventually she could see that the sparse countryside was making way for more built-up areas. Cesar took her hand and pointed out of the main window of the helicopter. She could make out a smudge of blue...*the sea*?

She glanced at him and he smiled. One of those rare smiles that made her want to smile back like a loon. She could see that they were flying over what had to be a city. The rooftops were terra-cotta, glinting in the sun. She saw a very majestic-looking castle on a hill.

They seemed, impossibly, to be heading right for the city centre. Lexie could see a bridge spanning a huge river, and the way the city was spread out on hills. It didn't look especially modern. There were trams and beautiful old crumbling buildings covered in coloured tiles.

She gasped and turned to Cesar and shouted over the noise, 'Lisbon?'

He nodded. So that's why he'd told her to pack her passport. A rush of incredible emotion and gratitude filled Lexie. She remembered standing in his study that day and exclaiming with a feeling of panic that she wanted to visit Madrid, Salamanca and Lisbon.

So far he'd taken her to all of them.

The helicopter set down on the rooftop of a building and Cesar helped her out. Lexie realised it was a hotel when the staff greeted them and led them inside where solicitous customs officials were waiting for them to check their passports. Cesar took her hand once they were done and she sent him a quick, dry look. 'No queues for you?'

Cesar smiled. 'My name, Da Silva, isn't strictly Spanish in origin. It comes from a very distant Portuguese ancestor. So I'm allowed…certain liberties…'

Lexie all but rolled her eyes as one of the staff got Cesar's attention. She'd just bet he was allowed untold liberties for the promise of his favour and business opportunities. The fact that he was obviously a regular visitor to Lisbon told her that he didn't take advantage of their respect and that made her feel soft inside.

They went one floor down and were shown into the most sumptuous suite of rooms Lexie had ever seen.

She explored on her own and found a terrace outside the bedroom's French doors. She went out. The view was astounding. She could see the huge imposing castle up on a nearby hill, lots of steep streets with distinctive yellow trams. And then what had to be the River Tagus, spanned by a massive bridge.

She felt a presence behind her and then arms came around her, hands resting by hers on the rail. Lexie shut her eyes for a second at the way her body wanted to melt, and when Cesar pressed close behind her she *did* melt into him, blocking out the voices screaming *Danger! Danger!*

One of his hands disappeared and she felt her hair being tugged back gently, so her neck was bared. Breath feathered there and then she felt his mouth, warm and firm. Lexie's hands tightened on the rail and the view became blurry.

She turned around to face him and looked up. His eyes were heavy-lidded, full of something dark and hot. A pulse throbbed between Lexie's legs.

'I have a whole agenda laid out for you today, Miss Anderson.'

Lexie arched a brow and tried to be cool. 'Oh, you do?'

Cesar nodded, and took some of her bright hair between two fingers. He tugged gently again and his eyes rose to hers.

'And right now I have something very specific in mind.'

Lexie was already breathless. 'You do...?'

'Yes.'

And then, with devastating precision, Cesar's mouth closed over hers and Lexie didn't care where she was in the world as long as she was right in this moment.

'A nightcap?'

Lexie looked at Cesar and nodded. 'That'd be nice, thanks.'

She watched as he turned and went to the drinks cabinet, her eyes devouring his tall, lean form sheathed in a dark trousers and a light shirt. He'd already shrugged off his jacket.

Lexie was reeling after the day. Not wanting Cesar to see how overwhelmed she was, she made her way out to the terrace that was accessible through the living room too. She heard the faint sound of a mobile and Cesar's deep tones as he answered.

A quiver of relief went through her—a moment alone, to try and assimilate everything. She sucked in the evening air, hoping it might cool her hot cheeks. They'd felt permanently hot since Cesar had made love to her that morning.

Afterwards, when she'd been sated and replete, he hadn't let her burrow back under the covers as she'd wanted to. He'd all but washed and dressed her, picking out a pretty shirt and jeans, sneakers.

They'd left the hotel and a car had taken them up to the impressive St George's castle, with its breathtaking views of the city. Peacocks had strutted on the paths, fanning their colourful tails much to the delight of the tourists.

Then, as if reading Lexie's mind, he'd taken her on one of the old yellow trams down a steep hill. It had been so packed that Cesar had pulled her into his body in front of him, arms wrapped tight around her. By the time he'd pulled her out at another stop she had been thoroughly turned on.

She'd found herself being led though a dizzying labyrinth of ancient streets. Cesar had explained that it was the Alfama—the old Arabic quarter.

Beautiful murals decorated walls at the ends of alleyways, little children darted dark heads out of tiny windows and called, *'Bom dia!'* Washing hung on lines between houses.

They'd had lunch there, on a tiny terrace overlooking the river. Afterwards they'd wandered some more, Lexie's hand tightly in Cesar's. At one point she had tugged gently, and when he'd looked at her she'd asked, 'No paparazzi?'

Something had flashed across his face but he'd smiled and said, 'No. Not here.'

Something very dangerous had infused Lexie's blood to think that here they were truly anonymous. That Cesar hadn't automatically thought of the bigger agenda.

Dangerous.

The car had reappeared then, as if by magic, and had taken them to see the stunning sixteenth-century monastery where Vasco Da Gama was buried in Belem. Afterwards Cesar had pointed to a blue-canopied shop nearby, where a queue literally about a mile long waited patiently.

They'd joined the back of it. Lexie had looked at Cesar, but he'd said enigmatically, 'Wait and see. Then you'll understand why all these people are here.'

Eventually, when they'd reached the shop itself, Cesar had spoken in flawless Portuguese. He'd handed Lexie what looked like a small custard tart.

'Taste it,' Cesar had urged as they'd found stools in the heaving shop with its beautiful ornate interior.

Lexie had obediently bitten into the flaky pastry and the smooth warm custard had melted on her tongue. She'd groaned her appreciation, much as everyone else had.

When she'd been able to speak again she'd said, 'That was probably one of the best tarts I've ever tasted in my life.'

A smug Cesar had just said, 'See?'

And then they'd queued again for more.

After they'd taken a circuitous sightseeing route back to the hotel, instead of leading her up to the suite Cesar had taken Lexie down to the spa, where he'd consulted in Portuguese with the receptionist, who had gone bright pink and giggly. Lexie might almost have felt sorry for her if she hadn't been feeling a disturbing rise of something else. *Jealousy.*

Cesar had turned to her. 'See you in a couple of hours.' And after pressing a swift kiss to her mouth he'd left Lexie there, gaping at his retreating form.

Two women had emerged and Lexie had been taken in hand—literally. The full works of an all-over beauty treatment, followed by a full body massage.

Then, when she'd floated back to the suite, Cesar had been waiting with champagne, and once Lexie had changed into the dark pink off-the-shoulder dress she'd brought with her they'd gone to dinner.

And now…now…Lexie took in the sparkling view of one of the oldest cities in Europe and felt overwhelmed. No more in control of her emotions than she had been ever since they'd queued a second time for the glorious *pasteis de natas* in Belem. When Cesar had looked so carefree and years younger.

Conversely, it had reminded Lexie that she harboured dark secrets, and they were rising up within her now— because she was going to be coming face to face with a very personal old scar on set the following week. The thought of it terrified her, and she knew she was feeling more vulnerable about it because being with Cesar…being intimate for the first time…had ripped away some vital layer of protection.

'Sorry, I had to take that call.'

Lexie tensed at Cesar's deep voice. He came alongside her and handed her a small glass of port. She forced a smile and tipped it towards him after sniffing it appreciatively. 'Appropriate—given we're in the land where port is made.'

Cesar inclined his head. He looked absurdly suave and gorgeous this evening. Tall and imposing. Yet with that very definite edge of virile masculine energy.

Lexie took a quick sip of her drink. It was smooth and luxurious. Her feeling of vulnerability and the darkness on her soul made her want to avoid Cesar's far too incisive gaze. Even now he was regarding her speculatively. She felt raw after the day, and on some perverse level she almost felt angry with him—for charming her, for making her fall for him.

A rogue desire to crack that impenetrable façade he wore so well made her ask, 'So how come you're not married…?'

Lexie immediately wanted to claw the words back. Regretting the impulse.

Cesar's gaze narrowed predictably and Lexie squirmed, cursing herself. Thinking frantically of a way to save herself, she sought to mitigate it by saying lightly, 'You're a catch. I mean you have all your own teeth, your breath isn't bad. You own property…'

Somehow Lexie was afraid she hadn't fooled him. Her voice had sounded too breathy, slightly desperate. She took another sip of the port.

But when she looked back at him he was smiling wryly. 'No one's ever mentioned the boon of having my own teeth before.'

No, thought Lexie, she'd bet they hadn't. They'd probably looked at him and seen a walking, talking dollar sign.

Inexplicable anger rose up within her to think of women seeing him as a target, and then just as quickly dissolved. Cesar was so cynical that he would never be taken for that kind of a fool.

Suddenly loath to think that he might consider *her* a vulture like that, she said quietly, 'Thank you. Seriously, this day has been…amazing. I never expected it.'

Something painful gripped her inside. Their time was finite.

Not wanting to think about that, she figured she had nothing to lose so she dived in, telling herself she wasn't genuinely curious. 'Have you ever come close? To being married?'

Cesar tensed. His fingers tightened fractionally on his glass. Then the line of his mouth flattened. 'I was abandoned at an early age and then left in the hands of two people who were little better than uninterested caretakers. They resented the fact that my blood was not pure. That experience hardly left me with the qualifications to create a warm, inviting atmosphere conducive to family and such frivolous things.'

Lexie's insides clenched in rejection of that. Creating a family, a home, was not frivolous. Cesar's words, however, had been emphatic. She realised something about herself then, in a blinding flash of clarity: on some fundamental level she hadn't given up hope for herself. She hoped that some day she might have a second chance and her own rather dismal experience of what a family was could be proved to be the exception rather than the rule.

'Your half-brothers…' she offered huskily. 'They looked happy in the wedding pictures.'

Cesar's jaw tightened. 'They're different. They had a different upbringing, different perspectives.'

Lexie thought of his grandmother, cruelly making him

cut out and paste pictures of them growing up with their mother—*his* mother. Together.

'They had your mother... But I wonder if it was any easier or better for them just because she was there?'

'Perhaps—perhaps not,' Cesar said, but it rang hollow.

Lexie wanted to slide her arm around him but didn't. 'Are you going to see them again?'

He glanced at her and his face was hard. As it had been when he'd looked at the portraits of his grandparents.

'I have nothing in common with them. Especially not now.'

He turned to face her more fully and Lexie almost shivered at the frost in his eyes.

'I made a decision a long time ago never to marry and have children.'

'Why?' Lexie breathed, not liking how that declaration seemed to affect her physically. How it felt as if he was giving her a distinct message.

'Because I vowed that the *castillo* is no place for a child. The legacy of my family is tainted, built on obsessive greed. Snobbery. When I die the *castillo* will be left to the local town and they can do what they like with it. And all the money will go to various charities and trusts. That's what I'm building it up for now.'

'But...' Lexie searched wildly for a way to penetrate the cool shell that surrounded Cesar. 'You said yourself that you wanted to renovate the *castillo*, but...why bother? Why not just leave it behind now?'

Cesar looked at her then, and for a second Lexie saw bleakness in those green depths. A bleakness that resonated in her because she knew what it felt like herself.

'Because...' he was grim '...it's in my damn blood like some kind of poison.'

Lexie was stunned into silence. She didn't like the way she wanted to do something to comfort Cesar. Touch him.

And even though he was only inches away it felt as if a chasm yawned between them.

Huskily she said, 'I'm sorry. I shouldn't have said anything.'

His mouth tipped up but it was a parody of a smile, a million miles away from the smiles she'd seen earlier.

'What about you, Lexie? Do you wish for a cottage with a white picket fence and a gaggle of cherubic children?'

For a second Lexie felt nothing. The words seemed to hang suspended in the air between them. But then it was as if a roaring flood was approaching and gathering speed from a long way off. *Pain*. Incredible pain.

A kaleidoscope of images bombarded her—a tiny baby, crying lustily. Nurses with rough hands and judgemental looks. Officials. And then...nothing. Silence. More pain.

'Lexie?'

She blinked. Cesar was watching her, his eyes narrowing. Face stark. From somewhere she found a brittle smile and said through the ball of emotion growing in her chest, 'You forgot the dog...there's a dog there too.'

'Ah...yes, of course. No idyllic picture would be complete without a dog.'

Cesar put down his glass and took Lexie's from her too. He reached for her with both hands and pulled her into his body. Lexie felt cold, and she shivered lightly. She desperately wanted to drive away the chill and feel warm again. She desperately wanted to blank out the dark images she'd just seen.

Coming up on her tiptoes, Lexie reached up and brought her arms around Cesar's neck, pressing her whole body against his. She saw the flare in his eyes and felt herself start to thaw from the inside out.

'Kiss me, Cesar.'

Cesar smiled briefly before a look of almost feral intent crossed his face. He moved his hands up to Lexie's face.

The kiss was fierce and passionate, and before Lexie lost all ability to think clearly she knew that they were both running away from the demons nipping at their heels. This time, though, it didn't feel like kinship—it felt bleak.

Much later Cesar lay awake in the dark room. Traces of the constriction in his chest brought on by Lexie's questions were still there, faintly. Even though his body hummed with much more pleasurable sensations.

She was curled into him now, her naked curves keeping him at a level of near constant arousal. If it wasn't so damned intoxicating he could almost resent her for her effect on him.

Her breath was feathering softly across his chest, light and even, and her hair was soft and silky. One hand lay right over the centre of his chest, where he'd felt the constriction most keenly earlier.

'*So how come you're not married?*'

Other women had asked him that question with a definite look in their eyes. Lexie hadn't had that look. He never talked to anyone about his upbringing, but he seemed to be incapable of holding it in whenever those huge blue eyes were trained on him.

He'd told her...*everything*. He'd never even articulated his plans for the *castillo* to his friend Juan. He'd never told another soul. And when he'd told her something incredibly bleak had hit him. Bleak enough to drive him to taunt her, ask her if she pictured herself in that idyllic scenario.

And she'd looked for a moment as if he'd run a knife right through her belly. Pale. Stricken. Shocked. Clearly the thought was anathema to her, even though she'd joked about a dog.

Cesar went cold in the bed beside Lexie as something slid home inside him. The joke was on him, because for the first time in his life he was aware of a yearning sensation, a yearning for something he'd always believed to be utterly beyond his reach.

The following morning Lexie woke up alone in the bed. She sagged back against the pillows with not a little relief. Images from the night flooded her head and her cheeks reddened even as a tight knot of tension made her belly cramp.

She'd been able to drive away the demons for the night, but now they were back. The conversation with Cesar replayed in her head. The bleakness she'd felt when he'd spoken about the *castillo*, about leaving it behind so no child would have to endure what he had.

It shouldn't be affecting Lexie like this. If anything it should be inciting a sense of protection within her. A sense that as long as she could count on Cesar's obviously deeply rooted cynicism then she would be okay too.

But she couldn't keep fooling herself. That discussion with Cesar had told Lexie that she wasn't half as cynical as she'd always believed she was. It had told her that at a very deep core level she *did* harbour a fantasy. A fantasy of family and security and happiness. Fulfilment. It might not be dressed up in a vision of a cute cottage with a white picket fence and a dog and children, but it wasn't far off.

And it made Lexie feel physically ill, almost as if she'd betrayed herself, to realise that. She'd been betrayed in the worst way possible by the very people who should have loved and protected her. And she'd always vowed to herself that she'd never allow that to happen again.

She'd vowed it. But deep down she hadn't wanted to become that hard inside.

Lexie could see now that that was why she'd allowed herself to believe she could trust Jonathan Saunders, even briefly. Even then she'd been trying to prove to herself that she could trust again. That she could believe that she wouldn't be betrayed. But he *had* betrayed her. And that should have proved to her that she'd been right all along not to trust. It should have shored up her defences. Made her even stronger.

But it hadn't.

Because Lexie knew that any illusion of feeling in control of what was happening between her and Cesar Da Silva was exactly that. An illusion. And this man had the power to show her the true extent of how flimsy her defences had always been.

CHAPTER NINE

'WOULD YOU MIND if we returned to the *castillo* this morning? Something's come up that I have to attend to in the
vineyards.'

Lexie was in the bedroom and had just finished dressing
in the jeans she'd worn the day before and a stripy Breton
top. For a second Cesar's words didn't even compute because she was just drinking him in, looking impossibly
handsome in jeans and a light wool sweater.

Then the words registered and relief rocked through
her. She'd been dreading facing Cesar so soon after her
recent revelations.

'No,' she said quickly—too quickly. 'I don't mind at
all. There's some heavy scenes next week so I'd appreciate some time to prepare...'

Anxiety at the prospect of what lay ahead for her
gripped her again.

Cesar crossed his arms and lounged against the door.
Instantly Lexie's skin prickled with awareness. She could
feel her nipples drawing into tight buds. Even more reason
why she would relish some space from this man...

'You don't have to sound so eager.'

She blushed and glanced away for a second, feeling
churlish. 'It's not that I want to leave...you've been so
generous...'

Cesar closed the distance between them so fast her head spun. He looked stern. 'You don't have to thank me.'

Lexie said weakly, 'Yes, I do… It's polite.'

'I don't want your politeness,' Cesar growled softly. 'I want you.'

He cupped the back of her head and kissed her. Lexie clung to his arms to stop her legs from buckling.

When he drew back she opened her eyes. *Lord,* she could barely breathe.

'Maybe I can convince them they don't need me,' Cesar said roughly.

It took a second for his meaning to sink in and then, despite the lurch in her chest, Lexie said hurriedly, 'No, you should go back. And I *do* need to prepare for next week.'

'You're staying with me in my apartment, though.'

She opened her mouth to object and saw the glint of determination in Cesar's eyes. She sighed, feeling weak. 'Okay.'

Much later that night Cesar finally returned to his apartment in the *castillo*. He was irritated and frustrated. The problem in the vineyards had been more complicated than he'd thought, and then he'd been waylaid by his house manager and that had evolved into a long impromptu meeting about the renovations Cesar was embarking on. Renovations that were now taking on a new resonance—as if something had shifted inside him with regards to his long-term plans for the *castillo*.

But he didn't want to think of that. All he wanted *was to see Lexie*. His apartment was quiet. Empty. When he considered for a second that she might well have gone back to her own rooms the rise of an even deeper frustration made him clench his jaw.

But, no… He saw her sneakers, thrown off near the couch where a low light was burning. Cesar walked over and his chest grew tight when he saw Lexie fast asleep. Her top had risen up, revealing a sliver of pale soft belly. One arm was flung over her head, the other was just below her breasts.

He came closer and wasn't even really aware of the way the irritation and frustration he'd been feeling moments before had just dissolved away. To be replaced by a different kind of frustration. A hunger.

He spotted the earphones of her mp3 player in her ears, the wires leading to the device. And that tightness was more acute as he thought of her dyslexia and how hard it must have been for her to overcome its challenges along the way.

As if aware of his intense scrutiny, she opened those huge blue eyes. It took a second for them to focus and then Lexie scrambled up, her cheeks pink.

'Oh, my God, what time is it?'

Cesar came down on the edge of the couch and pinned her with his arms. She lay back. She looked tousled and delicious and sexy as hell.

'It's way past your bedtime.'

She smiled and an incredible lightness infused Cesar. Addictive, seductive…

'Is it now? What are you going to do about it?'

Cesar said sternly, 'I'm going to make sure you go to bed right now and tuck you in myself.'

He stood up and reached for Lexie, swinging her into his arms, relishing the way she snuggled into his chest. Relishing even more the way her mouth unerringly found his neck and started pressing kisses there. Open-mouthed kisses, so that he could feel the tip of that wicked tongue.

Lexie sank back onto the bed and Cesar loomed over her, pulling off his top with one graceful move. She was still in a delicious half-dream haze. She didn't even have to be awake for him to have an effect on her.

But then, like a dream that became clearer on waking, the darkness of the material she'd been studying in the script came back to her. It made her mood change in an instant, dousing desire. She recalled too that just before she'd woken she'd been having disturbing dreams. Almost nightmares. And it was no wonder.

Cesar came down over her on his arms and just like that Lexie froze under him. In that instant she felt tainted, *damaged*. She could see now that the exhilaration of becoming more intimate with Cesar had helped her to forget for a moment who she really was. What had happened to her. The sheer extent of the dark secrets she harboured.

Right then it felt as if a chasm yawned between them. He wouldn't ever want to know who she really was. Why would he? This was just an affair. Fun. Lighthearted. Lexie felt anything *but* lighthearted. She felt acutely alone. As if she carried the weight of the world on her shoulders.

Cesar lifted a hand as if to touch her and Lexie flinched violently. Everything in her was screaming to get away *now*—before he could seduce her so much that she found herself spilling out all the awful ugliness that had no place here.

He stopped. 'Lexie…?'

Lexie scrambled out from under Cesar's arms and stood up by the bed, her whole body cold. Numb. Cesar was looking at her as if she'd grown two heads. Galvanised by panic, Lexie found her bag and started throwing things in.

'What are you doing?'

She shoved the blouse she'd worn the previous day into the bag, her belly swooping at the thought of that day. How perfect it had been. It felt as if it had happened to another person now. A person who *didn't* have the awful memories that were bombarding her right now.

'I'm going back to my own room.'

She picked up her bag but Cesar caught her arm. He was shaking his head, incredulous. 'What on earth is going on?'

She pulled her arm free and backed away, torn by the sense of increasing panic she felt and also by something much more disturbing: the desire to throw down the bag and launch herself into Cesar's arms, ask him just to hold her, to reassure her that she could feel safe with him. But that was not what he was interested in—Lexie being vulnerable. He'd run a mile.

Then he stopped looking incredulous. He folded his arms. 'I told you before that I don't play games, Lexie.'

Lexie felt sad. 'I'm not playing a game. I just can't do this right now. I need...some space.'

For a long second Cesar just regarded her, and then his face became unreadable. He stepped back and said coolly, 'By all means, Lexie, take all the space you need.'

Lexie gripped her bag and turned and walked out of the bedroom, and out of Cesar's apartment, adrenalin coursing through her system. When she got back to her own room it felt desolate. And then she realised with a sense of dread that *she* felt desolate.

The truth was that she was damaged and broken inside. For a brief moment in time she'd believed that she had somehow been miraculously cured. But she hadn't really. And this minor meltdown had just proved it to her.

'I need some space.' Cesar glowered so fiercely that his house manager saw him coming and scuttled out of sight. Those words had been eating away at him like poison for two days now.

One minute Lexie had been supine on his bed, flushed and sexy, huge eyes all but eating him up...and the next she'd become a different person. Cold. Stark. *Dios*, she'd flinched as if he might hurt her.

His skin prickled. He hadn't liked that feeling. And he

hadn't liked to acknowledge how feral she'd made him feel. When she'd said she needed space it had been like a punch to his gut.

The thought that she might have even glimpsed a tiny part of how ravenous she made him feel had made him go cold all over. He'd had to step back to stop himself from acting on the visceral impulse to prove her words to be a lie.

But even now he could remember the look in her eyes. It had been panicked. And he couldn't understand why.

The film unit was due to head back to London at the end of the week and Cesar was acutely aware of the fact— much to his chagrin. Especially when he'd set out at the very beginning to avoid getting involved at all costs.

For two days he'd deliberately avoided going near where they were shooting, in an old abandoned wing of the *castillo*. But today he found himself heading there even before he'd consciously taken the decision. The fact that he *needed* to see Lexie only put him into an even more foul humour.

Cesar saw the usual cluster of people as he got closer to the set—crew hanging around, waiting for someone to call for them urgently.

They nodded to him now. Said hello. He managed some civil responses. When he got closer he saw that the door to the set was closed. And there was a hushed air. He asked the third assistant director if they were shooting.

The young man shook his head and Cesar made to go onto the set, but the man stopped him. 'You can't go in there, Mr Da Silva.'

Cesar chafed at the obstruction. His need to see Lexie was like a burr under his skin now. 'Why not?' he demanded.

'It's a closed set. They're doing the rape scene. Essential crew only.'

The rape scene.

Cesar didn't know why, but he suddenly felt a chill in his blood. He looked around and saw the video assistant in the corner, with his wall of monitors which showed whatever the camera was seeing inside the room. Usually there would be a couple of producers or some crew watching the scenes, but today there was no one.

He went over and sat down. Just as he realised that he couldn't hear what they were saying the video assistant handed him some earphones. Cesar put them on and hunched forward.

They were about to shoot. The director was talking to Lexie and to Rogan, the male lead. Cesar's breath hitched when he saw her. Her hair was down, tousled, and she was wearing some kind of diaphanous white gown. It was open at the front, as if it had been ripped, and he could see the ripe curve of her breast.

And then the director disappeared, leaving Lexie and Rogan on the screen. The first assistant director called out the instructions to shoot and then the director called *action.*

Rogan grabbed Lexie by the arms and shook her, spittle flying from his mouth as he said crude, horrific things. She looked tiny and vulnerable. She was pleading with him. But he wouldn't listen. Then he brutally turned her and shoved her down on the bed, pulling her gown up over her thighs, undoing himself before he pressed himself into her, grunting like an animal.

The camera went close in on Lexie's face, pushed down onto the bed. Rogan's big hand was on the back of her head, holding her down. Her eyes were blank.

Cesar heard *cut.* But all he could really hear was the roaring of blood in his head. He wanted to move but he was paralysed.

On some rational level he knew it wasn't real. That it was just acting. He could see Rogan helping Lexie up. The actor looked faintly traumatised. Lexie looked impossibly pale, and sort of glassy-eyed. A shiver of foreboding went down Cesar's spine. He knew that it had obviously been a traumatic scene to shoot, but there was something else going on—he could feel it.

But then they were going again, and he heard the camera assistant say, 'Scene One Hundred, Take Twenty.'

Cesar pulled off the earphones and looked at the video guy incredulously. 'They've done this *nineteen* times?'

The man gulped. 'Yes, sir. We've been doing this scene all day from different angles. This is the last shot, but he's milking it.'

Cesar felt rage building inside him. The camera was close up on Lexie's face again and he saw a tear roll out of her eye and down one cheek. She hadn't cried last time.

Something rose up inside Cesar—something he couldn't even articulate. An overwhelming need to get to her. He surged to his feet, almost knocking over the wall of monitors. He stormed to the door of the set, swatting the protesting third AD aside.

He opened the door just as the camera assistant was saying, 'Scene One Hundred, Take Twenty-One.'

'*Enough.*' Cesar's voice cracked out like a whip.

Lexie turned her head and looked at Cesar. He saw only those huge bruised blue eyes, and something in their depths...a mute appeal. She wasn't acting any more. He knew it without even knowing how.

He walked straight over and scooped her up into his arms, and for the first time in two days he felt slightly sane again.

The director was standing up now, blustering. 'What the hell are you doing, Da Silva? You can't just barge in here like this.'

Cesar stopped in the act of turning around. Lexie was

far too slight a weight in his arms as he said coldly, 'You're on my property. I can do whatever the hell I want.'

'But we haven't got the shot yet.'

Even icier now, Cesar said, 'If you haven't managed to get it yet then perhaps you shouldn't be directing.'

He was barely aware of a suppressed snigger from one of the crew as he strode out of the room, Lexie curled into his chest, her head tucked down. It reminded him of how she'd curled into his chest after making love that first time. When she'd cried like a baby.

He carried her all the way to his apartment and took her into his bedroom. He sat down on the edge of the bed, still holding her. He was shaking from the adrenalin and anger coursing through his system.

After a long time, she moved in his arms. But she wouldn't look at him. She just said, in a quiet voice, 'I need to have a shower.'

Cesar got up and deposited her gently on the side of the bed, crouching down. Finally she met his gaze but her eyes were flat. As if she didn't see him. A shard of ice pierced him inside.

Reluctantly he left her to go and turn on the shower. When he came out she was standing, albeit shakily. 'Do you need help?' he asked.

She shook her head and went in, closing the door behind her. Cesar restrained himself from following her, making sure she was all right. The shower ran for long minutes.

Eventually it stopped. Lexie was so long coming out that Cesar was about to knock on the door when it opened. She was wrapped in his towelling robe. It swamped her. Her hair was damp and hung in long golden tendrils over her shoulders.

He handed her a glass of brandy. 'Here—you should drink some of this.'

Lexie wrinkled her nose, but she took it and sipped at it before handing it back. Cesar put it down on a nearby table. He felt unaccountably ill-equipped to know what to do. What to say.

'You shouldn't have done that.'

She was looking at him with her chin tilted up and Cesar arched a brow. 'Would you prefer to be back there doing Take Thirty right now?'

She paled so dramatically that Cesar reached out and put his hands on her arms.

'No,' he said grimly, leading her out to the living area and guiding her to sit down on the couch. 'I didn't think so.'

Lexie seemed impossibly tiny and fragile sitting on the big couch. Cesar stood over her and crossed his arms, because even now all he wanted to do was touch her. *I need space.* He cursed silently.

'So, are you going to tell me what's going on?'

Lexie glanced up at Cesar and then away again quickly. He was so…implacable. Determined. Stern. The numb shell that had surrounded her for the past two days was finally breaking apart.

When Cesar had burst onto the set and she'd seen him… He would never know the depth of the gratitude she'd felt. Because on some level she'd always needed to know that someone might have saved her.

She forced herself to look at him. 'Why did you do that?'

Cesar paced back and forth now, energy sparking off his tall, lean body. His mouth was tight. 'I don't know, to be honest. But when I saw you…I could tell something was wrong.' He shook his head, stopped pacing. 'You weren't acting, Lexie.'

Something huge inside her shifted to know that he'd

intuited something was wrong. 'No, I wasn't acting...not by the end.'

Cesar pulled a chair over to sit in front of her. Lexie gazed at him. Remembered how good it had felt when he'd swept her up into his arms. *Too good.* As if she'd been running for a long time and someone had finally allowed her to stop and rest.

She found that she wanted to tell him. She wanted to explain about the other night.

'Lexie...*what*?'

She took a breath and then said starkly, 'I was raped when I was fourteen.'

Cesar went white in an instant. His whole body tensed. 'What did you say?' His voice was hoarse.

Lexie bit her lip. She couldn't go back now.

'I was raped by my aunt's husband. One night my parents and my aunt had gone out—he said he'd babysit. He brought me into my parents' room when the others were in bed and raped me.'

'The others...?'

'My five younger brothers and sisters.'

'*Dios mio*... Lexie...that animal...' Cesar looked sick. 'You looked at me the other night like I was going to hurt you—you were scared...'

Lexie leant forward and touched his arm. 'No...'

But Cesar was almost recoiling now, and she could see the horror on his face that she might have thought for a second he was capable of something so heinous.

She shook her head, '*No*, Cesar. I wasn't afraid of you. I knew this scene was coming up... I was apprehensive about it... It's the first time I've ever had to do a scene like this and it was just too close to the bone.'

Cesar pulled free of her touch and stood up, pacing again. Lexie was tense, her hands forming fists in her lap.

He faced her, eyes flinty green. 'My God,' he said again—in English this time.

Suddenly a kind of hurt bloomed inside her. He was looking at her as if she was a stranger. A damaged stranger. The guilt that she had worked long and hard to believe wasn't hers reared its ugly head again. Her rapist's accusations were as clear today as they had been then. *'You were asking for it, you know. Always prancing around under my nose dressed in that uniform.'*

She felt cold and said tightly, 'I'm sorry. I shouldn't have told you.'

She stood up from the couch, hating that she'd been weak enough to confide in Cesar. Hating that she'd thought his intuition made her feel as if he deserved to know.

'Where are you going?'

She looked at him. 'Back to my room.'

She turned and headed for the bedroom, but Cesar caught her hand. This time when she looked at him his eyes were blazing. 'Dammit, Lexie, you're staying here.'

Hot tears pricked the back of her eyes, galling her. She hadn't even cried after she'd been raped—too shocked and traumatised—and yet with one touch, one look, this man could reduce her to tears and make her want to lean on him when she'd fended for herself for so long now...

'Damn *you*, Cesar.' She pulled her hand free and faced him. 'Just let me go.'

He shook his head. 'You shouldn't be alone right now.'

More hurt bloomed inside Lexie to think that he was acting out of a sense of duty. 'I've done my therapy, Cesar, years of it,' she sneered. 'You really don't have to act as my babysitter just because it turns out that your lover is damaged goods.'

Now Cesar was angry. He took her arms in his hands, gripping her. 'Don't you *dare* put words in my mouth. I don't think any such thing. And you are *not* damaged. You're perfect.'

Lexie's anger drained away, leaving her feeling shaky. 'I'm sorry. I just…I shouldn't have told you.'

'I'm glad you told me. It's just a lot to take in.'

He let go of her arms and stepped back, raking a hand through his hair. Lexie felt bereft.

'Look,' she offered, 'I'm fine—really. I always suspected this scene would be difficult. But it's one of the reasons I took the job in the first place. Initially I wanted to say no, but I knew I couldn't let it stop me. I dealt with what happened a long time ago, Cesar. But something like this would be difficult even under the best of circumstances.'

Cesar shook his head lightly. He came close again, touched Lexie's jaw.

'You shouldn't have had to face it alone.'

Lexie felt emotion building inside her. Terrified of it, she said simply, 'I've always been alone.'

Cesar looked at her with a burning intensity. Desire, pure and hot, sparked to life within her, mixing with the emotion to produce something volatile. She brought her hand up to cover his and saw his eyes widen slightly.

'Please…'

One word. She could see that he understood, and she trembled inwardly in case he might balk. He could never know the depth of how badly she needed him right now— for myriad reasons.

His voice was gruff. 'Lexie…are you sure? The other night…'

She nodded. 'I'm sure. The other night…it wasn't about you. It was about me.'

'I don't want to hurt you.'

'You won't…'

He didn't move, though. Frustration welled inside her. Maybe Cesar couldn't deal with the ugly truth of what had happened to her. She took her hand down, stepped back, dislodging his hand. She'd just exposed herself spectacularly.

'It's okay… If you don't want me any more because of—'

His hand shot out, caught her. She looked at him.

'Of *course* I want you.' He sounded fierce. 'I just have to look at you to want you.'

He came closer. Held her face with both hands. 'You're in my blood. I need you.'

Lexie's own blood sang. She needed him too. Her whole being came alive as he drew her close and lowered his mouth to hers. The kiss was so tender and gentle that she almost emitted a sob of emotion, but held it back.

When he drew back he took her by the hand and led her into his bedroom. There was no sense of hesitation within Lexie. No sense of that same panic that had gripped her the other evening. She knew now that that had been largely because of her apprehension of acting out being raped. And it was over.

Cesar stopped by the bed and she faced him. He said, 'If you want to stop…'

Something melted inside her. She shook her head, her hands going to the buttons on his shirt, her voice husky with need. 'I won't want to stop.'

Her hands were clumsy on his buttons and he gently took them away to undo them himself. Lexie sucked in a breath to see his chest revealed. She opened the knot on her robe.

Cesar looked down and she saw a dark flush slash across his cheekbones. He slid his hands under the shoulders of her robe and pushed it till it fell to the floor.

Lexie ran her hands over his pectorals, her nails grazing his nipples, making them stand up into hard little points. She reached forward and put her mouth there, swirling her tongue around one hard tip, feeling her core moisten with desire.

As she lavished kisses on his chest and nipples her hands were on his jeans, flipping open the buttons, feeling the hard ridge of his arousal brushing her fingers. She drew back and pushed his jeans down, taking his underwear with them, her breath disappearing when his erection was freed.

She wrapped a hand around him, awed by his sheer size and strength and the knowledge that he would never use it to hurt her. Cesar was kicking his feet free of his clothes and then he put his hands on Lexie's arms.

She looked up.

He sounded rough. 'I need you. I need to taste you.'

Her hand stalled on the thick column of flesh and gently Cesar removed it, pushing her down onto the bed. He came down beside her and his mouth was on hers, and Lexie moaned as she tasted him hungrily, sucked him deep. Wrapped her legs and arms around him as if she could bind him to her for ever.

Gently Cesar unbound her, spreading her arms out, his mouth leaving hers to explore over her jaw and neck. Over the tops of her heaving breasts. Taking each tight bud of her nipples into his mouth, making her moan even louder and her hips writhe against him.

But he kept moving down, over her belly. An arm came under her back, arching her into him, his other hand pushed her legs apart.

She felt dizzy. 'Cesar...'

His green gaze was blistering. 'Trust me.'

Trust me. Lexie sank back. She did trust him. She always had—from the moment she'd met him and let him kiss her. *Her*—with her history. The knowledge rushed through her. Wiping aside any trepidation or lingering hurt.

His mouth was moving down, kissing the top of her

thigh. Moving in. A big hand was splayed under her buttocks, tipping her towards his face. Lexie's breaths were
coming so hard and fast she had to consciously slow down
for fear of passing out.

And then his tongue touched her *there*. He licked her
with explicit skill. All the way up the seam of her body,
his tongue delving into her secret folds, opening her up to
him, baring every part of her.

Lexie's hands gripped the sheet. Legs bent, back arched.
Cesar licked and sucked and drove her more and more
mindless. His tongue swirled with maddening strokes
against her clitoris before leaving it to lavish attention
elsewhere and then returning just when those cells were
screaming for release.

When it came it was so huge...so all-encompassing...that
Lexie thought she'd passed out. Because the next thing she
was aware of was Cesar sliding into her, so deeply and thoroughly, and with such a fierce look of concentration on his
face that it was all she could do to wrap her legs around him
as far as they'd go and tilt her hips to take him even deeper.

They were locked in a dance that was as old as time and
as profound. Lexie couldn't look away from Cesar even
though she felt as though her soul was being turned inside
out and he'd see it as clear as day. *She loved him.* And it
went deeper than just loving him because he was the first
man she'd allowed herself to be intimate with. He was the
only man she could imagine being intimate with. The only
man she *wanted* to be intimate with.

That revelation came just as bliss split her body in
two, throwing her high into the air, where she seemed
to hang suspended on the crest of a huge wave until it finally dropped her again. Cesar caught her in his arms and
rolled them both so that she went limp across his heaving
chest, their hearts thundering in unison, their skin slick
with perspiration.

* * *

In the aftermath of her shattering climax and revelation Lexie felt as wobbly and vulnerable as a new foal trying to stand on spindly legs. So much had happened, and in the past couple of days since leaving Cesar's apartment she'd deliberately cut herself off from the people around her, dreading the upcoming rape scene.

It had reminded her of when she'd arrived in London for the first time, when she'd been completely alone and unsupported.

Cesar shifted now and she winced minutely as the connection between their bodies was broken.

He asked with obvious concern, 'Are you okay?'

Lexie nodded and looked at him. He was on one elbow, some hair flopping into his forehead, his face dark, eyes glowing like dark green gems. *She loved him.*

But even as she knew that she also knew, with a feeling of desolation, that he didn't feel anything for her other than desire…and maybe worst of all pity.

Cutting into her thoughts, Cesar asked, 'What happened to him?'

Lexie went cold inside. 'My uncle?'

Cesar nodded.

She braced herself for the pain that inevitably came whenever he was mentioned or she thought about him, but it wasn't as sharp. Lexie's mouth became bitter. 'Nothing. My parents didn't want to know when I told them. They were very religious—pillars of the community. My father was a salesman; he travelled a lot. The thought of the scandal was too much for them.'

Cesar was incredulous. 'You mean he just got away with it?'

She pulled the sheet around her and sat up against the pillows. 'He died in a car crash about a year after it happened. But, no, he never got prosecuted or punished.'

'How could they have done that to you? Just ignored it?'

Lexie glanced away from Cesar. There was an even darker stain on her soul than he could imagine. She suddenly felt jaded and weary. Knowing that she loved him, but that it would end when she left the *castillo* for London at the end of that week, she felt reckless. As if she had nothing more to lose.

'That wasn't all,' she said now in a quiet voice.

'What do you mean?' Cesar moved, sitting up too.

She looked at him. 'The rape resulted in me becoming pregnant.'

He frowned. 'Pregnant? You had a baby?'

Lexie nodded, suppressing the inevitable spasm of emotion. 'A baby boy. I named him Connor.'

Cesar shook his head, clearly finding this hard to digest. 'But...you don't... Where is he now?'

'I had just turned fifteen when I had him. My family sent me away to a distant relative down the country for the duration of the pregnancy, where I was pretty much kept a prisoner for nine months. He was adopted two days after the birth, and is growing up somewhere in the greater Dublin area—that's all I know. And that they kept Connor as his middle name.'

Lexie watched as Cesar, looking slightly stunned, blindly pushed back the covers and got out of the bed. A sinking feeling gripped her. This was it. Her ugly truth bared. She'd known on some deep level that it would be too much to take in. This relationship was about a flirty affair while they were filming—not about dark secrets.

She knew with a sick feeling that she had just ended it.

CHAPTER TEN

CESAR PULLED ON his jeans and then he faced Lexie again. She looked impossibly young against the sheets, eyes huge. He was literally speechless. Didn't know what to say. The knowledge of what she'd been through was…enormous. And it was making all of his own dark demons rear their ugly heads.

He felt tight inside. As if a hand was closing around his chest and heart and squeezing with remorseless pressure. He thought of her reaction when he'd first presented her with the option of staying in the *castillo* for the duration of the shoot. No wonder she'd looked panicked.

Lexie was a mother. She'd had to give up her baby. He knew rationally that she'd had no choice, but it impacted on him in a deeply raw place. He couldn't breathe.

'Why did you tell me this?'

Lexie's eyes widened. Her face paled. And then something in her features hardened, as if in response to Cesar's stoniness.

'I told you because I felt I could… But I can see I shouldn't have.'

Cesar watched as if slightly removed from his own body as Lexie reached for her robe and pulled it on, getting out of bed too. Belting the robe tightly around her.

So many different emotions were impacting on him that it was almost overwhelming. Among them was anger—

which he knew was directed at himself, for his less than coherent response, and at Lexie for bringing him face to face with things he didn't want to look at in himself.

'I don't know what you want me to say.'

Lexie stared at him, her hair tumbled around her shoulders. Right then she seemed like a tiny warrior queen. Majestic.

'You don't have to say anything, Cesar. I'm not looking for therapy. I had years of that. I told you…'

She stopped for a second and that tightening sensation in Cesar's chest grew stronger. He almost put a hand there, as if that could alleviate the pain.

'I told you because I've never been with another man.'

Cesar stepped back. Stunned. 'Since you were…?'

Lexie snapped. 'Since I was raped, yes. You were my first lover.'

Faintly, Cesar said, 'Why me?'

She crossed her arms. 'You were the first man I desired.'

Lexie had never regretted anything more than opening her mouth to Cesar. Self-disgust ripped her insides to shreds. She'd truly learnt nothing. For a long time she'd felt ashamed, dirty. That she was some kind of damaged goods. And then therapy had helped her make sense of what had happened and she'd begun the long process of healing and forgiving herself.

Healing. The physical process of that, which had started with Cesar's incendiary kiss in the stable, mocked her now. She'd confused physical intimacy with something deeper. Clearly it had never been about anything else for him.

Her own family had shunned her a long time ago, and she was damned if she was going to let that happen again.

Lexie stalked around the bed and into the bathroom, aware of Cesar's eyes on her. The fact that he was so silent, not making any attempt to touch her, said it all. She closed the door and with shaking hands that told her of the heightened emotion she was barely reining in, she took off the robe and put on the costume nightshirt she'd been wearing for the rape scene.

When she emerged Cesar had put on a top. He looked serious.

Lexie hated that even now she was acutely aware of her sensitised naked body under the voluminous robe.

She was brisk. 'I shouldn't have said anything.' From somewhere, Lexie even managed to force a smile—as if this *hadn't* just cost her everything.

'Lexie—'

She cut him off, dreading hearing some platitude, and a spurt of anger made her say, 'Cesar, we're wrapping here on Friday. It's not as if this was ever going to go further. The papers have already lost interest in us—we've done what we set out to do in the first place.'

'We have.' His voice was flat.

'Yes,' Lexie insisted, forcing herself to look at him even though it was hard. 'I wanted to salvage my reputation and avoid being dragged through the tabloids again as some kind of victim. You wanted to avoid unnecessary scrutiny into your family. It was a mutually beneficial affair—isn't that what you called it?'

Everything within Cesar rejected Lexie's terse words but something was holding him back. The feeling that the very walls around him were about to start crumbling—as if some sort of invisible earthquake was happening below ground.

Right at that moment the full impact of just how different Lexie was from any other lover he'd had hit him with the force of a blunt object. She'd turned him upside down and inside out.

'Yes,' he agreed, 'it was.'

Just then there was a knock on the main door of Cesar's

apartment. He cursed even as a very weak part of him welcomed the interruption. He strode through the main living space to get to the door, and opened it to see one of the film's PAs.

'Sorry to disturb you, Mr Da Silva, but the director is looking for Lexie.'

Cesar knew Lexie was behind him without turning around. His skin prickled. He felt disorientated, dizzy. Even now he had to battle an absurd urge to protect her and snarl at the young guy to leave.

Lexie was oblivious to the messy tumult in Cesar's gut. She stepped around him, didn't look at him, and spoke to the PA. 'Tell Richard I'll just change before I come to him.'

The PA hurried off, clearly relieved to have delivered his message. Cesar watched Lexie. She was avoiding his eye. He wanted to tip her chin up, force her to meet his gaze, but at the same time he didn't want to see what was in those blue depths.

'I should go and talk to Richard.' Lexie's voice was husky, her almost belligerent stance of moments ago less evident.

She looked at him then and Cesar tensed, but her eyes were clear. Unreadable. It irritated him—which irritated him even more.

'The next few days are heavily scheduled so that we get out of here on time. I think it's best if we just…let this be finished now.'

Cesar felt slightly numb. This was a novel situation: a woman who was ready to walk away before he was ready to let her go.

Humiliation scored at his insides. Lexie was right—this had only ever been about the short term. The thought of anything beyond this place was not an option. He did not chase women around the world. Whatever desire he felt would dissipate. He could not want her so badly that he was unable to let her go.

He was tight-lipped as he reached for the door and held it open. 'Goodbye, Lexie.'

Something flared in her eyes for a second, and then it disappeared. She didn't speak again, just turned and walked out, and as Cesar watched her go he thought numbly that she could be a ghost in the long white gown and in her bare feet.

He closed the door on her, on that evocative image, and pushed down the chilling sensation that she would haunt him for ever. Everything he'd been holding in since she'd told him about the rape, and then the baby, surged up in a tangled black mess of emotion.

He went to his drinks cabinet and took out a glass, poured himself a drink. Taking a swift gulp, he felt the liquid jolt him back to life. His hand tightened on the glass as he stared unseeingly at the wall in front of him.

His own mother had abandoned him and left him at the mercy of his grandparents. Lexie had given up her own son. For a moment pure unadulterated rage rose up within Cesar as he acknowledged what she'd done —but it was an old, reflexive anger that had more to do with his mother than with Lexie.

His rage dimmed when he thought of Lexie aged fifteen, a terrified and traumatised schoolgirl. What choice had she had? None.

For the first time in his life Cesar had to concede that by the time his mother had come back for him his grandparents had done such a number on him that he'd had no choice but to reject her.

And he had to concede too that perhaps there had been more to his mother's motives than pure greed and selfishness. Her distress when she'd said goodbye both times stung him now—hard. Like a slap across the face. This unwelcome revelation brought with it an even stronger feeling that everything he'd always counted on was falling apart at the seams.

Cesar pinched the bridge of his nose. All he could see was Lexie's face and those huge eyes.

Anger surged again. What had she wanted from him? Damn her! Had she expected him to take her in his arms and soothe her? Promise her that everything would be all right?

Cesar wasn't gentle. Or sensitive. Or kind. He was black all the way through, and he resented Lexie right then for making him see just how black he was. For showing him how little he could offer comfort. And for making him think of the bleak reality of his childhood, filled with a lifetime of resentment for his two half-brothers. How powerless he'd been under the influence of his bitter grandparents, intent on punishment and revenge.

Rage and a feeling of impotence wound up inside him so tightly that he exploded. He turned and raised the hand holding that heavy crystal glass and with an inarticulate roar of pain and rage flung it with all his might across the room at his stainless steel kitchen. He watched it shatter into a million pieces, amber liquid spraying everywhere.

An echo from a long time ago whispered across his soul, bringing a chill wind. It reminded him that no good came out of this dark, gothic place. And to have imagined otherwise, even for a second, was to have become weak.

Lexie Anderson would be gone in a few days, and right in that moment Cesar hoped he'd never set eyes on her again. Because she'd done the worst thing in the world: she'd made him forget who he really was.

Lexie was sitting in her chair on the set, waiting while they set up for a new camera shot. People milled around her, working, chatting. But she felt removed. She'd heard the helicopter leaving early that morning.

She'd known that Cesar had left the *castillo* even before she'd heard one of the producers say something about him having business to attend to in America.

She'd been awake for most of the night, alternating between seething resentment directed at Cesar for having awoken her body from a lifetime of numbness and anger at herself for being so stupid as to fall for him. She'd tried to tell herself that she hadn't fallen so hard…but the hurt was too real and too deep for feelings not to be involved.

She'd never forget the look on his face when she'd told him about her baby. He'd shut down. Lexie had only ever talked about her baby to her counsellor. No one else knew. It was one of the reasons she was paranoid about press intrusion—in case anyone ever dug deep enough to find out.

Her son would be thirteen now, and every day Lexie wondered about him—wondered how she would cope if he ever came looking for her, asking for information. Sometimes the thought was overwhelming. She went cold inside as something struck her. Had she, on some level, put Cesar in the role of confidante because she'd been so desperate for support?

Even as Lexie felt anger for being so weak she had to acknowledge that she could have asked for help before. She'd just been too stubborn. That had been borne out the previous evening, when she'd gone to find the director to try and explain to him why she'd reacted the way she had.

She'd told him about the rape, knowing instinctively that she could trust him.

He'd shaken his head and taken her hand, his eyes full of compassion. 'Lexie, you should have told me. If I'd had any idea of how huge that scene was for you I'd have approached it differently. We could even have got it out of the way in the first week…'

He'd humbled her, apologising for unwittingly causing her distress. It was as if another weight had lifted from her shoulders, and Lexie knew that if she hadn't already told Cesar there was no way she could have confided in anyone else.

That only made her angry with him all over again. He hadn't been able to get rid of her fast enough yesterday. His face had been hard. Clearly he'd rejected her unwelcome confidences. No doubt his other lovers didn't come with messy histories, or weep all over him after making love.

She was glad Cesar was gone because she knew all her bravado was very shaky and that if she saw him again her heart would splinter into a million pieces.

Over a week later Cesar returned to the *castillo*. It was as if there had never been a film unit on the estate. Apart from the flattened bit of grass where the extras' marquee had stood everything had been restored to its pristine state—and, perversely, it annoyed Cesar intensely.

For the past week he'd put in long days at board meetings he'd been neglecting. Because of a blonde-haired, blue-eyed temptress. Damn her. Those were his favourite words at the moment, and they beat a constant refrain in his head.

Damn her for coming into his life. Damn her for making him want her so badly that he seemed to have a constant ache in his gut. Damn her for being so light in spite of the horrific things she'd endured.

Just…*damn her.*

For making him think of things like his brother Alexio's wedding and how happy both his half-brothers had looked with their wives. And damn her for making him come to the uncomfortable realisation that he had to stop blaming his brothers for living their lives oblivious of his presence.

That realisation had hit him as he'd looked blearily into

the bottom of an empty bottle of whiskey in a dingy bar on the Lower East Side of Manhattan about two days ago.

Cesar stopped at the entrance of the *castillo*. It sat there, as forbidding and dark as it ever had been. But for the first time in his life it didn't feel quite so...oppressive.

It was quiet, though. And that quiet, which had never really bothered him before, seemed to reach around him and squeeze, bringing with it restlessness. Dissatisfaction.

Without even being aware of making the decision, Cesar found himself walking up the main staircase to the first-floor landing. He went and stood at the window where his grandmother had found him waiting, looking for his mother.

He felt the old pain like a bruise that would never fade. But it didn't bring with it that futile sense of anger. It only brought a sense of melancholy and a growing sense of something else. *Loss*. Acute, aching loss. Worse than anything he'd ever felt before—worse even the loss he could remember feeling as a child for his mother.

Cesar knew then that as much as his grandparents had all but imprisoned him in this *castillo* when he was a child, since he'd become an adult he'd happily inflicted the same punishment on himself, and self-disgust filled him.

Lexie's face and eyes filled his vision. How she'd looked that last time he'd seen her, in the ridiculous period night-gown. Pale. Yet strong. Defiant in the face of his frankly pathetic response to her pain and trauma.

Something had shut down inside him that day, as if to protect him from feeling the pain too acutely. But now that was breaking apart inside him as he stared out at a bleak view that was seared into his consciousness.

He was sick of bleak. He was sick of darkness. He was sick of himself.

Damn Lexie, indeed. Because she hadn't made him

forget who he was at all. She'd shown him *exactly* who he was and who he could be. If he was brave enough.

The street was stinking, narrow. Beggars lined it, calling out for mercy or money. Small children darted under people's feet. Lexie stepped out of the path of a horse and carriage only at the last moment and gasped as it whistled past. Her long skirts were splashed with mud. People jostled her. She was going against the tide. And all she could think about, even as the cameras were running, was *him*. Cesar.

She cursed him for about the hundredth time that day and hoped that her expression conveyed anger at her co-star, who followed her through the streets, tracking her like a hunted animal.

'Cut!'

Immediately Lexie stopped. All of the extras turned and went back to their first positions on the enormous set that had been built for the film on a back lot in the London studios. A swarm of crew moved in to rearrange things, fix focus marks, touch up hair and make-up.

Lexie felt removed, though. The director approached her and she smiled brightly.

He took her arm and said in a low voice, 'Lexie, are you all right? You just seem…not that focused.'

She grimaced inwardly, regretting having ever told him what had happened to her. He'd been overly solicitous ever since. 'Sorry, Richard… I'm fine. It's just—'

'Oh, my God.'

'Sir! *Sir!* You can't go onto the set without a pass!'

Richard frowned and looked past Lexie. 'What on earth is *he* doing here?' he said incredulously.

Lexie felt a prickling sensation and turned around to see a tall figure approaching them. But even now she couldn't really compute that it was *him*.

Cesar. Dressed in dark worn jeans. A jumper and a battered brown leather jacket. Dark golden hair glinting in the London sunshine. He was almost too gorgeous to be real.

She even heard one of the extras nearby say in an awestruck voice, 'Who *is* that?' and Lexie could almost sympathise with the inevitable impact he would be having on some poor unsuspecting person's senses.

He looked as intense as she'd ever seen him. A security guard caught up with him and took his arm. Cesar shook him off and kept coming.

Her mouth had gone bone-dry. She wondered if she was seeing things. Damn this corset that constricted her breath...

Cesar stopped just feet away and the security guard came panting up behind him. 'Now, look here—'

Lexie put out a shaky hand. 'It's all right, we know him. I...know him.'

Then all the anger and pain that had been her constant companion for a week now came flooding up, boiling over. She hissed at Cesar, 'What are you doing here? We're in the middle of a scene.'

'So I see,' he remarked dryly, taking in all the gawping extras and the crew, who were loving the interruption. He looked back at Lexie, and then spoke as if they were continuing a conversation that had stopped only moments ago. 'The thing is I should never have agreed with you when you said we should end the affair.'

Lexie gulped and darted a look at the avid crowd. 'Cesar, do we really have to do this here?'

Just then Richard stepped forward. 'Now, listen, Da Silva—interrupting my set once was—'

Cesar took his eyes off Lexie to stare at the man, and Lexie shivered when she saw the familiar steel in his expression.

'How much will it cost to shut down production for the rest of the day?'

Lexie blinked. Richard spluttered. 'I'd have to ask the producer...'

'Well, why don't you find him and ask him, and whatever amount he gives you tell him I'll double it.'

A murmur started through the crew and the extras. Lexie could see the PAs galvanised into action at the thought of an early wrap and a day off. The set started to clear.

Cesar stepped right up to Lexie and she was rooted to the spot. Terrified of the flutters that had started in her belly. Her heart squeezed. She loved this man so much, but he'd hurt her, and if all he wanted was to continue their affair...

'Cesar, if you've come just because you're not ready to end the affair then I'm not interested.'

His gaze on hers became assessing. Lexie's body hummed with awareness. With hunger.

'So what *are* you interested in?'

She blinked, confused. Fear gripped her... *What had she just said?* 'I just told you—I'm not interested in an affair.'

A ghost of a smile touched Cesar's mouth and she realised very belatedly how dishevelled he was, with stubble lining his jaw.

'One thing I do know is that I am not ready to end the affair—and I don't think you are either.'

A ball of pain lodged in her gut. She didn't have it in her to keep seeing Cesar knowing that it would end. Even one night with this man would kill her, even though every cell in her body was crying out for his touch.

She stepped back, her movement slightly hampered by her long dress. 'Yes, I am. And you should go and tell Richard you were joking about shutting down the production before too many people leave. You've caused enough disruption in my life as it is.'

Lexie went to walk around him, cursing her costume when she couldn't move more freely.

Cesar caught her and whirled her around, eyes flashing. 'I've caused disruption in *your* life? What about the disruption you've caused *me*?' He pointed a finger at his chest and glared at her.

Lexie pulled free, her anger matching his, boiling over when she thought of how naive she'd been, baring her soul to him.

'I did nothing but warm your bed for a few weeks! I was a convenient lover who also handily deflected some heat from the press about your family issues, and you were quite happy to take advantage of that.'

'On the contrary—you weren't *convenient* at all! The fact is, Lexie Anderson, you have been the most singularly *in*convenient lover I've ever known.'

Cesar was practically roaring now, and Lexie's eyes stung with tears. She bit back the lump in her throat to hear Cesar declare so baldly just how much he resented his desire for her.

Her voice was thick. 'Well, then, what are you waiting for? Leave me be.'

She went to walk away before Cesar could see the extent of her distress, but he caught her again. She cursed out loud, but he had both hands on her arms now.

Lexie felt a tear slip down one cheek and cursed again, struggling against his hold. She stopped and looked up. 'Just…let me go, Cesar. Please. I can't do this.'

He paled under his dark skin. 'I didn't want to make you cry.' His hands tightened. 'The reason you were an inconvenient lover is because you made me face up to myself in a way no one ever has before. Or will again.'

Now Cesar looked almost angry, but something in Lexie went very still.

'I was doing just fine without anyone challenging my

emotionally barren life. And then *you* appeared, literally like some kind of vision, and from that moment on something broke inside me. Something that needed to be broken.'

Cesar moved his hands up to cup Lexie's jaw.

'The truth is that you were…you *are*…the most beautifully *necessary* inconvenience, because you've brought me back to life. I don't want to end the affair, Lexie—*ever*. I want it to last for the rest of our lives.'

Lexie tried to shake her head, as if that might improve her hearing. But Cesar's hands held her immobile. She had to put her hands out to touch him, barely able to breathe. 'What are you saying?'

The tendrils of something impossibly light and effervescent were scaring her, beckoning her to a place where surely she would face the most epic fall of all if she was dreaming this.

'What I'm saying is that I'm in love with you. I think I have been from the moment I saw you. And I want to spend the rest of my life with you. I want it all—the picket fence, children, even *the* damn dog. *Everything.*'

His mouth twisted.

'When you asked me about getting married I taunted you because I couldn't bear the fact that you'd put a seed of something incredibly fragile in my head. A hope for the future I'd never even allowed myself to think about or imagine.'

Emotion was blooming inside Lexie's chest, making it expand, making her dizzy. She wanted to laugh and cry at the same time. But then she remembered his stark non-reaction that day at the *castillo*. The way he'd let her go so easily.

One of her hands on Cesar's chest curled into a fist and she hit him ineffectually. Her voice was choked. 'You hurt me. I thought you didn't care.'

Cesar looked pained. 'I'm so sorry—my response was... pathetic. I cared so much I shut down. I literally didn't know what to do or say. You were telling me those things... and all I could feel was my own pain. I couldn't begin to understand the horror of what had happened to you. I wanted to go out and find that man and kill him with my bare hands.'

Lexie paled.

'For the last week I've kept imagining you as a young girl, alone and scared, going through pregnancy and birth without any support.' He shook his head, his eyes glittering a little too brightly. 'You're the bravest person I know. You humble me.'

'I thought...' Lexie was whispering now '...that you hated what I'd told you because it was too personal. And that you didn't understand why I had to do what I did. I thought afterwards that it must have reminded you of your mother.'

Cesar's thumb caressed her cheek. 'If anything it's helped me to understand her a little better, because it's not so black and white any more. She wouldn't have been human if she hadn't felt some pain on leaving me behind— and God knows what nefarious bargain my grandparents struck with her to make her stay away.'

Feeling absurdly shy, Lexie said, 'I thought you resented the fact that I'd told you those things because our relationship wasn't about anything but...sex.'

Cesar grimaced. 'At first I did. I was angry because you'd forced me to acknowledge that what I felt for you went a lot deeper than I'd admitted to myself.'

Lexie could see it on his face now—in his eyes. Love. Blasting her doubts and fears. But it was huge. She was scared.

As if he could tell, he moved even closer and said throatily, 'What is it?'

'I'm scared,' she whispered, baring herself in a way she'd never done with anyone before. 'I'm scared because my own family turned their backs on me. Betrayed me in the worst possible way. I couldn't survive that again.'

Lexie could feel the tension in Cesar's body, see the ferocity in his expression.

'I vow to you with every breath in my body that I will spend my life protecting you from hurt and harm. I love you, Lexie. You're as much a part of my soul as I am myself. A betrayal of you is a betrayal of me…and whatever the future brings I'm going to be right by your side to deal with it. Including Connor.'

Lexie's eyes filled with tears. The fact that he'd acknowledged her son dissolved the last of her defences.

Cesar was blurry in her vision as she came up on tiptoe and slid her arms around his neck. 'I love you, Cesar… so much.'

He groaned softly and covered her mouth with his. The kiss was searing and passionate.

Lexie broke free and looked up. 'Take me home, please?'

Cesar smiled and his thumbs wiped away the tracks of her tears on her cheeks. '*Espere querida*…wait… There's just one thing I have to do first.'

Suddenly Cesar disappeared, and Lexie gave a little surprised yelp to see him kneeling at her feet, her huge skirt between them. He was holding out a black box which he then opened. He looked up, his slightly nervous smile making Lexie's heart flip-flop.

'Lexie Anderson…will you marry me?'

More tears filled Lexie's eyes. Pure joy bubbled up inside her. Her heart was in her voice when she said simply, 'Yes!'

Cesar took her hand and slid a stunning antique gold and diamond ring on her finger. The fact that she'd barely looked at it didn't seem to bother either of them, because he stood up and swept her and her voluminous dress into his arms before kissing her senseless—much to the entertainment of the security guards, who were the only people left on the set.

A week later Cesar had arranged to have his private jet standing by at a nearby private airfield. As soon as Lexie was wrapped after her final scene later that day they were going back to Spain.

Cesar's mobile phone beeped with a message and he read it.

Congratulations on your engagement. Alexio and I would like to meet you, if you're ready. Call me any time. Rafaele.

Cesar showed the message to Lexie later, when they were on the plane, and she was sitting in his lap. She looked at him and he saw the way her eyes grew suspiciously bright.

She pressed a kiss to his cheek and said, 'I'm ready when you are.'

Incredible joy gripped him—there wasn't a hint of the old darkness and pain. Cesar grinned and threw his phone down, and then got busy showing his fiancée just how ready he was.

EPILOGUE

Eighteen months later

'I MEAN...THEY look so innocent, don't they?'

Cesar smiled at Alexio's almost incredulous tone. Rafaele sighed deeply on his other side. They'd been standing and talking and were now watching the three women who were sitting around a picnic table under a huge tree, a few yards away. They were on Cesar's lawn, at the back of the *castillo*, where a new outdoor pool twinkled invitingly through some small trees.

The *castillo* looked the same on the outside but it had been almost completely remodelled on the inside, so that very few vestiges of the past remained apart from the parts that had to be preserved. It was light and airy, with vast spaces, and decorated with a sumptuous yet understated luxury. Lexie had personally supervised the storage of the portraits of Cesar's grandparents in a special airtight room deep in the cellars.

'I know,' Rafaele said now. 'And yet in spite of that innocence they all—

'Brought us down,' Cesar chipped in, sounding the happiest out of all of them.

Just then the three women's heads drew closer together: one dark, one bright blonde and the other reddish blonde. There came a very distinctive peal of laughter from Samantha Falcone, and then they were all guffawing inelegantly, heads thrown back.

Rafaele shifted uncomfortably. 'Why does that always make me nervous? As if they're talking—

'About us?' Alexio cut in.

'Because they probably are,' Cesar said equably, once again sounding like a Zen Buddha.

His younger half-brothers turned towards him and folded their arms, two versions of his own green eyes narrowed on him.

Alexio remarked dryly, 'I could take a photo of you right now and Tweet it and you'd lose your well-honed mystique in seconds.'

Cesar smiled and said ruefully, 'Be my guest. I think I lost that mystique somewhere around the first nappy-change, when my sense of smell got scarred for life.'

The tiny bundle wriggled against his chest and he looked down at the small downy head of his two-month-old daughter, Lucita, where she was burrowing into a more comfortable position. His hand supported her bottom in the baby sling protectively.

Just then a small toddler in a bright dress broke free of the women at the table and tottered towards the men with a determined expression on her face. A halo of strawberry-blond ringlets framed a heart-stoppingly cherubic face dominated by huge green eyes.

She'd already wrapped everyone within a ten-mile radius around her tiny finger—even Cesar's normally very taciturn housekeeper.

Cesar's chest grew tight as he imagined Lucita at that age. And growing older in a vastly different *castillo* from the one he'd experienced. One filled with light and love.

Alexio bent down and encouraged his daughter Belle the last few yards, until she fell into his arms with a squeal of excitement. Lifting her up, he settled her high against his chest, a distinctly soppy expression on his face as she rested her head between his neck and shoulder, thumb firmly in her mouth.

'How the mighty are fallen indeed,' Rafaele remarked wryly, observing this just as Milo, his almost five-year-old son, streaked by with his armbands on, ready to jump into the pool, followed swiftly by Juan Cortez's similarly aged son—Milo's new best friend.

Belle immediately straightened up to take her thumb from her mouth and pointed a clutching hand at where Milo was, exclaiming urgently in baby gibberish.

But Alexio's attention was fixated on his wife, Sidonie, who had followed her daughter and was sliding an arm around her husband's waist. She wore a long colourful kaftan over a bikini.

Cesar knew that they were sitting on the news that they were expecting again until Sidonie had passed three months. But Sid had already told Lexie, and Lexie had told Cesar, and he was pretty sure that Sam must know too—which meant Rafaele knew, which meant it was an open secret. But of course no one would acknowledge it till they did.

The look between Alexio and Sidonie was definitely carnal and very private.

She smiled as Belle wriggled to be put down. 'You know that now she's seen Milo she won't rest until she can play with him.'

Alexio scowled in Rafaele's direction and Rafaele raised a brow. 'What? It's not *my* fault she's hero-worshipping her cousin. She's displaying remarkably good taste in men already. That's a *good* thing!'

Sidonie just shook her head at the men's ribbing and took Belle's hand when Alexio let her down. She glanced fondly at where her new niece was cuddled against Cesar's chest. 'Lucita's due a feed, and Sam wants to take a nap, so I said I'd watch the kids. I'll take Belle to the pool.'

Alexio immediately declared, 'I'll come too,' and another hot, private look passed between them.

Samantha Falcone was walking towards them now, still graceful despite her seven months pregnant belly, evident under a stretchy dress. When she came near Rafaele drew her close and asked throatily, 'You're taking a nap?'

She looked up at him and nodded, and then said, far too innocently, 'You didn't sleep very well last night, did you? Maybe you should take a nap too?'

Cesar almost laughed out loud at the way Rafaele muttered something unintelligble and all but dragged his pregnant wife into the *castillo*. Rafaele had confided that this time was very poignant for him, because he'd missed Sam's pregnancy with Milo.

Alexio and Sidonie were now wandering off hand in hand, with Belle toddling in front of them, towards the pool.

Cesar looked over to where Lexie sat on the love seat beneath the tree, watching him. She smiled and crooked her finger. As if he needed any encouragement...

When he sat down beside her Lucita was already raising her head and mewling softly, clearly ready for her feed.

Deftly Cesar unhooked the sling and lifted his daughter out, holding her head securely as her huge blue eyes opened wide and she gazed back at him guilelessly. His heart clenched. Was it possible to fall even more deeply in love every time he looked at her? And then she smiled and the question became moot, because he fell fathoms deeper in a nanosecond.

'Look!' Cesar declared proudly, angling her for Lexie's inspection. 'She smiled at me.'

Lexie grinned and took their daughter from his safe

hands, settling her against the breast she'd bared, helping that seeking mouth to find her nipple.

As Lucita latched on, Lexie said wryly, 'I hate to burst your bubble but it's probably just wind.'

Cesar said nothing and when she peeked at him he was just smiling at her, a very private smile. He put his arm around her and said throatily, 'I could watch you nurse Lucita all day.'

Lexie rested her head back against him and smiled. 'Happy?'

Cesar looked down at her and felt his heart swell so much it might explode. Those huge blue eyes sucked him in as they had that very first time.

He shook his head and said quickly, '*Happy* doesn't even come close to how I'm feeling.'

He took Lexie's free hand—the hand on which she wore his rings. He brought it up and pressed his mouth there, over the rings that bound them together for ever.

He found himself admitting something he'd been too ashamed to admit before. 'Do you know…just before Lucita was born I was afraid…afraid that I couldn't possibly love any more than I already loved you?'

Lexie's eyes grew bright.

'But as soon as she was born I realised it's infinite. Love can't be bound to one person.'

'I know,' Lexie whispered. 'I felt it too.'

The pregnancy and birth had been incredibly emotional for them both, but especially poignant for Lexie, considering it had brought back everything she'd been through with her first baby. But Cesar had been with her every step of the way, and more supportive than she might have dared to imagine. With his encouragement she'd even been in touch with the adoption agency to leave word as to where she could be contacted should her son ever feel the desire.

A deep sense of peace and security pervaded her life now. And love.

Lexie huffed a small laugh then, even as emotional tears made her eyes glitter. 'You know, for someone who was deprived of love growing up you're remarkably good at it.'

Cesar smiled back and said, with not a little sadness, 'I can feel sorry for my grandparents now. They were so bitter and caught up in anger.'

Predictably, at the mention of his grandparents, Lexie's eyes flashed with emotion. But before it could rise Cesar pressed a kiss to Lexie's mouth, long and lingering, full of love.

When he drew back the fire of anger had gone out of Lexie's eyes to be replaced by another kind of fire, and she said, almost grumpily, 'That was blatant distraction.'

Lucita's mouth popped free and Lexie handed her back to Cesar while she prepared her other breast for feeding.

When their daughter had emitted a gratifyingly robust burp Cesar handed her back. With Lucita settled again, Lexie looked at her husband. 'Are you ready for tomorrow?'

'Tomorrow?' he asked disingenuously, clearly much more interested in his wife and baby. 'Tell me what's happening tomorrow again?'

Lexie smiled. He knew exactly what was happening. Even so, she reminded him. 'Sidonie's aunt is arriving and it's her first time out of France, so we all have to be very mindful of her. Alexio is going to Paris to meet her and bring her here so she won't be nervous. Rafaele's father and his new wife Bridie are coming from Milan. And Juan Cortez and Maria are coming to pick up Miguel— although you know they'll probably end up spending the night because it'd be rude not to ask them to stay for the barbecue...'

'And,' added Cesar dryly, 'because Maria is as thick as thieves with you and Sid and Sam.'

Lexie smiled, but couldn't stem a niggle of anxiety for Cesar. This was their biggest family get-together yet. And it would getting bigger all the time—especially as Sam's new baby would be born soon and added to the mix. And then Sid's.

It had been easier for Lexie, knowing what it was to come from a sizeable family, in spite of their estrangement. And also because she and Sam and Sidonie had formed a solid and genuine friendship almost within the first ten minutes of meeting each other.

She knew that even though Cesar's relationship with his half-brothers had taken a quantum leap ever since that first meeting in Rome, when she'd gone with him to meet them properly for the first time, it was still a novel experience for him to play at happy families having come from the exact opposite experience.

But then, it had been healing for Cesar to hear how Rafaele and Alexio had suffered at the hands of their unhappy mother in their own lives. Happy families didn't come naturally to them either. Once he'd seen they could empathise with him he hadn't felt so alone in his experiences.

Lexie saw the glint of determination in Cesar's eyes and castigated herself for underestimating how he might deal with this. He pressed another lingering kiss to her mouth and then pulled back, saying with a grin that transformed him into someone infinitely younger and even more gorgeous, 'Am I ready? As long as you're with me I'm ready for anything.'

Lexie answered huskily, with her heart in her voice, 'Well, that's easy—because I'm not going anywhere.'

* * * * *

LET'S TALK
Romance

For exclusive extracts, competitions
and special offers, find us online:

- **f** facebook.com/millsandboon
- **⊙** @millsandboonuk
- **🐦** @millsandboon

Or get in touch on 0844 844 1351*

For all the latest titles coming soon, visit
millsandboon.co.uk/nextmonth